Choose Me

Also by Kay Langdale

Her Giant Octopus Moment

What the Heart Knows (Rowolht, Germany)
Redemption (Transita, published as *If Not Love* by Thomas Dunne
Books, St Martin's Press)

KAY LANGDALE

Choose Me

HODDER &
STOUGHTON

First published in Great Britain in 2013 by Hodder & Stoughton
An Hachette UK company

I

Copyright © Kay Langdale 2013

The right of Kay Langdale to be identified as the Author
of the Work has been asserted by her in accordance with the
Copyright, Designs and Patents Act 1988.

A CIP catalogue record for this title is available from the British Library

ISBN Hardback 978 1 444 76682 0
Ebook 978 1 444 76683 7

Set in Plantin Light by Palimpsest Book Production Limited,
Falkirk, Stirlingshire

Printed and bound by
CPI Group (UK) Ltd, Croydon, CR0 4YY

Hodder & Stoughton policy is to use papers that are
natural, renewable and recyclable products and made
from wood grown in sustainable forests. The logging
and manufacturing processes are expected to conform to
the environmental regulations of the country of origin.

Hodder & Stoughton Ltd
338 Euston Road
London NW1 3BH

www.hodder.co.uk

For Finn, Georgia, Hal and Noah, with much love.

Acknowledgements

The publisher and author would like to thank: Virago Books for permission to quote from 'The Hurt Child' by Margaret Atwood, from *The Door*, copyright by O.W. Toad Ltd 2007.

Bloodaxe Books for permission to quote from 'Chapter 6: The Telling Part' by Jackie Kay, from *Darling: New & Selected Poems* (Bloodaxe Books, 2007)

The children's books referred to in *Choose Me* are:
'Dear Zoo' by Rod Campbell, published by the Penguin Group, 2008.
'Would you rather . . .' by John Burningham, published by Red Fox, 1994.
'The Great Pet Sale' by Mick Inkpen, published by Hodder Children's books, 2006.

The hurt child will grow a skin
over the wound you have given it
– or not given, because the wound
is not a gift, a gift is accepted
freely, and the child had no choice.
    (from *The Hurt Child*, Margaret Atwood)

Now when people say 'ah but
it's not like having your own child though is it',
I say of course it is, what else is it?
she's my child, I have told her stories
wept at her losses, laughed at her pleasures,
she is mine.
    (from *Chapter 6: The Telling Part*, Jackie Kay)

Prologue

2006

He'd woken to find her standing by his bed holding a blue balloon on a white ribbon in one hand and a box of Coco Pops in the other. *Happy fifth birthday!* she exclaimed. By his pillow was a present. When he'd unwrapped the book, she said *How clever is that? A book called* Dear Zoo *for your birthday present* (and here she pretended to blow a trumpet and sang toot-ta-toot-ta-toot) *and a trip to the zoo as well.* She clapped, and danced a little jig, and tipped all her money on to the table and counted out the right amount for the bus.

The monkeys were eating fruit. Billy couldn't tell what kind of fruit. In picture books it was always bananas, but this fruit was soft and round. When the closest monkey took a bite, Billy could see a row of very even teeth and a rim of pink gum. Occasionally, it spat out a pip or a seed. There was a baby monkey clinging to the underside of its mother and, as the mother walked along a branch, it swung beneath her from side to side. Mummy pointed at it and sang *Lulla lulla lulla lulla bye bye*, which was what she sang to him sometimes at bedtime, and sometimes when he wasn't sleepy at all. Once, she'd sung herself to sleep. There weren't any other words to the song. Now, she rocked backwards and forwards as she sang it, with her knees held close to her chest, and her body tipped back as if she was singing to the sky, and a lady sitting next to them on the grassy bank by the enclosure looked at them and then moved away to a bench nearby.

A big monkey started to flap its hands at another monkey and three of them started screeching and fighting. One threw a stick and it clattered against the bars. *What a caterwaul,* a man next to Billy said to his little girl, *what a shrieking and a shouting.* The little girl's lip was starting to wobble. *Don't worry,* the man said, stooping down around her so that she was wrapped by his knees and his arms, *they're just noisy, naughty monkeys.*

Mummy wasn't singing the lullaby anymore. Instead, she was laughing at the fighting monkeys. She joined in with their noisiness, and flapped her arms long and wide, and gave a huge screech. *Funny monkeys,* said the man. *Funny lady,* said the girl, and pointed to Mummy, who was now lying flat on her back and laughing at something Billy couldn't see. The little girl wasn't laughing, even though Mummy was being funny. The man picked up his daughter and walked away.

They continued to sit by the monkey enclosure until they were by themselves and the sun wasn't warm anymore and then a zookeeper came and told them the park was closing. Mummy wasn't singing or screeching now. She opened one eye carefully to take in the zookeeper. She nodded towards a monkey who was walking the length of a branch. Its bottom was huge and scarlet. She pointed at it. *If it asked you,* she said, beginning to laugh, *does my bum look big in this, you'd have to tick the yes box, wouldn't you?* The zookeeper gave a smile which didn't go the whole way along his lips, and he picked up some litter someone had dropped, and pointed the direction to the way out. His hand looked like it was shooing them away. Mummy was still laughing. Billy traced his fingers round and round the little blue badge he was wearing. *Five today.* Happy birthday to me, he whispered.

2007

'Shall I read to you?' Mummy said. 'Shall we read *Would You Rather?*'

She scooched him on to her lap, and reached behind the sofa to pick up the book.

'Think carefully now,' she said, smiling, 'I only want your best reasons and your best answers. Remember, now you're six you're clever as clever.'

Then she said *I think I'll stay six for ever and ever*, but she didn't seem to be saying it to him, more to the room, or to someone a long way away, and then she went quiet and looked sad.

'That would have been a good idea,' she said.

He looked at the book. Maybe they wouldn't be reading it after all. Maybe they would just sit and look at the wall. He hoped they were still reading *Would You Rather?* He loved it. It was all about deciding and choosing. The spine was peeling off from how many times he'd looked at it. The first page asked if you'd rather your house was surrounded by water, snow or jungle. He liked the jungle picture best; there was an alligator on the pavement and a monkey waving from the chimney-pot. The second page asked if you'd rather an elephant drank your bath water, an eagle stole your dinner, a pig tried on your clothes, or a hippo slept in your bed. He pointed to the elephant with its trunk in the bath.

'You have to say why,' Mummy said sternly, although he knew she wasn't cross. 'You know you have to tell me why.'

He told her it was the only one where nothing would be spoiled or broken; no dinner plate smashed, no ruined food, no stretched clothes, no collapsed bed. She nodded with her serious face. 'Good thinking,' she said. 'Super-smart.'

When he chose between supper in a castle, breakfast in a balloon, and tea on the river, she joined in. They decided on tea on the river and they named all the cakes and biscuits they'd like, and he chose lemonade and Mummy chose elderflower cordial. They pretended to drink tea from china cups and Mummy held her littlest finger curled and high.

On the next page, he didn't want to jump in the nettles for five pounds, or swallow a dead frog for twenty, and least of all stay the night in a creepy house for fifty pounds. Mummy hugged him. 'But I could be with you, all night long, in the creepy house,' she said, 'and we could sing, and tap dance, and tell jokes, and scare anything creepy away with our noisiness, and then we'd have one hundred pounds to spend on whatever we liked.' That sounded less fearsome. He told her he'd give it a go.

He chose a pig to ride whilst she picked a monkey to tickle. He preferred to be chased by a crab because it wouldn't catch him whereas the other choices most definitely would. She stopped reading when he said this and looked way ahead of her, and then kissed him and said 'My careful boy. My careful, careful boy.'

When they got to the picture where you had to choose between where you would prefer to be lost, she said what she always said, which was: if he ever got lost in a crowd he must find a lady with a baby or a little child and ask her to help him because she would be the person most likely to be kind. It was his job to nod when she said this, to show he was listening properly.

He took a long time to decide whether he wanted to live with a gerbil, a fish, a parrot, a rabbit, chickens or a dog. There were so many things to consider. He was still thinking about it when he turned to the last page, just for a peek, because it was his favourite. *Or perhaps you would rather just go to sleep in your own bed.* Mummy always added *your own* little *bed,* which made it sound extra cosy and inviting, and especially and only his. The boy in the picture looked so snug and sound asleep, and Billy was sure he could see the outline of a cat on the window sill outside.

Today, all his thinking and choosing must have worn Mummy out. When he looked up from the last page, his finger touching the perhaps-cat on the window sill, waiting for her to read the last line, her head was tilted back on the sofa, a strand of hair was across her cheek, her mouth was a little bit open, and she was breathing slowly and softly. She'd gone to sleep, even though she wasn't in her own bed, and it was morning. He sat very still, and looked at the maybe-cat on the window sill some more.

2008

Grandma spread the tartan rug on the ground. They were down by the river near her house.

'There, that's perfect,' she said. 'I'm going to make you a little fishing rod. I've brought some line from Grandpa's old tackle box, and a hook and a cork. Here, put out your hand and hold the hook for me. Now you are seven, you can help.'

She sat down and carefully tied some line to the end of a thick stick. The silver hook glinted in the palm of his hand. He pressed his thumb-nail into the rim of the cork. She reached into a plastic bag and took out some white bread.

'Chew this so it gets moist, and then we can roll it into a little ball. All the fancy bait people use to catch fish . . . Your mummy used to sit right on that stump there, that exact one, and catch perch after perch with balls of white bread.'

He spat on the bread and rolled it into a small, smooth ball. Grandma picked it up with her fingertips and rolled it some more. 'It has to be properly compacted, pressed in hard,' she said, 'and then it won't split when you put it on the hook.'

She spread the zip pack from her waterproof jacket over the tree stump.

'If you sit on this, you won't feel damp. Do you remember, Lizzie, when you used to sit here, and we'd always put something over it for you to sit on because you would recite the part from *Jemima Puddleduck* where the stump was *somewhat damp*. Do you remember? Surely you do?'

He looked at his mummy. She didn't seem to be remembering anything. Her face was as blank and as smooth as the moon in the sky last night.

'Lizzie,' Grandma said again, 'surely you remember?'

Mummy nodded. He thought it was one of her nods when she wasn't properly listening. Sometimes you could say anything – he'd tried it – and she nodded anyway.

Grandma busied herself with the picnic basket. She'd wrapped the sandwiches in crinkly greaseproof paper, and she'd put sugary tea in a thermos and said he could have it by his feet and drink it when he was fishing. She said she trusted him now not to spill it. He was saving the thermos. Maybe he'd reach for it only when he'd caught a fish, like it was a prize for doing so.

He sat on the stump and watched the river flow by. It didn't look very deep, but he couldn't see the bottom. The water was brownish at the edges and the strands of weed caught by the current looked like somebody's long hair. At school they'd done a project on the life of the river-bank. Otters, voles, water rats, mink. He looked carefully at the opposite bank but there was no sign of any of them. Maybe it was the wrong kind of river. Or the wrong kind of day. Or maybe all their own busy-ness had scared everything away. He looked at his line to check the cork. It was bobbing gently.

Grandma's voice was quieter now. He looked over his shoulder. She was sitting next to Mummy, her back straight, her arms wrapped round her knees. Her shoes were polished and shiny. Mummy was lying curled on her side, with her back turned to Grandma. Grandma's hand hovered over Mummy's head, as if she might be considering stroking Mummy's hair. Last night, after supper, she'd said 'I wish I could slap some sense into you', as they stood in the kitchen. He hoped she wasn't saving the slap till now. She hadn't sounded angry, or as if she meant to do it. She sounded more like someone who didn't know what to do. She'd stood wiping her hands on the tea towel as if she'd rather cry, not wash up.

'Surely there must be something else you can try, someone else who can help you. God knows I'd lock you in your old bedroom for a month and post food through the door if I thought that would work.'

His mother was stretching out on the rug. Her skirt moved, and he glimpsed the busted vein on her leg.

'I'll get there; I'll sort it,' she said. 'I've been better lately, honestly. I'm making progress. I'm on to it. Everyone tells you, it's got to come from me. In my own time.'

Grandma bit her lip.

'Daddy's avoiding me, isn't he?' Mummy continued.

'He's playing golf. Everything's not always about you.'

'And what's that supposed to mean?'

Grandma stood up from the rug and walked over to him. 'I want' (and here her voice returned to its cheery, usual volume)

'I want Billy to catch a fish, don't you?' She put her hand on his shoulder and said 'Lift up your line and let's check the bait is still there.'

His bread ball swung in the breeze. It looked like a tiny version of something that might dangle from a crane and demolish a building. A wrecking ball. That's what it was called. Last time they'd visited Grandma, his Grandpa had said it in the hallway. *Here comes the bloody wrecking ball,* he said when Mummy came through the door. Grandma had told him to shush. Now, Billy looked up at her. The bread ball swung between them.

'And you, my little man,' she said softly, touching his cheek with her finger, 'are the absolute image of your father. Like the spit out of his mouth.'

The way she said it didn't make it sound like a good thing. She pressed the bread ball gently, and her face looked sad, as if something had hurt her, or as if the fish hook had pierced her thumb, and had sunk in, silvery silent. He looked carefully at her hand, expecting to see blood.

2011

If watched, properly watched, Lizzie decided it was possible to track the gradations of light as they changed on the wall. If looked at intently enough, it might become her own personal sundial; grimy and grey and with a slew of April light reflected from the metal lift shaft in the block opposite, but an indicator all the same. The wall had been white once; she wouldn't hazard a guess as to what kind of white. She recalled her mother holding up a Farrow and Ball paint chart, next to her stone fireplace, her face focused in concentration. *Great White? Cornforth White? How about Lime White?* It would have been cruel to reply *Don't give a fuck which white,* especially as her mother's face was wearing the earnest hopefulness which was truly killing in its indefatigable belief that maybe this time Lizzie had turned a corner. *She's taking an interest in things beyond herself,* her mother would report to the doctor. How she had persisted in that illusion.

This wall, her wall in her crappy flat as opposed to her mother's immaculate wall with its Bath stone fireplace, was grubby. Drab white. Dingy white. White that no one had given a toss about cleaning or repainting in years. There was no adjective, she concluded, that could be gracefully or upliftingly applied to it. Occasionally, she wondered if the same applied to life itself. Certainly to her own life, although she was quick to acknowledge that for this she was entirely at fault.

Billy had had a sight test last week; school had suggested he might not be seeing the whiteboard clearly. She'd stood at the optometrist's desk, booked his appointment and had a moment of insight which felled her like a tree. The two receptionists were middle aged, one with thinning hair, the other broad of beam. They'd had a stab at flamboyance with the swirly patterns on their blouses, and both had coffee mugs she guessed they'd brought in from home when they started the job. She felt as if she were standing in a puddle of their evident decency. No doubt they got up each morning, made the bed, emptied the dishwasher, tidied the house, turned up at work on time, shopped carefully for food, came home, cooked, cleaned and tidied some more, and then flopped in front of the television. It was hard to fault. It had about it, though, a dreariness, a predictability, a work-a-dayness that killed her. Was that what she'd been trying to escape? In which case, she'd aced it. No one was going to feel ankle-deep in *her* decency any day soon.

When she left school there was a year book which everyone signed with comments about each other. There was a box to fill entitled *Girl most likely to . . .* No one had written in hers *Girl most likely to end up a heroin addict in a dump of a flat with Social Services on her back like a scarab.* That would have been inconceivable. Someone with prescience would have written *Girl most likely to implode.* That was surely what had happened and yet there had been none of the usual signs. She hadn't been one of the anorexics, burning with a destructive fierceness and hunger which turned them yellow, slashed the plumpness from their cheeks and covered them with downy hair. Nor one of the self-harmers, with the small, precise armies of scars marching up their limbs. No, she'd been chock-full of home-baking sent by her mother for her tuck box, rosy-cheeked from being outdoors, and issue free. Issue free. The very notion made her want to laugh – no, on reflection not laugh, but rather bark, bark with phlegmy bitterness.

Milo. It had all begun with him, and the shock of discovering that love could top all manner of self-harm in its reach and breadth; that it could in fact turn you inside out, flay you raw and leave you for dead in a pile of your own desolation. Cheers for that, she might have said to him, had he not spirited himself away one night and precluded any form of goodbye.

She recalled Miss Cartwright, her A-level Theology teacher. In the module on women in the Old Testament, she'd spent a whole lesson on worthy Ruth and her fulsome, devoted obedience. *For whither thou goest, I will go; and where thou lodgest, I will lodge: thy people shall be my people.* She'd held that up as a template of goodness – 'Imagine that, girls.' Inconceivable how that would pan out for Lizzie; following Milo to his dealers, to his dens, to his syringe-strewn alleyways. It had been, she noted with a degree of detachment, a surprisingly speedy process to de-rail a healthy constitution, to watch a blooming skin erupt with acne, veins splinter out of subcutaneous flesh, eyes mutate from bright to hollow. Now, today, looking at the wall and thinking about the Theology lesson, she recalled that Ruth had in fact pledged her devotion to her mother-in-law, Naomi, not a man. There was probably more of a lesson in that, if only she'd paid precise attention.

Her parents were devastated. Her mother's face frequently took on the dimensions of one of the Marys in an early Renaissance painting; anguished at the foot of the cross while Lizzie crucified herself with her drug of choice. *But you see so clearly what you are doing*, her mother said, as if the seeing made the doing easier to resist. Her father had begun with paying for expensive rehab, resorted to blind fury, and finally taken refuge in stony rejection. *Daddy's girl.* He'd refused to speak to her for months.

The therapy and counselling groups she'd been to – what a waste of time they'd been. The emphasis was on finding someone to blame, usually your mother. Mothers were the prime target, blame dolloped on them like icing on cupcakes. One foot put tentatively wrong in eighteen years of conscientious, selfless endeavour, and you could fling it all back at them. But no, Lizzie had repeated several times to an earnest therapist with a shock of wild hair, No I truly don't blame my mother for anything. She loved me, and cared for me, and gave me a wonderful childhood. Perhaps she should have added that she had gifted her adulthood and independence and been forced to watch while Lizzie smashed it to smithereens. Her father too. *Steady Teddy*, Milo called him, as if decency and reliability were somehow shameful.

If she closed her eyes, she saw the familiar image of her father leaving for work on a winter morning, so early the sky still sooty dark with a sliver of moon visible, and the feeling that only he was up and about in the world. If she knelt on her bed and lifted the edge of her pink curtain, she could watch him walk towards the paddock, carefully set down his briefcase by the gate, and pick up the mallet from beside the pony's water trough. He'd lift his arms in a crescent and bring it down to splinter the thick crust of ice, the sound ringing through the frosted silence, the pony stamping and shifting near him, and she'd watch him blow on his hands, brush a few droplets of water from his dark wool coat, and walk back along the path, the gravel crunching beneath his feet, to start up the car engine, throaty in the cold. She'd get back into bed and pull the duvet up tight around her chin, savouring the thought that the ice scattered on the paddock grass should spell *I love you*, because that was what it meant.

Billy probably had no such certainty. She tried. She felt she could say, some days with conviction, that she tried. It felt like burrowing very deep within the cavity of her own torso, scratching and scraping around the tip-ends of her ribs for energy to spend on him rather than on the all-consuming hunger for drugs that was burying them both alive. His little face was beautiful; it made her treachery, her persistence, seem even worse. Some days, she could hardly bear to look at him, so faced the wall instead, or webbed her fingers over her eyes so that she saw him as through blinds. Other days, he seemed to float just beyond her, as if she were seeing him through a paper screen, his outline beating against it like a butterfly, and then she'd have a moment of clarity, pull him towards her and smell his hair, the palms of his hands, or stroke the curve of his spine as he lay silently, loyally, curled next to her while she stared at the wall. *I love you*, she'd say to him, but the words tasted like tin in her mouth. Or, *It'll be better in the morning*, which it hardly ever was. All that made it better was what caused her troubles in the first place.

She'd read to him sometimes, or have bursts of enthusiasm, which might result in a walk looking for signs of Spring, of Autumn, or of Christmas coming. One raw day in November last year, the sky solid and unyielding and the light coming down in thick, grey slices, she'd walked him for miles looking for blackberries. Her mother phoned as they walked beside another empty hedgerow, Billy's hands blackberry-blue blotched with cold, and her mother had said *But Lizzie, there are no blackberries left in November, and anyway don't you remember about not picking blackberries after Michaelmas Day because the devil has spat on them? They don't taste right. Don't you remember, we made no more apple and blackberry crumbles after September 29th?* Did she remember? Evidently not. Maybe all that knowledge had fallen from her head as through an open drain. Maybe her brain cells had fallen out with it. That must be why she'd caught two buses out of town with a nine year old who was insufficiently wrapped up for the weather, and walked up and down country lanes telling him they'd find some soon, it was just a question of persevering. He'd trotted along beside her, uncomplaining, compliant, and her head was filled with the elusive scent of blackberries warmed by the sun, and she failed to notice that his shoes were soaking wet, or remember that he'd eaten nothing since breakfast.

What time had he left for school? What time was he due back? Had he got his bus pass? The details evaded her, floated beyond her like wisps of sea mist. *I am a very uncertain mother*, she'd told

Miriam Riley, the social worker, who'd taken that to mean she felt an overriding lack of confidence and had endeavoured to say something consoling and complimentary. It was evidently taxing. She'd decided to leave her with the illusion, rather than confess it was more pedestrian than that, and related mostly to what day it was, whether the boiler was on to allow hot water for a shower, and whether the fridge might be empty or contain just a jumbo packet of crisps.

Her legs felt numb. How long had she been lying on the floor like this? She opened her eyes. She'd told herself that if she waited until the shadow on the wall fingered the edge of the television, that would be longer than yesterday. It would count as weaning herself off, as going without for a little longer. That could count as progress of sorts. Billy surely wouldn't be home for a while. She could have it now. Now would be a good time.

She took up her syringe. She was ravenous. Ravenous. She spoke the word out loud. Ravenous and ready to be ravished. She'd looked that word up once, in the early days of their relationship, just to check it was exactly the effect Milo had on her. *To overwhelm with intense emotion; especially joy*. Ravenous. Ravished. The words bounced from her lips and scattered across the floor.

I

One of the girls at Mrs Oliver's – Billy couldn't remember her name – Kelly? Sarah? – said the only benefit of your mum dying was that people bought you stuff when it wasn't your birthday or Christmas, as if that somehow went some way to making up for what you'd lost. No show on the gift front yet, Billy thought, adjusting the bunched-up pillowcase of his possessions on his lap. Maybe Kelly/Sarah had got that wrong. He wasn't sure whether she had a mother anyway, so she might not be an expert. He was sitting in the corridor at the Family Centre, waiting to see Miriam Riley, his social worker, ten days after his mum's death. This was another surprise, that en route to not having a mother, you got your own social worker. Billy didn't think that was a fair swap, although Miriam seemed to be doing her best, something he'd also have said of his mum.

The thing about having a drug addict for a mother – and here Billy checked himself, reminding himself that he didn't have a mother anymore – was that you were no stranger to Social Services before you actually rocked up motherless. Miriam had been popping in and out, as she called it, of his life, since he was about six, and that was three years ago. Mrs Oliver too, who ran an emergency and short-term foster home for children who were between placements or on their way to somewhere more permanent. Three nights was usually her maximum stay rule, and for that she provided a clean bed and a hot meal daily, *and that's a novelty for most of them*, Billy had heard her say to Miriam.

Billy had been to Mrs Oliver's four times, when his mum had been hospitalised after either taking too much, taking something bad, or mixing something up; the details didn't matter, the upshot was the same. Either way, each time he'd come home to find her making broccoli soup which was what she always did after what she called a stumble, and telling him everything was going to be okay.

Lizzie, he'd heard Miriam tell Mrs Oliver, wasn't your regular addict. Nice middle-class girl, off the rails after a man; it was always a man, introducing the stuff and then disappearing, scot-free. The times she'd seen it. Like Whitney Houston and Amy Winehouse, Mrs Oliver had replied, and Miriam nodded. Billy wasn't sure if his mum *was* actually like Whitney Houston or Amy Winehouse. She'd had their CDs, and sometimes sang along, particularly when making soup. She certainly didn't sound like them. The bit about the man was probably true. Billy knew it was his dad, Milo, who'd introduced his mum to drugs; he was the one who'd got off scot-free and vanished. His mum didn't tell him much more. A musician, that's what she did say. *So beautiful*, she said, her eyes rolling at the memory, *so-ooo beautiful*. It seemed to Billy that his dad had left his mum not only holding *him* in her arms, but also some weed, cocaine, lots of tablets and finally heroin. That was probably more than anybody's arms could bear, particularly hers, which became more bruised, more needle marked, and more raggedy veined the older he got. He preferred to see her with her sleeves down.

The thing about having a mother who was a heroin addict was that it sounded very close to a mother who was a heroine, full stop, when it was in fact quite different. Spelling wasn't Billy's strong point, but recently in school, before his mum died, they'd had to write a story about a heroine of some kind. They could choose between Grace Darling, who'd bravely manned a rescue boat after spotting a shipwreck; Rosa Parks, who'd sat tight on the bus; and Marie Curie, who'd died because of her work in discovering X-rays. Alternatively, they could choose someone for themselves. Joey Meadows, his friend, said he was going to write about Emily Davidson, who had thrown herself in front of the King's horse to try and get votes for women. This was mostly based on the fact that he was proud of the way he drew horses, and was hoping Mrs Bailey might allow some illustrations in the margin. *Silks at the start,* he'd whispered to Billy, making his title look like a starting flag. Pen poised, Billy checked on the whiteboard for how heroine was spelt. Imagine, he'd thought, what a different life would open up if he could write 'My mum's a heroine' and leave it at that. Even if he could write My mum's a . . . and put in any of the words the other children in his class might use. (Doctor? Estate agent? Hairdresser?) All kinds of things might present themselves, none of which involved putting the washing machine on for himself or sticking forks in the toaster to retrieve the last half slice of bread. (*Chaotic home life,* he'd heard Mrs Bailey tell the new teaching assistant, *and yet his mother just enthuses about how well he's doing.*)

Enthuses. Billy wasn't sure what that meant. It sounded quite close to enthusiastic, and that word would definitely describe some of his mum's moods. Definitely the ones which started with her sweeping the kitchen floor a lot, and spraying Dettox over all the work surfaces, and muttering *new start, fresh start* to herself over and over again. The thing is, she'd told Billy on a number of occasions, I shouldn't be living my life like this, this is not the life I was meant to lead. I have no excuse.

Billy wasn't sure how having an excuse would make it any more bearable. In the last few months of his mother's life, even when she was sweeping very, very, hard and the dust was flying up in small, determined clouds above the skirting-board, he found himself a tiny bit less able to believe that this was going to be the long, much promised, fresh start.

The thing is, she kept telling him, I didn't grow up in hardship with horrible parents. I had a pony in the paddock, and flute lessons, and braces on my teeth. My daddy was chairman of the golf club, and my mother plays bridge. She said this last fact with a flourish, as if the ability to play bridge was a guarantee that nothing bad could ever happen either to you or to anyone you loved. This was a winning thought.

After a particularly bad episode, when his mother had shiny, gazy, eyes and hunched-up knees and sat facing the wall for two days, a neighbour, after rat-tat-tatting on the door a few times, had posted two slices of bread through the letter-box to Billy. He'd wondered, his teeth tearing through its flabby white softness whether this would happen if you could play bridge. He had a notebook, a small one with a wire spine which allowed pages to be ripped out. It had a plain brown card cover. *Things to remember*, he'd written on it in capitals, and on the first page, *Learn to play bridge*, just in case he forgot.

His grandparents had gone to live in Portugal two years ago, which had obviously seemed to them to be the answer. *I have to get away from you, Lizzie*, he'd heard Grandma saying to her in the kitchen, *I cannot take responsibility for the choices you make anymore*. Grandma had tried. Billy wasn't sure how she'd tried in the matter of choices, but she had invited them to her house a lot, and taken Billy fishing, and to the park, and she had a tall glass jar filled with Quality Street to which he was allowed to help himself. His mum had helped herself to the contents of Grandpa's wallet, so the visits stopped after that, but Grandma still came and visited them in the flat, but without Grandpa. She'd arrive with Tupperwares of stew. Grandma was not a great cook, or perhaps, in fairness, just not a great cook of things which could be delivered in Tupperwares. However, on bad days, when his mum lay down all day, or watched an old children's TV programme called *The Singing Ringing Tree* over and over again on You Tube, Billy would scoop out some stew, put it in two bowls and warm them in the microwave. Miriam had turned up once when he was doing it. *I think you're going to grow up and be on Master Chef*, she'd said. Billy thought this was a fine example of when grown-ups dig around to find something nice to say because what they are actually thinking is that your life is a bit rubbish, that the stew will not be properly warmed through, and that you will have a stomach-ache later.

He and his mum had visited his grandparents in Portugal when he was eight. Grandma bought them two flights to Faro on easyJet. It was just before Grandpa stopped speaking to his mum altogether. She'd lain by the pool turning very dark brown. The road his grandparents lived on was lined with smart villas, all built at the same time and each slightly different. The paint colours of the front doors and window shutters matched. The trees in the gardens were exactly the same size, and all fed by identical irrigation pipes.

Grandma kept asking Grandpa to take him for walks on the beach. His grandpa walked fast, strode out, and it was hard to keep up. Grandpa seemed not to want to look at him. In fact, he was becoming an expert at not letting his eyes rest on him at all. That was perhaps why he always walked way out in front, as if Billy were a dog, trailing behind on an invisible lead, looking mostly at the back of Grandpa's head. Billy had determined that if Grandpa didn't like the look of him, which he couldn't do anything about, he could at least work on how he sounded and try not to be irritating. Nobody liked a whiner. On the beach, he focused his attention on planting his feet in the less-sinky sand of his grandpa's footprint, and tried not to dwell on the fact that the sun was needling the back of his neck. He resolved to try never to complain. This, he was sure, was a route to being no trouble, which had to be in contrast to his mum, who seemed to be plenty. He'd stood in a newsagent's once, queuing to buy some sweets, and a woman with a baby in a pushchair had cooed to the man at the till that her baby was so good she hardly knew she had him. Billy thought this might be a smart strategy and had aimed for it since.

He was disappointed, after that particular walk, when he heard his grandpa say to his grandma *Hardly says a word*. This wasn't the effect he'd been aiming for and it seemed more than a little unfair. He had a huge blister on the side of his toe, and it had taken some effort not to complain about that, or limp.

On holiday, Lizzie had promised her parents she'd keep clean when she got back. He remembered she'd been wearing a bright orange sarong with a lizard pattern, and as she talked and waved her arms around, they made absolutely the same shape as the lizards' front legs on the fabric. *I feel a different person*, she'd said, *so rested, so healthy*. Grandma had given her some money at the airport. Billy wanted to shout *No, don't do that*. His mother lasted a week, and then Tom, her dealer, was knocking at the door again.

Grandma came and visited once more, before she had to come back for the funeral. *I am threadbare, Lizzie, threadbare*, she'd said, *I just can't do this anymore. I feel as if I've tried everything. You're shredding our hearts. Your father says enough is enough. And I have to be a wife, not just a mother*. She'd sat on the couch and kept patting Billy's knee, almost, he thought, to keep reminding herself that he was there too. He wondered if anything in the room was properly solid rather than liable to float up and away. His mother sat on the mattress she kept in front of the television and chewed at her bottom lip and crick-cracked her knuckles. It seemed to Billy that there weren't enough words to fill the room; the silence punctuated by the sound of his mother's hands collapsing, and his grandma's shallow sighs. When Grandma got up to go, she patted his knee extra hard, and turned and kissed him on the forehead, and he could see a tear, in a perfect tear-drop shape, glimmering in the corner of her eye, and as she bent towards him it splish-splashed on to the back of his hand and he worried that he felt so oddly empty and dry it didn't seem possible that his whole body might contain even one tear like that. When his grandma had gone, his mum had curled up into a ball and howled and howled like an animal caught in a trap, with an awful catching sound at the back of her throat, and he just sat by the mattress and patted her too, and wondered why she didn't have any tears either and if it was something else he might have inherited from her. He kept saying *It'll be all right, Mum, It'll be all right, Mum*, over and over, but his words felt like sawdust in his mouth. He didn't think she was really listening; she just kept making that terrible noise. The shadows in the room stretched and fuzzed around them both, until his legs looked long enough to touch the skirting-board, and he thought it was curious, really, because without meaning to, what he'd set out to achieve with his grandparents he had instead obviously aced with his mum. Like the woman with the baby in the newsagent's, she truly hardly knew she had got him. Good behaviour on his part didn't even come into it.

In the hospital, when he stood by his mother's dead body with Miriam beside him, he had been struck by how round and pink the nurse's arms were in comparison to his mum's. The nurse rearranged the bed sheet around his mother's lizardy-spiky blueness, smoothed the hair from her forehead, and then turned and patted Billy's hands which he held clasped in front of him. He wondered if he'd spend the rest of his childhood being patted by grown-ups who felt sorry for him and who were not sure what to do about it.

Miriam had gone to phone his grandparents to tell them, and he wondered how many glimmering, perfectly shaped tears his grandma would cry now, or if she would instead wail like his mother had on the last day she had seen her. He hoped his grandpa was good at patting, and wouldn't mind if Grandma hardly said a word. Enough had been enough; Grandpa had been right. There wouldn't be any more of his mum. Would Miriam be asking them if he could come and live in Portugal? He didn't think they'd say yes. Grandma might consider it, but Grandpa wouldn't want to spend every day concentrating on not looking at someone who lived in the same house.

Threadbare. That was the word Grandma used to describe herself. It was a good one. Waiting for Miriam, he'd poked his finger through a worn patch on the knee of his jeans. It felt pleasantly soothing, worming and wriggling his finger through what was left of the denim. He wouldn't blame his grandparents if they didn't want to have him. In Portugal, Grandpa had pointed to him sideways while talking to his friend and said *Addiction; they've shown on those new scans that they can locate it, see it, in the brain. You can inherit it, like a knack for anything. Some talent. With parents like his*, he'd added, *what chance has he got?*

The last night of the holiday, he'd lain in bed feeling all the bumps on his skull; some certainly seemed to stick out more than others. He pressed his finger on a particular one and wiggled it a bit. Might that be where a gift for addiction was ready for the off? At school the Head kept a list of the children who were gifted and talented; you could be gifted and talented in all sorts of things. So far, Billy felt he hadn't shown a talent for anything. What a kicker it would be if the only one he had was for addiction. School wouldn't want to list that. If it had been playing bridge, from his grandma, that might have been in with a chance.

Between waiting for Miriam in the hospital, and waiting for her now outside her office, he'd wiggled at the hole in his jeans until it was a perfect oval. His knee peeked out like a smooth, pink egg. He should leave it alone, he decided. If it got too big, who would buy him some more jeans? There might not be anyone in charge of that. That would have been his mum's department, although the hole would have had to get a lot bigger before she would have noticed.

His mum. He sat in the corridor outside Miriam Riley's office and tried to make her back alive. He thought of the curve of her ear, the smell of her hair, and the way she sat cross-legged. She was already blurring at the edges and she'd only been dead ten days. It seemed longer, longer in a way that made him feel tired and worn out, maybe because she'd seemed not properly alive for quite a long time. She'd been growing misty for a while, that was the only way he could think of it; half-dead before she actually, properly, was. He tried to picture her as a child his age, playing the flute, and riding a pony in a cherry-red pullover, with a mouth full of brace wires. She said she'd been rubbish at the flute; not the flute itself, but at the standing still. She blamed it on poor circulation, saying that at the end of the lesson she'd had big purple blotches on her legs and feet. That was why she gave it up despite gaining a Distinction at Grade Three and playing in the school orchestra. After she told him this, Billy had gone through a period of standing still for as long as he could bear and then checking for blotches. None showed up; perhaps that meant the talent for addiction wouldn't do so either.

She'd sold the flute about a year ago. *It's one of the last things to go*, she said to him, looking sad, *one of the last reminders of the peachy childhood I've blown*. Oddly, the person who bought the flute didn't want the case. This was a mystery to Billy, but his mum seemed fine with it, and knocked ten pounds off the price. By that stage, he knew, she was desperate to sell it. He could hear it in her voice, see it in her eyes, as she wheedled with the woman over the phone. Afterwards, the case stayed in the cupboard under the stairs, and when Billy sat there sometimes, when his mum had gone out to the shops or to buy her stuff, he flipped it open and ran his finger and thumb over the raspberry velvet lining, and into the hollows where the flute used to lie. There was a shiny, oval enamel plate which said *Boosey and Hawkes*. He liked circling its smoothness with the pad of his thumb. The pile of the velvet was crushed where the keys used to be. It faithfully bore all traces of the flute; its shape still clear and distinct in the rectangular, pretend-leather, case. Perhaps that was how it would be for him, he thought, focusing on the tree beyond the window; perhaps he'd carry the shape, the imprint, of his mother, despite the fact that she was completely gone.

She was difficult to describe. He'd found that out two days ago. He'd had a meeting with someone from the hospital, Samantha, who wanted to talk to him about his feelings, specifically, she said, carefully emphasising her words, about how *he* was feeling. She asked him to describe his mum, and how it was living with her. That was awkward. What made grown-ups think he'd want to talk to a complete stranger about what he felt, especially when he wasn't sure he was feeling anything at all? Lying in bed that morning, waking with a churning stomach and a tight throat, he'd pictured his heart with a small icing of frost around the edge, like the windscreen of the bus on winter mornings. Surely hearts weren't meant to feel like that?

Samantha said 'Don't worry if you feel upset when you are talking, or if you want to cry. We can take a little break if you need to.' Billy was more worried about the fact that he didn't want to cry; didn't seem to be able to cry. He'd been waiting to be ambushed by huge sobs, and so far, there was nothing. Samantha had boxes to tick on the sheet in front of her, whole paragraphs of white space that required filling in. It felt like a test he might fail; empty spaces of page where his words would not settle and which would not be interrupted by the tears she expected. He pictured his words as a big swoop of birds – Joey had told him that a group of crows was called a murder – so he saw his words as a murder of crows, thick-winged and soot-black, clustering together but not landing on Samantha Hollis's page. He'd looked at her blankly until she prompted him again.

His mum, he'd started to tell her, was a bit tricky to sum up. He told her that whilst she didn't take proper care of herself, injecting her body with things that should never have been near it, she tried to take care of him. As soon as he'd said that, he thought it might be difficult to give examples. Miriam knew about the bread through the letter-box. Might Samantha too? That wouldn't go down on a list of being caring.

She had all kinds of rules that were meant to keep him safe. He decided Samantha might like to hear about those. Not laughing when you were chewing in case you choked, especially if you were eating a bacon sandwich. Not walking close to the edge of the pavement in case you tripped and fell into the path of a car. Not walking outside in bare feet in case you stepped on broken glass or a syringe.

Samantha wrote it all down. Billy wasn't sure how much it had to do with how he was feeling, but the paper was filling up and maybe that was what mattered most. The last one – about the bare feet – had always seemed a bit rich. He had more chance of standing on a syringe when stepping out of the bath, although his mum was mostly careful that none of what she called her accessories were ever left lying around. Not that he needed to see them, he would have liked to say to Samantha; it was herself she left lying around, all too visibly affected by what she'd taken, her eyes shiny, her voice syrupy, and her hands spider-like, skittering through his hair and telling him she was sorry, she was happy, she was sad or that she loved him. Here, in my coal-black heart, she'd say, wrapping her fingers into a bruised fist and tapping herself on her breastbone, laughing softly. Once, she'd said to him *You're my sweet-faced tragedy*. He wasn't sure what that meant, but decided not to tell Samantha anyway.

Samantha, reading back what she'd written, didn't look as if she considered what he'd told her to be particularly good examples of caring or carefulness. Billy thought a bit harder, and added that his mum insisted that he always eat his vegetables, and that when she did buy meat she worried it might be full of chemicals. She hadn't seemed so bothered about her own body, he might continue, which seemed to be swimming with chemicals most of the time.

When it wasn't, because she couldn't get any, she sat turned to the wall, her fingers webbed together and pressed to her face. Then she was more likely to pass him, wordlessly, a packet of crisps and some Cheestrings, and he'd eat them in the cupboard under the stairs and wait for her to change. Samantha nodded almost enthusiastically at that bit. Billy wondered if he was supposed to feel pleased.

What he wanted to tell her, but couldn't quite bring himself to do so, was that his mother always said *There's no use crying over spilt milk*. She said that about lots of things, about what she referred to as his dad's upping and offing before he was even born, her own parents stopping giving her a monthly allowance, Grandpa not talking to her, and the vein on her leg which she said the doctor told her was so busted-up that she better not touch it again. And now, he couldn't help wondering if the same applied to whatever he was feeling, even if Samantha wrote it down. Crying over his mother was like crying over spilt milk, as spilt she definitely was.

He'd known it the moment he walked in from school and found her lying by the television, arms out like a scarecrow, some sticky bright blood from her mouth in a crusty puddle. He'd run next door to the bread-posting neighbour and then watched the paramedics pick up her body carefully (*Light as a wafer*, one of them said) and no light flashing on the ambulance outside. *That's always a bad sign*, Joey Meadows had told him afterwards. *With ambulances, when the light's switched off, it's curtains*. Billy wondered if his mum had been wrong about there being no point crying over spilt milk. She seemed worth crying over, even if he felt too dry to make any tears.

He turned his attention back to Samantha. She was handing him a tub of orange play-doh now, and told him he could play with it while he was talking to her. He remembered, in Year One, his class had made a huge flat sun out of petals of yellow and orange doh, and dressed it in a red hat with a jaunty feather. They'd stood in rows in front of it and sung *The sun has got his hat on, hip hip hip hooray; the sun has got his hat on and he's coming out to play*. Not exactly, Billy thought, squidging the dough between his forefinger and thumb. Not exactly.

He decided not to tell Samantha that he felt a little threadbare too. It wasn't only his grandma who could lay claim to that word. The last few months, he was tempted to say, what with knocks on the door at night, men's voices, and most of her money going on small foil parcels. Most days she seemed surprised when he got back from school, as if the day couldn't have gone by already, or as if she'd forgotten he lived there too.

She seemed to be forgetting her own rules as well; broken glass lay on the kitchen floor. She seemed too small, too thin, too raggedy, to get away from whatever chased her. She looked as if she'd had enough, that's what he wanted to say to Samantha. Enough of it all, and especially the trying. She mostly ate Haribo sweets; a heart evidently couldn't keep pumping fuelled only by Haribo sweets. The doctor had told him she'd died because it had stopped; her heart was worn out. Perhaps it hadn't been strong in the first place. He put his palm to his chest where he could feel his own heart steadily beating. Fingers crossed, like her poor circulation, he'd duck that as well. Samantha was looking at him steadily. He realised he hadn't said a word for some time. He squidged at the play-doh. Thinking was easier.

In the weeks before his mum's death, Miriam had popped in more often. He'd heard her talking on her mobile. *She's all over the place*, she'd said, *we must be approaching the time to apply for a Care Order*. He'd wondered what a Care Order was. Perhaps it was like a command which must be obeyed, and his mum would have to take more care because they would tell her to. He could have told them that telling her what to do didn't usually go so well; Grandpa had tried that, and look where that had got him.

At the end of the session Samantha asked for the play-doh back. That seemed a bit crummy. The least she could do, he thought, having expected him to tell her everything he was feeling, was to let him keep it, and not make him sit there while she neatly crimped it back into the pot. How many sad children, Billy wondered, had had a turn with that play-doh? Perhaps it absorbed all their sadness, and then sat in the pot swamped with the murders of crows' words children didn't want to speak. *The sun has got his hat on, hip hip hip hooray.* Not so much.

But, if she did give it to him and he put it into his pocket, he thought maybe sadness would seep into him. *Like with nuclear waste*, Joey would say. He'd want to experiment. That's what Joey would suggest, Billy decided, if Samantha Hollis hadn't asked for it back. They would have sat with half a tub each in their pockets, and tried to measure, at break-time, if they felt any sadder.

His mum's cremation was very small. He hoped this didn't mean she'd been unpopular for all of her life. He'd looked around the crematorium at Miriam, his teacher Mrs Bailey, Mrs Oliver, his grandparents, and his nextdoor neighbour, and hoped there might be a sudden flurry of grown-up pony club and orchestra girls, and men who were boys when she danced with them, her teeth newly even and straight. He'd wondered if his dad might show up. In a book that would happen, the man all ready to start over and be a good dad. No luck there, he'd concluded, no sign of anyone making his way sheepishly down the aisle, although the way Grandma kept looking over her shoulder at the door made Billy think she might be worrying it was a possibility.

They'd stood outside the crematorium afterwards, and Miriam went round to fetch her car to drive them back to Mrs Oliver's house. Mrs Oliver kept squeezing his shoulder, as if somehow she might pump him up into something bigger and sturdier. Billy tried to squint with his right eye, in order to block out the plume of smoke that was starting to come from the crematorium chimney. *That's my mum who is burning* was an oddly surprising thought.

His grandma hardly seemed able to look at him. Maybe she was copying Grandpa, who'd nodded to him when he came in but with his face almost turned sideways. Grandma said to Mrs Oliver *If only he weren't the image of his father . . . If only each time I looked at his face I didn't see Milo and the whole damn train wreck coming towards me again.* Perhaps Grandpa had decided that, long ago, when Billy was eight and visited them in Portugal.

Trains or ships seemed to crop up whenever his dad was mentioned. *Shipshape and Bristol fashion, post university,* was what his mum had said to him, *until your dad and the possibility of a thousand ways to shipwreck myself.* Billy knew his mother had gone to university in Bristol; he battled with where the ships came in, but thought better of asking her. Her voice had been at its syrupiest that day; he couldn't tell whether she was laughing or crying.

'Well,' Mrs Oliver had said as they got into Miriam's car, 'that's one version of grandparenting.' You can't really blame them, Billy said, and they both looked so surprised he didn't say anymore. What with, he could have told them, not just me looking the image of him, but this part of my skull which might be a sign of so much bad stuff to come.

As they drove away, he took one last look over his shoulder. The smoke from the chimney had dwindled to a thin wisp, like something from a cowboy and Indian film signalling bravely 'I'm here, I'm here'. But she wasn't. She definitely wasn't here anymore. Billy stiffened his shoulders and took a big swallow. She wasn't, actually, anywhere at all. Vaporised. Evaporated. Cindered. In Science they learned all kinds of words for processes which made something become nothing.

He should have guessed, he told himself, that a coffin made of woven willow wouldn't have lasted long in a fire. On Bonfire Night flames leapt and licked quickly through bundles of long twigs. He shouldn't be surprised that she was almost gone. He'd put his mother's favourite All Star sneakers on top of the coffin. Miriam helped him tie the long laces into very neat bows. She'd put some spit on her finger and wiped a smudge clean from the toes. He'd kept his eyes fixed on the All Stars as the coffin trundled its way towards the curtain. He recollected his mum tap-dancing wearing them, excited, her eyes shiny-bright, her bony fingers extended. She'd laughed and done jazz hands. Billy's eyes blurred with tears as the All Stars inched slowly forwards. Now, looking at the last wisps of smoke as Miriam's car gathered speed, he thought that if his mum was already burned by now, along with the willow of the coffin, and the canvas of the sneakers, all that remained might be the metal eyelets for the laces. Perhaps, in the powdery softness that was now her, the metal of the eyelets was melting and glistening. This was a comforting thought. He hadn't told Samantha, but it was a comforting thought. Should there be any chance of an afterlife in Heaven for a mother who was not a heroine at all, she would have her All Stars with her, ready for some dancing and a burst of bony jazz hands.

2

Miriam Riley sat at her desk, a folder before her with Billy Morris written on it in her large, looping handwriting. She could do with a cigarette. This was ridiculous; she'd given up as a New Year's resolution, had spent January and February looking like some kind of walking patchwork quilt with all the Nicorette pads she was wearing, and here it was, early May, patch-free for weeks, and still, at moments of stress, the desire to light up a cigarette, sit back, and hope for an answer filtered through a haze of warm, blue smoke.

She looked back at her notes from her meeting with Trudy Morris, Billy's grandmother, two days previously. Ted Morris had refused to come; that should have forewarned her. *He doesn't want to,* Trudy had said when Miriam phoned to arrange the appointment, as if it were an optional extra. *He's refused to discuss her for the last eighteen months.* Miriam wondered if she should point out it would not be Lizzie but Billy they were discussing; Lizzie was game over. Maybe in Ted Morris's mind there was no distinction.

Trudy's own response was not without appropriate hand-wringing and teary eyed-ness. She had sat before Miriam in a navy blue cardigan, a white and navy striped T-shirt, and well-cut taupe trousers, and she looked like a woman who still couldn't quite believe that she had been called to a meeting to discuss the custodial future of her only grandson, orphan of her recently deceased, drug-addicted daughter.

Trudy and Ted, Ted and Trudy. When Miriam repeated their names out loud, she felt they had an alliterative social glossiness, a little upbeat swing, which suggested that at a drop of a hat

Trudy and Ted might be game for drinks at the club, or for a whist drive; perhaps a party where one might be required to dress for the Roaring Twenties. What they apparently weren't up for, as became clear during the consultation, was taking on their grandson. There went that assumption, Miriam thought, and she was reminded of an old lover, a newspaper editor, who had written above his desk *Assumption is the mother of all fuck-ups.* How many times would it turn out, she wondered, that the route she assumed to be the automatic option was mostly the road not travelled?

Trudy Morris had not met her eyes as she told her, and had twisted the edge of her cardigan. Miriam had written down what she said, mostly in an effort to avoid looking at her and thus avoid any hint of what her own mother called her *sitting in judgment face* (this, on the occasions when she visited her mother and found her drinking ginger and lime gin fizz at three in the afternoon, alone, and spearing olives vindictively with a silver swizzle stick). Miriam had listened, composing her features into what she liked to think of as her patient, empathetic expression, while Trudy Morris faltered and stop-started, and ploughed through the awkward truth of not feeling able to take up where Lizzie Morris left off, which, as Miriam refrained from saying, was not a particularly high bar in terms of parenting.

I can't, I'm so sorry but I can't, Trudy said. *Ted is adamant; anything to do with her – with Lizzie – he won't countenance. It would be too much for me anyway; I'm too old and too worn out. Ted's had a small stroke recently. I need to be focusing on him. Lizzie has taken her toll on us all. Threadbare, threadbare is how it has left me. I can't explain how much. Last night I sat with a photo of her on her seventh birthday. She looks so happy, and all this was waiting to up-end and destroy her.*

She'd started to sob quietly, and finished by lifting her hands, palms uppermost, as if this might show to Miriam proof of her wornoutness, or of some form of crucifixion endured.

Miriam nodded. *I see, I see,* she said, which she didn't really but she thought it might smooth the way. Trudy rallied.

We could perhaps take him back to Portugal with us – for a week, maybe a fortnight – just while you get things sorted? I might be able to get Ted to agree to that?

Miriam thought it was not the time to disabuse Trudy of the notion that new families were found in seven days or so. Or, to say that tiptoeing around his grandfather's apparent hostility might not be the best environment for Billy, coming to terms with his mother's death.

I don't think that would be in Billy's best interests, she'd said. *It would be better for him to maintain his routine, his school, friendships, a familiar environment, and it would allow us to get started on the business of finding him a new home.*

And a business it was, Miriam thought, thinking of all the policy-bound criteria she would have to plough through, in contrast to the emotional desolation of the damaged woman sitting before her. Even if his grandparents *had* wanted him, it may not have been the optimum environment for the child. Too much damage, too much grief, too much – it appeared – resemblance to his father.

She'd spoken a little more gently.

I think what you need to do – and what in the circumstances seems to be in Billy's best interests for you to do – is to sign a Placement Order which absolves you of all responsibility for him and makes him a ward of court. Billy, and all decisions and information about him, would become our responsibility. You would be party to no information about him at all. You would be free to grieve for your daughter and resume your life in Portugal. For your husband, at least, that would seem to be a desirable outcome.

It didn't look like a panacea to Trudy Morris. Miriam's words seemed to be extracting her spine like drawing a splinter. She looked filleted. *We'll find him a new family*, Miriam had finished brightly, as if new families might be the regular outcome of a particularly specific treasure hunt. Afterwards Trudy appeared to limp out of the room; Miriam was relatively sure she hadn't limped in. Now, this morning, she determined to banish all thought of Trudy; Billy was who she should be thinking about.

She'd written out a preliminary list of options. Long-term fostering didn't look likely; that usually meant a return to the birth family when it became less chaotic. Lizzie's death and Trudy's obediently signed Placement Order scotched that. He was too young for short-term foster care; that was for older teenagers who were on the cusp of living independently. Adoption it should be. Miriam pushed back on her chair. Adoption should be the goal, even if at the outset the success rates for a boy of Billy's age were so low as to be worth weeping over.

Miriam looked at the photo of Billy on the first page of his file. She touched his cheek. *So I'd better find you a forever family*, she said out loud. Announcing it into the bald silence of the room somehow made it seem more achievable.

When Social Services found a child a successful adoptive home they called it a 'forever family'. The term was shot through with optimism and Miriam had some trouble with it. A forever family seemed to her to be a big ask, whether your circumstances were genetic or adoptive. (Her own mother drove her nuts.) The department had designed a little ceremony for it. At court, at the conclusion of a Placement Order, when adoption papers were signed, the judges made a bang of it and added a party feel. They gave the child a bunch of balloons, and let him sit in their chair. Miriam sometimes wondered if the ceremony wasn't more accurately an expression of mild disbelief and hysteria that a forever family had been nailed (*You're kidding, we've* really *found someone a forever family – crack open the balloons*).

Boys in care were thought to be violent, gobby, unschoolable, and not particularly loveable. Some with some justice, Miriam acknowledged, but never without extenuating reasons. Billy, however, wasn't any of those things. She'd never heard him even raise his voice. His request to put the All Stars on his mum's coffin had nearly undone her: the sneakers produced, God knows with what forethought and resourcefulness, from the grubby pillowcase he carried, and his fingers needing help with tying the long laces into bows.

She chewed at her lip. This was the part of her job when people expected a rabbit to be pulled out of a hat. Not just pulled out of a hat, but pulled out with an exuberant flourish. *Boy of almost ten, recently orphaned by his mother, absent and uncontactable father, copped-out, worn-out grandparents . . . BUT . . . ta – dahhh, the perfect prospective adopters and loving new home. Snug little bedroom, benign family dog, bright new aptitude at school. Vitamin count through the ceiling!* People wanted a child slam-dunked into a new life better-lived, the old one swooshed swiftly away with hardly a backward glance.

The truth was different. Children carried scars – all manner of neglect and injustice – and there was no guaranteed speedy panacea in home-cooked food, a calm space to do homework, and someone who could be counted on to pitch up when they were supposed to. So many children, thought Miriam, so many children born holding the shitty end of the stick. And now Billy; Billy for whom if she didn't find an adoptive home quickly, would most likely end up in a children's home, with all the emotional bankruptcy and chaos that entailed. She swallowed a mouthful of coffee still so hot it scalded her throat. For all the opportunity a children's home would give him, she might as well gather him up from the chair in the corridor and put him out with the rubbish. And not even, she thought bitterly, in the bin marked *For Recycling.*

She looked towards the corridor. He hadn't moved an inch. He was still sitting there clutching the damn pillowcase. He said it had all his things in, which was enough to make you weep. Lizzie had sold most of the stuff in the flat that wasn't nailed down. *At least,* she'd said to Miriam with something verging on pride, *I've never sold my body.* Miriam thought there was some consolation in this, but not in Billy's bare little room, his bed sized for a child much younger than him, a Buzz Lightyear cover on his duvet which was faded almost beyond recognition. There were pitifully few toys. Billy didn't go outside much, didn't kick around with the boys who hung around outside the lift. Lizzie said they were no-hopers, and she didn't want him mixing with them. What quite she thought she'd done with the allocation of hope that was his by birth, Miriam chose not to pursue. She sometimes wondered if by the end of her professional life she might lay claim to tact and diplomacy. They would certainly have been hard earned.

At school Billy was biddable. That was what his teacher, Cath Bailey, said. Biddable and sweet, if a little inhibited. *Never asked to play anywhere, never invited to parties, I think the head of the PTA scotched that; one of those whispers in the playground that might as well be sprayed in three-foot-high letters on the wall.* Lizzie had done well to get him into a village school outside of town, even though it meant he caught the bus, a pass round his neck when he was small. She'd lobbied for it, and appealed against their initial decision, during a clean spell when Billy was almost four. Smart thinking, a church school; it was an insight into the mother Lizzie might have been, had she not become consumed with shoving herself full of junk. It would have taken some foresight to anticipate the impact on playdates.

No outbursts. There had been no outbursts at all. Just his round, sweet, blank little face, with almond eyes and a dusting of freckles, his hair cropped short, his ears on the verge of protruding, his tongue often tapping his right front tooth. Miriam didn't doubt that the blankness was considered. It was an all too common characteristic; children in care learned quickly the upside of giving nothing away. His eyes, though, noticed everything, his eyes were always taking it all in. *C'mon Billy, what d'you reckon,* she'd say, and he'd shrug, lightly, non-commitally, refusing to jeopardise anything at all.

To get him to talk about himself, about what he wanted for himself, was going to be well nigh impossible. That was evident from the off. There would be the shrug again, a raising of the eyebrows and a downturn of the mouth all at once. Samantha Hollis had battled; she said he'd managed to talk a lot but say very little. *He asks questions,* Miriam told her, *questions about factual stuff. It's a clever strategy because he seems to be chatty without saying anything about himself at all, or if it is about him it's the baldest of detail.* Miriam could only recall one occasion, when she was waiting with him for the lift, bringing him home after his mother had been hospitalised, when he'd spontaneously offered anything about himself. *You'd think,* he said, *wouldn't you, if you were thinking about me,* (Miriam had found herself holding her breath) *you'd think with a dad who's supposedly a musician and a mum who got Grade Three Distinction on the flute, you'd think I might be musical, might be a bit talented at that. They've got recorder group at school now, at lunchtime on Tuesday. Mrs Bailey's put me in it; school have even given me a recorder, you know, one of those ones they keep in the blue bag for children who haven't got one at home, and I'm properly rubbish at it. We're playing* Merrily We Roll Along, *and my notes aren't going anywhere. It's like my fingers, my mouth and my eyes don't wire up at the same place at all.* He raised his eyebrows at her, and wiggled his fingers.

I'm sure you'll improve, Miriam had replied, *sometimes being quick off the blocks doesn't get the best results.*

He'd just looked at her and smiled, the smallest of twinkles in his eye, and it was all she could do not to scoop him up and make a bolt for the car. Upstairs, the flat would no doubt be smelling of broccoli soup. She'd take a bet on that before she even pressed the bell. *Screw the broccoli soup,* she wanted to say, *and all your bloody resolutions. You have a child to take care of, and that's about more responsibility than it takes to make soup.*

('Inclination to be a little terse with clients sometimes,' her supervisor Sheila had said in her appraisal. Who wouldn't be, Miriam rationalised afterwards.)

Even if she had said it, and it had taken some reining in not to, Lizzie would probably have agreed, would have nodded her head vigorously, earnestly, and said that she must get a handle on herself. *Be more responsible, yes, absolutely,* she'd have said. Miriam thought Lizzie had died of both a heroin overdose and her own poor, weak, good intentions. She had some sympathy with Lizzie's mother who'd put her shoulder to the wheel for years. *You can't save anyone,* she'd wanted to tell her, *that's what it boils down to. It's the thought that you can save someone that gets you into trouble in the first place.*

Sometimes, she wondered what kind of conversation her own mother might have with Trudy Morris. They'd both birthed daughters who hadn't lived the life they'd expected of them, although Miriam hoped she had some way to go before her own mother viewed her in the catastrophic terms Trudy saw Lizzie. Once, on the receiving end of her mother's tartness about her life choices, Miriam had said *At least I work for Social Services, rather than being the recipient of them.* Her mother's expression suggested that there wasn't much difference.

Miriam looked up from her file and out into the corridor. Billy still hadn't moved. Would it be wrong of her to wish for a streak of mischievousness in him, some unfetteredness that might mean when she looked up again he would be sitting with the waste-paper basket rammed on his head, pretending he was a robot and shooting at the figures in the posters on the wall? She logged into her computer.

Here was the moment she could no longer avoid, the one when she keyed in all of Billy's details and pressed *Enter* and waited for a list of possible prospective adopters to pop up, shiny with potential happiness. She always hated the search engine when it spat back *No available matches,* and it was odds on, today, that that was just what it would do. Good God, she thought (and that, she noted, was an expression with an irony all of its own) there was a child outside her office, sitting with the patience of Job, waiting for a conversation about a family he might go to, to be sent on little tasters of a life which might then possibly unfold before him, and all the computer was likely to come up with was *No available matches.*

Miriam rolled her eyes to the ceiling, stood up, and walked over to her office door. Opening it, she beamed at Billy in the corridor. *Sorry Billy, this is taking a little longer than I expected. I need to make a few phone calls. If you want to go and sit outside, perhaps under that tree where I can see you from my window, I can call you back in when I've got the details I need. Don't go wandering off.* (As if, Miriam thought, that was even a possibility.)

Billy nodded and, pillowcase in hand, made his way to the

exit. Miriam went back to her desk, and toyed with who to phone first. What did they say? It was easier to re-home a dog than a child. She banished the thought, and started tapping numbers on her phone.

Outside, Billy scanned the scrubby ground that surrounded the Family Centre. There was a wooden fence, once painted white, built around a tarmac area for cars; a patch of short, scuffed grass by a small red plastic swing and see-saw; and a tree, in full leaf, giving a broad ring of shade. There was a flower border, with a few little plants in straggly rows and a litter bin which looked like it hadn't been emptied for some time.

Billy watched for a moment, his eyes scanning left to right. There was a man with a hammer, a very tall man, who was repairing the gate to the car park with steady, patient taps. He was sweating in the heat, and there was a neat, damp V on his pale blue T-shirt. His hair was thick and curly, and looked as if it might get in his eyes. He stopped hammering for a moment, drew his forearm across his forehead, and reached into the van parked next to him and pulled out a bottle of Lucozade. He took a long, slow drink; if Billy scrunched up his eyes he could see his adam's apple moving. There was a bench by the swing and a young woman was sitting on it. She was with a toddler in a pushchair, who was licking an ice lolly. She was rolling the push-chair forward and back with one of her feet, her thumbs were busy texting; the toddler was asking to go on the swing. Billy looked again at the tree; Miriam had suggested the tree. He walked hesitantly towards it, and reached out, touching the bark carefully with his fingertips.

No singing, no ringing. Of course there wouldn't be. Billy sat down with his back to it, and pushed his shoulder blades gently into the curve of the trunk. This was a big tree, quite old, not like the one in *The Singing Ringing Tree* which could be uprooted at will, replanted, snatched by the dwarf, the princess, the prince, even the king. This tree felt as if it had been growing solidly, silently, reliably, for years. He consoled himself; the singing ringing tree couldn't possibly have existed, even though his mum seemed to have wanted it to have done so. The tree rings and sings, she said, in the presence of true love. Billy thought perhaps the person should know this for themselves, rather than needing the tree to point it out.

The dwarf in the story could magic up wind, snow, and floods; even turn the handsome prince into a bear. The princess started off cold, heartless and unkind to animals, and ended up loving the bear, who changed back into the prince. As she learned each of her lessons, she became prettier, until she looked like she had at the beginning but with a good, kind heart. His mum said she liked the story because it offered the chance to learn from your mistakes and end up better than you started. Billy could see why she found that comforting, even if she didn't seem as able as the princess to pull it off.

He turned to the tree he was sitting against, and placed his palm again on it. *Please don't ever sing or ring*, he said softly. The bark felt cool and thick under his hand. Billy looked around. The tall man had finished fixing the gate; now he was emptying the litter bin. The toddler in the pushchair had started to wail. *Oh shut up Dixon*, the mother was saying, *shut up, why can't you give me a break?*

Bets on, Billy thought, he and Dixon would be coming back to the Family Centre quite a lot. Miriam would make a plan – she always waggled her pen like a wand – and she would magic up meetings and there would be talking and talking and she'd write a lot of notes. That was supposed to mean everything was accurate and fair.

The dwarf wasn't treated fairly. Although he did bad things – changed a small thorny plant into an impossible fence, whipped up a snowstorm that buried a horse up to its neck – his wicked-ness gave the princess a chance to be good. She scooped away snow from the horse, and cracked ice from around a huge, eye-rolling, goldfish. His behaviour helped her to behave better, even though it wasn't obvious. He wasn't sure what this might mean in his own life, but thought it worth remembering. In what looked likely to be a possible shortage of permanent grown-ups around him, it might be sensible to hold on to anything that resembled wisdom. Perhaps he should write things down in his little brown pad?

He unknotted his pillowcase and rustled around for his pad and pencil. He found a clean page and wrote *Other people's bad behaviour can sometimes make your behaviour better.* Job done. He put the pad back into his pillowcase, and pressed his palms to the ground behind him. He grubbed his fingers between the raised tree roots, and felt an opening in the bark. There was a small, round hole. If he put something in it, he could check it each time he came back to the Family Centre. He patted it. It would give him a whole new idea of a tree, one that didn't do anything to give him the shivers, but instead stored things safely and carefully. He thought of his *Things to remember* notebook. Maybe that was where he could start. He took it out of the pillowcase, ripped out the sheets he'd already written on and folded them neatly into smaller and smaller squares. He tapped them for luck and pushed them into the hole. *My tree*, he thought, *my tree*. He considered blocking the opening with a small clump of moss. He scanned the ground around him but there was nothing thicker than the grass. *No one will find it*, he reassured himself, *no one will look here.*

He stood up and swung his pillowcase over one shoulder. He felt like Dick Whittington or a pirate, although that wouldn't stand up to closer examination. If they had what his pillowcase contained, he guessed they'd be strapped for a successful life on the high seas or the office of Lord Mayor of London. He looked across to Miriam's window; she was still at her desk.

He sat down again and started to examine the contents of his pillowcase. He wasn't sure what it was equipped to encourage, but everything in it felt dear. It didn't look much, examined in the bright afternoon sunshine.

There was an alarm clock which had long ago lost both the ability to alarm and, at the press of a button, to light up its frog face. It might only have needed a battery to get it croaking again, but batteries hadn't been top of his mum's shopping lists, and Miriam, he felt, had more important things to try and find for him.

He had a royal blue mouth guard which he'd been given at school when someone came to talk about the Olympics. His mum had fitted it for him, softening it first in a mug of boiled water. He hadn't used it yet but he'd looked after it carefully in case he should need it one day soon. In the interim he'd lost two baby teeth and gained a molar. He suspected that might be an issue.

He had a shin pad as well, just the one, which was perhaps also a problem. He took it out from the pillowcase and twirled it in the sun. Did anyone ever play with just one shin pad, he wondered? But it was such a fine one, such a smart one, with an Adidas logo and a gold line along the sweep of the calf. His mum had brought it home from a rummage sale. *I lost the will,* she said, *to keep rummaging for the pair. The woman said she wasn't sure it had ever had one.* It was worth keeping, just on the off chance.

On the grass he lined up a matchbox car, a transformer, and a set of false teeth that could be wound up to make jump. All of these had been birthday gifts from his mum, wrapped up in the same lollipop paper, re-used over and over again. He had a bobble hat which said Team GB and was red, white and blue. He'd won this at school for answering a question asked by the same man who came to talk about the Olympics. Right at the bottom was a book, *Dear Zoo.* He could remember his mum giving it to him, with a balloon, when he turned five. She'd taken him to the zoo on the same day for a birthday treat, and they sat on some grass and watched a cage full of monkeys. If he showed the book to the man fixing the gate, he would think it belonged to a toddler, not him. He was too old for it, and he should throw it away right now. He reached in and pulled the book out on to his lap. He touched one of its almost worn out audio buttons. The faint sound of an elephant trumpeting disturbed the stillness beneath the tree. He traced over the title: *Dear Zoo.* He thought he would be able to recite every word of this book if he lived to be a hundred; the story of a boy who wrote to the zoo to send him a pet, and got sent a series of animals which he sent back for an assortment of reasons, until the zoo finally cracked it and sent him a puppy. When he was smaller, he used to press the audio buttons one after another until he felt he had the whole zoo, calling and caterwauling, right there in his lap. He used to read it aloud to himself, his chest puffed out with confidence, loving the bit when he could say, with extra power and emphasis, *SO I SENT IT BACK*! He pressed the elephant button again. It was fainter this time.

He stood up again, and looked towards Miriam's window. He walked back into the Family Centre; maybe she would be finished soon.

Her door was slightly ajar and he could hear her talking; she sounded cross. He sat down quietly, and made a telescope of his fingers. Miriam's words threaded across the corridor.

'Look, Sheila, all I'm asking you to do is cut me some slack and let me play a little fast and loose with the usual procedures. If we agree it's in his interests, I can't see why that should be a problem. Think of it as speed dating. All I want is for you to agree that I can find some prospective adopters to start the Introduction process with but if there are any initial misgivings on either side I won't persevere and take ten months to decide and then have to go through a Disruption post-mortem. Instead, I'd like to act quickly and pull him out and start the Introductions process with someone else. Maybe we won't have to; maybe the first option will be perfect. Hooray. Pass me the balloons for the forever family ceremony. The thing is, Sheila, in reality I've got four months to find him somewhere and then he'll be ten and it'll be curtains, game over. Three strikes and he's out. You tell me the last time you successfully placed a boy over ten anywhere, especially one with a drug addict for a mother, which makes half of them stop reading right there. And don't even get me started on whether I'll consider different ethnicities. Bring it on, whatever the database can throw at me. In all likelihood even if we find two or three prospective adopters to start Introductions with, two will come back saying he's not quite what they're looking for.'

Billy looked down at his lap. Miriam didn't seem to be giving Sheila much time to answer. Her words snowballed in his head. If his alarm clock had been able to tick, it should start ticking now and most definitely be alarming, dud batteries or not. Four months until he was ten. Three strikes and he'd be out. He felt a bit sick.

He looked out of the window, and tried to focus on the bright green leaves of the tree. It looked quiet and still. His notes would be lying snug and safe in the dark cocoon at its roots. The possibility of it singing or ringing was obviously the least of his problems. His knee pressed against *Dear Zoo* in the pillowcase and the lion chipped in with a faded roar. It suddenly occurred to him, sitting there on a red plastic chair, his pillowcase on his lap, with Miriam's voice quieter now, it would be like in *Dear Zoo*, only it would be him that they were sending. It would be him who was not quite right for someone who had written to Social Services asking for them to send a child.

3

Billy sat on the bark chippings underneath the school climbing frame. Above him, Natalie Ferguson's white-socked legs dangled and swung as she tried to make it across the monkey bars. Beside him, Joey was trying to break a Wagon Wheel biscuit in half. Joey was big on absolute fairness. He'd started the deal that if either of them had anything for break-time, it should be shared absolutely evenly. He made an exception for fruit which he wasn't keen on. Joey was trying to draw a line down the middle of the biscuit with a piece of bark chipping. Billy wondered if he should point out this might not be hygienic. Joey wasn't big on hygiene. It probably wasn't the time to remind Joey that he'd peed on the bark chippings once, trying to write his name with the flow.

'So where's she go now then?' Joey asked.

It was Billy's first day back at school and he'd just given Joey a brief account of his mum's funeral, Samantha Hollis, and Miriam's idea about Introductions. The part about it being only four months until his tenth birthday he decided to keep to himself. Joey had a taste for countdowns and would probably have carved a calendar into the leg of the wooden climbing frame; perhaps really gone to town and illustrated it with progressively scuppered hangmen. Billy re-focused his attention. Joey's questions were never in sequence with the information he'd been given.

'My mum? Garden of Remembrance. Her name goes on a plaque on the wall. Grandma wanted her ashes, but Grandpa said no. You don't get to choose a flower or anything. You just go and sit there if you want to.'

'For remembering.'

'Yeah, for remembering. Although she never went there so it would be sitting there remembering her somewhere else.'

'I bet my Nan would go with you if you wanted to go. She's big on cemeteries and remembering. She came round last night. When my mum mentioned you, she said "Poor little sod" three times and then she said "Bless his heart".'

'What did she say after that?'

'"This hip will be the death of me", or "I could murder a Kit Kat." She's chatty. Your remembering visit wouldn't be all that peaceful.'

Billy wasn't sure remembering your dead mum would ever be peaceful.

'I told her she should look on the bright side,' Joey continued.

'What d'you mean?'

'I said that they're not going to leave you on your own like an orphan in a workhouse, are they, twisting hemp into rope all day or going up chimneys like we learned in Victorians. They'll find you someone, won't they, someone to look after you? That's what Miriam'll mean by her Introductions. It'll be a bit like *The Apprentice.*'

'*The Apprentice*? How do you get to that?'

'You know, the way the voice at the end of the programme says *And the search for Lord Sugar's business partner goes on* . . . That's what it'll be like for you.'

'Except nobody might want to do it and no Rolls-Royce.'

'Rolls-Royce maybe. Power of television, Billy. Perhaps you could search for a new family on television. People would love that. Ask Miriam. Cameras would focus on you in the Roller . . . *And the search for Billy's new family goes on.* Maybe Lord Sugar would lend you the car. We could write him a letter. My hand-writing's better but you'd think of all the sad phrases. Imagine it. You could go round in the Roller looking for a new family.'

Billy took the Wagon Wheel half Joey offered. He had to credit him, nothing ever meant game over. He'd tip his head to one side, open his arms out wide and make anything seem possible and a bit of a lark. Billy conjured up an image of himself in the back of a Roller, pulling up outside a house where a couple stood by a gate, hands clasped, waiting. There might be jam tarts on the table, and maybe chocolate milk shake.

'Mrs Bailey talked about you while you were away,' Joey continued.

'Did she say "poor little sod" too?'

'No. She says you might be less talkative. Might want to talk less. Might want to talk. Might want to. Might want. Might. M. Might want some space to feel sad.'

'What, like under a climbing frame you mean?'

'You know you're glad I'm here. We could go back to what we did in the winter, remember, you under here and me by the bins on the other side doing semaphore. You've got to admit we got that pretty taped.'

'We never got beyond "It's cold", and I'm not sure we got that right. We could have been saying something else completely.'

'What about when we did Morse code on the toilet doors? That was genius. If we did that now, and you were talking less, it would be quick to show. I could report back to Mrs Bailey with clear proof. Dot dash dot. Dot dash. Dot. D. Over and out real quick. Gold slip awarded to Joey Meadows for exact proof that Billy Morris has stopped talking altogether.'

Joey was trying to make things normal; Billy could see that. He was talking about his mum's death, not pretending it hadn't happened. At least he was asking about her, and it felt, briefly, as if she was under the climbing frame with them, even though she wouldn't be that keen on bark chippings which might smell vaguely of pee. He'd like to have told Joey that it was difficult to place her anywhere, even despite the Garden of Remembrance. She seemed like a balloon which had tugged free of its tie and floated away. However hard he scrunched up his eyes to try and see her, she was out of his view.

To be almost laughing, Billy reflected, was probably better than almost crying. Or actually crying, which he'd felt like doing, for the first time, when Mrs Bailey read out his name on the register. He suddenly felt so completely alone, so utterly completely without anyone who properly truly cared for him, it was hard not to put his head on his desk and start sobbing. He'd taken a big swallow before he said *Yes* to his name. Mrs Bailey had looked up and smiled at him when he spoke; with a smile that grown-ups seemed to have for him now, since his mum had died, which started with a wrinkle in their foreheads where they were probably thinking '*Poor little sod*' too. Joey's Nan wasn't that wide of the mark, just a bit more direct.

4

Climbing into it, Miriam Riley acknowledged that she loved her bed. In the absence of someone to love *in* her bed, this would have to count as enough to be going on with. Men, in her life, were mostly short-term. This, so far, had not yielded to scrutiny.

Her mother said there was something off-putting about her. *The way you stride into a room, Miriam, it's as if you are announcing a coup or a putsch. There's not an ounce of femininity.* Miriam privately wondered if her lack of success in relationships with men was more to do with the fact that her mother had totally done her head in on that front, and would continue to do so whilst offering additional helpful insights (*Maybe some highlights, Miriam, they can soften the face beautifully*). Her mother's beauty had only been gently softened and smudged by age. Miriam thought the book was yet to be written on the particular frisson engendered by being the not beautiful daughter of a beautiful woman; her entire childhood and adult life spent, she felt, with people registering, quick as a heartbeat, that no, she had definitely not inherited her mother's looks. Maybe that was why she strode purposefully into a room, defences up, ready for the palpable reminder that Beauty was capricious in its bestowing. Her mother also remained tack-sharp. Despite this being occasionally wounding, Miriam decided the upside was that she could hopefully rule out Alzheimer's; it wouldn't be nestling subversively somewhere in the near future, steel-edged, razor-toothed, like a trip-wire for them both. Each maternal barb could be filed, positively, reassuringly, away.

Miriam snuggled down deeper. It had become something of

an obsession, this dressing of her bed in perfectly toned layers. She loved The White Company brochure and in recent years had ordered multiple tastefully neutral bedspreads and throws, and had a cupboard full of high thread count white linen. Her own bed, she felt with a degree of pride, could give any of the styled beds in the catalogue a run for their money. Hers definitely deserved a wider audience, if only she could find one. She particularly enjoyed the catalogue sections entitled 'Top Tips' which provided helpful, soothing guidance on maximising aesthetic appeal. She occasionally wondered how the same approach might play out in her own working life; how a series of Top Tips might give her charges a corresponding lift. The potential was not the same. *Top Tip: try and avoid being born to a heroin addict mother; try, if you can, to discourage your mother from taking up with a man who'll resent you from the off and use you as an ash tray; avoid, if possible, being hurled against a wall by your birth father just before he returns to prison.* That wasn't going anywhere uplifting.

What she loved about lying in her own bed was that she felt safe; safe from all the chaos of her working life, and with the weight of pure white cotton, slippery satin, and ribbed, double-knit wool enfolding her like a cocoon. She could hardly move.

Billy was apparently too frozen to move. That was how Samantha Hollis had termed it, in a debrief held after her session with him. Cath Bailey, his teacher, had corroborated her view.

'What's happened,' Samantha said (they'd met in the local Costa, and as she waited for her, Miriam imagined a parallel life that might consist of school runs and conversations about whether to join a Bikram class or not) 'is that he's become disconnected; not right now, not immediately, like a fuse that's blown or a switch that's tripped. No, it's been more gradual I think. He's not showing any of the signs of panic and intense grief demonstrated by a child who feels himself to have been abruptly abandoned. I think he might feel as if he's been abandoned gradually, as his mother retreated into herself, ring-fencing him with a few rules and an oddly passive style of parenting.'

'Except for the soup episodes.'

'Yes, although I sense he was losing the will to believe in those as fresh starts. He's definitely withdrawn, disconnected. I think there are probably huge monologues going on his head, and yet all he does is nod. Look, let's be frank, you can't expect him to be running round laughing and joking. The child's lost his mother, but it would be a good sign to see a thawing, some kind of engagement. It's a tricky one. It didn't sound like he had a particularly communicative relationship with his mum. Do you think he did?'

Miriam shrugged. 'She watched TV a lot. I think she left him to his own devices. Once I went there and told her I was popping in to see Billy, and she showed me to the cupboard under the stairs. He was sitting there holding some old instrument case, and she didn't seem surprised. She acted as if it was like a kids' den and nothing remarkable. It was probably the only place in the flat where she never went, so what do we infer from that?'

'Not much that's positive. We're better off focussing our attention forwards. I just want you to understand him as partially disconnected. With all the social skills you'll be requiring of him in the Introduction process, you need to be mindful of that. One, it's a big ask, and two, you need to be watchful for any positive signs of thawing.'

'So that's all good then.'

'Careful, you're starting to sound bitter.'

'Not bitter. That's probably further down the track. Jaded. That's more professionally appropriate. Maybe excusable too, when you think what I deal with. And what, by the way, do you think of his grandparents' decision not to take him on board? Do you think that's compounded his frozenness?'

'What I think is less important than what Billy thinks. And again, oddly, he seems relatively forgiving and understanding. You said he revealed that in the car on the way back from the funeral. I'd love to know what's going on in his head, but there's not much chance of winkling it out. Perhaps he sees his grandmother as his mother's mother – in that Lizzie was her first priority – rather than as his grandma, who should be looking after him. That would be another example of him distancing himself. Or maybe he's secretly hoping his dad might show up.'

'He's never mentioned him. That isn't to say he doesn't think it's a possibility, although I've got nothing on him, not even a surname. Could have junked himself too for all we know.'

'What a mess.'

'No, not a mess, a life. And therein why it's got to be fixed.'

'Go to it, Miriam,' said Samantha. 'Atta girl.'

Miriam shifted underneath the weight of the bedclothes. If she'd brought home every child she'd felt compassion for in the course of her career, she'd be like Brigitte Bardot except with stray children not stray animals, and without the peachy youth spent on yachts in St Tropez. In fact, all she'd have was the line-raddled, careworn face. Her mind snagged on the expression *stray children*; nobody ever used that term, but it was what she dealt with. It all felt overwhelming.

Perhaps she should just whisper *I haven't a clue* into the multi-textured depths of her bed. She felt restless and agitated. How many times had she told herself not to think about work when she was trying to sleep? It was fruitless to expect inspiration or the answer to alight on her Hungarian goose down pillow. The more predictable outcome was that she'd wake with a tension headache, her jaw rigid from having her teeth clamped together all night. That sequence of events wouldn't make it into a White Company Top Tip box. You were only ever meant to wake up dewy-skinned, rested and refreshed, copping an eyeful of your bedroom and all its beautiful calming components.

5

Meg Oliver sat on the side of her bed and worked some hand cream into her fingers. Her hands always rustled and rasped when she rubbed them together at the end of the day. Too much water, always in and out of water, she thought. She stopped and listened. Seven children tonight, one at the last minute, now all sleeping. She slept like a dog, not a log, she thought; always one ear cocked, listening for a whimperer, for one who called out in the night, for ones whose dreams chased them somewhere, heart thumping. In the morning, she made all the beds, patting her hand casually beneath the duvet to see which sheet was wet and reeking.

She climbed into bed, turned off her lamp and pulled the covers up under her chin. She gave a small pulse of thanks that, for today and tonight, all the children under her roof were, at least, safe and warm. It wasn't a prayer she uttered; that would be a bridge too far. She'd long ago decided that if God existed he didn't seem to be paying sufficient attention. Suffer little children to come unto me? Not so much. Not in famine camps in Ethiopia, in orphanages in Romania, or shell-pocked houses in Syria. Not in the tattered debris of lives that washed up at her house each day; damage, neglect, abuse in varying degrees. Meg had to wonder sometimes at the capacity of the human race to totally screw up parenting. How hard could it be to birth someone, feed them, dress them, keep them warm, love them, maybe focus a little on the difference between right and wrong. Rustle up a birthday cake once a year, candles a bonus. The animals and birds had it sorted. A blue tit, in her garden this spring, practically killing herself with constant forays to and from the nest.

Cats with kittens in the scrub of the hard shoulder of the motorway; lions and cheetahs shown on television documentaries travelling miles to hunt for food for their cubs. It was only humans who got it so spectacularly wrong. Children caught up in the poison that rankled between their parents, or unfed, ignored, left in wet, stinking clothes. And that was not counting the physical and sexual abuse; the children who turned up at her house at all hours, bearing the brunt of an adult's inadequacies.

One of the latest Government initiatives had taken the biscuit: the proposal of a measure to make all schools provide breakfast clubs. It was meant to ensure that all children started the day with some food. How hard could it be, Meg thought, for a parent to put out some cereal, some milk, maybe a slice of toast?

Laying the breakfast table was the last thing she did at night, the children all in bed, the kitchen quiet and still. She lined up boxes of cereal, jars of marmalade, jam and Nutella, and put out a bowl, plate, spoon and mug for each child who was staying. She always laid one extra place. It was a habit she'd got into, so that the last child who arrived in the kitchen had a choice about where they wanted to sit. This seemed important, when choice was absent from so much of their lives, and also in case someone had pitched up in the night. It was disconcerting for a child to be reminded they were a late, unanticipated addition.

Meg had no children herself; she thought this was responsible for the way her life had unfolded. A daughter, born twenty-six years ago; grey-blue, premature, the bones of her skull narrow like a rabbit's. She'd stayed alive for twelve days, her heart beating, a small, livid pulse on her temple flickering to match. Meg had sat by the incubator, held on to her tiny hand and used the tip of her finger to stroke her soft cheek. When she died, they'd let her hold her, wrapped in a blanket stamped with the name of the hospital. It had caused Meg the most inexplicable pain, the fact that her daughter died wrapped in a worn blanket that wasn't her own.

Peter, her husband, had wept uncontrollably, not spoken much, just wept. Huge great racking sobs out in the garden when they came home that night, and she'd placed her hand, wordlessly, on the heaving space between his shoulder blades, and stood there, silent in the blue dark, her breasts leaking and sticky, haemorrhaging loss. *I'll not risk my heart again* was what he had said, turning to her in the morning in the light of a placid dawn, and it turned out he didn't have to, because she never conceived again. She kept a lock of the child's hair in a box by her bed. Over the years its soft gleam had faded; sometimes she still traced the whorl of it with her finger. *I would never have harmed a hair on your head*, she would whisper, her body bone-tired at night from picking up after parents who felt no such compunction. Peter's heart slammed to a halt of its own accord when he was forty-four; sweeping snow from the path, his face misleadingly, cruelly, rosy cheeked in death.

The trickle of children that had begun during his lifetime turned into a flow after that; the house full of them, constantly coming and going. She'd filled up bedrooms with bunk beds, bought great stacks of pyjamas, T-shirts, trousers. For any child who came to her, she could provide the basic necessities. *Can I wear the blue striped ones, the ones I wore last time?* a child would ask, brought to the door wrapped in a blanket, clothes filthy, smelling of pee. Nit combs she had by the dozen, worm medicine, ringworm cream; some of them were almost feral such was the degree of neglect. A neighbour, Doreen, complained about all the cars coming and going; Social Services approved drivers for school runs, social workers for meetings, health visitors to check on children who had sustained injuries. Meg had stood on her doorstop, her arms folded over her bosom, and listened while Doreen's voice whined and wheedled, saying it was spoiling the character and tone of the street. Meg invited her in; the children were all having breakfast. Seven of them lined up, an older one divvying out Weetabix. *Children*, she'd said, *this is one of my neighbours, Doreen Walker, would you like to say good morning?* and each one of them had chimed in, like something from *The Sound of Music*. The littlest said it, and then licked his spoon and stuck it to his nose. Meg shepherded Doreen out, and on the doorstep, turned to her and said *So which ones precisely do you take exception to?* She'd not heard from her again; she'd scuttled off down the path.

Some nights it was wearying. Some nights it was soul-destroying when she acknowledged that all the clean pyjamas, all the lined up cereal bowls in the world couldn't begin to ameliorate the fact that these children were not being cared for as they should have been. She had sympathy for the social workers, trying to make the best of a bad job, trying to have rules, policies, guidelines, taut nets of words and accountability which wouldn't allow children to slip through or be failed. She liked Miriam Riley. She liked how she got things done. If a building were on fire, people should follow Miriam Riley. Once, Miriam had said to Meg, in the days when Miriam smoked, and they'd been out in the garden, Miriam talking about a child, her hand waving, the cigarette making ribbon-looped streams of smoke, *I don't know what I'm going to do about her, Meg. Frankly I'm whistling in the dark*, and Meg had been discomfited. She did not like to think of Miriam unsure.

Miriam had brought her Billy now. Sweet, earnest-faced Billy; he was an unusual case. She'd met his mother, once, when she'd taken Billy home after a stay. She'd reminded her of a horse, easily spooked, skittish. Billy didn't say much; they were always the ones to watch, the ones to keep an eye on for any turbulence within. The ones who let it all out, they were always the least of the problem. They were on the fast track to being fixed; she'd seen that time and time again. Once, a girl called – what was she called? sometimes their names eluded her – but she could see her now in the kitchen, must be at least five years ago – defiant and furious, a bag of frozen Brussels sprouts in her hand. Meg kept a bag of them in the freezer – no chance she'd ever persuade a child to eat one – and she used them as a cold compress on bruises and bumps. This child had stood there, incandescent, brittle; pulled open the bag and steadily pelted Meg with frozen sprouts. *Fuck you, fuck you, fuck you,* she'd said as each one bounced off Meg, or the chair, or the window sill. Meg had said nothing until the bag was empty. She'd stood there, calmly, in a hail of frozen Brussels sprouts and fuck yous. When the child had finished, she'd walked over and scooped her up in her arms. *You probably feel better with getting that off your chest,* she'd said, *your fingers must be cold.* The child had started to sob; huge great choking sobs, and Meg had held her, and rocked her, until she was almost asleep on her lap.

Meg Oliver had a vast bosom like a bookshelf; she viewed it as one of the best assets for her job. If God didn't seem preoccupied with gathering up children to comfort, she considered herself well equipped for the task.

She wasn't long falling asleep. She stirred when a tom cat scrambled over the gutter. The house was quiet and still. Later, a child called out Meg's name, and she rose from her bed, her plenteous nightgown swooshing with her tread, and she walked purposefully to the child's bedside, saying *Hush hush little one,* and Billy Morris, lying awake but completely still in the opposite bunk, thought that if angels existed, they should be properly big and solid, and look just like Meg Oliver. Then, if you were falling through frozen air, spare and light as a clean, smooth bone, an angel would be able to catch you properly, deftly, no question.

6

When Billy woke up, it took him a second to remember where he was. Then it came back; Mrs Oliver's, Bedroom Two, bottom bunk. Night ten. This was a first. Mrs Oliver's was meant to be three or four nights and then home, or on to someone else.

'Special circumstances,' Miriam had said. 'Meg must like you to break her own rules.'

Billy wondered if it didn't just mean there was nowhere else to send him. Joey's more positive take on it was that he must be *exceptional*. He said the word with a flourish; he took great pride in his vocabulary. *Exceptional at what?* Billy had said. *Exceptional at being at Mrs Oliver's – that's obviously enough.*

Joey had angled to see if Mrs Oliver might consider any sleepovers for friends; he was fascinated by the idea of the long breakfast table, and being allowed mugs of tea with two spoons of sugar. He was also curious as to how the pyjamas got allocated. (Joey prided himself on being a details man.) *What if two people want the same ones, what happens then? Does she flip a coin, or is it first one to bed? Or maybe is it taking it in turns depending on who wore them the last time?* Billy had shaken his head. It was hard to explain that tussles like that simply didn't happen. Maybe everyone there was a bit too grateful to stake a claim so boldly, or maybe there were simply enough appealing pyjamas to go round. Joey had changed tack.

If I did get to sleep over, would we be allowed to go on the same set of bunks?

You wouldn't be allowed to sleep over. It's not like that. Your mum and dad would have to mess up.

My Nan clipped me round the ear once, do you think that would count?

No, especially as she made you a fish finger sandwich afterwards to say sorry.

It would be cool though, wouldn't it, in the bunks, like in a pyjama club.

A pyjama club did sound cool. Billy toyed with suggesting one at Joey's house. He'd hardly ever been there. Joey's mum said she had enough unexpected small boys about the place. Joey had been born when his mum was forty-four. His sisters were already grown up with babies of their own. (*I was a surprise*, Joey said, and would pretend to jump up like a jack-in-the-box.) His mum had a hairdresser's shop in town, and she loved working there; that was why Joey's Nan looked after him before and after school, and Saturdays too. Women came to his house in the evening to have their hair done. Sometimes, Joey had to sit and fold the foil parcels for the highlights; he said it was the dullest thing ever. That was probably why there would be no possibility of a pyjama club there, if the kitchen was full of women having their hair cut and coloured. *They start talking about something*, Joey said, *and then Mum remembers I'm sitting there doing the foil and she makes her eyes go wide and nods towards me so that they won't say anything interesting.* Billy thought it all sounded interesting. In his flat, with his mum, it was only ever the two of them, or Miriam, or Grandma, and that usually meant something was up. A kitchen full of chattering sounded appealing.

He looked down at his chest. Dennis the Menace pyjamas. He'd worn these before. The top had Gnasher printed on it but his face was cracked where Meg had caught it with the iron. Dennis's face was printed on the left knee of the bottoms, and remained pinkly unscorched. If you considered it, most things could be put down to luck and chance; there was Dennis, off scot-free, whilst Gnasher's nose was completely melted. It all came down to the wrong place, wrong time, hot iron looming, Meg lifting her glance at the wrong moment to check on a child, and curtains for Gnasher.

Billy stretched his hand from beneath the duvet, and felt beneath the bunk. His pillowcase was still there. He patted it softly. He'd chosen not to put it in his locker in the hallway. He felt for *Dear Zoo* and pressed an audio pad randomly. He settled back into his pillow and listened to the monkey screech. In the quiet of the morning it seemed surprisingly vigorous. The monkey got sent back because it was too naughty.

What counted as good, he wondered, for a Social Services Introduction? Miriam hadn't been super-clear about that part: she said it was really just like a meeting. Not with an agenda of things to consider, not that sort of meeting. *Just perhaps going for lunch, or doing something nice, and seeing if you like the person, you know, find them easy to talk to, maybe laugh at their jokes.* It seemed a tall order.

Good manners were probably helpful. His grandma had told him that. Most table manners were worked out so that nobody had to watch anybody else use cutlery like shovels and chew with their mouths wide open like a cement mixer. Perhaps he could have asked his grandma what counted as good manners for Introductions. If she still was his grandma – which he hoped technically she still was – it would have been useful to be able to pop her a question now and again. Even if they didn't want to bring him up, that would have been comforting. He hoped all record of his connection to them hadn't been wiped out. If that kept happening – his dad, his mum, his grandparents – he wouldn't have a family tree, it would be just him, by himself, no connections going anywhere.

Both of his grandparents might have had some suggestions with regard to the right manners for Introductions. With other people, at the golf club, in Portugal, his grandpa had done lots of firm hand shaking. He always looked people smack in the eye when he did it, and sometimes used his other hand to slap their shoulder. He wasn't sure Miriam would think much of that. When people came into her office, she mostly smiled and then waggled her pencil to show them which chair to sit on. Would Meg know? She was a hugger, a picker-upper, a scooper into her big fat arms. Introductions probably didn't work like that. Last night when she'd come to Archie's bedside, she seemed vast in the half-light of the room, her flesh substantial and solid beneath the folds of her nightdress. There was no hint of anything within her that might be sharp or poky. He'd fallen asleep thinking her bones must be as solid as pillars. She looked as if she could never be blown over by anything.

Bowing. That could be part of Introductions. He remembered a tape he'd had, when he was much younger, of sing-along songs. It came back to him now, something about gentlemen bowing. The gentlemen – ah yes, he had it now – *bowed most politely and bowed once again*. If that was an Introduction, it couldn't possibly be interpreted as naughty. It would be extra-polite and guaranteed to make a good impression.

The tape, he remembered, got all scrambled in his Early Learning Centre player. His mum had tried to repair it, using a pen to rewind the spools that glittered like fish. It hadn't worked. When he pressed Play afterwards, all the words had melted into each other. The gentlemen weren't bowing anymore, and didn't sound like they would do so again. He lay back on his pillow and made his index fingers bow. He made them bow to each other, and then, more deeply, to his face.

Downstairs, he heard Meg calling that it was time for breakfast. He got swiftly out of bed. Some days his mum didn't even manage that; just put her face in her hands and turned and faced the wall. He patted Dennis on his knee; Dennis-smooth, scot-free, undamaged by the iron. Miriam said that the Introduction process usually took months, but for him they were going to speed it all up. Perhaps that would mean he had less time to worry about how he was supposed to behave. Maybe he wouldn't even have time to think.

In the kitchen, Meg was pouring tea from the huge spotted teapot. Billy looked at the whiteboard on the wall by the table. Each morning, Meg looked at the list sent to her by Social Services, and wrote out clearly what each child was doing. Some stayed with her and waited for their guardian or key worker to come; some went to the Family Centre and had supervised contact with their parents. One day soon, Billy thought, Meg would write

Introduction next to his name. Today, she just wrote *School*. That was a relief.

Joey thought that coming to school in a taxi was super-smart. He mostly walked down the hill with his Nan after his mum had gone to the shop. His Nan liked dawdling past the churchyard and Joey wasn't allowed to run ahead. When Billy arrived in the taxi, Joey hung on to the wire fence of the playground and whooped as the driver parked in the lay-by and got out to open the door. *The Big Man's arriving*, he'd shout, and Billy would get out, blushing.

Today they were practising for Sports Day. They didn't used to have proper races, in case anybody's feelings were hurt when they came last. After the man came to talk about the Olympics, the headmistress decided that just as some children were encouraged to be brilliant at maths, it was good for others to be allowed to run like the wind. Billy didn't expect to excel at either.

Meg watched him as he did up his trainers for school. She gave him a tube of sun screen in case it got hot. She reached into the cupboard and gave him a Kit Kat for his snack. She'd already given him a banana but said he could eat the Kit Kat if he promised to eat the banana first. Joey would be chuffed. Kit Kats were easy to divide. Mrs Oliver took out a comb and did some sort of smoothing thing with his hair. When she finished, she tapped her finger on the tip of his nose and said *Now little man, off you go and be brilliant!* He thought it was nice that she said that, even if there was no evidence that he could be. He thought of his sing-along song and gave her a formal bow, except it came out a bit cramped and he suspected looked more like a bird bobbing on a stump. Meg looked puzzled, but Billy had gone off pleased. If bowing were ever actually required to make a good impression, that would no doubt count as some nifty early practice.

After school, the taxi dropped Billy off at the Family Centre. Miriam wanted to talk to him. Joey said maybe she'd got an Introduction sorted. Billy thought it was more likely a check that he'd understood everything properly. Social Services were very big on explaining stuff until they were convinced you'd completely got it.

His taxi arrived at the same time as Miriam's car pulled up. She got out of her car with a coffee cup in her hand, her bracelets all jangling, and a big stripy bag over her shoulder.

'Hey Billy, how was school? You look hot.'

'We practised for Sports Day, all the races.'

'Are you thirsty?'

'No, I'm fine thank you.'

They fell into step and walked towards the building. The tall man Billy had noticed three days ago was replacing a pane of glass in the entrance.

'Hello Andrew, how are you, how's things?' Miriam asked.

'Good thanks. Lovely afternoon. You look hot, mister,' he said to Billy.

Miriam's phone rang.

'I'll just be a sec,' she said to Billy, lifting her index finger in the air and stepping to one side.

'Sports Day practice,' Billy said, watching how the man rolled the putty around the edge of the new sheet of glass.

'Win anything?'

'Second in two races. One was the wheelbarrow, we'd have won but my friend Joey kept dropping my legs.'

'Takes time to get your pace back when that happens.'

'Hopefully he won't do it on the real day. What's the word for someone who fixes glass?'

'That would be a glazier.'

'Is that what you are?'

'Nope.' He pointed to a van in the car park. 'That's my van over there – see the writing? Carpenter, handyman, decorator. Jack of all trades more like but mostly a carpenter, a chippy.'

'Why's a carpenter called a chippy?'

'From being covered in woodchips and shavings I think, from the old days, when they only worked with wood. All manner of stuff now.'

Miriam's voice drifted back towards them.

'I can't talk anymore, I've got a meeting. Yes, him, that's the one. Hopefully, yes.'

'Maybe your ears should be burning,' the man said.

Billy nodded.

'What's your name?'

'Billy. Billy Morris.' He gestured towards Miriam. 'Miriam's trying to find me a forever family.'

'Good luck with that.' The man smiled and started to sweep up the broken pieces of glass on the paving. Miriam beckoned to Billy to follow her.

He turned to go.

'What's your name?'

'Andrew Walker – see, it's on the van too.'

Billy nodded.

'Come on, Billy,' said Miriam, 'sorry about that; I'm switching my phone to silent.'

'See you around, I expect,' said Andrew.

Billy nodded again. He wasn't sure he agreed though. What life seemed to be teaching him so far was that it wasn't good to expect anything.

7

Caroline Fraser stood in the sanitary protection aisle at Tesco's and tried not to cry. Other women might have fixated on nappies, or babygrows, but the thing that stopped her in her tracks was boxes of tampons. For some, she acknowledged, this might require an explanation. It was ridiculous, anyway, standing motionless in the aisle like someone mouth half-open with memory loss, fingers gripping the trolley handle as if it might save her from being swept away. It was ridiculous – evidently so – because if you were pregnant you didn't need tampons. She chided herself that she should at least be more logical in the things which brought her to a halt. On one occasion she had stopped there and actually wept, her palms up to her cheeks like the pages of a soft-skinned book. An older woman had walked past and patted her on the arm. Caroline was taxed as to whether it was meant in solidarity, in pity, or as a rallying call to buck up. She took a deep breath. Mindfulness. That was what she was supposed to be practising when everything came crashing in.

The thing about sanitary protection, and she was mindful that Toby often teased her for making too much of things, was that they were symbolic of fertility, much more so than a babygrow or a nappy. If your ovaries were working, if your hormones were chiming in perfect accord, what you had was a period, and you needed to buy protection. If you were pregnant, you didn't need it. If you weren't pregnant and still didn't need it, it was indicative of two life stages: girlhood or post-menopause. Caroline was beyond the first, and technically not meant to be at the second. At forty-one, however, an early menopause had ambushed her, explaining her failure to conceive in the second half of her thirties.

She gathered herself and looked in her trolley: lemons, curly kale, spelt flour, chicken. She seized on their ordinariness and named them mentally – over and over – to inch her away from the desire to burst into tears. An assistant was by her shoulder. How long had she been standing there? Had she spoken aloud?

'Can I help you?' the assistant asked. 'Is there something you're looking for?'

'No, thank you, I'm fine, thank you. Sorry, just trying to remember the ingredients I need for a recipe.'

The assistant nodded, and left her. How would the woman have responded, she wondered, if she'd said *Yes, actually, you can, I'm looking for another child, although not in this particular aisle obviously. Might you be able to help me with that?*

Some would consider her greedy, considering she actually did have a child, although the word child seemed to sit less easily on Horatio now that he was twelve; the line of his jaw changing as puberty began to jostle its way into view. If she lived in China she would already have her allocation, and a son would be considered additional good fortune. Except she lived in England, and it didn't feel enough. As mother to one child, she felt under-capacity. That was the expression she had come up with to try and make sense of it to Toby. He'd given it his best shot; he'd humoured her through it all.

Caroline couldn't remember being alive without having had a plan to have at least four children. It was tattooed on her beginnings, that was how she saw it – imprinted right through her like a stick of rock. As a child, she covered shoe boxes in Fablon to make little beds, and knitted a series of blankets in matching colours. Each night she would tuck up four of her dolls and pretend she was kissing her children goodnight. She'd kept a notebook where she listed all of their names. If she found the notebook now, it would have made her cry, her neat pencil script infused with the optimistic, childish certainty that what you hoped for, you'd achieve. Evidently not.

Now, when the Boden catalogue came through the door, she would sit at her kitchen table and mournfully turn the pages, looking at tousle-haired children holding shrimping nets and wearing striped flannel hoodies, beaming out from lives crammed with wholesome chaos and warmth. It was hard not to feel that it was her own life she was looking at, the life she was meant to have lived, and which, had she found the right door to, she would have slotted into with ease.

She would have been good at shepherding a small squad of children into a people carrier, a Land Rover, something with many seats. 'Come on chaps', she would have said, as they followed her like ducklings. She would have suppressed a frisson of pride when she saw that half the front row of the school orchestra consisted of her offspring. At Christmas she'd have accompanied the card with a photo of them all taken somewhere exotic, a note scribbled on the back (*The Taj Mahal – God it was beautiful but hot!; Barcelona, Gaudi's bench – we're taking up more than our fair share!*) The children would be beaming, wearing artfully semi-matched clothes and brightly-laced funky sneakers.

She still had names for them, all her unborn children. Boys' names came to her easily; she could have named a platoon. She had always envisaged a raft of fine, broad-shouldered sons. She'd made herself cry once imagining her death, her sons manfully, poignantly, carrying her rose- and hyacinth-strewn coffin.

Roman names, for boys, remained her first choice. That was why Horatio was Horatio. She'd kept Lucius, Julius and Hercules for later. The names for her daughters were a nod to her friends from boarding school and her chalet girl days. Tati, Bonnie, Fizz, Teddy – what larks. She'd imagined her daughters in rose-sprigged cotton nighties, blonde hair rebelling from plaits, running barefoot through long meadow grass, refusing to come in for bed.

She shook her head. She hadn't told Miriam Riley any of that. No doubt she'd have given it short shrift. Miriam wouldn't be big on fantasies of children which involved unmown meadow grass and specific nightwear. At their first meeting, Miriam had been pragmatic, self-assured. Caroline felt it was not, and would never be, the right occasion to say to Miriam that what she actually needed was rescuing from living a life which was not meant to be hers.

Miriam had asked what had made her contact the adoption services. To say only having Horatio would have begun on the wrong note. That was, however, the truth which nestled at the heart of her application. That, and a consultant who'd blithely said four years ago that it was game over for her as far as another pregnancy was concerned. Caroline wanted another child. Horatio said he wanted a dog. She wasn't sure what Toby wanted. She suspected he might be perfectly satisfied with their lot; his job in the city, his weekend cycling, his immaculate home. Maybe everything he wanted and wished for he'd already got, and he'd had the grace not to challenge her with that. For Toby, Horatio seemed to be plenty. He called him Rach for short. He played cricket in the garden with him on long summer evenings, bowling good-naturedly, and calling *Howzat!* when the wicket fell, his voice rippling through the leaves of the vast purple beech. He had a wine cellar which was a source of some pride, a road bike which weighed practically grams, bespoke ski boots, beautiful golf clubs, and gold cufflinks which felt as heavy as jacks in her hand. It seemed to be enough.

What was more, he seemed to Caroline to be unmarked by any form of anxiety or doubt. In fact, had always seemed so. She wondered if generations of affluence had bred all trace of it away. When she married him, the service had taken place in the church in his village. He'd been christened there, wearing his great-grandfather's robe. Most of his ancestors lay peacefully in the churchyard beneath lichened headstones. During the service when the congregation sang hymns, his family seemed utterly at ease with all that was promised (*Bestow upon this woman the gift of children* if she remembered correctly), in perfect pitch with the prospect of a full life, well-lived, that was conjectured that day.

Miriam Riley was intimidating. Subsequent meetings hadn't lessened Caroline's first impression. *She's intimidating,* she said to Toby, *even if she doesn't mean to be. It's as if she has a greater claim to moral purpose, or moral outrage, than anyone else.*

Toby had said mildly that it was more likely she was just fizzing with resentment at spending her working life mopping up other people's crap, and having to drink really appalling coffee every day at the Family Centre. He seemed mostly to joke with Miriam. When she'd asked him what he thought Horatio wanted, Toby said it was a toss-up between a sibling and a dog, but dogs made Caroline sneeze, whereas a sibling wouldn't.

Caroline loaded her shopping bags into the boot of the car. She and Toby had passed the assessment but maybe Miriam would never call her about a prospective child. Then, Horatio would leave home in six years' time and she would turn into a middle-aged woman who knew a lot about herbaceous borders, or learned Italian simply for the mental stimulation of it, or who had all her Christmas presents purchased and wrapped by December the first. When Horatio, as an adult, rang for a chat, it would be for conversations increasingly pause-filled and dreary as she metamorphosed into a woman who kept herself gainfully occupied in the face of the desire to ask someone, anyone, calmly yet plaintively, how this life had ended up being hers.

Caroline came through the front door, shaking a light shower of rain from her hair. She carried the shopping bags into the kitchen, piling them on the island to be unpacked. The light of the answer machine was flashing. She pressed the button to listen to the message. Miriam Riley's voice asked her to return her call.

Billy was right; Miriam had wanted to go through it all again, just to check he was happy with what she called The Plan. The word plan suggested it might not work and also made it seem a bit fragile, but he didn't say that. He wondered about asking her if there was any alternative, but the answer would probably be no, so best not to. Perhaps big chunks of his life might now be spent deciding his thoughts were better not spoken. Maybe this was a sort of progress, compared with the last few months with his mum when it seemed better not to think, let alone say, much at all. Some days, when they sat and looked at the wall, he almost felt he became part of it; solid and still and blank. He refocused his attention; Miriam was telling him he could wait by the tree and Meg would be along to fetch him shortly.

As he came out past the car park, he saw Andrew Walker leaning against his van with a box and what looked like a fishing rod. He had a bucket of water, and a cloth, and was cleaning something. Billy walked over.

'Hello you,' said Andrew, looking up from his rods.

'Hello. What work are you doing now?'

'This doesn't count as work. That's done for the day. I'm cleaning my fishing rods and my reel. I'm off down to the river.'

'Why does the reel need cleaning?'

'A good fisherman always cleans his reel; it keeps it smooth flowing, means it reels in right when you've got something feisty on the line. He also keeps a tidy tackle box; that's as good a way to judge a fisherman as any.'

He flipped open the lid of the box beside him. Billy crouched down and resisted the temptation to touch. There was an assortment of lead weights, different thicknesses of line, silver- and brass-coloured hooks, and things he couldn't begin to name. He remembered the cork and line from when he used to go fishing at the river by Grandma's. That obviously didn't count as the real thing.

'Do you go fishing a lot?'

'As much as I can,' Andrew smiled. 'Early on Saturday mornings, everything peaceful and still, a bacon sandwich in my bag. Paradise. You can't beat it.'

Billy thought that was probably true. He imagined a fish, twisty-silver, held on a taut line. He'd never actually caught anything at Grandma's. Maybe bread balls weren't as good as they used to be. Grandma said the river had changed so much since Lizzie's childhood, so much less wildlife, so many fewer fish. The way she said it made it sound as if everything had got steadily worse since his mum grew up. The lack of fish couldn't be his mum's fault, even though Grandpa had shouted once, in the kitchen *She's taking us all to hell in a hand cart,* which sounded like it might be. His mum's arms couldn't have pulled a hand cart, they could hardly carry a shopping bag. Maybe Grandpa hadn't realised that.

He looked at Andrew. He was spraying the reel with a can of WD40. Billy thought about asking what that was for, and then suddenly felt so tired of asking questions, he just watched as he sprayed the reel and put the tin carefully back in his tackle box.

'That's me set,' Andrew said. 'Looks like the perfect evening for it.' He loaded his stuff into the van. 'Have you ever been fishing?'

Billy shook his head. This wasn't a lie; if you'd never caught anything, you probably hadn't been fishing properly.

'You should give it a try some day. When I was your age my rod was never out of my hand. Except I was brought up by the sea so it was sea-fishing. Mackerel – hundreds of mackerel. I used to gut them and sell them. Nice little business.'

He slammed the van door shut.

'See you later,' he said. 'You're supposed to wish me tight lines.'

'Tight lines,' Billy said, and waved as Andrew pulled away. He saw Meg walking towards him. A fishing rod, a bacon sandwich and a nice fat fish. He could see how that might count as a version of Heaven.

When Caroline called back, Miriam's voice was crisp.

'It's not a baby,' she said first. 'And it's not an under-five.' Miriam paused. 'And in fact, it's not a girl either.'

'Oh,' Caroline said.

'So that's your wish list taken care of; I think it's best if we get that out of the way.'

'Yes, of course. I see.' (In her mind's eye, the image of a baby girl swaddled in a pale pink blanket pixellated and dissolved.)

'The situation is exactly as I tried to describe to you at the end of the assessment period. It's as much about who is in need of a family and whether we think you might be a successful match for them as the preferences you put on your form in terms of age and gender. Everybody wants a healthy baby which is increasingly rare because we make every effort to keep mothers and babies together. And so, in an admittedly less than ideal world, when I phone a prospective family about a child, it's not so much a turn-up *for* the books, which is what a baby would count as, as a turn-up *on* the books, if I'm making myself clear.'

'Yes, absolutely clear.' Caroline wondered how many more negatives Miriam might be about to drip-feed her. Was the child healthy, did he have any special needs or disabilities? What exactly had turned up on the books?

Miriam paused again.

'This part of my job sounds awful I think, describing a child as if he were something on a market stall. I can only repeat that, sometimes, in my experience, getting what you didn't think you wanted turns out better than what you thought you wanted in the first place.'

'I see; yes, I can see that, so who exactly might be better?'

'Billy. I'm talking about an almost ten-year-old boy called Billy who has never had a father in his life and whose mother died recently from heart complications due to drug use. His grand-parents have backed off, and so he has been placed with us.'

A drug addict's child, Caroline thought. It was hardly surprising Miriam parcelled out information in bite-size pieces.

'I see, how dreadful for him. What a series of complex attach-ments and adjustments.'

'He's surprisingly well-adjusted, even if a little withdrawn. He is well-balanced and sweet and very engaging. He's good at asking questions, and he has an enquiring mind. He attends a small village school with excellent levels of pastoral care, and they've been very effective at keeping him on track.'

'I see, that's good.' (Caroline bit her lip; how many times was she going to ineffectually say 'I see' like an idiot while Miriam steamrollered on?)

'During the course of your assessment we talked about a younger child, not someone who might also qualify as a playmate for Horatio, which Billy evidently would. In fact, the age gap between them is about two years, which is often thought of as ideal. I just thought, you know, that it might be something fruitful for your whole family, which is a great possible outcome.'

Miriam's voice trailed off. When she'd been to the Frasers', Horatio's playroom looked like a sports' shop. She'd never seen so much equipment. She thought of catapulting Billy into that, clutching his solitary shin guard. It felt like a long shot. The potential prize, she resolved, was unquestionable social mobility. *Onwards and upwards.*

'I see,' Caroline said again. (God, what is it with me?) 'Yes, I can see how that might work. I can see how there would be immediate overlap.'

Miriam spoke again.

'Look, all this is putting carts before horses. You need to take some time to think about it, you need to talk to Toby and you need to sound Horatio out too. And when you've done all that, you need to tell me whether you are interested in me setting up a meeting. If you're not, I completely understand, and it won't count in any way against you in relation to other children. It's better to be frank and truthful from the off. This process has no chance of working if not, and he's most definitely not a girl under five.'

Caroline took a deep breath.

'I would like to meet him. I do know a little about ten-year-old boys as I've already had one.' She tried to keep a tremor of pride from her voice. So much of the process had been about inadequacy.

When Miriam put down the phone, she sat back in her chair and pondered. Caroline's speedy willingness was a surprise. Had she even begun to comprehend the galaxy of differences that probably existed between Billy and Horatio at ten? Why puncture her optimism? At least she had something to report to Billy: one iron in the fire.

Caroline went upstairs and lay on her bed. Her head was spinning. Be careful what you wish for, she thought with a surge of energy; in some form or another you might just get it.

He wasn't a little girl. She'd have to let that go. His mother, his dead single mother was a drug addict. She'd have to let that go too. His grandparents didn't want him. Ditto. Miriam had dropped into the end of the conversation that his mother had a degree in Theology from Bristol University. Toby had gone there; he might like that detail. It suggested Billy might be bright.

He'd been mothered by someone else for almost ten years; that was more significant. She pressed her fingers to her eyelids.

She thought of someone she knew who had adopted a one year old from Romania. The child had spent most of her life tethered to a cot. When they brought her home, they'd had to teach her how to be held. She was like a feral kitten. *How dreadful,* Caroline had said. The woman had replied, with a little stiffness, that there was an upside. 'Maternally there's a clean slate,' she'd said. 'No attachment. She felt absolutely mine from the off.'

Billy wouldn't be. He'd been his drug-addict birth mother's from the off. She rubbed her hands together and flexed her fingers. Surely there was something she could be doing right now, something to prepare? If Toby were here, he'd sit back in his chair and smile, knowing that internally she'd be spinning like a top. Always his serenity in the face of her intensity. She'd need to think about how to forge a way forward with Billy and how to make good what must have been ten years of inadequate mothering. She kneaded her brow. What must the child be feeling? What memories did he have? Toby once said that she rolled her shirtsleeves up without looking right or left. She'd laughed and accused him of mixing his metaphors, but it had rung true. Her problem was that she tended to think that most things could be solved with an afternoon's focussed application, nervous energy fizzing from her fingertips.

She got up from her bed. Horatio was playing in a cricket match later that afternoon. She'd promised to make chocolate scones for the tea. She'd busy herself in the kitchen, as if a mountain of chocolate scones might be a start to addressing Billy's needs. At least making them was symbolic of intent. Miriam would not be able to fault her endeavour when it came to it. Always at cricket matches, she reflected, she ended up feeding half the batsmen who weren't on the pitch. It was another example of her excess capacity.

8

Billy was laying the dinner table at Meg's; the children had a rota for taking it in turns. She liked it properly done, no knives and forks facing the wrong way, everything lined up neatly. She liked big jugs of water to be put down the centre of the table. When eating, she liked you to ask your neighbour *Can I pour you some water?* rather than just helping yourself. She always had a roll of kitchen towel handy, and a square had to be laid out for each person. She said it was good to have something that meant fingers weren't wiped down the back of the chair, or mouths on sleeves.

Billy liked it when his name came to the top of the rota. He sometimes dawdled in the kitchen when it wasn't his turn. The other children were usually watching the television, or playing a game on the computer. It was peaceful in the kitchen, with Meg going about making the dinner. In contrast to his mum's, there was no frantic sweeping, no phrases said over and over again, no soft laughter in response to something he couldn't guess. Meg never held her palms up to the ceiling because she'd opened the fridge door and been astonished to find it empty again.

Laying the table properly, Billy felt, seemed a daily thumbs-up that what was meant to happen would in fact do so. Food would be cooked; the children would sit down together; and Meg would sit at the head of the table and ladle the food out on to their plates. As he laid the table, Meg stirred the stew pot and hummed to herself. He didn't know the song but thought it was a hymn. She looked over her shoulder at him a couple of times but otherwise left him to what he was doing. He liked that she didn't constantly need to be chatting. At least she didn't expect him always to be explaining.

When the phone rang, and Meg told him it was Miriam, Billy was surprised. Evidently, she was speedy.

'I've got an Introduction for you, Billy. I'm very excited. I'm going to arrange for you to meet someone called Caroline. She already has a son two years older than you. I thought that might be nice.'

'What's he called?' Billy asked. (It was better to be prepared for the questions Joey would ask.)

'He's called Horatio. Horatio,' she said with added commitment.

'You're kidding me? Horatio?'

He put the phone down and resumed laying the table. Meg restarted with her humming. Then, after a pause, 'Horatio?' she said. 'That's mighty unusual.'

Toby Fraser settled himself into his seat on the train, flicked open his i-Pad, and prepared to get his head round what his day held. On his screensaver, Caroline and Horatio smiled up at him. He studied their faces. Caroline looked at him in a way that might be described as beseeching. Beseeching? Maybe it was steelier than that. She had been relentless in her conviction that their family should be larger.

She's not straightforward; that's what his mother had said, years ago, when he first brought Caroline home. She implied that being described as straightforward was a compliment, and that her use of the preceding negative was as close to criticism as good manners permitted.

Toby wasn't sure – then or now – that he'd ever met a woman who might be described as straightforward. He'd disregarded his mother's remark, however, with the unflinchingness of youth, and yet now, on this morning, on the early train into town, he wondered if it wasn't the most perspicacious thing she'd ever said to him. His wife was *not* straightforward. Whether taking it on board, all those years ago, would have changed anything, was pointless to consider, but that Caroline was not straightforward was irrefutable.

On the day of that first visit he remembered his mother had

shown Caroline into the guest bedroom, where she had obediently slept each time they visited until their marriage. Through
the half-open door, he could see her sitting at the end of the high
bedstead, her feet barely touching the floor, subsumed by the
William Morris wallpaper, while his mother gestured towards
the basin, with its unwrapped bar of Floris soap. Caroline listened
intently to his mother's murmured directions – here a towel, here
a lamp switch, here a carafe and glass on the bedside table – and
he could sense in her the desire to please, to be liked by his
family. *Yes, that's lovely, no, I shall be absolutely comfortable, what a
chocolate-box view from the window.* She'd stood up and looked
out beyond the branches of the catalpa, over the meadow with
its Friesian cattle, towards the church spire, and it all looked
exactly as it had looked during his childhood when he felt his
world was ring-fenced with a bucolic, satiny certainty which took
the form of family rituals, and seasonal patterns, and a deep-
rooted knowledge that all would be well. Downstairs he could
hear the kettle whistling on the Aga, and his father calling to the
dogs after a walk, and the church bells struck the hour, and he
honestly felt, as Caroline stood by the window, her palms pressed
to the sill, exchanging pleasantries with his mother, that she
slotted into his life, into his future, like a coin into a fat-bellied
piggy bank, part of all that he knew, and all that he was to know.
Marry me, he'd said to her a month later, and when he told his
parents he thought his mother pursed her lips, just fleetingly, the
lightest of shadows across her expression, before saying, with a
broad smile, *Darling, what wonderful news, a wedding!*

Sometimes, when he missed the train home, Toby would stand
in WH Smith at Marylebone station, queuing to buy a paper,
and he'd glance up at the books on the shelves, all the self-help
manuals blithely confident that they could lead the reader to a
life better lived, and he'd wonder whether any book – particularly
self-help books with their lists of to-do points at the end of each
chapter – could get to the heart of what it was to grapple with
being alive, to make the decisions which constituted, and totalled
up to, a life well lived. *Good humour,* his father had said to him

when he was sixteen, *good humour oils the wheels of most things.* Toby had taken it to heart, and made it his mantra, and so far, professionally, socially, it had not let him down. Emotionally might be an altogether harder question. *It can't oil the wheels*, he might have said to his father, *of a woman who is unfulfilled by having only one child.* Caroline, he might have told his parents, is most unstraightforwardly stuck.

Once, up late at night, away on business, and looking too clearly into an almost empty whisky bottle, Toby had reached – and then tried to banish – the painful conclusion that whilst the overriding image of marriage was a woman and a man, standing bedecked before an altar, promising a life spent joyfully together, it was in fact much more naked than that. If asked – and if forced to answer rather than seek refuge in his customary good humour – he would have said that marriage was really a protracted diptych, two people asking, with an increasing degree of bewilderment, *What is it that you want of me? How do you want me to make you happy?*

Because, and here he switched off his i-Pad, as to continue looking at Caroline augmented his sense of failure, it seemed he could not make her happy because they could not have a large family, with the irony being that it was because of her, not him. Would her unhappiness have been worse if she could have blamed him, rather than herself, which she did with an unrelenting focus that pained him. Each time he sat at the supper table, Horatio to his right, Caroline to his left, the spare placements beyond them seemed to her to be an active reproach. *Would you like to invite a friend for supper, for a sleepover?* she would ask Horatio, gesturing to the empty places. Perhaps a smaller table would have helped. Perhaps living in a tiny caravan would have helped. A further irony, Toby reflected, was that his financial success had made it worse not better. *I am under capacity*, she said to him, *we are under capacity*, and she'd throw out her arms to include their spacious home.

And now, there was her plan to adopt, which he'd gone along with because agreement seemed kinder than resistance, and because he hadn't really thought it would come to anything. Miriam Riley had trounced him on that assumption. There was a child, Billy, whom Caroline was going to meet. *His dead mother*, she told him, *read Theology at Bristol*. He felt himself being played like a fish on a line.

Last night in bed, she had told him what Miriam said, her eyes shining with excitement at the thought of fixing, of making good, and he was reminded of all the reasons that he loved her, and all the reasons that he would always love her. So he determined now, sitting on the train, to banish the feeling of inadequacy that came with the knowledge that it was something beyond his capacity to fix which had made her so happy, and he resolved to put his best foot forward, to summon up his sunniest good humour, and to try and make whatever constituted the so-called Introduction process work.

It was not without irony, he thought, as he got off the train, that sometimes the choice which seemed to require the most effort, actually carried with it the promise of a more peaceful life. *Billy Morris*, he thought, passing through the ticket barrier, with the slight fatigue of a traveller long on the road looking for a solution to a problem that is not actually his own.

Billy whispered to Joey during Maths 'Miriam's arranged the first Introduction. She phoned last night. I'm not coming to school tomorrow morning. I'm going to the Family Centre to meet the mum.'

'I knew she'd find someone. Maybe now's the time you should suggest to her about Lord Sugar.'

'Meg's taking me there on the bus; no Roller required.'

'Would be nice though. Does she have any other children? The car'd impress them.'

'He's called Horatio.'

'Horatio?'

'Are you going to say that's mighty unusual too? That's what Meg said.'

'Has he got a middle name?'

'No idea. I didn't ask that.'

'Horatio and Billy. If she likes you, d'you think she'll want to change your name?'

'Change my name?'

'So they match.'

'You don't get your name changed if you're adopted.'

'You get a new surname, why not a new Christian name?'

'You're kidding.'

'Or perhaps they could just tweak what you've got, you know, tweak what your name is already. You could be Billio. Maybe Billius. I think that's my Nan's word for feeling sick. I feel Billius.'

'Joey Meadows,' Mrs Bailey said from the front of the class, 'every time I look over in your direction I see that you are in fact not doing your Maths but instead you are talking or laughing. Concentrate on your work, please and don't distract others who would prefer to be doing their work.'

'Sorry, Miss.'

Joey ducked his head.

'You are never going to get told off again. Do you realise that Billius boy? No teacher is ever going to tell you off again because they're so grateful you're talking. It'll just be me, taking it for the team. If ever the Roller does appear, I've earned my place. Shotgun the front seat.'

Billy looked down at his Maths. Surely they couldn't change your first name too? Miriam hadn't mentioned that.

9

Billy sat very still in the corridor. Meg had dropped him off; she'd let him choose where they sat on the bus. Before they left her house, she'd given his face an extra wipe with a warm flannel and some yellow soap. She said, *You are not just clean, you are polished.* Billy thought there might be some soap left in the crease of his nose or perhaps behind the lobe of his ear. If he sniffed, he could definitely smell lemon. Lemon-fresh for Miriam and Caroline Fraser; that had to be a good start.

Being a little bit talkative might be a good thing too. Miriam had hinted as much. Joey had been more direct. As they left the playground after school, he'd told him not to look like a nodding dog in the back of a car. He'd done an impression, hands held up like paws. 'Be sharp, Billius,' he'd said. Billy rolled his eyes.

He shifted on his chair. Andrew Walker came into the corridor near to where he was sitting. He trailed a hose-pipe from the open door to a radiator.

'Hey, Billy,' he said, unwinding the hose-pipe from a coil under his arm.

'Hello,' Billy said. This kind of talkative was easy. 'What are you doing now? What's that for?' He pointed to the pipe.

'Draining down the system,' Andrew said. 'One of the radiators has got to be taken off the wall in the corridor so that I can paint it. The hose-pipe drains all the water, then I'll bleed any air out from it.'

'Bleed it? That sounds like you're a doctor.'

'A radiator doctor, then. That's what I'll be today, thanks to you.'

Andrew rummaged in his tool box. Billy peered over. He

wondered if this one was tidy too. It wasn't. Evidently the same rules didn't apply.

'Do you have a favourite tool?' he asked Andrew.

'That would be saying. Do you?'

'I don't really know the names of many tools; just the obvious ones like a hammer, a spanner, a saw.'

'Well then, I'll choose a bradawl. I'm not sure it's my favourite, but I expect it's a new one for you. I collected tools in my head before I ever had any.'

'What does a bradawl do?'

'I'll show you one and you see if you can tell me what you think it might do.'

Miriam appeared at the door of her office. 'Come in Billy, I'm all set now. Sorry to have kept you waiting. Are you being taken on as an apprentice?'

Andrew smiled. 'The bradawl can wait. Another time,' he said.

Billy stood up and made towards Miriam's office. As she stepped inside, he heard her phone ring again. He paused for a moment and then took a few steps back.

'How did your fishing go? Did you catch anything?'

'When?'

'The other night, when you were cleaning your reel.'

'Oh yes, nice big pike. Put up a fight.'

'Did you have a bacon sandwich?'

'No, that's only in the morning. I had a cold beer, and Lorna, my wife, came down when she'd finished work and we had a little barbecue. She'll be having a baby soon, so it'll be different next summer.'

'Was it quiet and still, even though it wasn't the morning?'

'The water was flat as a mirror. Beautiful. I saw a woodpecker, a kingfisher, and heard a cuckoo too. That's a hat trick, that's special.'

Miriam came back out of her office and called him again.

Billy smiled hesitantly, nodded and went in. As soon as he sat down, the phone rang on her desk, and she pulled an apologetic face and answered it, flipping quickly through a file on her desk.

Billy wondered how many children Miriam was in charge of. It always sounded like she had a lot on her plate. He peeped back down the corridor. Andrew had gone. Perhaps there was another radiator down the corridor that needed draining or bleeding because the wall behind it had to be painted. He twisted a little on his chair. Bradawl; he liked the word. The barbecue sounded nice too. And the cuckoo, the kingfisher and the woodpecker.

Maybe the dad in the Fraser family went fishing. Maybe he had a tool box. Maybe Horatio had a fishing rod too, and a boy-sized workbench and knew what a bradawl was. Miriam would tell him if they were good Introduction questions. She'd put down the phone and was staring right at him.

'Anything you'd like to ask me before Caroline comes?' she said.

'If you get adopted can your first name get changed too?' His words came out in a rush.

Miriam clapped her hands together. 'Only if you wanted it to be.'

'And, in an Introduction,' he said, 'is a question about fishing or tool boxes the right kind of thing?'

Caroline Fraser appeared at the door. Miriam stood, reflecting that you couldn't script or predict what came out of a child's mouth. Fishing, she thought, striding forward to shake Caroline's hand, where the hell had that come from? It was only later she realised she'd neglected to answer Billy's question and that he hadn't repeated it. What that said about his expectation of adults she didn't want to dwell on. Likewise what it told her about herself.

Caroline Fraser hoped Miriam wouldn't notice that she was trembling. She'd got dressed about four times that morning, leaving the rejected clothes in a heap on the bed. She wanted to look warm, approachable, and kind, and that seemed quite hard to conjure up in one outfit. She'd finally chosen a duck-egg blue sweater and jeans. She'd taken off her largest ring.

As Miriam gestured for her to sit down, Caroline tried not to stare at Billy. He was sitting in a chair by Miriam's desk and seemed to be looking up at her from beneath his eyebrows. He had a sweet little face. He was small – small for his age? – or was that just smaller than Horatio had been at almost ten? She tried not to become distracted. Comparing the two boys was probably not productive.

'I'm really pleased to meet you, Billy,' she said, sensing no formal introduction was going to come from Miriam. 'This is a very exciting day for me.'

He didn't reply *Me too*. He squirmed in his seat, and seemed to nod or bob in acknowledgement. She reminded herself that hoping for enthusiasm on his part was too much to expect. Given a choice, he'd no doubt prefer his mother still to be alive, and a meeting like this never to have to happen.

His fingers were clutching the edge of the chair; she could discern a visible whitening of the skin over his knuckles.

'How are you?' she tried again, and then flushed in embarrassment. How might a child who had recently lost his mother answer that? Miriam would think she was an idiot; Miriam who seemed fascinated by a file in front of her and happy to watch Caroline drown in her own poorly executed, good intentions. He answered her though; there was a pause but he lifted his head and almost made eye contact.

'I'm fine, thank you. I'm staying at Mrs Oliver's.'

In his tone there was a scrap of tenacity, of pride. She suddenly remembered a book she used to read to Horatio about pets in a pet shop competing to be bought. *Choose me! Choose me!* the rat kept saying, hopping up and down. There was an atom of steeliness in Billy's quietness which, she thought, meant he would never say *Choose me* in any shape or form. That might go down well with Toby, she reflected; she couldn't begin to anticipate how Horatio might feel.

'I suppose I should tell you a bit about our family,' she started. 'My husband's called Toby; he works in London and commutes every day on the train. I have a son called Horatio who is twelve. I'm hoping, if you want to come and meet us all, you and he might have fun together. He likes sport a lot – do you?' (Oh God, was she gabbling? Surely Miriam should be chairing this, somehow smoothing the way; she shot a look in her direction but Miriam was opaque.)

'Yes, but I haven't played much, only what we do at school and the playground is very small. We go on the bus to swimming; I'm in the improvers' group. I've got a mouth guard from the Olympics talk. I've got a mouth guard if I need one.'

'That's very organised. Horatio is always losing his; I've stopped getting them from the dentist and I buy them in multipacks.' (Was her tone too bright? She was putting her own teeth on edge.)

Miriam looked at Billy. 'Is there anything you'd like to ask Caroline?'

He shrugged, it was more like a twitch of his shoulder blades.

Miriam continued. 'Maybe we could talk about something you might like to do with Caroline, Toby and Horatio? You could visit their house, or go out somewhere. Maybe you and Caroline could talk about something that would be fun to do?'

Thank God, thought Caroline, Miriam's finally remembered who's meant to be leading the process.

Billy seemed to have spent all his available words telling her about the mouth guard. He was biting the edge of his lip. Caroline took a sharp intake of breath. She should take the initiative.

'I wondered,' she started again, 'if you might like to go to a place where you do climbing, high wires, that sort of thing. You jump from platforms, obviously with a harness on, and help each other scramble to on things. Horatio has been to some birthday parties there. Have you ever been to a place like that?'

Billy's eyes widened. Had he ever been in a million miles of a place like that?

He shook his head.

'Would you like to go to a place like that?' Miriam asked.

Billy paused, and then nodded, hesitantly.

Miriam turned to look at Caroline. She had to credit the woman, sitting there in her blue jumper, everything just so, but resembling a swan who appeared to be still and serene but who beneath the waterline was paddling in a frenzy. Miriam had deliberately stepped back from direct involvement when Caroline came into the room. It was always important to see if bridges could be built without help, especially in the awkwardness of first interactions. Billy seemed to have decided not to ask anything about fishing or tool boxes. After his one sustained answer, he had reverted to nodding. Maybe he had used his allocation of chattiness in the corridor with Andrew.

'Perhaps we could go this Saturday,' Caroline was saying, 'perhaps Miriam might organise for me to collect you from Mrs Oliver's?'

'Yes,' Miriam said. 'If Billy's happy with that, it can certainly be arranged.'

'I'd like that,' Billy said, with what seemed to Miriam to be determination.

'Okay, let's go ahead with that then. Billy, if you want to go and wait by the tree for Meg, I'll sort the paperwork and permissions with Caroline.'

Billy stood up and paused. He looked directly at Caroline and gave a little bow. 'Thank you,' he said, swallowing hard. 'I'll see you on Saturday.' He walked out and shut the door behind him.

'You're probably thinking how inept I am, how dreadfully I managed that,' Caroline blurted.

'No, it's tricky. It's all new, uncertain, and best that I don't interfere too much.'

'To look on the bright side, at least he said yes. He seemed positive about coming. I'll sort out booking tickets. I feel a little flustered; I'm sure you understand. It's all familiar to you, but quite daunting when it's the first time.'

'I appreciate that; I really do. Let's sort out the logistics for the weekend. At least you've met and now things should be less nervy going forward.'

Caroline thought this was as close as Miriam Riley could get to reassurance.

Andrew Walker sat in his van drinking coffee from a thermos. Lorna made him his lunch every day, even when she'd felt vomity from the baby. *I know you,* she said, *if I don't, you'll be eating junk.*

He liked her concern. She cut him big thick slices of brown bread and mashed up egg and mayo, added two rosy apples, plums, sometimes a big, fat orange. He'd peel it in the van, the juice squirting into the air, and it smelt of Lorna, clean and blossomy, standing in her nightie, barefoot, tapping the lid of the Tupperware to check she'd closed it properly. She worked in a care home looking after old people. Everyone they knew said *Please God if ever I'm old and in a home, let it be Lorna who is looking after me*. Even if the time-frame was nonsense, their sentiment was valid. Lorna was one of those people who was genuinely good, and had a really good heart. Once the baby came, they'd have some deciding to do. As Lorna pointed out, what was the point of paying someone to care for their child, while she got paid to care for someone else's parent? The maths didn't really add up either. Everything she earned would go on childcare. Both sets of parents lived too far away to help.

Andrew re-filled his thermos cup and thought back to Billy. Pale, still, little face, but his eyes looked as if they didn't miss a trick, and his questions proved it. It was odd to chat to a child and realise afterwards that you had given more away than they had. His face had lit up at the mention of the fishing; he'd crouched so carefully by the tackle box, taking it all in.

He finished his lunch and made his way to the tool store. The edges of the grass needed strimming, particularly around the trunks of the trees. He put on the safety goggles and made his way back to the car park and worked his way carefully round the edge of the fencing. From the corner of his eye, he saw Billy approach and wait by the big tree, and he waved as he then walked away with Meg Oliver. He strimmed around the tree by the road entrance, and the one to the side of the drive. Lastly, he came to the one where Billy had been waiting. As the thread of the strimmer whipped at the grass at the base of the trunk, a sliver of white caught his eye, and he stopped strimming and bent down to look. From a small hole at the base of the tree he took out some neatly folded sheets of paper. He unfolded one: *Learn to play bridge*, it said. Was that some kind of resolution?

The second note said *Other people's bad behaviour can sometimes make your behaviour better.* True enough, Andrew thought. He looked down the path to where Billy had walked to the bus stop. Were they his notes? It seemed likely. He'd waited by the tree. There was a third one, the corner of which had first caught his eye. Billy must have pushed it in in a rush, as Meg approached. *I don't think I like heights,* it said. *Is it bad manners to say?*

Andrew re-folded the notes neatly and tucked them deep into the tree. Was it wrong to have read them? He looked around guiltily. They were evidently meant to be secret, or perhaps just personal. Billy was out of sight.

Why was the child fretting about heights? Maybe Miriam was supposed to know about something like this. It was probably part of her job spec to know all the available details. It certainly wasn't part of his, he thought, checking the notes were back in the hole, and wiping the strimmer cord clean.

Andrew tapped on Miriam's door. He did his best to look purposeful, although Miriam, he conceded, probably owned that territory.

'Hey Andrew,' she said mildly, 'what can I do for you?'

Andrew thought perhaps it got to be a habit, with a job like hers, to assume it would always be her who would be doing the fixing.

'Just thought I'd check your window seals if that's okay. Won't take me a couple of minutes. Is it okay to do it whilst you're at your desk? I'll come back later if anything noisy needs doing.'

'No problem, go ahead. I was just about to make a coffee anyway.'

Andrew opened and closed the window, and ran his finger down the frame. He kept his eyes fixed on the tree. Behind him, Miriam was filling the kettle.

'Billy said you were finding him a new family. Did you have a meeting with someone about it this morning?

'Ah-huh.'

'Was it the woman wearing a blue jumper and driving a BMW?'

'You haven't missed a trick this morning, Inspector.'

'Does whatever happens next involve heights?'

'I'm sorry?'

'Heights. Is what happens next anything to do with heights?'

Andrew sensed Miriam had stopped making coffee and was staring at the back of his head. He pressed his thumbs more obviously into the window insulation tape.

'Obviously this is confidential, but, in the light of your new interest in Social Services procedure, we arrange a few meetings, outings, whatever, to allow the child and the prospective parents to spend some time together over a period of weeks and we call it the Introduction phase.'

Her voice ended on a questioning note, even though she hadn't asked a question.

'I see, and so where are they going then, on their first Introduction meeting, outing, whatever?'

'What, in this non-specific case we're talking about, as any specific case would be confidential.'

'Yes, in this non-specific . . .'

'I can't believe I'm telling you this, but some kind of high wire, climbing, family fun zone.'

'High wire, platforms, oh I see, I see, I get it. Heights.'

'I'm sorry?'

Andrew stopped fiddling with the window, and paused with his palm flat to the glass.

'So was there anything wrong?' Miriam asked.

'I'm sorry?'

'Anything wrong with my window? Does it need sanding or insulating?'

'Oh no, nothing wrong with it at all. Tiptop.'

'Great, good to know. Thank you for checking. At least my window frame is in perky, tiptop condition even if nothing else in my life is.'

'Good.'

Andrew continued to stand by the window.

'And . . . was there anything else you needed to check?'

Miriam's gaze was quite piercing now.

He opened his mouth.

She stirred her coffee. It wasn't like Andrew to be so hesitant, so awkward.

'Miriam . . .'

'Yes?'

'It's okay. It's nothing. Your window's fine.'

He left the room with a slightly awkward wave. Sheepish would have been a better way to describe him, not a word she would normally have used for him. She went over to the window. The thick insulating tape was clearly visible. What had that been about? She shook her head, and turned her mind back to Caroline Fraser.

She winced at the memory of the meeting with Billy. Had Caroline any idea of the minefield involved in helping a child like Billy adjust from his experience of life to her own? Mouth guards in multipacks; that said it all. She screwed up an appraisal form she'd started to write and tossed it into the bin. She pushed back in her chair.

Class and race. She didn't have time to dwell on what spanners in the works they could be. And if, as issues, they weren't complex and inconclusive enough, they'd added in a few extra issues of their own. They had a new policy not to place any child under five in a home where a prospective parent smoked. The intention was to achieve a non-smoking policy across all age groups. Imagine that, Miriam thought, rolled out and stamped across the general population. Compulsory contraception until you had given up the fags. All of it hovered around the elusive equation of what defined good parenting. If only good parents came with a visible mark; that would help things along, if not avert disaster. The killer question – whether children should be matched with families from the same race and the same socio-demographic background or not – remained unanswered. Was any kind of loving home better than remaining in care? *You tell me*, Miriam sometimes wanted to shout at any bystander available. *You tell me with all that confidence you can scoop up from the sidelines.*

Miriam webbed her fingers around her coffee mug and blew on it, and wondered irritably about people whose working lives consisted of designing new packs for supermarkets, or baking bread in a bijou deli. Surely they slept easier at night, in the knowledge that the downside of screwing up was simply a dip in sales, or a burned-black crust, rather than a child failed? She sometimes envisaged, when thinking of her distant retirement, that what she'd say at a farewell party, probably clutching a glass of not properly chilled Freixenet, was *Truly, truly, I really tried my best*, and then she'd weep copiously. That would be a shocker.

And what had she spontaneously agreed to for Billy? Some kind of high wire, family-action day place? Was that a little remiss? Maybe something tamer would have been better for a first trip. A boating lake? Flying a kite? Maybe she should have chipped in with some alternatives. Billy's expression wasn't exactly eager. Please God, she thought, can all the health and safety checks have been thoroughly done; please God let every wire, pulley and load-bearing item on the site be in meticulous condition. If Billy returned with concussion or a broken arm, that would take the biscuit. Negligence, as well as what looked like a brewing disregard for due process, would be slapped at her door, along with some disciplinary action for scant attention to detail whilst Billy was on her watch. The retirement party, the lukewarm Freixenet, the uncharacteristic tears would evaporate in an instant. She'd be stacking shelves in Tesco's or Sainsbury's, absolutely no question. Miriam wondered if this wasn't actually an appealing outcome. A further upside would be not having to deal with a mystifying handyman behaving out of character, and looking for all the world like a man with something to tell who had decided not to.

Caroline rang Meg's doorbell, and stood on the step, her hand lightly on Billy's shoulder. He didn't shrink from her touch. It had been such a day of buckling on harnesses and helmets she felt as if a degree of physical intimacy had been established. He certainly didn't shrug away from her now, and she felt a flush of pleasure as Meg answered the door.

'Here we are, all safe and sound. It feels like we've climbed Everest! Billy did really well. He'll probably be exhausted tonight as some of it was quite difficult!' Caroline wondered, as she spoke, if everything she would ever say in relation to this process would be bright in tone, and studded with implicit exclamation marks. She wasn't speaking, she thought, but exclaiming. She had been exclaiming all day. She had caught Toby looking at her once or twice, as if bemused at this speeded up, wide-eyed, over-enthusiastic version of his wife. She felt as if she'd spent the day steeped in one long sugar rush.

In the car, on the journey there, she'd directed her energies to pointing out things they were passing: a kestrel on a hedge, some rape seed being sprayed, a rabbit which looked as if it had myxomatosis hunched blindly by the verge. Billy had craned his neck each time to see, perhaps more out of politeness than in interest. Horatio was fed up because she'd said he couldn't use his play station or put on a DVD. Toby reasoned that it might be more of an ice breaker with Billy, but Caroline worried it spoke of lazy parenting – what would Miriam think? She might rush to a judgement if she thought they were the sort of family who didn't chat on car journeys. So she'd chattered: she felt as if she had chattered for England, and as Meg Oliver stood by the door she would like to have said *I have never felt more exhausted in my life; frankly I'd like to sink down on your front step and suck tea through a straw to avoid lifting the cup to my lips.* God, she thought, listen to me, now I'm babbling about Everest.

Billy turned to her, and said 'Thank you very much for taking me out.' He gave what appeared to Caroline to be a stilted little bow.

'It's been a pleasure, an absolute pleasure, you've been a delight.'

By rights, she thought, they both should be standing knee-deep in the soapsuds of all her chatter. Meg Oliver nodded politely and ushered Billy inside.

'She didn't really respond, just took him inside,' she said to Toby as she got back into the car. 'I'm not surprised he's so quiet if she just nods a lot as well.'

'He nods all the time,' said Horatio, from the back.

'Don't be mean; it must be difficult for him, difficult for everybody. Please don't be unkind.'

Toby reached over and patted her leg.

'Darling, you've made a huge effort today. Frankly, we're both left staggered in your slipstream. I wouldn't take it personally that Meg Oliver's not chatty. She probably has so many people turning up at her door, she must be a past master at keeping it short and sweet. You've done well; it was a good idea and a good venue. He seemed to enjoy it.'

'He wasn't very good at it,' Horatio said. 'You have to admit, Mum, he wasn't very good at it.'

'I think he made a really good effort. He'd obviously never done anything like it before. You're older too, two years makes a big difference.'

'When we went for Beau's birthday, his brother was the best of the lot of us and he's only eight.'

'Well, Beau's brother's obviously destined to be a mountaineer or a high wire walker in the circus. Billy will have other talents that will reveal themselves to us shortly.'

As she closed the door, Meg said 'So what was it like?'

'High. Very high.'

'I imagine that's the point. Do you want a cup of tea and a biscuit?'

'I'll just go up to my room for a bit if that's okay.'

Billy lay on his bunk. It felt beautifully still, low and solid. Each time he closed his eyes, all he could see was the ground far beneath him spinning like a plate. High didn't even begin to cover it. It was evidently possible to feel on the verge of being sick for several hours and yet not be.

The Platform of Trust. They'd climbed up a tall pole which wobbled as each person came up it. Once on it, there was nothing to hold on to, and only just room for four pairs of feet. Billy pulled the duvet up over his face at the memory. Getting back down meant free falling backwards, suspended by a harness. Billy concluded that was where the main Trust came in.

Horatio had asked to go up first; Toby suggested Billy go second. 'You two can show us how it's done,' he said.

Horatio had climbed quickly. He'd stood looking down as Billy struggled to heave himself on to the platform. Billy felt so dizzy he wanted to close his eyes. Caroline was shouting encouragement from the base of the pole. *You're a star! You've nearly done it! One last pull!* After several minutes of him flipping around like a fish, Horatio bent down to help and said quietly, firmly, as he grabbed his arm and hauled him up on to the platform, 'I am always going to be stronger than you.'

'Fair enough,' Billy had said. 'Fair enough,' he repeated, with extra emphasis.

He'd opened his eyes to see Caroline starting to climb up. She made the pole sway even more. Horatio made no effort to hold or steady him; he stood with his arms at his side like a soldier. If he were with Joey, Billy decided, they'd be clinging to each other like what Joey said was called a clag of worms.

When Billy looked to the left, he could see the mirrored flat glassiness of a lake. Straight ahead he saw feathery treetops. To the right, far below, he could see the shiny bumpers of parked cars. If he looked behind him, he thought he'd see the spot on the ground where he'd crash, faulty harnessed, and die; like Icarus.

He'd crash to the ground with a wallop, but minus the wax and feathers. Joey would probably have encouraged him to take consolation in going out with a bang, and with the added benefit of making the headlines in the paper.

His descent, as it turned out, wasn't that bad. *Hooray!* said Caroline. *Well done, chaps!*

The afternoon ended with a leap from a platform to grab a trapeze bar. The length of the leap matched your age. (Toby laughed and said that part didn't apply to grown-ups.) *Twelve, almost thirteen,* Horatio called when it came to his go, and flung himself confidently and caught the bar.

Billy thought of Joey when it came to his turn; he'd have probably yelled out *I'm six me,* and leapt out looking like a flying squirrel. Horatio might have laughed. When Billy called out *Nine,* his voice didn't seem to be his own. He leapt for the trapeze bar but could see it dangling far before him. He crashed towards the net, thinking Miriam definitely hadn't thought this through properly.

You almost did it! You almost did it! Caroline said, coming to help disentangle him from the net.

Billy rubbed his face with his duvet again. He was exhausted. He shouldn't lie here much longer. Meg would think something was wrong.

He went downstairs. In the Rumpus Room, someone was playing on the computer. Meg was in the Receiving Room, which was the tidy one at the front. She was sitting peacefully in her chair.

'Mark's dad is coming to collect him at six and he's staying over at his flat tonight, so it's just you and me,' she said. 'I thought I might order a take-away and we can break all the rules and eat it in front of the television. What do you think? Are you hungry?'

Billy nodded. 'Yes, yes please. Not so hungry, you know, during today, with all the activities.'

'To my thinking, the only creatures meant to be that high up in the trees are monkeys and chimpanzees. Or maybe fruit bats – don't they do some leaping too?

Later, after dinner, when Billy got up to go to bed, he stood by the Receiving Room door and said *Thank you very much for the Chinese*.

'You're very welcome,' Meg said.

Through the open door she watched him walk slowly up the stairs. There was something so resigned in his tread it made her place her hand to her heart. Tomorrow she'd do something low key with him; perhaps take him down to the boating lake. She could rent one of the white swan paddle boats and he could pedal it, even if her weight skewed it so they went round and round in circles. She sensed he'd had the living daylights frightened out of him on the high wires. He was brave not to say; it probably came from a lifetime of not expecting his feelings and needs to be put first. The woman who brought him back – Caroline – seemed full of good intentions. Good intentions, Meg knew, were frequently not enough.

Caroline sat on Horatio's bedside, smoothed his hair from his forehead and gave him a big kiss.

'I was so proud of you today, darling, you were brilliant. You chatted so nicely to Billy and were so kind, showing him what to do. I'm hoping you two can get along. My next plan is to ask Miriam whether I can pick him up after school and bring him to Mountford and he can watch you play cricket. Lots of younger boys watch; he might find it fun.'

Horatio said nothing, just raised his eyebrows and pushed out his bottom lip.

'And what's that supposed to mean?' Caroline said, squeezing his chin.

He shrugged.

'Come on, say. Remember, you can always say anything to me. I'm always listening.' She kissed him extravagantly on the cheek. His body felt stiff, reluctant.

'Horatio?' Caroline tugged at his pyjama top. 'Come on,' she coaxed, 'out with it.'

He didn't meet her eye.

She stood up and checked the curtains were properly closed.

Where had she read that children found it easier to say difficult things if you weren't looking at them? Like when you were driving a car, the article had said, eyes fixed on the road. She neatened and straightened the edges of the curtains where they met.

Horatio paused, then said, 'It's just I understood when it was meant to be a girl, a little girl, a baby and all that, someone like Felix's sister. I just don't understand why you'd want another boy who's just a bit younger than me.'

'Oh, darling,' she said with a sweep of relief, 'it doesn't work like that. There are so many children who need homes, sometimes you just experiment and see what works. That's why we're getting to know Billy, in case we all think he would be nice to have as part of our family. And, of course, if he feels the same about us.'

Horatio seemed to be looking beyond her. His face was unreadable.

'It's meant to rain. The match will probably be cancelled.'

He made as if to settle into sleep. His final glance at her, she thought, as she switched off the bedside lamp and kissed him again, contained something of a reproach, wordless but potent all the same.

Oh God, she thought, as she stepped, suddenly weary, across the landing. Jealousy. She hadn't even thought of that. How had it not crossed her mind? Of course he might be feeling jealous and threatened when he'd had her undivided attention for his entire life. Caroline's brow puckered. Now she'd have to think not just about how to build bridges to Billy, but how to avoid burning them with Horatio.

11

'Nightmare,' said Billy to Joey underneath the climbing frame at playtime on Monday morning. 'Nightmare. I don't even want to look up at these monkey bars.'

Joey looked up, considering them. In Year Two, Matthew Phillips had broken his arm on them. It hadn't put them off climbing, they'd been more preoccupied at the time with saluting his choice of a bright pink cast.

'At least you didn't bottle. And think on the bright side. Now you know some of the jobs you don't ever want to do.'

'What, like a high wire walker in the circus, or jumping out of planes with a parachute?'

'No, a tree surgeon for example – one of my cousins is one of those. Or a window cleaner. Or putting up scaffolding like my uncle. If you ever have to fill in one of those forms at the Job Centre where you say what kind of job you would really like, you could write in capital letters ONE ON THE GROUND.'

Billy nodded, and made a mental note to jot down in his notebook the jobs Joey had come up with. Tree surgeon would definitely be out.

'Meg took me to the boating lake yesterday. We went on one of those swans that you pedal. We had an ice cream on the bench afterwards.'

'Maybe that girl who said you got presents if your mum died was wrong. Maybe it's just loads of day trips. How about asking if a friend could come too? I could make myself available. All I did yesterday afternoon was watch *Bargain Hunt* with my Nan.'

'Caroline Fraser's coming to collect me from school tomorrow.

Miriam phoned to tell me last night. I'm going to Horatio's school which is called Mountford to watch a cricket match. I'll have tea there, because if you watch that's what you get and then we're going to meet Toby in an Italian restaurant. Then, she's taking me back to Meg's. I have to be back by nine o'clock.'

Joey lay back in the bark chippings. He breathed out loudly.

'Billy, you are the man. Drivers and taxis and restaurants and cricket at Mountford. Maybe if they become your forever family, that's where you'll go to school, all in a blazer and a tie or something, leaving me here in the bark chippings with a Kit Kat.'

Billy almost smiled.

'Maybe you could persuade them,' Joey continued, 'to include me. You know, buy one get one free. My Nan's probably fed up with walking me to school every day. I could be sitting next to you on the bus to Mountford looking like this.' Joey crossed his eyes.

The whistle blew and they scrambled up to join the line by the door. What Billy couldn't shake off, as they started History, was that if Horatio met Joey, he'd probably think he was all right. He most likely wouldn't haul him up on to the Platform of Trust and say *I'm always going to be stronger than you.* Joey would probably have made him laugh before Horatio had a chance to think of anything mean. He'd have popped his head up round the platform, managed a rubbish salute and said *Aye aye Captain,* or told Horatio some nonsense about flying foxes, or bats, or something loopy which sounded pleasingly believable. Horatio would have been laughing in the car, instead of looking out of his window but actually watching the reflection of Billy's face so that keeping completely still felt the best thing to do.

Horatio didn't look like he was going to take a shine to him anytime soon. When he'd told Joey what he'd said on the platform, Joey had shrugged and said *That's because you're like a cuckoo in the nest, taking up the cosy space that was all his. D'you know cuckoos sometimes boot the other chicks out?* Cuckoo boy. He wasn't trying to boot Horatio out of anything.

Billy turned to feel a hand on his shoulder.

'You haven't been writing much,' Mrs Bailey said softly. 'Look, you're still on your first paragraph, try and do a little more.'

As she walked past, Joey rolled his eyes and shook his head.

'See,' he whispered, 'you could be as lazy as you like and never, ever get in trouble again, and still get to eat cricket tea at Mountford.'

Caroline stood in the playground, clutching her passport and driving licence. She had to show photographic evidence to Cath Bailey to prove she was who she said she was, and she'd brought both along to cover all bases. She felt ridiculously nervous. She bit at the inside of her cheek. The other mothers and childminders were giving her a wide berth; she could see she was the topic of conversation, eyes askance. She pulled her suede jacket closer around her; the sun kept going in and she wasn't sure whether she was warm enough or not. For a day in May, it was cool; she hoped Billy wouldn't be cold on school field. There was always a breeze that came up from across the river. She'd brought one of Horatio's old fleeces along, just in case. That would ensure Billy was warm, but now she was worrying it might put Horatio's nose out of joint. It was evidently a fine line. She hadn't mentioned her conversation with Horatio to Toby; she didn't want to fan that particular fire. Maybe jealousy could be pleasingly fleeting; she'd pump up her efforts to make Horatio feel secure. In the Boden catalogue, sibling rivalry never looked as if it would rear its head. Those children looked as if they would say *Oh is your crabbing line broken? No problem, share mine,* in a spirit of constant, considerate harmony. She sighed. Could she be accused of idealising family life? Sharing your mummy was no doubt in a different league all together. Why did this whole process increasingly seem like tiptoeing across broken glass? They hadn't even hinted at that in any of the leaflets supposed to guide you through it. *Help change a child's life for the better,* they were titled, not *How to cut yourself to parenting ribbons.*

Billy was walking hesitantly towards her, the teacher's hand on his shoulder.

'Hello Caroline,' he said, 'thank you for coming to collect me.'

Cath Bailey greeted her and looked at her passport and driving licence. In a spirit of sudden reckless optimism, Caroline reached out for Billy's hand, took it in hers, and led him to the car, her arm swinging slightly. Billy's hand felt unresisting, although he wasn't holding hers back. As they came out of the gate and walked past a length of chain-link fence, a boy with a shock of flame-red hair and a face like a fox cub's was pressing himself up to the fencing, one eye speed-winking, and giving a thumbs-up. Billy seemed to be carefully studying the ground where he placed his feet. She peered at him sideways. His mouth was twitching; was he trying not to laugh? As they got into the car, the same boy had emerged with an elderly woman and was standing in Silver Street. As she pulled away, she could see in her rear mirror that he mimed bowling a cricket ball and then hitting a perfect six.

'Is the boy with the red hair a friend of yours?'

'That's Joey Meadows. His Nan says he's a card.'

'He looks like a card, although I've never really known what that means.' She laughed brightly. He didn't respond. It was probably best, she thought frantically, not to pursue it. She paused. 'I've made cakes for the tea, butterfly ones with wings. I hope they haven't collapsed in the basket or they'll be a sorry sight. I probably should have done brownies instead.'

Billy nodded.

'Did you have a good day at school?' Caroline went on. 'Your teacher looks nice.'

Billy sat in what he learned was called the out-field. He felt cold. Caroline had offered him a fleece from her basket. He guessed it belonged to Horatio, so thought it was better refused. Better to be freezing, he thought, suppressing a shiver, than have Horatio walk off from batting and see cuckoo boy wearing his jumper. Joey would have given that as a top tip.

Billy concentrated on the chatter of the boys in the team. They were all sitting in a row watching the game, the next one in the batting order all set to go on if the wicket fell. Such a lot of equipment they had, that was what struck Billy first. Huge great kitbags with pads for batting in, pads for wicket-keeping, bats, gloves, and helmets with grilles over the faces, and red and grey caps to wear for tea.

We'll win by at least six wickets; we blasted them at hockey last term; have you done your History prep, I got an Alpha for mine; our house is miles in the lead.

Billy edged nearer to listen more closely. Caroline smiled approvingly. When they arrived, she had taken the time to explain the rules of cricket. *I'm a little vague at the edges,* she said, *I can't tell you all the different sorts of bowling, I mean I know there's fast and medium pace and spin, but then it gets more complicated – something about off stumps and near stumps and Yorkers and goodness knows what. And the fielders – you'll have to ask Toby or Horatio – they can be arranged in defensive or attacking positions. Where they stand has names.*

Billy looked at the length of the field. It was almost impossible to think that he might be at home, having bread posted through the letter-box or sticking forks in the toaster, and all the while on perfectly green grass that looked like it had been sewn rather than grown, boys would be playing cricket. A college clock would strike in the background, a river run peacefully alongside, and next to a tree, there'd be a white wooden pavilion with a board that flick-flacked when the score changed. Inside, cakes and sandwiches were laid out neatly on a table, with orange squash in huge jugs, and all of it as real and as everyday to them as going home to the graffitied lift and the flat had been to him. Had his mum's school been like this? There were pictures of her in the tennis team, racquets across the lap of the person in the middle, and a certificate which said she'd been awarded colours in netball and hockey, and a photo of her in a smart dress with Grandma wearing a hat at an occasion called Foundation Day. How had she got from all this to that, from her beginnings to where they ended up? It must have been hard for Grandma, one day baking cakes for tea in a pavilion and then making stew in Tupperwares to carry up to a dingy flat in a lift that smelt of pee.

Billy, Billy, Caroline was saying (Had she said it lots of times?). 'It'll be time for tea shortly. I'm just going to walk up to the pavilion and take the cling film off the sandwiches. Do you want to come with me?'

Billy shook his head. On the pitch, Horatio thwacked the ball with confidence, and lifted his bat to acknowledge the clapping as it went for a four. Caroline beamed. 'He'll be thrilled with that shot, it's one of his favourites,' she said, getting up from the tartan blanket and brushing grass from her trousers.

At tea, Billy sat at one of the long tables, and ate an egg sandwich, a scone, half an orange and one of Caroline's butterfly cakes. She introduced him to the cricket master who smiled at him broadly and asked him if he played.

'No,' Billy said, 'but it would be nice to learn.' He toyed with telling him he already had a mouth guard, but wondered if cricketers actually needed one. That might count as overdoing it if the helmet already had a grille.

After tea, the opposing side went into bat. Billy watched as a boy on Horatio's team polished the ball on his trousers, and hooved at the ground like a bull before he ran up to bowl. He definitely had what Caroline said was called 'his eye in'. In the course of the next three overs, he sent seven wickets tumbling to the ground. Each time he did it, he held up the correct number of fingers for the total number of wickets he had taken. He ran between the wickets as his seventh one fell. As the team came off the pitch, all the boys in the team were patting his back and telling him what a great job he'd done. *Well done! Victor Ludorum! Victor Ludorum!* chanted two of the boys.

The boys came over to their bags and started to pack away their pads and bats. Billy stood awkwardly beyond them, wondering whether to speak his first words to any of them. The bowling boy had been very impressive. He caught his eye.

'Well done, Victor,' he said awkwardly, nubbing the grass with the toe of his trainer. 'Well done, that was very impressive.'

'Victor? Victor?' interjected one of the other boys, laughing. 'Do you think he's called Victor? He's Thomas. Victor Ludorum means winner of the games, silly. Don't you know any Latin?'

Billy blushed. Evidently not.

Toby arrived at the table when Caroline was already sitting with the boys. She'd ordered some bread sticks and Billy was watching Horatio snap them briskly and dip them into olive oil. He'd cast his eye over all the cutlery and given thanks that Grandma had always been such a stickler for table manners. At least he wouldn't make an idiot of himself over knives and forks.

Toby sat down, and flicked the large napkin out on to his lap.

'Hello boys. Good days both I hope? Rach, I heard from Peter Ellis you played a couple of blinders. That's my boy.'

Horatio flushed with pleasure. 'Thomas's bowling was really why we won. My thirty-two just helped rattle them a little. I edged it a few times.'

'And prep, when we get home are you going to be scrambling for prep?'

'Not really. Mr Field's given us two sessions for History. We're working on the *Titanic*. We have to decide whether it was the faulty rivets, the arrogance of the captain, or the flaws in the design which were the main reason why it went down.'

'That, and the not inconsiderable matter of an enormous iceberg, I assume?'

Horatio laughed. 'That, and the iceberg.'

'And Billy,' said Toby, 'what did you learn at school today?'

Billy stifled the impulse to sit up straight.

'Fire of London, the baker and his oven,' Billy said, 'and also the meaning of Victor Ludorum.' He blushed.

Toby smiled quizzically at Caroline.

'Victor Ludorum,' said Joey, the next day, when they were sitting in the playground shed, perched on an old piece of canvas that was used for the Ascension Day picnic.

'Victor Ludorum,' Joey said again, breathing softly. 'That's a good one, I'm going to be storing that up.'

'What like clag of worms, and murder of crows?'

'Yes, but better. Better.' In the dim light of the shed, Billy could see that Joey's green eyes had the faraway gleam they got when he was hatching a plan.

'Now we know that expression, thanks to you making a complete idiot of yourself.'

'Caroline said it was an easy mistake to make.'

'Plus point for Caroline. *Victor Ludorum:* I'm bagging that. Shotgun me. Do you think we can persuade Mrs Bailey for Sports Day, now that we're actually allowed to have races that someone can win, that the winner of the most races gets to be called Victor Ludorum? We could ask her if, in DT, we could make a crown from leaves, like the Romans wore. That'd be History too. Then it might count as one of her joined-up projects. Imagine if she says yes. Victor Ludorum, Victor Ludorum 2011. I'd run till I felt sick just to be called that.'

'Even if you were, and you did win, I'm not calling you that. I'm not making the same mistake twice.'

Joey laughed and threw an old tennis ball at him.

12

Billy sat with his back to the tree in the Family Centre grounds. His chest felt weighed down as if his heart were unusually heavy. If he moved from side to side, perhaps it might roll, like a ball bearing, rumbling and hefty, from one side of his ribcage to the other.

He'd been collected from school for a meeting with Miriam. When she'd phoned Meg's the night before, she said she'd just wanted to have what she called a proper chat. Billy squirmed at the thought. That would probably mostly mean questions. He preferred to ask, rather than answer them. He recalled the way Horatio had looked at him after he'd called Thomas *Victor Ludorum*. He'd prefer not to tell Miriam that.

Billy was early. The taxi driver had said it was 3.35. He looked around. The red swing was swinging by itself; someone must have just got off. There was something lonely, he thought, about the sight of a swing swinging empty. It was minus the happiness, the feeling of flight, that came with soaring high and free. By itself, and moving less as each moment passed, the swing looked forlorn. That was a word from his spelling list this week. He'd copied out its meaning too; the swing was definitely forlorn. Billy hoped it wasn't infectious. He thought of Samantha Hollis's orange play-doh and how it might seep sadness into your pocket. Unhappiness might be catching; he should be on guard. Today had not been a good day.

Andrew Walker's van was in the car park. He must be somewhere around. Billy cast his eyes around the perimeter of the fencing. There was no sign of him outside. Perhaps he was working inside the building. If he did see him, he guessed Andrew would be cheery. Andrew, he'd decided, was in a good mood with life, which seemed to be unusual for grown-ups.

He checked again. There was no sign of anyone; just the slightly heat-flattened feel of the end of a warm afternoon. He crouched, and squirrelled his fingers into the hole at the base of the tree. The notes were still there; he took them out and carefully counted all three. They were still folded neatly; the tree had kept them safe. He patted the trunk. It unexpectedly made him want to cry. He fixed his eyes on the white picket fence and concentrated until everything stopped being blurry.

He reached in his bag and took out his notebook. He'd write another note. That could help; it would be like putting the orange play-doh somewhere other than in his pocket. Maybe he'd walk away with a heart that was lighter, if not light like Joey's. Joey was not sad, Billy had seen that clearly today. This afternoon, they'd been practising for a singing concert; lined up in rows. Joey, from Billy, was two along, in the row behind. They were singing a song that celebrated Spring. Mrs Bailey had tied some soft green willow around the recorders, and brought in a jar of lilac, cut from her garden. The class sang *May time, May time, God has given us May time. We thank him for his gifts of love, and sing a song of Spring.* Billy turned round to peek at Joey, expecting to see him stifling a laugh, or impersonating an opera singer, but instead Joey was singing with enthusiasm and a big broad smile on his face. He looked properly happy, as if he were on a different planet from Billy, not two along, row behind.

Gifts of love, Billy had sung softly; what might they look like? It was hard to tell. Yet when he got into the taxi at hometime (and that was a word that was increasingly starting to cause him some bother), there was Joey, doing his usual thumbs-up routine, his face pressed up against the chain-link fence. Maybe, Billy thought, a gift of love could look like that; a little bit bonkers but on your side. Perhaps he shouldn't feel so upset by Joey's enthusiasm for the song.

He took his pen from his rucksack and started to write. He

lifted his head when he saw Miriam's car come into the car park. It didn't make him feel hurried; she'd have a phone call to make, or something to sort out. She was always on to something. She'd call from the open window when she wanted him to come. He carried on writing.

'So,' Miriam said, half an hour later, putting glasses of water down on the desk for them both. 'How's it going? How's it with Caroline, Toby and Horatio?'

Billy looked as if he were trying to become as colourless as the water in the glass before him, as if, with extraordinary effort, he might blend into it and become invisible.

'Mmm,' he replied.

'Mmmm?' said Miriam. There was a pulse of silence. It looked as if he wasn't going to be forthcoming. She suppressed her impatience.

When her supervisor Sheila opined that Miriam was occasionally inclined to terseness with clients, Miriam thought later she'd got off lightly. What Sheila had failed to identify was that she was frequently ineffective at encouraging children to open up. How she struggled to get them to sing like canaries. Her mother nailed it; she said that Miriam's directness, her frankness, made tunnelling in the opposite direction appealing. Thinking of this, she softened her tone.

'Would it make it easier if I went through the things you've done and that might jog your memory about how you felt at the time?'

If she channelled Patience on a monument, she wondered, might she somehow become gloriously infused with it?

'Mmmm.'

'So, where to begin: high wires, climbing, free falling, all that bit, which thank God didn't result in any injuries or you breaking an arm, was that fun? Did you enjoy that, was it a nice day?'

'It was very high.'

'I expected that.'

'Mmm.'

'What were they like to talk to? Were they easy to talk to?'

'Caroline talks quite a lot, trying to be kind, checking I'm okay, so you don't really have to.'

'Have to what?'

'Talk. Talk much. She points out things to look at, so you can just look at those if you want to.'

'Oh. And what about Horatio?'

'Horatio?'

'Yes, Horatio.'

'Mmm.'

'Should I be reading more into that *mmm* than the others you've spoken since you sat down?'

Billy shrugged. Miriam looked at him fixedly.

'Horatio is used to being the only one, their only one,' he said.

'That doesn't mean he won't be happy to have a brother, or a sister, for that matter. You're an only one so you know that.'

Billy looked surprised to be reminded of the fact. Miriam wondered if he'd never equated it with any possibility of excessive attention.

'Mmm.'

'Do you think Horatio doesn't want a brother or a sister?'

Billy shrugged again. Miriam bit her lip. Patience seemed to be itching to take a hike.

'Billy, I promise you there's no right or wrong answers here. You can just say what you feel or think, or you could just say what you noticed, if you've noticed something. Maybe we should talk about what you've noticed.'

She resolved to sit out the silence. Silent it was. She thought she could hear her own watch ticking. Perhaps even her heart beat. Billy shifted in his chair. He cleared his throat. Miriam realised she was holding her breath.

'The field they play cricket on is very beautiful. Very flat. Very striped. Cricket tea is very nice, like a birthday party probably.'

'Ah, so you enjoyed that. Were the other boys nice to you? Did you talk to them?'

'Just the once.'

'Did you feel shy?'

Billy shrugged. 'They know a lot of things. Horatio's homework is about the *Titanic*. He's also got to think about how a play about an inspector shows the politics of the person who wrote it.'

'Hmm,' said Miriam. 'Well remembered, and go Horatio on the homework front. You'd know all those things too if you were in Year Seven. Don't forget Horatio is twelve, that's more than two years older than you.'

'He called out twelve almost thirteen.'

Miriam looked at the file in front of her.

'Sorry?'

'When you jump for the trapeze bar, you have to call out your age. He said almost thirteen so the bar went further away.'

'It says here he was twelve in April, that's only a few weeks ago.'

'You're supposed to do it to match your age.'

'Oh I see. Maybe he's very good at jumping. Maybe he likes a challenge.'

Was this getting them anywhere? Miriam wondered. *The problem with you*, her mother had told her in another ostensibly well-meaning insight, *is that you're never content to go with the flow, you're always wanting to set the course.*

'Mmm.'

'So, you've been for a day out, you've been to the cricket, you've been out for dinner – how was dinner?'

'Italian. Toby told Horatio that if he squirts lemon on his fish, he's supposed to stick the fork into the lemon to do it which is better manners than just squeezing it when you might get lemon juice by accident in the eye of the person who is sitting next to you. I learned a new piece of good manners to go with what Grandma taught me.'

Miriam looked at Billy quizzically.

'Did you get lemon juice in your eye?'

'Lemon juice is not sore. Not properly.'

Miriam looked back at her notes.

'And isn't the next part of the plan that you are going to their house on Saturday?'

'Yes, for the whole day. They're collecting me from Meg's.'

'Well, shall we meet here on Monday after school again, and you can tell me some more, or sort of tell me some more?'

'Okay.'

'Do you want to wait by the tree for Meg to come and get you? She's got a review meeting going on with Jayden's parents. It's meant to finish at half past four, so she won't be long. She can take you both back to the house.'

'Okay.'

'And Billy, are you sure there's nothing else you'd like to say, or like to tell me?'

'Uh-uh.'

'Okay. I'll see you on Monday then, and I hope Saturday goes well.'

Miriam watched Billy walk off down the corridor. Andrew had appeared by the notice-board; Billy had stopped and was talking to him. More likely just 'Mmmm-ing' to him, Miriam thought.

She'd been on training courses which focused on how to talk to children; how to skilfully and deftly encourage them to express their feelings. Her accrued learning, she felt, wasn't evident in her attempts with Billy. He was tight as a clam. How great would it be if she could just cut to the chase; ask him, plainly, *Has this got the remotest chance in hell of working for you?* She thought back to her original conversation with Sheila, and how she had lobbied her to play a little fast and loose with the process. The question it now raised was just how quick a quick decision might be. How quickly should a plug be pulled and the whole bloody caravan move on?

She looked down the corridor to where Billy and Andrew were talking. Prior to Billy's interruption, Andrew was no doubt focused on something practical, necessary and in the realm of the completely resolvable. (*Hey Miriam*, he'd say to her as she walked past the stationery cupboard, *see, I've replaced the latch; it won't bug you with sticking anymore.*) Miriam frowned. Lemon juice at dinner. Was that something, or nothing, he was telling her? She could have kicked herself. As the adult who was supposed to be

Billy's primary interpreter, could she look herself in the mirror and say she was doing a good job?

Either way, she couldn't sit here contemplating. One of the few consolations of her job was the fact that there was only limited time to beat yourself up about how you might have done something better. She had an assessment to do. Her directness was a strength for that; no mincing words. Would she ever, she wondered, become more subtle, more tactful? Perhaps a relationship might change her. If a man loved her with tenderness, might it somehow seep osmotically into her? Would she wake up one morning with a whole new skill set, sensitive, intuitive and ready for the off? Gentle, patient men, she mused, collecting her things together, tended not to fall for women routinely described as ball-breakers. That would likely be her first obstacle to success.

Andrew watched Miriam drive away. She'd given him a wave as she got into her car. The receptionist was the last to leave. She walked down the path and out to the bus stop. Andrew made his way to the tree.

Lorna had said it wasn't a breach of trust. He'd asked her. It was forgivable, that's what she'd said: that for a vulnerable child, it counted as a safeguard. If it revealed something important, she said, he could tip off Miriam and that would be a good thing. She made it sound such evident good sense, rather than unacceptable snooping even if it felt like that now.

Billy had been sweet in the corridor. He'd asked about screwdrivers, and Andrew had shown him the difference between a Philips and a flat-headed one. Andrew had asked him how his trip to the adventure park had gone.

'It was high,' Billy said.

'Can't stand heights myself,' Andrew had answered. 'They make me feel sick to the point of passing out, and roller-coasters do, and the view once from a very tall skyscraper in Toronto where part of the floor was glass and you could see right down to the people below who looked like scurrying ants. I couldn't walk across it. Lorna just laughed.'

'So what did you do?' Billy asked.

'Crawled across it, on my hands and knees, palms sweating, all six foot five of me. The lift attendant was laughing so much he had to use a handkerchief to cover his mouth.'

Billy had digested the image.

'From my point of view,' Andrew continued, 'you're either a bird or a fish. I'm much more comfortable in water, me; give me a surfboard over a high wire any day.'

Billy paused, and then, leaning forward, almost whispered 'Maybe I could be an excellent surfer then, because I was properly scared.'

'Surfing's the way forward. Far cooler gear too.'

Billy nodded, and turned to wave to Meg who was walking towards him.

The note in Andrew's hand had been folded with careful precision. This time, Billy had written a list.

1. Jobs to remember I can't do – definitely tree surgeon. Park attendant in charge of the boating lake, definitely a possibility.

2. When you are meant to be grateful, when people are kind, it's difficult to say you don't like something.

3. If you don't know Victor Ludorum means winner of the games and is not a boy's name, it doesn't mean you are stupid, even if it looks that way.

4. Lemon juice in the eye properly hurts even if you say it doesn't.

5. Horatio thinks I am cuckoo boy. Am I?

6. How are you supposed to know what a gift of love looks like?

Andrew re-folded the note. Cuckoo boy. He's called himself cuckoo boy. Surely Miriam should know that?

13

Trudy Morris sat by the pool and smoothed her thumb over her perfectly painted toenails. She'd just returned with Ted from the supermarket. It was full of couples their age, shopping together, their trolleys filled with a combination of Portuguese and British groceries: fresh fish, avocados, peaches, Marmite, cornflakes, fig rolls. She didn't like looking at all the imported English goods; they seemed a dismal snatch at a life left behind, an acknowledgement of things remembered, things missed, and mostly indicative of stubborn, concrete yearnings. Such nostalgia seemed pointless; none of it tasted the same. The heat seeped into everything; softening, flattening, altering.

Everybody still bought English newspapers. Some subscribed to the web versions, and read them on laptops or i-Pads, but most drove to buy a paper, carrying it from the car under their arm like some vestige retained of routines at home. Mostly, she felt, the trip for the paper was another mechanism designed to fill up the day. Sometimes she wondered if that was all they did on this ribbon of clean, identikit, developed coastline: filled their days with untaxing activities, reminding themselves as they walked, loose-limbed, in the joint-warming heat, that in England they'd probably be scurrying, shoulders hunched, jaw clenched, into horizontal rain.

All the women had painted nails – fingers and toes. She stroked the glossy coral on hers. They wore broderie anglaise blouses, crisp linen shorts, dresses with a little more colour than they would have worn at home. They were carefully tanned, the men less so, their faces ruddy from more alcohol than they'd consumed in England, their scalps hyper-pigmented from too much sun.

Leisure and recreation were all-consuming endeavours here. Sometimes, Trudy felt exhausted by the orchestration of all their pastimes. Pastimes. Pass time. There was a word, she thought, that carried more meaning than was first apparent. Lunch parties, drinks parties, tennis sets, bridge, golf. *Having the time of their lives at this time of their life*, said the advertising billboards outside villa developments under construction. The images showed people who looked exactly like them.

Recreation. If she split the word, Trudy thought, it became re-creation; something entirely different in meaning. And that was what they had done, she reflected. She and Ted, in coming to Portugal, had re-created themselves. They had sloughed off the pain and weariness and the repetitive cycle of being the desperate parents of a drug-addicted young woman, and emerged, here, beside a turquoise sea and a sweeping beach, ready to reconfigure themselves as creatures of leisure. *We've no dependants*, she'd overheard Ted say.

Some of her friends still watched the TV series they'd watched at home: *EastEnders, Coronation Street*, beamed to them by satellite. Some listened avidly to what they could get of Radio Four. All of them listened to the Queen on Christmas Day. This was Trudy's only exception. She liked to think it was a scrap of patriotism, but in reality recognised it as more self-serving than that. Instead, some kind of self-flagellation in listening to a small, elderly woman who had so wholly embraced the notion of duty when Trudy felt she could fairly be accused of a dereliction of her own.

Out of season, there were no children in the resort. They came, like the swallows in England, at the start of the summer, and when September arrived, they disappeared again, lured by the scent of fresh pencil cases, stiff new shoes, over-sized school uniforms. There were Portuguese children beyond here, she thought, now lifting her head towards the hinterland. Her maid, Maria, had a child; she lived a few miles inland. Trudy had never been to her home. Perhaps it was on a street where there was a church, a school, a post office, a chemist. The old life.

Billy couldn't have lived here, of that she was sure. He'd have been totally isolated. It had started to prickle at her, like nettle rash, the feeling that perhaps she had been too hasty in her decision. Billy had seemed one more Lizzie-related problem to take care of; one more thing that would have, no doubt, ended in failure. Ted would not have agreed to return to England which was what Billy would have needed. Perhaps he *was* actually having the time of his life, and it was only she who was beginning to feel guilty at absconding.

It was a blur; Lizzie's death, Miriam's phone call telling them what had happened. Lizzie's pathetic, bruised, thin, needle-marked body in the mortuary. The grey blanket they'd covered her with which she wouldn't have used for a dog. Trudy chose to go and see her; Ted wouldn't come. *I know what she looks like*, he said, so she had gone alone. Afterwards, he hadn't asked her anything about it. She was surprised by his lack of curiosity, if not his lack of empathy and support. The mortuary technician had been kind, polite. She'd left them alone. Trudy held Lizzie's hand. It was all she could think of to do. She suppressed the temptation to lift her daughter on to her lap, and rock her, wailing; what a clattering of things made of stainless steel that would have caused, and the quick footsteps of attendants. So, instead, she'd held her hand and looked carefully at the detail of its stiff blueness, and tried to remember it chubby and pink and warm as it had been when she was little. How many times, in childhood, had she held her hand to protect her from harm? Not enough, evidently. Either that, or she had failed to pay attention when attention was still needed. When she finally left her – which felt like yet another abandonment – she kissed Lizzie's forehead as if she might be kissing her goodnight.

Nobody tells you, she thought, how to mourn the loss of your child; how to pick a path through the visceral keening, the palpable collapse of the heart, the torrent of memories. An avalanche of grief, that was what she had felt, and she saw now, with the perspective of a little time, that the same avalanche had swept even the possibility of supporting Billy away.

Perhaps she should have asked Miriam for more time. Perhaps she should have suggested to Ted that they stay in England a little longer. Perhaps she should finally have spent time with her grandson without him being overshadowed by his mother's needs.

Trudy shifted uneasily. She had failed him. Always he'd been a side show; small, quiet, obedient, while she tried to fix Lizzie. She put her face in her hands. Ted would be home soon. She must rally. He would not be prepared to discuss it; perhaps never be prepared to discuss it. She determined to bury it deep; bury it like something beneath the shoreline, its jaggedness, its intractability, worn smooth by the waves and time.

She had signed Miriam's Placement Order papers the day after their meeting. She'd sat in the hotel lobby and signed them on a tacky, faux-mahogany desk with a cheap biro contained in a mock ink-well. Her maternal sign-off; that was what it had been. She'd dropped the envelope off at the Family Centre reception rather than face Miriam. They'd returned to Portugal, and she was surprised to find that, rather than wakefulness, she slept like someone who had been on a march for weeks.

She stood up, and carried her tea tray into the kitchen. She changed the water in a vase of flowers she had on the counter. She took a peach from the fruit bowl, and sliced it brutally, cleanly. Wholeness, wholesomeness, she reflected wearily, was so easy to destroy.

14

Toby watched Caroline from his vantage point of the couch in the kitchen.

She had got up before him, and been downstairs making ice cream. He'd rolled his eyes a little – just a little – at the sound of the machine churning by seven fifteen. What nine-year-old, he might have said (now watching her, whilst appearing to read the The Times on his i-Pad, as she sprinkled sugar over little star-shaped shortbread biscuits), would discriminate between home-made and shop-bought ice cream? Ditto shortbread. But he didn't say. She was singing as she did it. She had her hair tied back with a vibrant blue ribbon, and she was singing as she worked; her hopes for the day, and her fizzing energy, as tangible in the kitchen as the couch he was sitting on.

Endeavour. She deserved a medal for endeavour, and always had done. All the years of their marriage, he could see her *maxing the moment* as she called it; her face determined as she climbed on the runners of her car to unstrap a vast Christmas tree from the roof, or, on Bonfire Night, carried a fat-bellied tureen of tomato soup that she had pushed through a sieve for hours to eliminate all the pips and skins.

Now, she was brushing caster sugar from her fingertips. She came towards him, and kissed him.

'Thank you,' she said. 'I can tell you're trying not to conclude that most of what I do is superfluous to requirements.'

Toby shrugged. 'Whatever makes you happy,' he said, as she turned and began to plump up cushions.

It *was* that, he reflected. Whatever made her happy. He'd recognised sometime ago that that was where the bar was set, for him.

If Billy Morris, adoption, this whole episode, home-made ice cream and shortbread biscuits made her happy, so be it.

Horatio came into the kitchen and poured himself some cereal.

'Hey, chap,' Toby said good-naturedly.

Horatio didn't respond.

'Not the morning to get out of bed the wrong side,' Toby said, nodding towards Caroline who was now tidying a stack of mail. (Surely a nine-year-old wouldn't notice that?)

Horatio flashed him a glance.

Toby went back to his i-Pad.

Women were complicated, children were straightforward. That, up to now, for him, had been a sufficient take on domestic life.

Their house was enormous.

Billy stood in the hallway which was paved with smooth black and white flagstones. He craned his neck backwards to look up the circular stairway. Ahead of him, through a door that was ajar, he could see a large stone fireplace and, down the hallway, in the kitchen, a long table with four lights hanging over it, and a huge oven.

'We did the house up after we bought it,' Caroline was explaining. 'It belonged to the church. It was the rectory, which it still is, of course, but just without the vicar. When we were knocking some cupboards down on the landing, I found a whole suitcase of sermons.'

'Think yourself lucky,' said Toby, who had appeared in the kitchen through a door from the garden, wearing cycling clothes. 'She gifted them to the church warden so they're no longer here, or they may have become compulsory reading before lunch. Maybe even compulsory reading out loud.'

Billy wondered if the vicar, when he lived here, had a wife and children, and enough coal or wood to go in the huge fireplace. It would have been a cold and empty space if he hadn't. His sermons might not have been all that cheerful.

'We rented a cottage down the road while the house was being done,' Caroline said. 'I came here every day. I even had my own hard hat.' She smiled at the recollection and Billy thought he should smile back. He did so, but his mouth felt tight at the corners.

Horatio came down the stairs.

'Hey Billy,' he said.

'Hey Horatio,' Billy replied. Now Horatio would decide he wasn't just cuckoo buy but parrot boy too.

'Why don't you show Billy your playroom?' Caroline said, putting her arms round Horatio's shoulders. 'I'm sure there will be something he wants to play with in there. I'm just going to finish off lunch. I've made some ice cream for pudding, Billy. I'm experimenting with my new ice cream maker. It's chocolate and peanut butter flavour, which I hope is going to be delicious.'

Billy thought the ice cream probably would be delicious. What had Toby said? *Think yourself lucky*. Maybe that was possible. Perhaps if you were like Caroline, chock-a-block with enthusiasm, things maybe turned out all right simply because you willed them to be. Maybe luck, he thought, was something to do with determination. Caroline looked like the person least likely to be shipwrecked. He couldn't imagine her life ever being blown off course. Her kitchen, with all its smooth surfaces and no visible handles, would never be the setting for soup and fresh starts.

Horatio opened the playroom door.

'Ask before you touch anything,' he said quietly. 'It's my stuff.'

'Sure,' said Billy. No danger of any gifts of love coming from Horatio's direction.

It was like a toy shop; a toy shop, or a sports shop, Billy would have been pushed to decide. Along one wall there were hooks from which hung equipment for every game Billy could think of. There was a tennis racquet, a net of rugby and foot balls, a hockey stick, a baseball bat and a pitching glove. There was a snorkel, flippers and a mask, and three sets of brightly coloured swimming goggles. There was all Horatio's cricket stuff, some running spikes, a badminton set, table tennis bats, and what Horatio told him was a lacrosse stick.

On another wall there were photos of Horatio doing all different kinds of things. The one that caught Billy's eye was a sequence of pictures somewhere sunny, in a glass-bottomed boat. Horatio was holding a snorkel and a mask in his hand. In the next shot he was swimming amidst a shoal of carrot-coloured fish. He was holding something in his outstretched hand for them to eat.

Billy looked back to the wall with the snorkel. He reached out his hand and traced the curl of the mouthpiece.

'That counts as touching,' Horatio said.

Billy put his hands back into his pockets. Caroline came into the room.

'Have you ever been snorkelling, Billy?' she asked brightly.

He shook his head.

'Well, I always say if you can breathe through your mouth you can snorkel. Didn't you say you were in the improvers' group at swimming? I'm guessing with a pair of flippers on, you'd be snorkelling away in an instant.' She made a flip-flapping gesture with her hands.

Billy looked back at the photo. Surfing, snorkelling, maybe they took similar skills. He'd ask Andrew when he saw him.

Caroline seemed to think most things were achievable. Maybe thinking this got you halfway to actually being able to do them. Perhaps if he lived with her, he'd magically be able to. Alternatively, she might cheerlead from the sides while he failed at everything. He took a last look at the fish. They were the same colour as Joey's hair. If he'd been snorkelling amongst them, he would have completely matched them, perhaps even become invisible. It would be an invisibility cloak made from swimming fish. He'd tell him that on Monday; Joey would like the thought that somewhere (Caroline was now telling him it was in the Seychelles) there were fish that could help him achieve this particular ambition.

Toby was coming down the stairs. He'd changed out of his cycling clothes and had wet hair from the shower.

'How about some cricket, boys? I'll bowl and you can whack me around a little before lunch.'

In the garden, which Billy thought was big enough to pass as a small park, Horatio set the barrels on the stumps and stood before the wicket. Toby motioned to Billy, showing him where to stand, and then ran slowly towards Horatio, the ball curving from his hand in a smooth, flowing motion. From the corner of his eye, Billy could see Caroline watching from the kitchen window. She was clapping and beaming. Horatio struck the ball, and Billy scrabbled for it in the flower bed. Each time Toby bowled, Horatio sent it soaring over the lawn, sometimes in Billy's direction, sometimes to the other side of what Toby told him was a purple beech tree. Finally, Toby caught him out, standing beneath the ball until it fell into his cupped hands. *Howzat! my boy* Toby shouted, and Horatio laughed and offered the bat to Billy.

'Your turn,' he said to him.

'Good boy,' said Toby.

Billy wiped his hands on his jeans and took the bat carefully.

'It won't break,' Toby said.

Horatio didn't look so sure. 'It better not,' he said quietly.

The first ball Toby bowled clattered through Billy's wicket.

'Sorry, there was a bit of spin on that,' Toby said, 'it wasn't intentional. Let's go again.'

The second and third did the same.

'Let's try under arm,' said Toby. 'I'm forgetting you're nine, not twelve. My fault. Under arm should be much better.'

Billy struck the ball and it rolled feebly across the lawn towards Horatio.

'Shot!' called Caroline from the kitchen. Billy couldn't lift his eyes from the ground. If this was his forever family, maybe all his time would be spent being rubbish at things while Caroline enthusiastically pretended otherwise.

'Perhaps that's enough cricket,' said Toby. 'Rach, I'll just go and give Mummy a hand. Why don't you show Billy your den? Come in for lunch in about ten minutes.

'There's a no-adults-allowed rule in the den,' Toby continued, turning to Billy. 'I know better than to trespass.'

Horatio began to walk towards a corner of the garden. Billy

followed him down to a small wooden shed tucked in a semi-circle of trees. Above a door that opened in two sections was a sign which said 'No adults allowed'. If he lived here, Billy wondered, would Horatio add 'or Billy' to the sign?

Inside the den, his first thought was that Joey would have died of joy. His second was that he might too. The shed had a rug patterned with the Union Jack, and a square plastic table with four chairs. There was a biscuit tin that actually had biscuits in, and some mugs and a tin of hot chocolate. There was a glass jar of pillowy pink and white marshmallows.

'I've been allowed a kettle since I was eleven,' Horatio said stiffly, twirling its plug in his fingers. There was a dartboard on one of the walls, and two beanbags, and a table football.

'Sit down,' Horatio said to him, gesturing to one of the chairs.

Billy sat down on the chair opposite Horatio and met his eyes for the first time.

Horatio started to speak.

'We've met three times, and I've got three things to say. Number one. The only reason I went along with this idea of my mum's is because you were meant to be a girl aged five and under. Felix in my class got a Guatemalan four-year-old sister, and then a new X-box Kinect to say congratulations on becoming a brother. You're not a girl and you're not under five.'

'Point taken,' said Billy. It was indisputable. He could also see the appeal of the X-box that was part of the package of the four-year-old girl. He didn't imagine any such strings would come attached to him.

'Number two. I am always going to be bigger than you, cleverer than you, braver than you and better at sport than you, and they are always going to be properly my mum and dad. You see that, don't you?'

Billy wondered if he should nod. Horatio didn't seem to be requiring that.

'And number three. Before all this started about adopting, I wanted a dog, but dogs make my mum sneeze. If I'd been allowed a dog, and I wanted a chocolate Labrador, I was going to call him Billy and teach him to fetch sticks. You probably can't even do that.'

Billy looked out of the tiny window of the shed. The last part was a bit harsh. Across the lawn he could see Caroline approaching and waving.

'Your mum's coming,' he said. '*Your* mum.' He deliberately emphasised the first word. 'She probably wants us to go in. We should go.'

He stood up and turned to Horatio who looked as if he was trying not to cry. He was biting his bottom lip.

'They just feel sorry for you, that's all it is. Everything else I've got covered already. Everything,' he said, with sudden determination.

Billy nodded. Horatio stood by the table, his hands balled up by his sides. Maybe he'd have benefited from a turn with the orange play-doh too. He could have filled the pot with his own murder of crows' words. Billy paused. Maybe he should say *It'll be all right, they won't want me, I'll get sent back.* But it wouldn't have made any sense to him. Might Horatio have read *Dear Zoo?*

'It would have been nice to play table football,' Billy said, gesturing to the table.

'If you'd just been coming to play, just to play, for that kind of normal visit, and going back to your parents like everybody else, I would have. Happily.'

Billy wondered if Horatio might realise how much more happily that would have been for him too.

'Boys,' Caroline was calling, 'lunch is on the table.'

'You're not that bad, Billy.' Horatio said, pushing the chair underneath the table. 'If that doesn't sound weird, you're not that bad.'

'Obviously better if I'd been Guatemalan, and a girl aged four,' Billy said.

Horatio smiled.

Victor Ludorum, Billy thought.

Billy looked at the painted shelf in the corner and the jar of pink and white marshmallows. It felt as if some sort of decision had been reached, even though Miriam, Caroline and Toby were meant to be in charge. The marshmallows spoke to him of a life that might have been. Not holidays in the Seychelles when he might or might not have been a whizz at snorkelling, but the possibility of going quietly down to a den in the garden, boiling a kettle (which he'd been doing safely for years already), and making hot chocolate, and topping it with melting marshmallows, and lying on a rug of the Union Jack, or sitting cosy on a beanbag and feeling like the king of the world.

'Coming,' shouted Horatio to Caroline. 'We were just playing table football.'

Billy stepped out of the den, his eyes watering as they adjusted to the slice of sunlight that came from beyond the semicircle of trees.

In her bathroom at bed-time, Caroline used a pristine white facial mitt to wash off her cleanser.

She looked at herself in the mirror, chin up, her hand to her throat.

Happy? Toby had asked, when she'd returned from taking Billy back.

Giddy, she was tempted to say, although she wasn't sure whether it was from exhilaration or exhaustion.

She'd kissed him. She'd leaned over in the car when she dropped him off at Meg Oliver's and kissed him, quickly, on the cheek. Fleetingly, a little embarrassedly, but she'd kissed him all the same. It felt like staking a claim, like a little bold flag on the moon, and she'd flushed afterwards and hoped he hadn't noticed. How different, she thought from kissing a newborn baby, but it was a gesture of intent. She felt proud of that.

She'd had to call *Boys, boys*, a couple of times in the afternoon, calling them from the playroom, or from the den. The word had bubbled up from her throat, and she felt her heart quicken with gladness. She should have been saying that for years.

Toby had kissed her and said *Well done, you were a triumph.*

It's not about me, she'd replied, and yet, now, several hours later, staring at her clean, still, face in the mirror, she suddenly thought maybe that was what he thought it was about; appeasing her, gratifying her. Maybe Toby didn't see it from any other perspective.

Horatio had been quiet. Quiet, or possibly mutinous. He'd gone to his room and said he wanted to read his book. He stared at her blankly, coolly. Now, as she started to brush her teeth, she felt ripples of unease.

Billy lay in bed. He felt exhausted. All the listening, and trying, and concentrating at the Frasers' house. After lunch, Caroline had suggested a game of what she called family ping-pong, and they took it in turns to be partners playing table tennis. *This is great*, Caroline said, *usually we have to play two against one!* The Frasers had their very own table tennis table. It was kept in a room which was called the games room, which was not the same room as the one called the playroom. When it was his turn to be on a team with Horatio, Billy could feel them both trying their hardest for the outside of their arms to not even touch. Caroline and Toby won that game easily. The ball kept going down the middle of the table, straight through the gap between the boys.

Toby was jolly. That seemed a good word for him. He seemed to find everything a little bit funny. He teased Caroline, he teased Horatio, he called snacks snakes. *Would you like a snake*, he asked, offering Billy a bowl of crisps. He timed how long it took the boys to put on and zip up a raincoat. Billy was quicker, and Toby had lifted Billy's arm in the air like a winning boxer and called him the champion. Horatio hadn't looked as if he were properly trying. Billy was wearing Horatio's old jacket anyway; the zip was probably slipperier, more worn. Perhaps Horatio would have been happier if they'd actually been boxing. Maybe Billy's nose, bloodied, would have cheered him up.

They'd gone for what they called a tramp through the woods at the back of the house. Billy could see that was where a dog would have come in handy. Sticks a-plenty, just there on the ground for the picking and throwing. Caroline told him that the flowers on the horse chestnut trees were known as candles. *Remember, Horatio,* she said, *how we used to walk a route through these trees when you were very small, and pretend they were candles, lighting your way?* Horatio hadn't seemed much bothered. Caroline, for a moment, reminded him of Grandma. *Remember, Lizzie, remember, Lizzie,* she'd keep saying, when his mum obviously didn't. If his mum were still alive, if he'd got to be a grown-up and she'd got to be old, what would she have asked him to remember? Nothing that sounded pretty.

Billy was beginning to think that being a mother was perhaps not the happiest of things. Maybe you ended up reciting a whole lot of memories that your children didn't much care for. Perhaps it got a bit whiny, mothers saying *remember, remember* when grown-up children just wanted to think about now. Maybe, in fact, being a mother wasn't as good as having one.

Caroline had driven him home. Outside Meg's, when she'd stopped the car, she'd leaned over from the driving seat and kissed him goodbye on the cheek. She looked a little bit embarrassed afterwards, as if perhaps she'd surprised herself as well as him. *We've loved having you today,* she said, and beamed.

Billy had got out of the car and stood on Meg's doorstep with his hand touching his cheek. He wasn't sure how he felt about her kissing him. The last person who'd kissed him was Grandma. She and Caroline were starting to blur in his mind which probably wasn't a good thing. Also, it was weird for another reason. For an odd moment, in the car, he felt older than Caroline, even though she was the grown-up, driving, and he was the child in the passenger seat. She couldn't see it was all doomed, so she was sitting there, beaming, as if it might all work out.

He thought back to Horatio in the den. He must have planned his words carefully. Even if given time for a proper answer, Billy wasn't sure he would have come up with one. Of course they would always be more Horatio's parents, *actually* his parents. Of course it would have been easier if he'd been a baby girl. And, Horatio *would* always be better than him, except perhaps in crummy things like putting on a rain coat fast.

The thing was, what was he supposed to do now?

Miriam had phoned when he got back and he would be seeing her on Monday. She'd ask him lots of questions and look at him in that way when she went all beady-eyed. A back-to-front bala-clava would come in useful, he thought. Then he wouldn't have to spend so much time looking down at his trainers while Miriam attempted to look right into his eyes.

15

Andrew waited until Billy was inside Miriam's office before he went to the tree. He reached in to remove a freshly folded note. It was headed *Things I know now.*

1. Dads bowl cricket balls and call out Howzat.
2. They call you 'my boy' or say 'that's my boy'.
3. They stand in the kitchen and make a very big room seem smaller.
4. Horatio would like it better if I were a girl from Gwotemarla aged four. That would probably make it okay.
5. Horatio is always going to be better than me at everything and they will always only properly be his mum and dad. That is accurate.
6. Horatio wants a dog to call Billy and teach to fetch sticks. That would probably be more fun for him.

Wherever Billy's dad was, Andrew thought, may there be a plague of locusts on his head, something biblical and terrible, like being covered in boils and sores. Toby sounded decent. But Horatio – would Miriam even be aware of what he had obviously made clear? Cuckoo boy. Andrew shook his head, and looked across at her office, and wondered how she was picking her way through it all.

Miriam sat at her desk staring into the middle distance. It was like skating over very thick, milk-white ice. She'd just spent half an hour with Billy and he'd told her about Horatio's array of sports equipment, which she already knew about, and about peanut butter and chocolate ice cream which he said was delicious. He'd told her about some sermons in a suitcase in a cupboard, and playing ping pong, and going for a walk in the woods. He made it sound like an activity list. When she'd probed about Caroline and Toby, he'd told her Toby's new road bike was so light Toby could balance it on one finger, and in fact had, in the kitchen. Then he asked her if she had any children she was finding homes for who came from Guatemala.

'Guatemala?' she said, bemused.

It had been a singularly unsatisfactory debrief. Everything he had said came down to things he had noticed rather than thought or felt, other than the question about Guatemala which was inexplicable. Should she have probed that rather than just told him it was a different department? There was not a scrap of anything personal or non-factual in what he had told her. Nothing that gave her a clue about the possibility of attachment. Was this what Samantha Hollis meant by being frozen? Maybe he needed more time. What else could she arrange for him to do with the Frasers? Maybe the cinema? On current form, she thought, Billy's feedback would likely be a précis of the film's plot.

She looked up from her desk to see Andrew about to knock on her door. She gestured for him to come in. He'd got that slightly bashful expression again. She looked at him intently. She'd got too many cases to think about to spend time second-guessing him. Maybe that was another key to her fatal flaws; maybe she consistently failed to pay men enough sympathetic attention. What should she resolve from that insight? Must try softer? She smiled to herself, which seemed to wrong-foot Andrew. He gestured to the light fitting.

'I just need to check this, check the bulb's okay, and check the thermostat on your radiator. I might need to order some new ones with clearer settings, so that the temperature in the building can be controlled more accurately. All part of the sustainability objectives . . .'

'Go ahead,' Miriam said briskly, 'check whatever you need to check. Sustainability is obviously very dear to my heart.'

Andrew knelt down by the radiator. From what Miriam could

see there wasn't anything particularly focussed going on. If she hadn't been 'trying softer', she'd have called it a bit of random twiddling.

'About Billy,' Andrew began.

'Yes..ss,' said Miriam, 'about Billy, whose circumstances are obviously confidential so I'm not going to be doing any chatting about them.'

'Yes, not his circumstances. Just something I could tell you, something that might be helpful to you, in whatever you were thinking, you know, thinking about deciding.'

'Fire away, I'm all ears,' Miriam said, thinking there was something uncannily similar in the way both Andrew and Billy addressed her without meeting her eye, the radiator as fascinating to Andrew as Billy's footwear had been to him half an hour previously.

'I'm not going to say how I know. I just think you should know he calls himself cuckoo boy. Horatio would prefer it if he was a girl – from a country I think might be Guatemala, hard to tell, and also Horatio wanted a dog before all this and he planned to call it Billy and teach it to fetch sticks. Also, he's wondering if you are meant to be grateful, because when people are kind, it's difficult to say you don't like something. Something else about how to know what a gift of love looks like. That's about it.'

Miriam looked at him, still crouched by the radiator. He had the air of a man who had tipped the entire contents of his pockets on her desk.

He paused and wiped his hands on a rag. 'That's me done. No need for you to say anything. The radiator's fine, all very sustainable, you'll be pleased to know.'

'Evidently I am very pleased about my radiator, and evidently also pleased to learn everything else that's somewhat unexpectedly come out of your mouth. Can I just check one thing. You said cuckoo boy. Cuckoo boy was the term he used?'

Andrew nodded.

'And Guatemala?'

'I'm hedging my bets a little on that one. It's very hard to spell.' Andrew paused. 'I'll be off now, what with your radiator being perfectly sustainable.'

She watched as Andrew retreated down the corridor. Jesus, he might just as well have lobbed a grenade into the room. Cuckoo boy? If Billy was referring to himself as that, the whole thing was doomed, and how on earth did Guatemala come into it?

Miriam kicked back on her chair. Billy the stick-fetching dog. If Horatio had thought that up it was a master-stroke in belittle-ment. If he hadn't, and it was an unbelievable coincidence and he really *had* wanted a dog called Billy, they ought to add a new question to the potential sibling assessment. *If you had a pet, what would you call it?* The assessor would have to write the chosen name in big red capitals on the form. Any overlap with a proposed child and it would be curtains for the placement.

How the hell did Andrew know any of this? Last time she'd listened in, they'd been talking about tool kits. And yet he'd come in to her now, having no real business with the radiator, to tell her about Billy, information achieved God knows how, and put to her, a little shyly but with a degree of tenacity. It reminded her of the huge marmalade cat her parents had when she was a child, who used to bring her fledglings and mice with the sure certainty that they were a gift even if she didn't look fully appre-ciative of the fact. And what Andrew had told her was, in fact, a kind of gift, just one that could be more correctly described as a spanner in the works.

She'd have to call Caroline. She'd have to get Caroline to come in for a meeting and see if any of it made any sense to her. Last time she'd touched base it was all going swimmingly; cricket on the lawn, table football in the den, and home-made ice cream around the extensive kitchen table. Win win.

Shit, said Miriam aloud to herself, *shit shit shit*. The child was worrying about love. Gifted or not, her own experience told her it was a taxing, and potentially lifelong, preoccupation and accom-panied by no guarantees.

16

Was he still sulking? Caroline tucked Horatio into bed, and drew the curtains. He'd never been a sulky child; he'd never assumed the cold distance he'd achieved since Sunday night. She felt as if a shell were setting over him, brittle and taut. She reached over to tuck him in a little more. He still didn't meet her eye. She moved away and stood by his door. It all felt abruptly hopeless, her arms like useless, broken wings by her side.

'Night night, darling,' she said with extra conviction. 'Sleep tight, I love you.'

He didn't answer.

Before he was born, her waters had broken in a spectacular swoosh across the kitchen floor. She'd interpreted it, afterwards, as symbolic of the outpouring of love she felt for him when she first held him. She felt a similar whoosh now, but it felt as if her hopes, her good intentions, all the things she thought she wanted, might be leaving her body in a frantic flush. She felt curiously light and empty. She walked out on to the landing, her feet feeling as if they might leave no tread on the carpet, and pressed her forehead to the cool smoothness of the pale wall. Her legs felt weak. She sat down on the blanket box and put her head in her hands.

She rubbed at her temples. Ever since all this had started with Billy, she'd had persistent face ache, either from smiling forcefully and trying to make every expression buzz with encouragement, or from her face in repose increasingly puckered with strain. She'd never worked so hard in her life. And yet, if she could bear to admit it to herself, it felt flawed, invisibly, minutely flawed, however much she enthused and babbled about trying to make everything perfect.

Horatio's body, hunched wordlessly beneath his duvet, was an eloquent reproach. It was as if he were floating away on a raft made by her own hand. How surprising was that, she thought: trying to gain another child potentially triggered losing the one she already had.

Horatio wouldn't talk about what he was feeling. It felt catastrophic. Surely she should have seen this coming? She saw it now though, as she sat on the blanket box and felt clarity of thought ricocheting through her.

Caroline picked up a photograph from the window sill of herself, Horatio and Toby. Toby was looking at her and Horatio was facing the camera. She was looking at Horatio on her lap. For the first time – how inexplicable was it to be asking herself this question now? – she wondered why she had never considered him to be enough. And why had she never considered it from his point of view? Did all of this, all of this frantic effort, achieve nothing but underline to Horatio that he wasn't enough? She had, she realised, with sudden devastating insight, allowed a childish, Fablon-coated fantasy to cast its shadow over her entire adult life.

Horatio was jealous, hurt and insecure. Of course he was, and it was all her fault. She had spent time priding herself on having elastic, excess capacity as a mother, and yet had failed in making her son feel he was enough. To feel in fact, that he might be exactly what she dreamed of.

Was it stubbornness, or blindness, that had driven her so relentlessly on? Now, she was sweeping up Billy in her determined progression forward. Through the open window she could see dusk beginning to skirt the edge of the trees. By the purple beech, a pair of bats winged in sweeping arcs. She looked at the photo again. Toby was looking at her. In all of this too, how little she had considered him. Of how many forms of blindness was she guilty?

Toby had indulged her. He had loved her enough to let her pursue this. How odd that tonight she understood it for the first time.

When he came home later, she was sitting quietly in the kitchen. A candle threw its shadow long on the wall.

'How was your day?' she asked him.

'The markets gave us the runaround this afternoon but otherwise same as same as. How about you?'

'A big day, or at least a big last couple of hours. Everything tumbling into place, things I should have known but didn't. I'm sorry. I should start with that.'

Toby poured himself a glass of wine. He fleetingly had the expression of a man who thought he might be in for a long night of it. How smart, she thought, that he so mildly assumed his best listening face.

'I've been such an idiot. I need to talk to you about Horatio, and about Billy, about mistakes, my mistakes. I think we may have run aground. When I say we, I mean me. I definitely mean me.'

Caroline found herself fighting an overwhelming desire to sob.

Toby looked at her carefully. 'This is unexpected. Unlike you to accept defeat. It all seems very sudden; I thought we were progressing to an overnight stay. I was gearing myself up for sunshine pancakes for breakfast.'

'I know, I know, and you've supported me so brilliantly. I can hardly confess what I'm thinking, even to you. It's hit me tonight, like a plank in the face, after I said goodnight to Horatio. I think I may have got everything wrong. I feel like I've woken up from some kind of sleepwalk. I don't know anymore' (and here she spoke carefully and clearly) 'why I'm doing this. How ridiculous is that, to understand, all in a rush on the landing tonight, that I may have got it all wrong, all wrong for years?'

She clasped her hands together.

'Don't say anything. Just listen to me. I'm an idiot. An idiot. I should have thought all this through months ago. Years ago. I've been so selfish. All this is unfair to Horatio. And to you. And to Billy.'

She started to cry. Toby made to step towards her, but she shook her head.

'I've behaved like a fool. I haven't seen what's plainly in front of me, and I have spent the last few years chasing the dreams of a child, and tonight' (and here she clicked her finger and thumb) 'it has just popped in my face, like an enormous bubble.'

She lifted her hands towards him. 'See what a total idiot you married.'

Toby wrapped her, unresisting, in his arms. He'd always hated seeing her cry. 'Shuush,' he said, holding her close. 'Please don't cry. Nobody died, nobody lost a war.'

He took her face in his hands.

'It feels like that.'

'It is what it is. I guess it's good – if a little inconvenient all round – that you're seeing it now. I'm to blame too. I went along with it all.'

He gestured to the kitchen around them.

'We seem to have so much, and yet you couldn't leave alone what else it was that you thought you should have. A bit like a mole in a tunnel,' he said with a hint of a smile, 'just forward in one direction. I wasn't sure whether you were trying to save a child or save some idea of yourself. I'm sorry if that sounds brutal. I sound like I'm agreeing that you've been an idiot which I'm not. I'm just being truthful, which I should have been some time ago, so it's my fault too.'

'I've hurt Horatio, and I've hurt Billy. That's unforgiveable.'

'If this conversation is headed where I think it is, your decision will turn things around for Horatio. He'll rally and move on. And as for Billy, I don't know. Even if we had adopted him, I'm not sure if we would have been great for him or a prolonged exercise in demoralisation. He didn't look sure either. Miriam may have some insight into that. Isn't this where her speed-dating process is supposed to make everything easier? Billy gets to move on, and so do you.'

'I want to stop the whole thing tomorrow.'

'That's okay. If you're sure you're sure, that's okay.'

'Why didn't I register to be a child minder or something, and just had my fill of armfuls of babies during the day when Horatio was at school?'

'You still could, if that's what you decide you want to do. Or you could do any number of things if the thought of Horatio growing up fills you with horror. You just don't have to do *this* thing, if you don't want to, if it doesn't seem right.'

He kissed her gently.

'Caroline, I'd have loved you if we had no children, or one child, or six of them. It didn't ever have to be just about that. I think that's where you kind of missed the point.'

All these years, she thought, preoccupied, obsessed with the idea of herself as a mother, while Toby had been steadily, warmly, loving her as a woman, as his wife.

Later, she lay awake, as Toby slept beside her. What should she tell Miriam tomorrow? That she'd suddenly emerged from the shadow of a row of dolls in decorated shoeboxes, from the aura of the Boden catalogue, from a fantasy about Christmas cards? How could she tell her that sitting on a blanket box at twilight, on her landing, she'd finally seen that what she actually wanted was the life she already had. She was Toby's wife and Horatio's mother and that was enough.

The moon shone through the edge of the curtain. Poor Billy. Their life would sweep on, leaving Miriam to fix and to sort, to remedy the mess that was the upshot of her stupid blindness. Should she see him to say goodbye? Should she write him a letter? The last thing she had done was kiss him. What a Judas kiss.

Toby had counselled *Least said soonest mended.* Caroline wept silently in the dark, her body curled into Toby's as he slept.

17

Miriam's first phone call of the morning was unexpected. It was Trudy, Billy's grandmother. She said, with almost no preamble, her words spilling out in a rush as if she had been practising them, that she'd like to see Billy.

'Just for a short while, half an hour, fifteen minutes?'

Miriam hesitated, and steeled herself against the implicit pleading in Trudy's voice.

'I'm sorry, I'm just not sure if it's in his interests, Trudy. I know that probably sounds unkind but you can't step back and then still expect to see him. It doesn't work like that I'm afraid. I did try to go through this with you at the time in as much detail as possible. Signing the Placement Order means you have no rights to see him, no rights to know anything about him at all. All I can say is we're making progress with finding him a new home, and I don't want to disrupt that.'

'I'm not trying to disrupt that, I'm really not trying to do that. It's just I find myself thinking about him, wondering, how he is, you know.'

Miriam thought, impatiently, yes, she *did* know about thinking about Billy. It was her task to be thinking about him because his grandparents had signed the Placement Order and made him her professional responsibility. It probably wouldn't be helpful or soothing to restate that.

'He's fine, Trudy, it's my job to ensure that.' She tried to avoid, sounding shirty. 'He's physically well, he's doing fine. That's about all I can tell you, I'm afraid.'

Trudy started to cry. Did it count as bullying, Miriam wondered, making an old lady cry? Except she hadn't made her cry, Miriam reminded herself; Trudy's own decisions were what were making her cry. *I am not responsible for this, or for you*, Miriam thought, imagining herself as a non-stick pan. *It's a good job Meg and I aren't crying about him. Too busy trying to sort it out.*

'I understand,' Trudy said, 'I understand what you have to do, and I know we set it all in motion so there is nothing more I can expect. I know it's all my fault. All of it.'

Miriam looked up at the ceiling. Trudy's self-blame was harder to deal with. *Don't beat yourself up*, she thought, *it's actually Lizzie's fault*. She could feel herself softening. She hesitated. 'Look, I promise I'll tell Billy you called. I'm not committing to anything else but I will tell him you called. I'll phone you if I think there's an appropriate time for a meeting, but just not now, when things are at a delicate stage. It would be disruptive for Billy, and he's my first priority.'

Trudy sobbed some more. Miriam couldn't help but feel sorry for her. Anything to do with her offspring seemed to have resulted in heartache.

'He mentioned you the other day,' she said, with an unexpected flash of appeasement. 'He recalled how you'd taught him good table manners. He went out to a restaurant and I think they came in handy.'

Trudy halted her sobbing. 'Did he say that? Bless him,' she said, then cried some more.

Miriam ended the conversation and put down the phone. Billy had, she mused, in his family tree, an unfair proportion of poor decision-making adults.

She looked at the clock on her desk. Ten past nine on a Monday morning and she'd already had someone in tears and had to be officious, and that was before she'd tried to speak to Caroline about what Andrew had told her.

When the phone rang again and it was Caroline, Miriam started to say 'You've beaten me to it' but stopped when she realised Caroline was crying too. This was turning out to be quite a morning, even by her own standards.

'I'm sorry, Miriam, I'm really sorry. I've made a dreadful

mistake, and been so blind. It's all my fault, not Billy's at all. I want to pull out.'

When their conversation ended, Miriam didn't know whether to laugh bitterly or bite someone. All the hours spent on careful assessment and then the outcome was a woman realising she hadn't properly thought it through, and was, in fact, in thrall to some fantasy she should have junked long ago. Caroline was apologetic, she was remorseful, but the fact of the matter was she'd decided that she didn't want to progress towards adopting Billy. She asked if she might explain herself to him.

'I can't see that as being productive,' Miriam said crisply. 'And that's what I am here for, to explain things to Billy.'

Form a queue, both of you, Miriam thought angrily, Trudy and Caroline, women who had rejected Billy but would still like the luxury of a chat.

She tried not to sound cold. She wanted to get off the phone. My time is better spent, she wanted to retort, finding someone who wants the child you don't. Caroline reiterated that she was withdrawing from the adoption process altogether. 'Even,' Miriam said, with the tiniest detectable whip-edge to her voice, 'even from the prospect of a little Guatemalan girl?'

Caroline sounded puzzled. 'I'm sorry, I'm not with you,' she said. 'Guatemala? One of Horatio's friends, Felix, has an adopted little sister who is Guatemalan.'

Ah, puzzle solved, thought Miriam; that configuration obviously makes it acceptable to Horatio.

Caroline cried a little more. Miriam found herself losing concentration.

'I'm sure Toby's been fantastically supportive, that's great, and yes, I'm sure Horatio will move on quickly.'

Afterwards, she sat at her desk, having switched the phone to answering machine. She needed to talk to Andrew.

What was it about standing by outbuildings, Miriam wondered, that still made her want a cigarette? Also, she thought, where was a six-foot-something handyman when you needed him?

Certainly not within eye or ear shot. Miriam scanned the car park. There was no sign of his van. Perhaps he wasn't in today; or maybe he had other work to do and would be in later in the morning. Might she leave a note pinned to his workboard? – *Please come and check the radiator thermostat.* It could all become terribly cryptic, this not talking about Billy. She looked up to see Andrew walking towards her.

'I was looking for you,' she said, 'or your van,' and she gestured towards the car park.

'I'm parked round the front. I had some stuff to unload for Reception.' He looked at her, puzzled. 'What's up?'

'Radiator's fine, everything else not quite so brilliant.'

'Why?'

'Difficult to say really, especially in the knowledge that I'm not actually meant to say anything at all.' Miriam contemplated briefly whether if in the eyes of her superiors this conversation might count as a first step towards professional suicide. (*So you were discussing a case with whom? Oh, the site handyman, I see. I'm sure you have an explanation for this.*)

'I understand if it's difficult to say.'

'That said, there are two things I might perhaps mention to you, should you then come by any additional information which might shed further light on any of it. In the case of the child we may or may not have discussed, the potential adoptive family pulled out this morning. Game over, finito benito, and back to the drawing board for me. Any insight into his feelings would be helpful. Hopefully that's an end to the cuckoo boy thought. Now I'm going to be looking for another family who have no children at all. Coincidentally, and not of the same significance, the child's grandma phoned this morning and asked how he was and whether it was possible to see him. I've said I'll just tell him she called and get back to her. Again, any thoughts about Grandma would be useful.'

'I see. Right. Mission understood.'

Miriam watched him walk away. He was warming to the role. If she ended up with a more rounded picture of what was going on in Billy's head, would the ends justify the slightly dubious means? Maybe she should broach it with Sheila. Any extended loitering by the tool store was bound to set tongues wagging. That would be rich; to be collaborating, somewhat bizarrely, in Billy's interests and to be suspected of having an affair.

A cigarette would be brilliant now, she thought, and something of an alibi. It wouldn't, however, stop her feeling sick at heart. How was she going to find the words to tell Billy that the Frasers wanted out? *You know that affluence you just got a glimpse of,* she hypothesised, *well, now we've shown it to you, so you can conjure up in detail a life with a playroom like a sports shop, and a den in the garden, and holidays in the Seychelles and private school cricket pitches, just to let you know it's actually not going to be yours, for reasons, it appears, that have little relation to you at all. Try not to take it personally.*

She was surprised by the anger she felt. She went back to her office, dreading Billy's arrival.

Billy waited to go in.

Miriam was looking very busy through the glass.

Meg had picked him up at lunch-time from school. Joey said this counted as another advantage.

Billy had told Joey at break about the carrot-coloured fish and the den. They decided they'd have called it the Clubhouse and taken all their meals in there. He hadn't told him what Horatio had said, just that he knew he didn't like him. I am properly cuckoo boy, he told him. Joey said there were worse things to be.

Now, as Miriam called him in, he thought she looked a bit awkward. Had Horatio spoken to Caroline? Had it all been decided? He thought of *Dear Zoo*. He would be the elephant. The elephant was too big. That was mostly the problem. There wasn't an animal in the story that was sent back because it was useless. If there had been, he'd have qualified as that too.

'How did your day with the Frasers go?' Miriam asked him. 'Did you have a nice time?'

'Mmm, sort of,' said Billy.

'Only sort of? Why's that? Did anything happen that you didn't like?'

Billy shook his head, and then paused. It was now or never.

'I just think they might decide that they are all right as they are, and that they don't need another boy aged nine when they already have Horatio.'

Miriam looked as if she was trying to keep her mouth from falling open.

Billy reached down and re-tied his shoelace.

Miriam stared at the top of his head. He was unfathomable. He spent most of his time passing her off with a 'mmm' and then, from nowhere, out came an emotionally literate observation. She gave herself a moment.

'And if they had decided that,' Miriam said, 'let's just imagine for a minute that your guess was brilliantly clever and right, how would that make you feel? Would you be sad, or would you be okay with that?'

'It would be spilt milk,' said Billy, looking up from his trainers, 'that's what it would be.'

'It was bizarre,' she told Sheila afterwards. 'He seemed almost relieved. As if he had seen it coming and the actuality was easier than the anticipation.'

'He has a perspective on what's the worst that can happen that most children of his age are lucky enough not to have,' Sheila noted drily.

Miriam nodded. It was good to be reminded how different his perspective might be from hers.

When Andrew opened the note, it was the first one to have drawings as well. Beside a picture of an elephant, Billy had written *But I was too big so they sent me back.* The elephant seemed to be holding a mug in its trunk, and behind it was drawn something which looked like a children's playhouse. The next point said *Grandma must still be my grandma because she phoned.* The third point was written in capital letters. *AND THE SEARCH FOR BILLY MORRIS'S FAMILY GOES ON.* He'd drawn a huge car, with a small stick figure sitting pertly in the back seat. There was a chain-link fence running alongside the car, with another child drawn behind it. When Andrew looked closely, he could see the second figure was winking – his closed eye was shown with comically long lashes – and giving an exaggerated thumbs-up. It was also, somewhat surreally, surrounded by a shoal of small fish.

18

Miriam sat in Sheila's office, going through her supervision session. They'd covered the couple who seemed unable to hand over their child to each other for contact without an aggressive scene; they'd discussed a mother being sent with her baby to a unit in the hope of attaining some parenting skills: they'd skipped through three foster placements, and a teenage girl who kept absconding from a children's home, even though the department was paying a small fortune for them to keep her safe. Miriam felt protective at the sight of Billy's name on the agenda. He didn't seem to fit with all the other turmoil.

'So,' Sheila said crisply. 'Billy Morris. Bluntly, our first attempt at speed-introducing has failed, yes?'

'Yes.'

'And could any of the reasons for the failure – which of course I'll expect you to detail in his file – be because of the process? Did we rush anyone?' She looked intently at Miriam. Miriam shifted in her seat. On a previous occasion Sheila had accused her of impatience. Miriam had retorted that there was hardly an abundance of time and resource.

'It wasn't the speed process which was flawed, more like the assessment process. Caroline Fraser had a complete change of heart. The process isn't designed to anticipate that. Did we rush anyone? Maybe. But then we got to a speedier conclusion, even though it wasn't the one that we wanted.'

'Have you got a plan B?'

Miriam envisaged, momentarily, progressing despondently all the way to plan Z.

'I'm considering a childless couple; a gentle, understated

childless couple, very traditional values, very calm lifestyle. Unusual, but very solid. I've got their file here if you want to see it.' She handed it to Sheila, who read it through quickly.

'I can see your logic. In your terms, worth a go. Anything else that is relevant to Billy Morris?'

'Mmmm. Maybe.' (God, Miriam thought, she was starting to sound and stall like him.)

'Maybe?' Sheila raised an eyebrow in a way that Miriam had always found disconcerting.

'It's just that Billy seems to be communicating with Andrew, the site handyman, about things that he's feeling. I'm not quite sure how, and don't know whether I should ask Andrew for more detail. Thing is, I don't want to make Andrew feel self-conscious or clam up because what he's telling me is helpful and pertinent, and it's evident he has Billy's interests at heart or he wouldn't be telling me. Mentioning it to Billy might cut it off altogether. It's unorthodox, but I kind of feel best left well alone. I just wanted you to know about it in case anything significant came of it.'

'And you're confident Andrew personally poses no risk to Billy? It's our job to be suspicious.'

'Oh God no, absolutely not. They talk in the corridor, by the tree, in the car park. It's all very public. Billy seems to have taken to him. I think it's something to do with his props – toolkits and things – Billy's fascinated by all that. It fits with a fatherless boy. Sometimes I think if I had a toolkit on my desk rather than a bunch of files, things might progress a little faster with him.'

'Well, let's leave it as it is then. We need all the information we can get. I presume you'll progress with plan B. B for Bridges,' Sheila noted, handing Miriam back the file.

Miriam sat outside on the bench eating her sandwich. She'd read an article recently about Alzheimer's sufferers, and one of the women described believed herself, day in, day out, to be taking her lunch break at work, eating a sandwich on a bench. That would be a grim prospect, Miriam thought, to be trapped in a life composed of how her lunch breaks – if she got them – felt.

Plan B. Malcolm and Elspeth Bridges. They were unusual, unusual in a way that Miriam hoped might be soothing. If not for Billy, she thought ironically, maybe for her. They were a couple in their late forties who'd married only three years previously and had no children of their own. She could not think of them without conjuring up beside them, from the depths of her memory, an old oak table of her grandmother's; plain, smooth, and well-scrubbed, quietly exuding familiar, placid, wholesomeness. They were gentle and unworldly. Miriam reflected how out of step that made them with much of contemporary life. Malcolm spoke slowly and carefully, in a way that suggested words were not to be treated lightly, to be babbled or wasted like water. He was a religious man, although, she recalled, no longer churchgoing. He used to belong to – what was it – the Brethren, some kind of Quaker offshoot – something where silence was cherished and much of the world shunned because of its materialistic noise. Everything in their house, Miriam had noticed, was made of materials which looked like they would stubbornly, quietly, endure. Cream stoneware on the table, woollen tweed chairs, an absence of anything plastic, or gaudily coloured. A television that was so old she wasn't sure it would survive the digital switchover. The phone in the hallway had no chair beside it; there seemed an assumption that time would not be spent on it chattering.

Some winter afternoons, when visiting their home to carry out their suitability assessment, Miriam endeavoured to sit more neatly, to discipline her long limbs on the sofa, careful not to nudge the lace antimacassars. As darkness gathered outside, Malcolm rose from his armchair to switch on the pendant light, the bulb gleaming softly through the frosted rose glass shade, the room increasingly enveloped in duskiness and dark smudgy colours. Miriam felt it to be some kind of retro cocoon, and thought how easy it would be to doze off, the grandfather clock ticking, Elspeth making tea in china cups in the kitchen, and to be woken by the sound of the wireless, for that was surely what it should be called. Sometimes, when leaving, rustling for her car keys in her bag, her hand would alight on her i-Pod and it would seem a thing of miraculous impossibility. Likewise, the thought of Malcolm's feet in trainers rather than solid shoes, Elspeth wearing jeans, or buying a heat-and-serve meal. They had eluded, somehow, any brush with modernity. What remained, at their heart, Miriam felt, was kindness and innate dignity. In the face of much of what she saw, that was to be valued.

She decided she would ring them, see if they were interested in Billy. If she recalled correctly, neither of them had a mobile phone. Would Billy, she hoped, one day be teaching them to text?

19

Elspeth Bridges sat on the bus, and arranged her skirt around her. She caught sight of her reflection in the large pane of the window and adjusted her expression. Sometimes in repose she worried she looked as if she were frowning. Today she had filed Mr Woodward's accounts at Companies House; another year accounted for, another year fastidiously in profit.

She had been working for Ry Woodward for eighteen years and had called him Mr Woodward for the duration. She thought the Ry might have been long-ago truncated from Raymond. Certainly it had an air of dash which was at odds with his pains-taking gangliness, his long spidery limbs, his desk piled high with seemingly chaotic legal papers. He was a solicitor; she was his secretary, his office manager, his book-keeper, his accountant, whatever myriad of terms that might cover the fact that Ry Woodward worked alone, had never wished to have any sort of legal partner or assistant, and found all that was extraneous to his effort to be adequately taken care of by Mrs Bridges, née Matthews.

His accounts showed another year of steadily incremental profit. He was particularly good at wills. Elspeth frequently shepherded the grieving, the grasping (sometimes a combination of both) to hear a will being read in Ry Woodward's ponderous tone. He had the right air of gravitas, she had concluded, to make the business of death seem well-organised and within his control. Heavens, hadn't she herself sat on the Ercol chair in his office, with him reading out her own mother's will to her, telling her she had been well taken care of?

Stella, her mother, had aspired to Ry Woodward being more

than Elspeth's employer. She knew him first, from Bowls Club;
that was how Elspeth had first been nudged towards the job. *Set
your cap at him, Elspeth,* she'd said, *set your jolly old cap.* Elspeth
wasn't sure jolly was something she'd ever lay claim to. *You'd be
well looked after,* her mother said keenly. Elspeth thought it took
her mother about eight years to abandon all hope; each Friday
night asking, when Elspeth came home, *And how is Mr Woodward,*
followed by *Do you have any plans for the weekend?* Elspeth never
had plans. This, she reflected, might count as a phenomenal
achievement, to have so sloughed off all resemblance to a young,
social, friend-filled life. By her thirties, she could no longer conceive
of a life which didn't revolve around being at Ry Woodward's
beck and call, or dancing attendance on her mother. Her mother
continued to supply her with helpful pointers. *Get yourself a girdle,*
she said once, lying back, grey-lipped, on her day bed; *that might
give you a lift in the look of your daywear.* Elspeth, wordless, had
smoothed her palms over what was evidently the unseemly
rumpled plumpness of her hips (did girdles still exist?), and taken
her mother's supper tray back to the kitchen.

Each Christmas Ry Woodward presented her with a box of
Thornton's chocolates with a bow. On her birthday, and the
day of the filing of accounts, he gave her flowers tied with a
ribbon and taped with a sachet of plant food. His choice, at the
filing of accounts, was usually chrysanths. *They have a vase life
of three weeks,* he'd told her last year, which made her suspect
that his selection was based on longevity and thereby value for
money. She wondered if he assessed her in similarly pragmatic
terms.

It accounted for why, this evening, she was sitting on the bus
clutching a raggedy bunch of flowers. Malcolm wouldn't like
them, vase life of three weeks or not. Malcolm was of the opinion
that soil was too precious to be spared for that which could not
be eaten. *Every rose could be a carrot,* he'd told her once. It was
true if looked at in that way, although grievous for roses. Elspeth
also wasn't sure if it bore wider application. Where, on that spectrum, she thought, might it leave circuses?

Stella, Elspeth was sure, would have been hard-pressed to disguise her disappointment, had she lived to see that Elspeth never managed to captivate Ry but instead attracted Malcolm, who delivered office furniture and tended his allotment.

It was the allotment that had done it; Elspeth had signed up for one not long after Stella's death, wanting to breathe air that was not of Ry Woodward's office or of her mother's (now her) net-curtained home. The allotment she was allocated was next to Malcolm's. She watched him working steadily, attentively, with careful economy of effort, and found herself absorbed in a way that was entirely unexpected. She was drawn to his capability, to what seemed to be his fastidious, muscular integrity. *Set your jolly old cap*, her mother's voice rang again in her ears. She wore a polka dot blouse, smudged a little lipstick hesitantly on to her mouth. Shyly, he began to offer her produce, standing awkwardly at the makeshift divide, her own plot a failed tangle of mostly weeds. She had blushed, and been able only to look at the ground, at the soil, which, subversively, magically, vividly, was cascading with life. The vegetables he gave her evoked things beyond their own wholesomeness. A cauliflower, she remembered, white, plump and dimpled like the inside of her thigh, and as if it had been lace-wrapped in a frilled edge of spring-green brightness. Radishes pink as flushed lips, and peas so fresh they seemed to Elspeth to leap from the pod.

Miriam Riley, during their assessment, had asked how they had met. *You could say he wooed me with vegetables* is what she wanted to confess. Malcolm would have been scarlet with embarrassment if any such words came from her lips.

He'd progressed from giving her vegetables to asking her to his home for supper. He'd cooked a beef stew and served it with a vast wooden spoon, and before eating, put his huge hands together and said Grace.

It was evident from their beginnings that there were things they shared; both living, she felt, in their respective parents' homes like large, slightly clumsy, abandoned children. A predisposition for understatement, a preference for stillness. The assumption of an inner life that was likely to remain so.

They'd gone out on his little boat, *The Girl Jane*, and to Salisbury Cathedral, to a talk at a horticultural society, and to an agricultural show. He'd first taken her hand as they watched cattle being judged, and she had felt like weeping, her fingers folded within his. He had courted her. There was no other word for it. He had courted her in a manner that was gentle and tentative, his huge frame at odds with his hesitant cautiousness. When he'd asked her to marry him, he seemed surprised that she'd said yes. On their wedding night, a clumsiness on both of their parts; an uncertain clambering and shyness of unaccustomed limbs. Afterwards he'd said *Thank you Elspeth* as if she had given him a gift. They were both virgins; their virginity preserved through the years, she felt, like something dried and forgotten in the pages of a book.

Elspeth bunched the chrysanthemums under her arm and put her key into the front door. Malcolm would be home; he only worked a three-day week. He would have cooked something for their supper and that still felt like a gift, from years of coming home to her mother demanding querulously, imperiously, something to eat.

As she opened the door, she saw that he had tidied the hallway. On the phone table, he had displayed a tall ship he'd constructed entirely from matches, which he'd made from a kit the previous Christmas. She thought that had been relegated to the back of the cupboard on the landing. When she came into the kitchen, he was humming and shelling peas into a colander.

'Accounts have been filed then,' he said, with a twinkle in his eye, nodding towards the bunch of chrysanths. Ry's habits, for reasons Elspeth couldn't ascertain, always seemed the source of some amusement to Malcolm.

'Job done,' Elspeth smiled, 'and don't worry, I know you can't stand them. I'll put them in in a vase and tuck them out of sight in the back bedroom.'

'No, put them in the front room, or in here,' he said, gesturing expansively around the kitchen. She noticed that he had also cleaned the windows.

'Miriam Riley's phoned to ask if she can bring someone here Saturday. A little lad's coming. She's got a little lad she wants us to meet.'

Next morning, Elspeth put the kettle on to boil, watching, as she did so, a robin alight on the feeder in their tiny garden. It swooped beneath the orange blossom to the left of the window, some nigella seed tight in its beak. She guessed there would be a nest beneath the foliage, the robin would be feeding her young. She looked across at the table. She'd eaten half a grape-fruit and some muesli. Would a child eat that? Shouldn't she know?

'Would you like a poached egg?' she asked Malcolm, who was finishing his cornflakes.

'No thank you,' he said, beginning to read the newspaper.

She hesitated, pulling at a tendril of her hair.

'What would a child choose for breakfast, do you think. Eggs? Do you think a boy would like eggs for breakfast?'

Malcolm looked up at her, evidently giving it some thought.

'I can't think why not. A boiled egg and soldiers. I think I ate that sometimes for breakfast when I was a boy. Porridge too, although perhaps not in the summer. I think there's all kinds of cereal made especially for children.'

'My mother used to make porridge with sterilised milk when I was a child. It was delivered in long thin bottles, with a metal cap like beer. I'm not sure I liked it.'

'You don't need to be fretting about what he might eat for breakfast. He's not coming for breakfast, is he? He's coming in the middle of the afternoon. Perhaps think about some cake or some scones, that'll probably be right.'

Malcolm went back to the paper. He seemed almost jolly. Elspeth began to wash up.

'Did Miriam Riley tell you anything else about him?'

'She said his mother died recently – drugs. She was an addict.

Of his father there's been no sign since before he was born. He's officially an orphan, that's why Miriam is in charge.'

Elspeth looked down at her soap-sudded hands. Boiled eggs for breakfast could surely never repair those kinds of wounds? She felt a judder in her own chest at the thought of what might have careered through his. She looked out at the bird feeder. There was no sign of the robin.

It had been last November when Malcolm had first raised the idea of adoption. It had come, unprompted, from him. If she'd had anyone to tell, she'd have said *Extraordinary, right out of the blue*. Eggs, that was right, he was cracking eggs into a bowl; his hands so huge that from her vantage point, it looked as if he were magicking yolks from his palms.

'What about a child,' he'd said, 'what about us trying to give a child a home? There's so many without and we have so much.'

She remembered blinking, blinking slowly and with intent, as if she might somehow ingest his words better that way. Her first thought was that surely it should not be a surprise. She alone would never have expected to be enough. She was too hesitant, too timid, to fill all the available space in a heart. Her second thought was that she should perhaps hold her breath; to cradle the moment where a child might be a possibility. And soon afterwards, Miriam had come, with her clipboards, her files, her jangling bracelets. She reminded Elspeth of some kind of exotic heron, leggily perched on the settee, asking question after question. And now there was Billy, coming to see them tomorrow. A living, breathing, moving child coming into their home.

She paused at the sink. Malcolm was getting up from the table, and had started to whistle. In the winter, beneath the bird table, a tiny wren had died. Insects had eaten it; she'd found the skeleton stripped clean. She'd reached down to look at it, and run her finger across the scoop of the skull. The wings had disintegrated but the ribcage cradled, delicately, gamely, its contents of pure air. She had picked it up, carefully, and placed it on the window ledge. It felt lighter in her palm than the mist of her breath. She'd stood by the window, her feet chilled by the frost, feeling that the moment was infinitely precious. Now, she looked down into the sink, her hands motionless before her. Were they capable, properly capable, of keeping anything safe?

20

Joey and Billy were standing by the chain-link fence in the play-ground next to the road waiting for the whistle to blow for the start of the day. Joey had suggested a new game, which was to stand very still, pressed against the fence, and appear like prisoners of war to passers-by. He was clear that they weren't to look miserable. Some prisoners of war were made to build railways and only given a ping-pong size ball of rice to eat daily. They, in contrast, had to achieve the look of prisoners of war with a plan: they were going to steal a guard's uniform, dig a tunnel and make a dashing escape for the Channel. *Like in a film, like it's Colditz*, he said. Billy was reluctant.

'They're not looking at you any differently from when it's your usual face,' he said, indicating a couple walking past. 'I think maybe this game doesn't work.'

'You're not helping. You're looking miserable rather than like someone with a secret plan anyway. Game over.'

'It's game over with the Frasers.'

'What, just like that?'

'Yes, properly pulled out.'

'No more Horatio? No more cricket matches?'

'Nope.'

'Mountford gone?' (Here Joey clicked his fingers.) 'No more Caroline telling you you're going to be great at everything?'

'Uh-huh.'

'Chocolate and peanut butter ice cream?'

'All of it, Joey.'

Joey paused.

'Well then,' he said. 'I salute,' (and he did so) 'Horatio – great name – Mountford – and all the words it might have taught us – and the hot chocolate with marshmallows in the Clubhouse.'

'You're forgetting who was supposed to be getting adopted and who'd have been drinking the hot chocolate in the Clubhouse. And, you can stop saluting now because that old man is saluting you back.'

'That's because he's spotted I'm officer material. He can see I'm going to tunnel my way out whatever the odds. The Channel or bust. Good morning, sir! Mission will be accomplished.'

'There's probably a special school somewhere for boys like you.'

'Well, it's not going to be Mountford, that's for sure. I'd have looked so cool in one of the cricket caps.'

'Again, Joey, it was never going to be you. Me neither. I've done so many nights at Meg's now there's been time for the ones who come back each month to still find me there.'

'See, you're just like the kind of prisoner who never makes it beyond the perimeter fence. They've escaped, been recaptured, and come back again and you're still there looking miserable and eating your rice ball.'

'Maybe I've laid a lot of train track in the meantime.'

'I'll give you that, although my Nan says the miserable ones always died first.'

'Where's your Nan come into this?'

'The film; I was watching a film about Colditz with her at the weekend. She loves a good war movie.'

'That explains a lot.'

'So what's Miriam going to do now? Has she said?'

'Plan B.'

'Go Miriam. She'd have been an escaper, I bet you that.'

Billy nodded. Joey had never met Miriam, but his words rang true. Miriam, in his mind, took on the aspect of a Spitfire zooming into battle for him, determinedly on his side.

21

Samantha Hollis had been right, Miriam thought, it *was* a big ask. As she stood on the Bridges' front step in bright sunshine, bringing a nine-year-old boy to the home of two perfect strangers to see if they got along seemed a big ask of anyone. Billy stood patiently beside her. She felt like giving him a hug. That was always controversial territory. Sheila had said sharply to her once, in another case, that her role was to find a substitute mother, not to be one. *Professional distance*, she'd said to Miriam, *it exists for a reason*. Miriam hugged him mentally; Billy seemed to be focussing all his attention on the heavy, black door knocker.

She'd decided against bringing the Bridges in to the Centre for their first meeting. She couldn't transpose them on to the bright plastic chairs, offer them coffee in polystyrene cups, watch their slow careful movements under the glare of the yellow strip lighting. They would have been like fish out of water, awkward and uncertain. Better, she'd decided, for the first introduction to take place in their home.

'Remember I'll stay as long as you like,' she whispered to Billy. 'I can stay for the whole thing if you are not feeling comfortable.'

She lifted the knocker, and rapped with resolve on the door.

'Here we go,' she said to Billy.

Billy's first impression was that Malcolm was very, very big. He had a huge face, and a bald head, which somehow, as a whole, called to mind a slightly blue, full moon. He was tall, and broad, and his hands were as big as joints of meat. His words came out slowly, as if he were picking each one with particular care.

'You must be Billy,' he said. 'I'm very pleased to meet you.

You're very welcome in our home. We give thanks that you're here.'

Billy's second impression was that stepping into their home was like stepping into the very middle of a wood. A glade, that would be it, like into a glade. The light was emeraldy yet dim. The air felt very still, and as if it might not have moved for some time. Heavy curtains stood guard, and all of the furniture was made of dark wood. The carpet was so thick it seemed to be swallowing his feet. The windows looked as if they might never consider opening. The front door closed behind him with a solid click so that the sounds in the street beyond it were instantly extinguished. Walking down the hallway, Billy peeped into the front room. Gauzy net curtains made everything outside look hazy. He felt like a diver – he reminded himself to breathe – as if he were moving through a world which was submerged, far from the surface. He blinked purposefully to see if anything looked any brighter or clearer. It did not.

Malcolm led the way into the kitchen where a woman was standing. She wore an apron with roses on, and held out a plate of something in one hand and a pot of jam in the other.

'Elspeth is very glad to meet you too,' Malcolm said.

'I thought you might be hungry,' Elspeth said, 'so I made these.'

Miriam smiled broadly. 'Hello, Elspeth. Goodness, I can't remember the last time I ate a scone warm from the oven.'

Billy was momentarily distracted, wondering if he'd ever eaten a scone warm from the oven. He concluded probably not. He thought for a moment of the cupboard under the stairs, and the smell of a packet of Cheestrings, torn open in the almost dark, and the weight of the empty, raspberry velvet flute case on his lap. Where had the flute case gone?

Malcolm was pulling out chairs.

'Sit, sit,' he said, with a wave of his vast hand. He picked up a large brown teapot and began to pour tea into thick-lipped cups. Everything in this house, Billy thought, felt solid and heavy. Even the air felt as if it weighed a little bit more. It seemed to be pressing on his shoulders as he sat down to eat; when he took a deep breath it was as if his ribs had no space to expand. He squirmed on the broad base of his chair.

'Billy, Malcolm's a delivery man, for an office company,' Miriam was saying brightly. 'I expect he has a van or a truck you'd like, probably with lifting devices at the back and all manner of clever things.'

'The company I work for doesn't favour technology,' Malcolm said. 'They are Brethren, and so don't encourage mobile phones or faxes or e-mail or computers. We have orders, on paper and in envelopes, and I have road maps to show me where to go. There is a plainness they feel is more in keeping with the Lord.'

Billy hadn't seen Miriam lost for words before. She looked all out of place in this kitchen, with her brightly coloured clothes, her chunky necklace, her turquoise nails. She looked, Billy decided, like an exotic bird, perhaps a parrot, who'd made a mistake in migration and ended up in the wrong country.

'Oh,' she said, 'oh, I see. Well, it takes all sorts.'

'I have a suggestion,' Malcolm said, 'after we've had our tea, we might go down to the allotment, if you'd like. There's some crops that need picking, some raspberries, some vegetables. I thought you might enjoy that,' he said, gesturing towards Billy.

Miriam looked at him expectantly.

'Yes, that sounds nice, yes let's do that,' Billy said.

'You don't have to stay,' he said to Miriam. 'You can come back for me later if you want.'

Miriam looked surprised. 'Are you sure that's okay? I'm happy to come with you to the allotment.'

Billy nodded.

Miriam left a little while later, and Malcolm went to get his tools. Billy got up from the chair. Standing up, he felt he was dislodging a lapful of minutes which had gathered there during tea. Time, he would tell Joey, can take on solid form. How much would a minute weigh, or an hour, an afternoon? A kilogram of minutes. He imagined them clattering to the floor.

'Shall I help you wash up?' he asked Elspeth, who had moved to the sink.

'No, it's no bother, but that's very kind of you.'

Billy watched her hands, pale and fluttering like butterflies over the crockery in the sink. She patted her throat with her fingertips, and Billy could see a glisten of detergent bubbles on her pale, freckled skin. She looked as if she was thinking of a question to ask him. Caroline would have been chattering away, he thought. Chat chat chat. Maybe, at the Frasers', he should have tried harder, tried differently. Maybe he should have tried to persuade Horatio that he posed no more of a threat than a Guatemalan four-year-old. Truth be told, he thought, looking at the long spidery leaves of a dark green pot plant on the window sill, he most likely didn't.

Malcolm came to the back door with a spade, a fork, and a large basket.

'For the pickings,' he said, holding out the basket to Billy. 'Rich pickings.'

Elspeth crouched to lace up her shoes in the hallway. Billy could hear a clock ticking in the room to the left of him. The sound was slow and steady, loud in the stillness. Malcolm held the front door open for them both.

'The Lord shall preserve your goings out and your comings in,' Malcolm said as they went past him. 'Psalm one hundred and twenty-one. Good for going out into the world which can be a dark place.'

Billy's first thought was that the world, in fact, was not dark. It appeared to be lit by doubly-dazzling sunshine after the gloom of the hall. The brightness exploded across his eyeballs. His second, and not for the first time in the process, was to wonder whether Miriam had properly thought this through. Surely there was no danger in going to an allotment?

Did Malcolm repeat the prayer every time they went out? In RE they had learned how Jewish people touched the mezuzah on the doorway as a measure of safekeeping. Mrs Bailey had explained how this made a great deal of sense, considering the terrible persecution, all the fleeing, and sudden dashes they'd had to make. Had Malcolm and Elspeth ever had to flee? He couldn't imagine so. Speediness didn't look their thing. As he walked behind Malcolm, who held the spade and fork aloft in his right hand, Billy thought he looked like Moses leading his people out of Egypt. They had a picture of him on the classroom wall. Moses was enormous; his left hand was raised to encourage those behind him to follow, and in his right hand he held the staff ready to kill the snake. Malcolm walked at a pace that was slow and steady. The spade and fork didn't wobble in his grip. He looked very strong. If *he* said the psalm each time he left the house, perhaps it was because he truly felt the world outside to be a dangerous place, which it most likely was, all things considered. Maybe Malcolm saying his prayer was like touching the light switch six times before going out. Billy had done that for a while at home when his mum was particularly bad. He couldn't claim that it worked, but who was he, he reflected, to think that a psalm wouldn't either.

The rows of vegetables in the allotment were lined up as perfectly as soldiers. Malcolm stood amongst the runner beans, the peas, the raspberries, his palms held broad to the sky. 'God's gifts,' he said with a smile. 'Have you ever been shown how to pick any of these?'

The snapping sound of the bean stalks was pleasing to Billy, and the staining of his fingers from the ruby juice of the raspberries. A bird was singing from the top of the canes, the sun felt warm on his back, and Elspeth was humming softly as she picked tiny tomatoes. Billy stopped for a moment and watched Malcolm fork the dark brown soil which seemed to be miraculously sprouting small, thin-skinned new potatoes. He felt unexpectedly peaceful. It was not suffocating here, unlike inside the house. He suddenly felt brilliant at noticing everything; a small caterpillar curling itself on the underside of a leaf, and a ladybird crawling across the lip of a pea pod.

'Come and pull some of these carrots,' Malcolm was saying, 'you can eat one if you like, just brush the mud from it before you take a bite.'

Billy pulled out a hand of carrots, shaking the soil from the lean, long fingers of the bunch. Out of the blue he thought of his mum's hands, her long bony fingers, and he wondered how they would look now if she had been buried in the ground.

'Take a bite if you want, lad,' said Malcolm. Billy shivered and shook his head.

'Look at this courgette then,' Malcolm said, holding the yellow flower in his hand. 'See how this one has withered and the courgette is starting to come?'

'Perhaps you'd like to stop for something to drink,' Elspeth suggested.

'Yes, please,' Billy said.

Elspeth produced some orange squash from a thermos, and Malcolm took out two folding chairs from a lock-up chest in the corner of the allotment. 'You sit, you sit,' he said to Billy. Billy sat down next to her and sipped the cool orange squash, and brushed a storm fly from the rim of his beaker. He half-listened as Malcolm talked to the man on the neighbouring allotment about curly kale, and about how the last frost in early May had done it the world of good. Elspeth leaned over and told him that allotment used to be hers, but that it didn't look like that then, as she'd been a terrible gardener. It had been, she said softly and with particular emphasis, a triumph of weeds. Billy resolved to share the word with Joey on Monday; a new collective noun, he'd say, a triumph of weeds. Elspeth said the words with the merest suggestion of laughter in her voice, but kept in check as if it was somehow shameful, and not to be shared. At the side of the allotment was a small plaque which said *God sees everything and all of us*. Billy wondered if she was worried that He might have spotted she was rubbish at allotment-keeping.

'Malcolm used to give me vegetables; mine produced almost nothing,' she said. 'I think he was glad when I gave it up in case all my weeds came on to his.'

She spoke quietly and carefully. Billy closed his eyes and listened to the soft humming of a bee, and the bird on the canes which was still singing.

Malcolm stopped talking to his neighbour and started to clip some orange flowers at the end of a row of broccoli. 'Look at these I'm dead-heading,' he said to Billy, 'these are here on purpose. They work to attract the bugs instead of using chemicals. Everything's useful, we just have to find out how.'

Billy stood beside him and hoped he could be useful; it didn't seem like too much to ask. It had none of the optimism of wanting to be gifted or talented, just not wanting to be useless, which, if he admitted it to himself, perhaps his mum was, at the end.

She seemed more present today; she kept popping up in the cracks of the quietness. The slim carrots had reminded him of her fingers. He shook the thought away. Malcolm was handing him a basket to carry back to the house. It looked just like what they put at the front of the school hall when it was Harvest Festival. It was just like Harvest Festival, he affirmed to himself, but without having to sing.

Stepping back into the house, Billy had a sensation of being pressed down by all the dimness and gloom. It was like being a jack-in-the-box, only without the jumping out part.

'That's nicely done,' said Malcolm, washing his hands at the sink. 'Shall you put the kettle on, Elspeth, and we can have some more tea?'

Malcolm pulled out the chairs and they sat again at the table, and Billy sipped from a glass of water. It was very quiet. Elspeth asked if he'd like to take some raspberries for Mrs Oliver – did he know if she liked them?

It turned out she loved them. She put the little ones to bed, and then sat with her feet up in the Receiving Room. The children didn't want them so she ate the whole bowlful with a mound of softly whipped cream. After she'd finished them, she smacked her lips together and laughed.

Billy lay in his bunk later, feeling proud of himself. He'd gone to the quiet, emerald-dim house and brought back raspberries warm from the sun.

When Miriam had come to collect him, Malcolm and Elspeth had stood on the step to say goodbye, and Malcolm had raised one of his huge hands to wave. It looked as big as a flag. He didn't repeat Psalm 121 as they left, but Billy imagined that was because Miriam never looked as if she needed protecting.

In the car, she'd ruffled his hair and said 'I'm proud of you; I'm really proud of you' and she looked so pleased with him, Billy wanted to feel as relieved as she evidently did. It probably wasn't the right time, he decided, to tell her that the house made him feel as if he had to hold his breath; that he was worried, if he stayed too long in its gloomy stillness, he might start to feel he was drowning.

22

Elspeth held a runner bean and began slicing it in smooth, swift, strokes into a colander. At the kitchen table, Malcolm was sitting with his vast Bible, reading aloud as he did each Sunday morning. The pattern was always the same. Time for prayer, his lips moving with intensity: time for silence, when she sat beside him and they contemplated the Word, and then the Book, when she would begin to prepare lunch as Malcolm read aloud.

The words, this morning, wouldn't stick. They were off, like bees, buzzing beyond her reach. She tried to concentrate, construing it as a gesture of loyalty to Malcolm if not an affirmation of her own faith. Elspeth was unsure whether it was possible ever to be truly certain about anything. She had never shared this thought with Malcolm, who was. Today, he had chosen Luke chapter one, verse seven, the story of Zacharias and Elizabeth, who had given birth to John in her forties when considered barren. Its significance did not escape her. *And you will have joy and gladness*, he read. Was that what Malcolm was feeling? Last week, in bed, after Billy's visit he said *I think that went as well as we could have expected or hoped.* Was that how he might express a joy and a gladness that perhaps had set his heart singing? Elspeth glanced at him, his head lowered in reading, his palms flat to the pages of the Bible. He gave no clue. Never, she thought, would she shed the instinct that it was somehow impertinent, improper, to ask someone, anyone, what they were thinking, what they might feel.

Billy was coming for lunch. Elspeth looked at the clock. Half an hour until he arrived. Malcolm continued to read. Elspeth checked her thoughts; heavens, she was not listening at all. Had her entire adult life had been spent paying attention to her mother, Ry Woodward, or Malcolm? On occasions, what they said surely didn't require it; her mother complaining peevishly about the weather, about the weight of a rug on her knees; Ry confirming a schedule of meetings which she could see perfectly well for herself in the diary; and Malcolm, now, reading from his beloved Bible, the words familiar and resonant in his mouth yet skimming over her skin. Maybe the fact that they talked to her, and that she listened, confirmed her existence. She existed because her mother had called to her for more tea, another almond slice, because Ry Woodward asked her to set up a meeting; and because Malcolm read to her the story of Elizabeth and Zacharias. If at the end of her life she did, in fact, face the Lord, she concluded she could say, with some conviction, that she had patiently listened.

The boy was lovely. His quiet intensity had made the breath catch in her throat. She felt as she did in the presence of something wild, fearful; careful not to move too loudly, or too abruptly lest she scare him into starting or fleeing. As she hovered beyond him at the allotment, she saw his eyes take in everything; a caterpillar on a leaf, the carrots he pulled from the ground, his face clouding momentarily with a shadow of something. He'd closed his eyes as he sat in the chair drinking his squash. Malcolm's voice had washed over them, and she saw he was watching them through his eyelashes.

The world was divided, Elspeth thought, into those who felt it their right to emote, to express, to have the light of others' attention shone goldenly upon them, and those who skirted at the edges, the shy, the uncertain. Those who masked what they felt and looked on warily, remaining steeled, poised to duck, should life throw a punch.

Surely he was too young to have settled for that?

Perhaps loss could disfigure the heart, the spirit, like a bruise. She winced at the image of him carrying vivid blue-green pain.

Malcolm intoned *These are the words of the Lord,* and smiled broadly. And what might the Lord say of all this, Elspeth wondered, if He were actually witnessing their scurryings, their fastidiousness, in their kitchen, on this day. *You will have joy and gladness?*

She looked again at the clock. Perhaps she might make a pudding; something which spoke of an exuberance which she would never dare to express. Her hands might. Queen of Puddings; she would whisk egg whites and bake them to a billowing cloud of browned meringue-softness. She would carry it from the oven, a small tribute to possibility. Elspeth reached for the raspberry jam and began to spoon it thickly into a bowl. Malcolm was laying the table, adding the place for Billy with excessive care and attention. His hands looked like vast crabs on the oilcloth. It was like in a fairy story, Elspeth thought, a woman making a pudding, a man laying a table, like the couple who made a snow child and next day watched her skip into life. A tiny child nestled in an apricot; or Thumbelina who sailed downriver in a walnut shell to a couple who couldn't believe their luck. This morning, this morning in the placid stillness of their home, it felt like a fairy story. How unexpected was that?

'Shall I go down to the corner shop and perhaps buy some lemonade?' Malcolm asked. 'He might like that with his dinner, a treat for a Sunday.'

'Why not, yes, why not,' Elspeth said, thinking of a shimmering new world which involved lemonade and exuberant puddings, and where a small boy might stand before raspberry canes, his fingers smudged with juice, and for a moment seem perfect recompense for all that had gone before.

Billy sat at the table, his elbows pressed to his sides. Grandma had told him it was poor manners to stick out your elbows. Lunch smelt delicious. Joey had been quick to notice that one of the upsides of Billy's search for a family had been food. Elspeth had cooked what she said was a rolled rib of beef. Malcolm was carving it with a knife so large it looked capable of chopping off someone's head. Elspeth spooned out the vegetables, and poured gravy into a jug. Beside him, the bubbles fizzing in the lemonade glass sounded as loud as fireworks. The meat carved, Malcolm signalled to Elspeth and she caught Billy's eye, bowed her head, and pressed her hands together in prayer.

'Dear Lord,' Malcolm had said, 'we thank Thee for these Thy gifts, the food on this Thy table and for the presence of Billy here today with us. May Your word be forever in our hearts and in our mouths. Amen.'

He turned to Billy.

'Take a moment to add any thoughts of your own,' he said.

Billy's mind went blank. If he sat perfectly still might that count? He peeped at Elspeth, whose head remained bowed but who seemed to be having some thoughts of her own. He reclosed his eyes and tried to think of something he might add. He wasn't confident that his prayers would attract God's attention. On occasions, in the past, when he was smaller, He hadn't appeared to be listening. Perhaps a sound bet was to give thanks for the allotment. That was a place, he decided, where Goodness was evident. He peered through his eyelashes and saw Malcolm was watching him. 'Start eating when you're ready,' he said with a broad smile. Elspeth had made a pudding called Queen of Puddings; Joey would like the triumphal note that sounded.

It wasn't like at the Frasers; there was no chattering through lunch. The focus was on the business of eating, and of paying due attention to what was on the plate. Eating, for the Bridges, seemed a serious, quiet endeavour. Billy tried hard not to clink his knife and fork. Elspeth asked him quietly if Mrs Oliver had liked the raspberries. *Yes thank you, she said to say thank you very much*. He decided not to tell them she'd eaten them with her feet up in the Receiving Room. It seemed so feast-like. Perhaps they might think she didn't behave with good manners when given food from the allotment; food which, potentially more seriously, was not only from them but also from God.

'Now for another Sunday ritual,' Malcolm said, when lunch was over, 'time for the winding of the clock. Do you want to see how it's done? There's a knack.'

Billy nodded. He followed Malcolm into the front room, and

watched as he crouched, breathing heavily, before the cabinet of the clock. It was made of dark wood, and on its pale cream face there were ornate roman numerals and a picture of a half-moon. Its slow steady tick seemed to be crossing the thickness of the carpet and pushing its way into the soles of his feet.

'It belonged to my father, and his father before that,' Malcolm said. 'See where the crank here has a little dip; that's the imprint of their thumbs, winding, each week through all the years. Come forward, step forward, look in here and I'll tell you what's what.'

Billy peered in. The clock's innards smelled fusty. He pressed his fingertips to his nose, to disguise the fact that he wanted to wrinkle it.

'See, here there's two weights, and two corresponding winding points. This one keeps time and drives the hands and the pendulum. This one is for the hour strike. Each one needs winding fourteen times each Sunday. Best done in the middle of the day when the room is neither too cold nor too warm. Here, I'll do this one, and then you can do the other.'

Billy stepped backwards hesitantly. Elspeth was behind him, having come silently into the room. Her hand hovered above his shoulder.

'It's all right, don't worry,' she said, 'you won't harm it or break it. There's a seat-board – isn't that what it's called, Malcolm? – the seat-board stops it being over-wound. It's fine to have a go.'

Malcolm passed him the crank. It felt cool in his hand. His own thumb pad, he saw, was tiny compared to that of the imprint of all the Bridges' men's thumbs.

'Then there's this,' Malcolm said, gesturing towards the china-blue image of the moon. 'That's the dial feature and it shows you the phases of the moon. You just have to check that's keeping pace with the calendar. When the moon's full in the sky, it should be full on the clock. Looks like it's spot on.'

Malcolm stood back and patted the polished cabinet with affection.

'It's a thing of beauty, is that.'

Billy nodded.

'And,' he continued, rubbing his hands together, 'if clocks are of interest to you, I've pictures of another one that might be.'

He gestured to Billy to sit down, and he went over to the dark wooden sideboard and tugged open the drawer. It stuck a little on its slidings. 'We want to be putting some candle wax on that,' he said, looking over to Elspeth. 'That's what my mother always did and it gets it running smoothly in no time.' Elspeth nodded.

Malcolm took out a small booklet and sat down next to Billy.

'Sunday afternoons, when I was a boy, I always read my comics – *Marvel* and such like, and sometimes *Look and Learn*. I'd read out fascinating facts. This counts as a fascinating fact, this is a thing to be seen.'

He pointed to a photograph of what appeared to be a clock, contained within a wall, behind a curved pane of glass.

'A chronophage,' he said, chuckling. 'They call this a chronophage. They even had to go to Greek to make a name for it. It means time eater. It's on a street in Cambridge; it belongs to one of the colleges. I was making a delivery there and I walked by. It's just built into the corner of a building. I stood watching it work. I bought this little book about it in a shop afterwards. Chronophage means time eater. It sits there, everyone going by, and eats up all the hours.'

Billy wondered what they weighed.

Malcolm flicked through the booklet.

'Look, see . . . the clock face is like a golden curled shell. It's got no hands or numbers, just blue flashing lights. It looks like an ammonite fossil, but you don't need to bother yourself with that. It's properly plated in gold. They say it cost a million pounds and that two hundred people helped to make it. On top of it sits the insect – look, can you see it has pincers, antennae? It's a grasshopper or a locust, you can't really decide which. Here's the clever bit, the motion of the clock makes the insect move its mouth. Open and shut, like it's chewing. It actually eats up the time. What a blessed invention. If you watch it carefully, it blinks, every now and again, not to any pattern. I stood there long enough to catch it doing it. Like in this picture here, its eye briefly skins over all golden like a lizard's. To top that, it makes a terrible grinding sound, and when it gets to the hour there's no lovely bell chiming; no, it's tolled by the sound of a chain clanking into a wooden coffin hidden at the back.' Malcolm chuckled. 'For whom the bell tolls, that's what the man next to me said. Can you imagine the wizardry in inventing all of that? And look, this is what the inventor says – I'll just put my glasses on to read it correctly – he says *I view time as not on your side. He'll eat up every minute of your life, and as soon as one has gone he's salivating for the next.* Can you credit it? And here's the ticket; he also said it should be able to run accurately for at least two hundred years. It stopped three times in the first month. There's proof that you can't believe everything you hear, no matter how clever the chap who says it. This bit here, it's a Latin inscription underneath and what it means is . . . let me find the page . . . what it means is *The world passeth away and the lust thereof,* which also shows however clever a thing is, it's best to let the Bible have the last word.'

Malcolm sat back on the settee, the leaflet on his belly. He chuckled a little more. 'There's a thing for you, don't you think? Do you want to look at it a little further?' He proffered the brochure to Billy.

Billy thought the spirit of the chronophage seemed to be entering the grandfather clock. Each second it ticked was one chewed and swallowed. He imagined a chain clanking, a coffin gaping. His hand hung in mid-air before him. Malcolm went to pass him the leaflet. Billy could see Elspeth was looking at him carefully.

'Perhaps that's enough of the chronophage,' she said hesitantly, reaching forward as if she might take the leaflet herself. 'Maybe it's not suitable for children really.'

Malcolm looked puzzled.

'There's children walking past it on the street,' he said mildly, 'stopping and looking.'

'Would you like to do a jigsaw puzzle, Billy?' Elspeth said. 'I don't know if I have one with the kind of picture you would like.

I'm afraid I have mainly country cottages and gardens full of rose bushes, although I have one of an old-fashioned sweet shop.'

Billy nodded. She beckoned towards the table and he sat down on a high-backed, wooden chair.

'Let's start with sorting out the corner pieces and edges, shall we? I'm guessing you'll be sharp eyed at that. Do you want to make a start while I just fetch Malcolm's paper from the kitchen and bring him some tea? After the winding of the clock, there's always the papers with tea.'

A little later, Elspeth sat sorting jigsaw pieces with precise, careful hands. Malcolm sat in his armchair reading the paper, tutting to himself and saying 'Follies, follies.'

She set Billy to finding the pieces for a child holding a bag of aniseed balls. The leaflet about the chronophage was on the arm of the settee. Billy kept casting a look at it, half-expecting the fabric of the couch to be smouldering. He strained his ears to see if he could hear the sound of a chain clanking. What had Malcolm said? *He'll eat up every minute of your life, and as soon as one has gone he's salivating for the next.* His mum was gone. Did that make him the next?

He felt a bit sick. Maybe he had eaten too much Queen of Puddings.

23

Billy sat in Meg's kitchen later in the evening, watching her make scrambled eggs. Miriam had brought him home and tried to make conversation in the car. She asked him about lunch, and about what he had done. Billy had told her he had a headache, so she let him sit quietly. The fib started off feeling unfair, but then felt less so, because as he shut his eyes and leaned his forehead against the car window, the chronophage insect popped up goldenly on the inside of his own eyelids, mouth chewing determinedly, and Billy started feeling his head pound for real. Miriam had squeezed his hand when he got out of the car. He wasn't sure what that meant.

Jayden was watching television in the Rumpus Room. The sound of it was audible in the background, along with Meg's fork whisking the eggs in the Pyrex bowl. Meg was humming as she worked, and the toaster was popping up with a ping, and a dog was barking out in the street, and someone was mowing their lawn three doors down. He could hear the whack of bat against ball as a child next door played Swingball. They were, Billy reassured himself, all normal noises, all the sounds of life. No insect clock could consume those. He gave a little shiver.

In the Bridges' house nothing sounded normal. It was as if every sound fell into a thick pillow of silence, making ever-fainter ripples of noise around itself. The tick of the grandfather clock, the click of each jigsaw puzzle piece slotting into place, the catch in Malcolm's breathing as he snoozed in the chair after reading the paper. He thought of Elspeth, her pale grey eyes, her hesitant voice, her hand hovering above his shoulder as he stood behind the clock. Her not touching him felt as physical as Miriam squeezing his hand.

It came to him that if Elspeth had been an animal, she wouldn't have come from a zoo, but from a forest. That was where she'd be sent back to, if she didn't already have her dark, greenly-lit house. She'd be a deer, watchful but camouflaged, gentle through the trees. As he sat doing the puzzle, she seemed to fade into the dappled colours of the room around her, and all that he was aware of was her eyes, looking at him while he searched for the pieces. Malcolm slept on. The catch in his breathing increased to a slow, steady snore. Billy kept thinking Elspeth might speak, but she didn't, and the image of the sweet shop spread shinily beneath their fingers on the dark satiny table, and when Miriam rapped the door knocker, he nearly jumped out of his skin.

Miriam, on the doorstep, looked smaller than usual. She looked uncertain, her hand held out to him on the step, and he wondered if he should have so much trust in her ability to make everything come right.

Now, in the kitchen, he could hear someone kicking a football against a wall. Jayden had taken her skipping rope outside and he could hear it thwacking against the paving stones as she tried to learn to skip. Someone further down the road was having an argument: *Don't you try and tell me what to bloody well do.* All these sounds, he wondered, all these sounds jammed together, might they be chronophage-proof and scare the locust grass-hopper away?

'Do you think time goes quickly or slowly?' he asked Meg, who was now spooning the scrambled eggs on to toast.

'Depends if you're having fun or not,' she said, which seemed sensible to him.

He didn't want to think too closely about whether this afternoon had been fun. The Bridges were kind; they'd bought him lemonade. Elspeth's hands, he saw, when she took the sweet shop puzzle from the box, shook like ferns.

Elspeth lay in bed, and waited for Malcolm to finish saying his prayers. He prayed every night by the bed. When she hoovered the bedroom, she paid special attention to the two smooth scoops his knees had made over the years in the carpet. She wasn't sure what they demonstrated. Consistency? Devotion? Persistence? His lips never moved. Sometimes she lay there wondering what he prayed for. Had he prayed for a wife, for her to materialise in the adjacent allotment, hands outstretched, to receive the gift of a cauliflower? Now, was he praying for a child to whom he would teach the things his own father had taught him? He took off his slippers and settled heavily beside her.

'Well, that was a lovely day, a lovely lunch, thank you, my dear,' he said warmly, patting her thigh. 'It was nice to wind the clock with the little lad, a child after all these years. I think he enjoyed it. And on the settee, fascinating facts. The chronophage. Brings a smile just thinking of it.'

Elspeth lay there, heart-sore. She'd never heard him speak as many words as he had done today. *What an effort you are making*; why couldn't she say that to him? Billy seemed terrified of the chronophage; she couldn't say that either. Malcolm hadn't seen it at all. Nor, that when he tried to hand the booklet to him, Billy looked as if he thought it would scald him. Everything about it – the thought of it, the sight of it, the words about it – all of it had scared him, it was written clearly on his face. When he sat with her for the jigsaw puzzle, she could see a small pulse in his temple, beating, beating. *Dare I*, she had thought, *reach out my hand and smooth the hair on his forehead, rest my finger, for a moment, in the hollow of his temple until the flickering stops*? Her courage had failed her. It would be such an invasion, such an intrusion. All of her life, she thought, mastered by a shyness which was steely in its grip. Her hand had remained, trembling, poised above the puzzle pieces in the box.

Malcolm could not see it. He could not see the truth of the boy. The mist of his own nostalgic happiness blinded him to what was in front of his eyes: a small boy, terrified at the talk of a clock which ate lives, just as his own poor mother's had been consumed. A coffin: Malcolm had chuckled about the ingeniousness of the wooden coffin. Her inept, fearful hands; how she railed against them now in the silence of the bed. She had wanted to take them and press them against Malcolm's unknowing mouth, to smother the sounds or suck them away through her veins. Malcolm had, she knew, not an ounce of malice or unkindness in his bones, and yet he had talked on and on, drawing attention to the detail of the photos, and all the time the boy stiffened and stiffened, and Malcolm did not see it at all. And yet she had seen, which might have been enough to save him, but she had not been brave. She had failed him too. She had stood there, frozen, passive as always, longing to rip the booklet into small, impotent pieces.

And so were they doomed, she wondered, like the old men and their wives in the stories, who had children brought to them by fairies rather than by Miriam Riley? Doomed because Malcolm could not see, and because she was not brave? She had carried the pudding from the oven to the table with a small pulse of hope. The sweet smell of the hot raspberry jam was like an affirmation of the possible. After Billy had left, she had scraped what remained of it into the bin.

'Goodnight, dear,' Malcolm said, patting her hand.

'Goodnight, dear,' she said, feeling as if they lay together on a cold stone tomb.

Billy lay in bed. The house was silent around him. Was it possible, he thought, for his heart to beat any faster? The inventor's words were looping shrilly around and around in his head. *He'll eat up every moment of your life, and as soon as one has gone he's salivating for the next.*

The locust grasshopper's eyes blinked goldenly at him. Its jaw gaped wide. The chain clanked into the coffin. From behind it peered the dwarf from *The Singing Ringing Tree*, grinning wickedly. The tree chimed in with its silvery, sinister ringing, and the prince, who was turned into a bear without knowing if he'd be turned back, rocked his head in his hands. All of it rolled into a smothering, dark thunderous cloud which knocked between his temples and rattled at the base of his skull. He fell into an unsettled sleep.

In his dreams, he was chased by the grasshopper locust. It cranked, ground, and munched, and a coffin gaped open like a crooked smile while a grandfather clock ticked. The dwarf shook his fist and hurled a thorn bush for good measure.

Billy heard himself cry out as the insect drooled wetness, and he was aware of Meg lifting him gently from his bed, carrying him to the bunk opposite and sponging him with a flannel. She put new pyjamas on him and tucked him carefully beneath a dry, clean duvet. All the time she was saying *Hush, Billy, hush, nothing is eating you* and he sank back into sleep, his heart slowly ceasing its racing, and in the morning he woke in the different bed, his own already changed, and he knew Meg Oliver wouldn't mention it at all.

24

Home from work, Elspeth was upstairs in the bedroom changing her clothes. The phone rang, and she heard Malcolm answer it, and talk, she presumed, to Miriam Riley.

She took off her skirt, and carefully hung it up in the wardrobe. Sometimes, when she reached into the back of cupboards and disturbed their stillness, she imagined she was breathing the same air, untouched, as Malcolm's long-dead mother. Their home, she felt, was coated in a sediment of age. It felt like old, yellowed glue, seeping from corners, from edges, from skirting-boards and casements. How could a child be expected to soften and dissolve all of that? She took off her slip, and kneaded a stiffness in her left knee, listened as Malcolm put down the phone and came upstairs to the back bedroom. She heard the sound of furniture moving, a shifting, a dragging. She put on her dressing-gown and went to him.

He had moved the bed from the length of the wall to the window. The sun-faded wallpaper revealed a perfect outline where the headboard had rested.

'I thought by the window, a view of the tree, the garden,' he said.

'For whom, for when?'

'For if Billy stays; give the lad a sense of his own room. How it might be. I've suggested to Miriam him coming with us on *The Girl Jane* for a day. I've said to her that to get the most out of it – an early start – he could stay the night before here if he likes.' He patted the bedhead. He looked pleased with himself.

Elspeth looked around the room. The wallpaper was flock; the bed had an eiderdown and blankets. At the foot of it was a blanket box covered with a ruby toile de jouy fabric. It didn't feel like a room in which a child would want to sleep. Didn't boys have computers, hockey sticks, posters, board games?

'It doesn't feel much like a boy's room . . . yet,' she added apologetically. She edged carefully around what she saw as the fine tissue of Malcolm's hope, his pride. She paused and flushed. He had suggested the trip to Miriam; he had thought it up on his own initiative. Who was she, she chastised herself, to stand here fretting about bedspreads and wallpapers? He had thought boldly of the boat, of Billy on the boat.

'Look what else,' he said, 'I've just remembered.'

He opened the chiffonière and lifted out something from the back of the top shelf.

'Look at these, look at what I have in here. I can't believe I've never shown you these. They were my pride and joy.'

The tin was full of toy soldiers, some so much-played with as to be devoid of paint. Malcolm smiled and nodded. 'I'll show these to him when he comes. I think, at a push, I can remember the Charge of the Light Brigade.'

Elspeth allowed herself to smile. Miriam had agreed in principle.

'I suppose we could buy a duvet and a cover, something bright,' she said.

'This old wardrobe doesn't have to stay, the wallpaper neither. I'd have that off in a jiffy. Paint, a lick of paint's the thing I think. Blue for a boy?'

Elspeth nodded.

'If she says he can come this Friday and Saturday, we won't have time to do any of that for then,' he said. 'It'll just have to be as it is now. I'm sure he will understand.'

Running a bath later, Elspeth thought of the little old lady and man who had baked the gingerbread boy; a little gingerbread boy who they wanted to treat as their own. The thought of Malcolm and his long-kept tin of soldiers made her want to weep.

25

Miriam waited for Billy to arrive. On the phone to arrange logistics, Meg had been cryptic. *I'm not sure he's comfortable,* she said, *something's bothering him.* She wouldn't be drawn any further. Miriam sighed. Was it the Bridges, was it the situation, was it her constant questions, or was it the realisation that his mum, however inept, was never coming back? The finality of death often took time to dawn on children. If only he were transparent, her job would be so much easier.

When he arrived, and sat before her, she told him what Malcolm had suggested.

'A boat?' Billy said. 'A day out on a boat?'

'Yes, on his boat, their boat, and a sleepover the night before so that you can get a nice early start. That's what Malcolm and Elspeth are suggesting. It sounds like a lovely idea to me. What do you think?' (*Idiot*, Miriam thought, *don't jump in with your view before he's had a chance to express his.*)

She looked at him. She'd bought him an ice lolly, but it was a little bit melted from the warmth of her car. He was licking it strategically, trying to stop trickles running down the stick. The fan on her desk whirred softly. *An abacus would be good,* she thought, *I could make myself thread all the beads before I try and cajole an answer from him.*

'A boat,' Billy said again. 'Is it one that you row or pedal?'

'No, nothing like that, it's a little cruiser, with fuel. I've even checked there's a life-jacket.'

'Okay,' he said decisively, 'I'll go. I've never been on a boat like that.'

'Good sport,' Miriam said. Maybe that expression wasn't entirely appropriate?

'Good. That's good,' she ploughed on. 'Now that you haven't got a headache, do you want to tell me a little bit about Sunday?'

'They bought lemonade for me to drink with my lunch.'

'That was thoughtful.'

'Elspeth made a pudding called Queen of Puddings which has meringue on top and raspberry jam in the middle.'

'Sounds delicious.'

'Their carving knife is huge.'

'I'm sure Malcolm uses it sensibly.'

'He has a grandfather clock he winds up every week. He showed me how to do it.'

'Good for him for remembering. If it were mine it would stop.'

'I did a jigsaw puzzle with Elspeth.'

'Which sounds nice too. What did you talk about?'

Billy paused.

Miriam looked at him carefully.

'So what did you talk about?' she ventured again.

'Thing is, they're not so talky.'

'Maybe they will be as you get to know them. Grown-ups can be shy, just like children. They haven't had any children so they might just be a bit unsure what to talk about. Maybe it will get easier, maybe on the boat there will be lots to chat about.'

Billy nodded. Miriam kicked herself. Why had she jumped in with the up-side rather than encouraging him to elaborate? Now, she could see, the shutters had come down again. He was looking at his laces in the way that meant game over.

'Do you want to wait for Meg by the tree?'

'Okay.'

'So I'll see you after your day on the river, and after your sleepover. Come and tell me all about it. Anything you want to say at all.'

Billy nodded.

Walking towards the tree, Billy could see Andrew mowing the strip of grass beyond it.

'Hey Billy,' Andrew called, waving and switching off the mower. 'How's it going? What have you been up to?'

'Allotment. The new family have an allotment, so I've been picking fruit and vegetables.'

'A proper farmer.'

'Not really, but Meg liked the raspberries a lot.'

'Lorna wants to eat nothing but strawberries. My bet is the baby's going to come out red.'

'Can Strawberry be a name for a girl?'

'Don't think so, but didn't someone famous call their daughter Apple? Cherry's a girl's name.'

'Not Berry, though, Raspberry or Blackberry.'

'Nor Damson, but hey Plum is, there's another one. Peach at a push, but not Apricot. Not any vegetables either I don't think. You wouldn't want to be calling your baby Potato or Carrot.'

Billy nodded. 'Sweetcorn. She might not thank you for that.'

Andrew looked down at the mown grass.

'So, are you all right then? Everything all right with you, for you, I mean.'

Billy paused and nodded. 'I'm going on a boat on Saturday. I'm having a picnic on the river. Before that I'm sleeping at their house but then I'll be outside. What are you doing?'

'I'm going fishing in the morning. Then I'm starting work on the little bedroom which is becoming the nursery. Lorna says it all needs painting, and she's wanting me to make a wardrobe and a unit for all the things you need when you're changing a nappy. I'm hoping that counts as my bit towards the nappy business.'

'Sounds fair.'

'Although probably unlikely.'

Andrew looked at his watch. 'I have to get going. It's ante-natal class tonight. That's when they tell you everything about having a baby. Lorna decided last week there are things she'd prefer not to know. Those are the parts when she says I'm supposed to be in charge of listening. I'll just be putting the mower away and be off. I'll think of you down at the river on Saturday. Any luck and it will be minus one massive fish.'

'Tight lines,' Billy said.

Andrew gave him a big, broad grin and waved as he walked away.

Billy sat down at the base of the tree, and reached into the hole. All safe and sound. He closed his eyes. If he'd said no to the sleepover and the boat trip, Miriam would have thought it was game over like with the Frasers.

He took out his notebook and wrote a note for the tree. He hesitated and looked up. The toddler Dixon was back; his mum was kissing a man while Dixon went to and fro on the swing. Had his own mum taken him to a park when he was little? Maybe she had; maybe she'd put him on one end of a seesaw and pushed the other end down with her hands. *See saw Marjory daw*, Dixon's mum was singing now, which Billy thought would probably be more fun for Dixon than the kissing.

Andrew was building stuff for the baby's room. That was obviously another thing dads did. The unit for storing nappies could be for toys when the baby was older, and he would know his dad had made it for him before he was even born. Made it just at the thought of him. In his own case, the thought of him had made his dad run a mile. His mum said she woke up one morning and he was gone. Offski, she said.

Billy finished writing his note, folded it into smaller and smaller squares and posted it into the tree. He could see Meg walking towards him, carrying shopping bags of food. She looked hot and bothered, as if the shopping bags were heavy. Billy jumped up and waved, and ran down the path towards her. He offered to take one of the bags, and hoisted it on to his shoulder.

They walked to the main road and Billy put his hand out for the bus to stop. This life, he thought, this life with the Introductions, was turning into *his* life, but it was almost the end of June. Two and a bit weeks more and it would be the end of school for the summer, and then there would be the holidays, and then the last day of August would come and there it would be – his tenth birthday – lying in wait. Ten years old, when maybe no one would want him. There wasn't exactly a rush on now. Unless something worked soon, his tenth birthday would jump up holding a sign that said 'Off to a children's home' like long-ago kings said 'Off with his head'. Billy wondered, sitting on the bus and looking out of the window, if maybe they'd turn out to be the same thing anyway.

'Hey little man, you're looking bothered. What's bothering you?' Meg said, touching his chin with her finger to turn his face towards her.

Billy tilted his face so his expression was no longer visible in the pane of the window.

'Nothing,' he said, shaking his head.

26

Billy lay in bed.

The Bridges' house creaked and wound down around him. Water gurgled in a pipe, Malcolm moved, heavy-footed, in the bedroom next door, and something – was it a boiler? – clicked and whirred in a cupboard on the landing.

The bed was broad and very high. Sitting on the edge of it and pulling off his T-shirt, Billy waggled his feet to confirm that they didn't reach the carpet. It had sheets, and a blanket, and a padded eiderdown which felt like it would be too warm for a night in June. He pushed it back, and it slithered, thickly, on to the floor. He pulled the sheet up to his chin. The blanket was the tiniest bit scratchy. The mattress was full of coiled springs which, if he pushed one down with the palm of his hand, meant his body pooled in the dip in between. He gave a tentative bounce. One of the springs creaked; the sound was unexpectedly loud. He turned softly on to his side.

It was very dark. The curtains were made of thick, plum-coloured velvet. When he reached out and touched them, he could stroke the pile both ways. Maybe the thickness was why it was so good at blotting out any light that may be outside. A street light? The moon? The beam of a car headlight going past? Nothing doing. It was darkness as thick as soup. Darkness soup. Elspeth had asked if he wanted a night light, perhaps the landing light left on and the door ajar?

'The lad won't need that, he'll be asleep in minutes,' Malcolm said, 'all set for a busy day tomorrow, eh Billy?'

Billy nodded. 'This is fine, no light's fine,' he said.

Perhaps he should have asked for a quick demonstration before saying so. Elspeth looked like she wouldn't have minded.

It seemed, now, as if he could not only feel, but hear, his heart thumping. It was making advances into his ears, its rhythm steadily increasing. Did he need the loo again? He'd gone to the bathroom four times in the evening. He was mindful of Meg's and the night of the chronophage. He had drunk very little tonight. Elspeth had offered him hot chocolate and he'd said no thank you straightaway. She'd looked sad when he'd said it; perhaps she'd bought it especially; she'd bought Rice Krispies for his breakfast tomorrow. He could hear a low murmur of voices from their bedroom. They were probably talking about him, talking about the evening.

Malcolm had showed him a tin of soldiers he'd had when he was a boy. Some had painted plumed hats and kilts, some looked like ones from the First World War. Malcolm had got down on his hands and knees on the carpet and arranged them into what he said was a battle formation. He had a tiny metal cannon and Billy was supposed to say *Boom!* when Malcolm tapped it, and then with a sweep of his great hand he'd knock a whole battalion down. Billy tried to give it his all; to say *Boom!* with a degree of enthusiasm when the cannon was tapped, and then re-scramble the fallen soldiers into a new, freshly determined, formation. The problem was it all felt joyless, what with the soldiers getting repeatedly swatted aside, and the ones with no paint looking forlorn anyway, and Malcolm so keen for it to be fun. After three battles – Billy had found the Charge of the Light Brigade particularly mournful – Malcolm put them back in the tin. He sat back on his knees, his face a bit red, and wiped his forehead, which was shining, with the back of his hand. *Well, that's a game,* he said. Billy worried that Malcolm perhaps hadn't enjoyed it as much as he hoped either, and that he had somehow disappointed him in the business of toy soldiers.

Malcolm put the tin away and got out a draughts set, and said he could teach Billy to play. He set up the board with all the smooth chequers, and gave Billy the white ones which were yellowed with age and smelt funny in his hand. Malcolm showed him how to try and criss-cross the board, how to pile a second chequer on top, how to leap over the black pieces and then take them off. Billy thought that if he'd been at the Job Centre, filling in the form which said he didn't want to be a tree surgeon, he'd also have to add *Rubbish at draughts*, in case that revealed anything about how suitable he might be for a particular job. Malcolm was patient; he kept saying 'Maybe look at this one', or 'I think you were just about to move this one and take this one of mine from here' when Billy wasn't at all.

Elspeth hardly spoke but Billy could feel her watching, like a deer again through the trees, every sense straining. She sat in the chair knitting, her needles flashing and clicking. The rows streamed from her hands, a gauzy web of wool, and the draughts clicked on the board, and the needles clicked in Elspeth's fingers, and the room was heavy with so much clicking and trying it made Billy feel a little bit sick.

Malcolm said 'There's another thing to tell you; you'll like this,' and he chuckled with the anticipation of the telling. Billy looked with horror at the sideboard, and the prospect of another booklet. Malcolm sat back in his chair, his arms crossed on his belly. He started to give an account of someone at work, another driver who was not a Brethren, who had offered him a dual-screen baby monitor set. He'd bought it to keep a check on his puppy, for when the puppy whined in the night, so that he could see it in its basket and calm it via the monitor.

'He thought I might like it for you,' Malcolm continued. 'Imagine, to keep an eye on you in the night. I'd said we'd all be out like lights, early doors, what with the games tonight and the prospect of tomorrow. He didn't say, now I come to think of it, if it had worked on his puppy. The terrier my parents had when I was a boy would have chewed it to bits, that's what he'd have done. Nice little dog, though. Sometimes I think about getting a terrier. He could do a bit of ratting at the compost heap in the allotment, and sit on the boat at the bow.'

'If you had a dog, what would you call it?' asked Billy, with a sinking feeling.

'Rex, that's what this dog was called. I'd name it after him.'

If Malcolm had said yes to the baby monitor, Billy wondered how would it have worked? Would he have been able to see Malcolm and Elspeth sleeping, and would they have been able to see him? He imagined Malcolm's big, bald, smooth head on a pillow. Over dinner, Malcolm said God could see everyone, watch everyone. If so, Billy thought, he'd have been tucked up in this bed with a whole team watching him not being able to get to sleep.

He turned over again. The blanket seemed to be getting scratchier. He wondered if Elspeth was sleeping. While he was brushing his teeth in the bathroom she had hovered outside, asking him if he needed anything. There was plenty of everything. As he washed his face he could feel her outside the door hovering, and he thought of a bird he'd seen once fluttering up against a window pane, its wings beating and beating, and that was how it felt with Elspeth and he was glad when he scooted into the bedroom and she and Malcolm stood on the landing and said goodnight.

Malcolm said *O Lord keep us safe this night from all wickedness*, and now, in the soup dark, Billy thought he didn't feel very safe at all, and the world felt full of all sorts of possible wickedness. He tried to summon up Meg in her big white nightgown, standing on the Bridges' landing, saying *Hush, Billy, hush*. He imagined Miriam striding up the stairs, her brow furrowed because she'd been like a whirlwind all day. There was comfort in the thought of them both. Then he felt guilty because he hadn't thought of his mum. Perhaps it was because she hadn't really kept him properly safe when she was alive, and now she was dead she couldn't do it at all.

When he fell asleep, it was listening to a cat yowling out on the street. If he concentrated very hard, the notes seemed like a proper song, looping and curling their way into the room. Perhaps he could make it into a lullaby of sorts? He tried to smooth it into *lulla lulla lulla lulla bye bye*, but that didn't work. He counted bobbles on the blanket between his finger and thumb. Eventually he slept.

Elspeth was lying awake in the blue dark.

When he got into bed, Malcolm had said 'A smashing evening. I think it's coming along well. He'll pick up the draughts better on a second go.'

Elspeth wondered if it crossed his mind to ask whether she had a view, or whether to question, for himself, whether what had obviously been so idyllic, so reassuring, during his boyhood might not be so for another child forty years later. Was he still awake?

'Malcolm,' she hedged, her voice a whisper.

He did not respond. His out-breath was long.

'I'm not sure we have what it takes to make him happy,' she ventured. 'I'm not sure we even know how.'

No response. But she had said it, she had dared to say it out loud, after an evening when she felt foolish, inept, knitting frantically in her chair, and as ill-equipped to parent him as to hold water safe and contained in the web of her hands.

27

Andrew was running, running with everything he could muster. He felt like a rhino, crashing through bush. He'd been running for miles. What he'd said to Lorna was going to be a short run had turned into something else. He'd run through the streets and beyond, out along the towpath, and on to where everything thinned to the wide flat bowl of the meadow, beyond the curve of the ring road, past where cattle were grazing, to the overgrown banks of the river. Still he ran, his muscles on fire, his calves and face scratched by brambles, and a soft gauze of midges suspended in the dampness around his hair.

If he ran for long enough, he reasoned, if he kept on running, through the twilight, through the sooty dark, on from where the odd star had started to hang silver in the sky, to where the moon made way for the dawn, would he feel better? Would he have shed what was bothering him or come up with some kind of plan?

The most recent note was killing.

1. They are kind. They try so hard it feels like something is going to snap.
2. Malcolm told me about the cronofarge clock. It eats up your life. There's a coffin that clanks.
3. Their house makes me feel like I can't breathe. The air comes into my nose like pond water. At night, it's soup-dark.
4. I don't know how to tell Miriam because she's trying hard too.
5. Also, if a dad is happy about a baby coming, he can make a storebox to put nappies in. If he's not, he can run away without a word.

Andrew shoved an overhanging branch out of his face. An owl flapped low over the surface of the river. Something called out, something cried in response. For the first time, he wondered if he should be able to name the sounds. As a father, how would he teach a child how to name their world? He stopped by a willow tree and vomited with exhaustion. He needed to work out a way to tell Miriam.

Halfway through last week's ante-natal session, the group leader said she wanted to address all the men. They'd bunched together looking a bit wary, thinking they might be called to account. Most of them were there under pressure from their partners. Their primary preoccupation seemed to be what would happen to sex. What had she said?

It will make men of you in ways you can't yet imagine. You will become fathers, with all the protectiveness, responsibility, love and wisdom that involves, and you'll know that it's someone else's turn to be the child now; that before the birth you still held some scraps of your boyhood in your hands, and the day after you'll wake up a man, and a father.

They'd looked stunned; shifted awkwardly. There'd been a lot of shrugging, and some nervous laughter. Now, on the towpath, running again, but back towards Lorna, what Andrew found he was battling with was something that he would not be able to say to her. His own child, his baby, was not due for more than three months. And yet all those things, all those things he was meant to feel on the day he'd wake up after the baby was born, all of that he was feeling already, reading Billy's notes, and watching him walk towards him, by the tree, with his sweet little face. It wasn't meant to be this way. All of that, surely, should be reserved for his baby? Billy couldn't breathe in the new family's house. What kind of man would stand by and knowingly let a child secretly worry about that? He started to run faster. His shin splints were scorching.

Lorna was sitting at the bottom of the stairs. When he came through the door, she burst into tears.

'Where have you been? You've been gone so long. I was worried. I thought perhaps you had tripped, fallen into the river, that something dreadful had happened. I've been out of my mind. The team midwife came for the check-up. Everything's fine, but I told her you'd gone running, and that you hadn't gone running for ages. She laughed and said it gets some men like that, the dawning responsibility makes them want to run a mile. Tell me, please tell me, that isn't why you've been gone for so long.'

He stepped forward, and held her. She was so clean, and he was sweaty and rank and bloody, snagged by brambles, splashed with river sludge, and vomit, dead storm flies pressed to his shoulders, his cheekbones. He kissed her hair. 'I promise you, I promise you,' he said, 'I have never felt so ready to be a dad as I do now.'

28

The boat was called *The Girl Jane*. It was moored on a floating pontoon next to a little café by the river. *The Girl Jane* was written in looping blue lettering. The canopy was white with blue stripes. Billy sat with Elspeth on a bench by the pontoon while Malcolm did what he called 'readying the craft'. He swept a little debris from the deck with a dustpan and brush. He wiped off duck mess from a chrome rail that ran along at the rear. He poured some fuel into the tank from a metal canister, and opened one of the under-seat boxes and shook out a life-jacket for Billy.

'The captain likes a tidy vessel,' Elspeth said to Billy, and just for a moment, the slightest flicker of a moment, Billy wasn't sure if she was teasing, maybe even joking, as Malcolm huffed and puffed on the deck and Elspeth sat patiently with a picnic basket on her knees.

He'd eaten two bowls of Rice Krispies. He hoped that might go some way towards balancing the rejection of the hot chocolate. He'd come downstairs at quarter past seven and found her making flapjacks for the picnic. She'd offered to pour his cereal and he'd said he'd do it himself, and so she moved around the kitchen melting butter, spooning syrup, and he got the cereal, a bowl, and milk from the fridge and he thought they were like two bees, dancing around each other, or moths around a light, something that came near but avoided coming too close. She went upstairs to give Malcolm a cup of tea. *My whole adult life,* she said to him, *I've started the day taking someone tea,* and Billy wasn't sure, from her voice, whether that was a good thing or not.

Malcolm came downstairs and sat beside him at the table and ate a bowl of Weetabix. In the curl of his ear was a tiny fleck of shaving foam. The Rice Krispies sounded like guns going off. Malcolm finished eating and went outside to check the rainfall measurer, the thermometer and the barometer he kept by the kitchen door. He pronounced it would be a beautiful day. *Praise the Lord and give thanks*, he said. Billy nodded. Elspeth stirred in the oats.

Sitting on the bench now, the sky completely blue, Billy craned his neck back to check for one small scrap of cloud. Not even a wisp. Meg had given him sun screen and he began to rub it into his arms and his face. His skin glittered with a milky white sheen. Elspeth put on a hat with a broad straw brim. 'Malcolm, don't forget your cap,' she said to him, passing it from the basket. 'The sun's hot and you don't want to go burning your head.' Billy wondered if this was what marriage was like: taking tea up in the morning, saying don't forget your cap, doing the crossword in the car together as they had done driving here. It seemed very peaceful, with little room for an unexpected 'offski'; maybe his mum hadn't been clever in her choices.

'All set,' Malcolm pronounced. 'Do you want a hand on board, Billy? Welcome to *The Girl Jane*.'

Billy climbed on and Malcolm gave him the life-jacket. 'Best to wear that,' he said, 'I think it's a rule of Miriam's.'

He stood by the wheel and looked around him.

'All shipshape and Bristol fashion,' he said with satisfaction.

Billy felt momentarily wrong-footed. His mum said that too, and look what happened to her. Maybe his day would not end well. He looked across at Elspeth who was packing the picnic basket away. She didn't look like she thought being shipwrecked was a risk.

Malcolm started the engine. Billy sat at the bow of the boat, and watched it cut through the water, making an arrow of white foam. 'Look, Billy, look,' said Elspeth, pointing to a moorhen and her chicks busying themselves in some reeds. Malcolm steered past some men fixing willow hurdling on the bank. He waved at them and they called out *Lovely day for it!*

'A kingfisher, look,' said Elspeth, but he saw only a flash of blue. The Introduction process, he thought, consisted of a lot of pointing out Nature. They came to the lock and Malcolm tied the boat to a metal loop with a thick snake of rope. He asked Billy to hold it taut as he tied up the other end. The rope felt warm and coarse in his hand, and stung just a little, and when Malcolm said *Now you can let go*, he rubbed his pinked palms together and felt proud that he'd been useful. The lock drained out, and *The Girl Jane* lowered with the water, and the stone wall of the lock gleamed green with algae and rusted metal loops, and a man in a long boat said 'You can't do better than this,' his arm taking in the water, the sky, and the hollyhocks on the towpath.

A little later, Malcolm moored the boat in a scoop of water beside a willow tree, and a swan came looking for food and he shooed it away with his hand. Elspeth took out lunch, and gave Billy a smooth, cool, hard-boiled egg. She handed him a teaspoon with which to tap it, to help him crack and peel off the shell, and showed him how to dip it in salt. It was neat and precise. He looked up to see some teenagers coming past in a rowing boat. One of them got pushed in. *Charlie, you idiot*, he yelled, *I'll get you back. Waahh!* screamed one of the girls. Malcolm looked severe.

'It's foolish to behave like that, especially in rivers when you don't know the current.'

Billy checked himself. It had looked like fun. The boy was clambering back on board, wringing out his shirt and laughing; his skin shone wetly. The girl was holding on to his leg and laughing as well.

Everything, it seemed, for Malcolm, was more dangerous than Billy might have guessed. The river looked so lovely, but danger lurked everywhere. Across on the other bank, a man was treading water next to his boat. He was trying to encourage a small blonde girl to jump to him; his arms were raised out of the water. *You can do it, come on I'll catch you*, he was saying.

'I think it's safe here,' Elspeth said hesitantly. 'Look at that little one jumping in.'

'You never can tell,' said Malcolm. 'The surface of water is often deceptive, with weeds or even a supermarket trolley to tangle you beneath. It's always better to be safe than sorry. It's a good rule for life, Billy.'

Billy nodded. The little girl whooped and jumped.

They sailed on through a stretch of the river that was shallower, wider. People were paddling on one side, splashing each other with great arcs of their arms, silver droplets flying. Malcolm nodded to the opposite bank which had been churned and hooved by some cattle. 'The stock drink here,' he said, 'that can bring bacterial infection. Possibility of broken glass, sharp stones on the bottom too. People just don't take proper notice.'

Billy sat still. The river only seemed safe if you didn't actually touch it. Water splashed up on his arm and he wiped it carefully away. He held on to the chrome rail. The boat rocked beneath him. All the people shrieking and splashing and laughing and larking seemed to be in a different world, one that wasn't dangerous or threatening and which didn't need God to safeguard their each and every move. The sun felt too hot on his head.

'Watching the world go by . . .' said Elspeth, and Billy nodded. That was what they were doing, but was that always a good thing? The Bridges were kind. Their house was suffocating but they tried to be kind. There was no Horatio to upset. There was no one to upset. They didn't expect him to be brave or clever. But he wondered, with a start, his stomach spinning, his head feeling hotter, that if he lived with the Bridges was that exactly what he would do? Watch the world go by while other people larked in it; be afraid of what might be beneath the water while other people jumped in? He would sit stiller and stiller, and become more and more silent, and the silence and the stillness would seep first into his toes, and then his knees and his tummy and his arms and his shoulders, until it settled on him like ice and froze him entirely. He would not grow into a teenager who would tumble into a river and laugh that he was soaked through to his boxers, but would be like a cautious creature in a story who was made partly from stone.

He was aware of Elspeth looking at him. She was worrying at

her eye with her fingertip. Malcolm looked straight ahead, steering through the bathing people, serious and intent. Billy released his grip on the chrome rail and watched a swan glide by. He wondered if Andrew had caught the giant fish he hoped for. He imagined how Joey would run, top-speed, Victor Ludorum, into the water.

He tugged to loosen his life-jacket; it felt tight and restrictive. It was rubbing a patch of skin at the back of his neck. He fingered the seam. A life-jacket was evidently a sensible thing. Perhaps he was being too hasty, too quick to judge. Maybe the life-jacket was just like the Bridges: something Miriam hoped could save him from disaster. Safety first. That was one way of living.

And yet, if he thought back to the soup-dark, to the swamping feeling of being in the Bridges' house, he felt his throat full of thick, slippery pond weed. He cleared his throat – once, twice – and he saw Elspeth look at him straightaway, thinking he was going to speak. He looked down at his feet.

He'd have to find the words to tell Miriam, however unkind it felt. When she asked him about it, he would have to try and say. Even thinking about it, he could not meet Elspeth's eyes. Caroline Fraser had kissed him goodbye and then decided she didn't want to see him anymore. He looked up to the sky which, in the heat, now seemed a glittering blue. Beneath him, the water shone luminously clear. The life-jacket glared orange; he turned his face away. Perhaps it was silently scolding him for not seeing what might be best.

29

As Miriam drove into the car park, she could see Andrew loitering near the space where she usually parked.

'Let me guess,' she said, getting out of the car, 'out of the goodness of your heart and beyond your job spec you're doing a visual check on the tyre condition of all vehicles, which is going to mean I need to stand here for a few moments while you clock mine.'

Andrew knelt down by the front nearside tyre.

'That would be it,' he said, 'you can never be too careful with the depth of tread on your tyres.'

Miriam folded her arms and leaned against the driver's door.

'And, while I'm standing here, we might as well be chatting about anything or nothing in particular,' she said.

Andrew's voice was a little muffled from down by the wheel. 'Yes. I googled chronophage.'

'I'm sorry?'

'I googled what I think is chronophage and it's a clock in Cambridge with a locust grasshopper insect on the top which eats up time.'

'I see, that's unexpected. Surprising even. Google's a wonderful thing.'

'He's scared of it. Terrified.'

'I see.'

'The house too. He can't breathe in it, even though they are kind.'

Miriam's heart sank. Billy had given no clue as to this level of distress. He'd described them as 'not talky,' which didn't even begin to cover what he was evidently feeling. Andrew's voice had an urgency that wasn't present before. He also had a huge scratch across his face which she thought was best not mentioned.

'You have to do something,' he continued. 'He's properly troubled. And he's worried about telling you, because he knows you're trying hard.'

Miriam felt sick. As if the child didn't have enough to worry about; now he was worrying about what to say to her.

'I'll fix it, I'll sort it, don't worry,' she said wearily. 'I'm on to it. I'll juggle things around today.'

'Thank you,' said Andrew, his voice – surely not? – sounding emotional. He paused. He reappeared from behind the car. 'And sorry, I know I wasn't meant to be doing this, but your front two are actually down to between about one and two millimetres which is borderline. You might want to go to a garage and get them checked out – maybe your MOT is soon – because I don't think they'd pass like this.'

'Thank you.' She said it with a pulse of real gratitude. 'Case input and an actual tyre check. Beyond your job spec but very much appreciated.'

Miriam walked slowly to her office. A chronophage? Perhaps she should google it for herself. She looked back at her car, momentarily distracted by the thought of a life lived where a man who loved you might keep an eye on your car, top up the windscreen wash, and buy the right kind of oil. Possibly the same man who might empty the gutters of leaves at the end of the autumn, mow the lawn, rinse out the filters of the washing machine, and hammer in a hook while you stood there confirming the height you wanted the picture hung. All the things, Miriam reflected, which she paid people to do, and which didn't look like changing soon.

She sat down at her desk and thumbed through the pile of files. Today she was meant to be starting with a hospital visit to discuss a child protection case with a consultant paediatrician. There were two foster carer assessments to get through, plus a home visit to carry out where she was considering taking a child into care. That wasn't going to be pretty. And now Billy. Miriam decided to phone Meg. Perhaps she could stop by later and try and tease out what he was feeling. She already had enough information to stop this Introduction and move on. She could feel a tension headache starting to thrum in her temples. It was only nine-fifteen. Miriam scowled at her files. It seemed incredible that for such a neat pile, they could contain so much chaos, so many unresolved issues.

After school, the taxi dropped Billy off at Meg's, and the driver waved to Meg who was taking a baby back from its mother after a contact session.

She stood on the step, dandling the baby, as Billy walked up the path.

'How was school?' she asked. 'If you're hungry there's cake in the kitchen.'

'I'm starving. We played rounders in PE and I scored one.'

'That's great. Come inside, and don't forget to wash your hands first.'

Billy sat at the kitchen table and cut a slice of cake. Meg put the baby in a high chair and started feeding her some mashed banana.

'Miriam's stopping by later,' she said casually, 'to catch up.'

Billy paused, mid-chew. 'Why? Catch up on what?'

'Just everything, I think. How you are feeling about things.' Meg's lips were copying the baby's attempt to eat.

'I'm fine, everything's fine. Everything at the Bridges is fine.'

'Well, maybe that's what she just needs to check. It's always good to check.'

Billy paused. Meg seemed to be avoiding looking at him.

She scraped the spoon around the bowl of banana, fed the baby the last mouthful and used the tip of the spoon to clean her lips. 'Good girl, who's a good baby girl?' she said. 'That's all your lovely banana.' She didn't meet Billy's eye.

'Meg . . .'

He thought the tiniest raising of her eyebrow signalled that she was waiting to hear what came next.

'What happens if you know someone is kind, is trying really,

really hard but you still don't feel comfortable? Not uncomfortable, for some of the time, mostly outside in the fresh air, just not comfortable, especially inside. But it's not their fault.'

She looked at him intently. 'Then you say so. You just say so. You must say so.' She waggled the banana spoon like a baton at him. 'Miriam is listening. I'm listening. Comfortable is what counts. Comfortable, little man, is king.'

Billy reflected. 'When is Miriam coming?'

'Whatever time her crazy schedule allows. Soon as, I'm guessing.'

He went outside and waited on the garden step.

Miriam saw him in the Receiving Room. As soon as Meg showed her in, Billy felt his stomach start to churn. That meant Miriam wasn't thinking of being casual, or they'd be in the kitchen while Meg sorted out something, or sitting outside with Miriam drinking a mug of tea.

Miriam sat on the couch opposite him. She'd got his file on her lap which would mean she was taking notes. Billy bit his bottom lip.

'So,' Miriam said, gently but purposefully, 'the Bridges, shall we talk about the Bridges? About the Bridges, not what you eat there or the size of their carving knife? I think perhaps we ought to.'

Billy nodded.

'You start.' She leaned back on the couch.

'They're very kind,' he said.

'That's why I thought it was worth giving them a try.'

'They try very hard, what with draughts and Rice Krispies. They try very hard even though Elspeth doesn't make a big thing of it. She notices things. I know that.'

Miriam waited. If she kept her tongue between her teeth, she thought, no words could spill out.

'It feels ungrateful not to be happy there when there are nice things: the raspberry picking in the allotment, the boat, Malcolm teaching me to play draughts and stuff . . .'

'Stuff . . . ?'

'Stuff like that.'

'But . . .' She clamped her teeth down harder. She thought she might draw blood.

'But . . . but it's very quiet. Very still. Elspeth . . .'

'Elspeth?'

'She would be a deer.'

'I'm sorry, a deer? What, like an animal deer?'

Billy nodded.

He'd caught the measure of her – Miriam could see it – hesitant, wary.

'A deer. I see. I guess that's tricky. I can see how that would be tricky. What about Malcolm?'

'He tries to play. I think he wants it to be like when he was a boy, with all the things he did and liked.'

'Could you imagine them being your forever family? Would you want that or not?'

Billy bit his lip, looked down at the carpet, and shook his head. He started to cry. He hadn't kissed Elspeth goodbye which would have been worse, but he had eaten her cooking, and learned how to peel and salt a hard-boiled egg. When Miriam collected him after the boat trip, he had waved goodbye, and Elspeth was still holding the picnic basket so she hadn't quite managed to work her hand free. She had half-waved back, but was trying to do it properly. The basket handle was all tangled on her wrist.

'Elspeth bought the Rice Krispies and the hot chocolate, and Malcolm, with his tin soldiers . . . They will think . . .' he faltered.

'They will understand,' Miriam said. 'I will make sure they understand. That's what I'm here for. Thank you for telling me. Truly, thank you for telling me what you really feel.'

She went back to the office to pick up some other files on the way home. On her answer phone was a message from Malcolm suggesting that Billy might want to stay again on Friday night.

Miriam picked up the phone. She hoped it would be Malcolm who answered. To tell Elspeth, who would forever appear in her mind as a deer now, would be to inflict some kind of invisible bruise.

30

Elspeth came back from the supermarket with more groceries than usual. She'd allowed herself to stand in front of the biscuit fixture and pick some chocolate-covered bars. Wasn't that the kind of thing children ate between meals? She'd bought popcorn which apparently just popped in the saucepan. She'd bought Nutella spread which Billy mentioned he had for breakfast at his foster carer's. By the checkout there had been a special offer on some wide plastic bats with a soft neon ball. She'd put a set in the trolley thinking that might be something that could be done in the garden. She'd bought cartons of smoothie which said they were *for kids*. She'd shopped slowly, carefully, looking at a whole new range of eating possibilities. Beefburgers? Finger rolls for sausages? Coco Pops? There was even cheese that came in strings.

When she came through the door, Malcolm was sitting with the tin of soldiers in his lap. He was staring straight ahead.

'Billy's not coming at the weekend,' he said. 'The little lad won't be coming again.'

His eyes were wet with tears. She went to him, wordlessly, and sat beside him in the gathering shadows.

In the morning, Elspeth woke early, swept the kitchen floor in smooth, methodical strokes, tied on her apron and made chicken and leek pie. She made the pastry with lard, and sliced carefully through its composed marbled whiteness. Beneath her fingers it felt cool and measured. She balled the pastry and held it up like an offering. An offering to God, she thought, to Malcolm, or to the altar of her life lived in domestic quietude? She would have liked to utter a prayer but none came. Beyond the kitchen window a bird offered one of its own, the melody as limpid as the pastry was solid in her palms.

Billy did not want to come. He did not want them to want him. It would be dressed in kind words. A feedback report would be delivered in the post, or perhaps handed to them, hastily, slightly apologetically, by Miriam. Whatever it said, however they dressed it, she would see it for what it was. She and Malcolm, together, did not strike the right note. It was not for want of trying. Their life was plain, but not plain in a way which gave satisfaction, like a slice of Madeira cake served on a white plate. No, it was plain in a way that spoke of severity, of a lack of perception, of humour, or warmth. Of a life which smothered spontaneity even though it was not their intent. A life dominated, certainly for Malcolm, by a God who welcomed silence amidst the babble of the world, but who expected life beyond actual worship to be conducted in hushed tones. And she herself was at fault, she felt that with conviction, for having spent her entire adulthood steeped in her inner life, which, she thought now, she would never have the courage to express.

Elspeth stood in her kitchen and thought of Billy's face on the boat, when a slow horror seemed to be dawning on him that their life might become his. *You can jump in too,* she'd so wanted to say as he watched the blonde girl jump into the outstretched arms of her father. Those words would not come. She could not say them, and Malcolm would never think them, and never see them for what they might signify to a child. Her eyes had brimmed with tears as she felt the boy see the measure of them, properly see them, his silence speaking to her more eloquently than any words he might use. He was not settling for the spectator seats; in her heart, she thought, she would endeavour to find gladness in that. She would hope for him to live life at full tilt; for any wounds in his own heart to heal so that he would live fully.

She recalled a young man she'd once seen walking in a meadow in May who suddenly, spontaneously, leapt into the air and kicked his legs out like a frog. He whooped with what seemed to be luminous joy, joy that rocked round the meadow, shivered through the froth of cow parsley, and made her feel, at the fringe of the field, old and parched. What age had she been then – thirty? Thirty-two?

Billy did not want to come. There was prescience in his decision. She envisaged her table at supper that night; the chicken and leek pie neat before Malcolm, their plates evenly spaced, the cream pitcher filled with water. She saw Malcolm's hands, clasped, as they would be, for Grace; his fingers webbed together, their solidity and his humility seemingly at odds. He would say Grace, the words as familiar and softened as well-thumbed coins, and she would sit beside him, as she had done each night of their married life, and the prospect of a child accompanying them would recede further and further until she wondered if even the hope of it would fade from her memory. This would be their life, together, the one she had chosen, and she prayed, in words that came to her as the blackbird stopped singing outside, that her heart would be reconciled to it, that she would not be audacious and question why, and that she would not dream of a sweet-faced boy-child holding out his palm to receive a softly speckled egg, or words which tumbled unbidden and spoke hotly, quick-lipped, of a life lived otherwise.

3I

'Properly over-k-dover?' said Joey, the next day at break-time. 'We didn't see that coming.'

Billy shook his head.

'Or,' Joey said, crouching to peer up into Billy's downcast face, 'you didn't say so if you did.'

Billy shrugged.

'But the search, the search, you know . . .' Joey said valiantly.

Billy shrugged again. The words were starting to ring hollow. Lord Sugar's Roller was disappearing over the horizon.

'What reasons?' asked Joey. 'What reasons did they give?'

Billy turned away. 'No reasons. It was more me this time.'

'You? Even after the boat, the lemonade, the triumph of weeds, the Queen of Puddings, the trying to teach you to play draughts?'

'Uh-huh.'

Joey reflected for a moment. 'I'm guessing you had reasons.'

Billy nodded.

'Reasons you might want to talk about?' Joey asked in a brighter tone.

Billy shook his head.

'I might have to talk to Mrs Bailey.' Joey smiled. 'You know, when she said to watch out for signs that you were stopping talking. Maybe there's been a bit of a delay.'

'Dot dot,' Billy responded.

'Dot,' said Joey. 'Why didn't you like it?'

Billy looked across towards the chain-link fence. 'Just stuff,' he said slowly.

Joey nodded, looking down at the bark chippings. They sat side by side in silence.

'They were properly kind,' Billy added. 'Properly kind.'

'Sometimes,' Joey said softly, 'grown-ups get things wrong. Even when they don't mean to. That's what my Nan said about my sister's bad boyfriend.'

Billy nodded. If he closed his eyes, the grasshopper locust no longer gleamed golden on the inside of his eyelids. That was a relief. He thought of Malcolm, crouched on the carpet, his great hand swatting away his forlorn toy soldiers. Elspeth, her grey eyes watching him through the dim, green light that seemed to have been poured from a forest floor into their house.

'Sometimes,' he said, 'they want you to be like they were.'

Joey rocked back on his heels. 'So is Miriam on to it again?'

'At this rate, Miriam's going to be always on to it. She'll have introduced me to everyone in the area who wrote to Social Services for a child, a dog or a cat.'

'Maybe the next one will be it,' Joey said firmly. He patted Billy on the back.

Billy's heart sank. This was a disaster. Now Joey was feeling sorry for him, instead of thinking it was all high jinks.

32

Andrew pulled up outside the care home where Lorna worked. Her car was being serviced so he was picking her up.

He came to a halt in the circular driveway, and looked across the gravel to the bay windows of the day room. He could make out Lorna, standing by a chair, leaning forward, her hands on her knees, talking animatedly to one of the residents. When he looked more carefully, he could discern that the woman she was talking to wore a sun visor – Edith, one of Lorna's favourites. She wore the visor to help regulate the light for her failing sight. Lorna said it gave her a raffish look, an air of someone who might just have walked off the golf course, which, as Edith was ninety-five, would have taken some doing. Edith was American, and would sometimes say to Lorna *Lord, my sweetie, what I would give for a decently made vodka martini*. Lorna would laugh, and offer her tea instead, and help lift her from her armchair to the table. Andrew watched now as Lorna leaned forward and carefully manoeuvred Edith up and on to her feet. Should Lorna still be doing that, he wondered, lifting people in and out of chairs and beds, on and off commodes? Edith was now standing beside her: he saw Lorna straighten her uniform over her bump. Edith reached out and patted it, and said something which made them both laugh. Perhaps he should talk to her about stopping the lifting. Maybe she should check with the midwife?

Lorna said ageing was mostly a process of getting lighter; flesh, bone density, muscle solidity decreasing until, she said, lifting the very oldest of the residents was like lifting a desiccated child. Skin, she said, so thin as to be translucent. When someone died, she and the other carers adhered to the practice of opening the window just after the passing. *It makes sense,* she told him once, *all that getting lighter, all that evaporating. It feels part of a process which is completed by letting the soul fly away.*

Andrew got out of the van and walked towards a tree with a bench around it which formed the turning circle of the drive. Ridiculous, he thought, as he approached it, to be scanning the roots for any protruding paper. He was becoming obsessed. He sat down on the bench and stretched out his legs. They didn't feel light; he didn't feel light at all. He felt heavy and strong and solid and muscular. It begged the question, he thought, sitting and rubbing his quads, how, in what was deemed the prime of life, you were meant to turn it to best effect. What did his old headmaster say? *Go out into the world and do well, but more importantly go out into the world and do good?* And what form might that take, he wondered, when his day job, unlike Lorna's, dealt with nails and screws rather than the business of doing good?

He started as a pair of hands was placed over his eyes.

'Penny for them,' Lorna said behind him, and kissed his cheek.

He smiled.

'No, I mean it,' she said. 'Penny for them,' and she flipped him a coin from her pocket with her finger and thumb. 'What were you so deep in thought about?'

He shrugged.

'Nice try,' she said, 'but you know I can't bear it when you go all silent on me. Spill.'

He took a deep breath. 'I was thinking about being a parent, whether you should try to know stuff, you know, like what a particular bird call is, or the name of the highest mountain in Spain. Is that being a good parent?'

'I expect good parenting takes lots of different forms, some of which aren't anything to do with knowledge. And anyway, Professor, isn't that a little premature? From what I gather, we've got about a year of babbling and just working out whether he or she is hungry, wet, too hot or too cold, with maybe a colicky tummy thrown in to confuse us and then it's mostly words like ball, teddy or biscuit. I don't think we'll have any problems naming those.'

Andrew smiled, but persisted. 'But older, if he's – or if she's – older, what then? Or when he or she is older, I mean.'

'Then you learn stuff together, find out stuff together. Go on holiday to Spain and read a guide book which tells you the highest mountain, or buy an app of bird song and sit on a river bank listening until you've cracked which one it is. Aren't children meant to be super-curious? I think they're supposed to want to find out things for themselves.

'And anyway,' she continued, 'I'm not sure this is what should be worrying you now. Aren't you meant to be concerned with how much sex you'll be getting, or whether I'll suddenly love the baby more than I love you? That's what the book says you might be thinking about.'

'Ah, but that's because most men reading that bit haven't had an ante-natal pep talk about how I'm going to wake up feeling different and responsible and protective the day after the baby's born.'

'Sounds to me like you're feeling that already, which is a bit premature as we've still got twelve weeks to go. Are you aiming for super-dad? Or are you just trying to work out exactly what that might mean?'

'Some of the notes, you know, the notes he puts in the tree,' (and here he avoided meeting her eyes,) 'he talks about what a dad does. I guess he's working it out for himself, what with his own doing a disappearing act before he was even born.'

'And what's he decided?'

'Playing cricket, that seems to be the ticket, saying *howzat*, and *my boy*. And making things for them . . .' (and here, curiously he still could not meet her eye, and he found himself gesturing towards her stomach, and trying to maintain the evenness of his voice) 'stuff that shows you are pleased they are there.'

'It all sounds a good recipe, nothing too complicated, thank goodness. It sounds like he notices a lot.'

She reached forward and placed her hand on his.

'Are you okay? I'm not sure where all this is coming from, or where it's going.'

'Yes, I'm fine, of course I'm okay.'

He fixed his gaze on his van, and tried to suppress inexplicable emotion.

'Is there anything you're not telling me?' Lorna persisted.

She looked at him carefully.

'No, of course not. Too many random things just crashing about in my head. It's been a weird kind of day. Let's go home, shall we? Are you starving?'

As he started the van, Andrew was aware that he hadn't felt able to say Billy's name. What was that about?

'Shall we think about baby names again tonight?' Lorna was saying. 'My favourite is still Sophie for a girl if you're really not going to let me have Freya.

Andrew stared fixedly at the road. They had their baby to think about. Lorna had their baby to give birth to. Thinking about anything else was stupid, totally stupid.

33

Miriam stood in front of her washing machine and stripped to her bra and pants. Just like the man in the Levi's ad years ago, she thought, adding detergent and starting the programme, except less well-toned, and he, presumably, hadn't emerged, reeking, from one of the filthiest flats she'd ever encountered. She'd applied for an Emergency Protection Order on the spot; whipped the children away and into foster care. The mother had screamed abuse, an Alsatian had looked as if it was going to take a chunk out of her, and a pale-faced, nit-ridden, urine-stinking two year old had sat in the middle of a shit-strewn kitchen floor and wailed. The five year old was licking the turned-out inside of an empty packet of crisps and wearing only a pair of grubby socks. Words had almost failed her. *How can you, how can you?* she would have liked to say to the woman, but instead she marshalled all her professional vocabulary, called for back-up, got the children into the car and drove off as the woman banged on the roof shouting *Fuck off, you fucking bitch.* Some of the neighbours came out to watch; one threw a can at her bonnet and Coke spumed up all over her windscreen.

Miriam walked upstairs and into the shower. She turned the temperature to the hottest and scrubbed the place off her. She rubbed at her limbs with a mitt until they were red from both friction and heat. Afterwards she wrapped herself in a white towel and lay on the bathroom tiles. She let the mild warmth of the underfloor heating begin to dry her. She rolled back her shoulder blades and tried to lie flat. Her left calf was crooked around the foot of the basin. It was exhausting, completely bloody exhausting. Other people's crap. Other people's inexcusable parenting.

The government's latest initiative involved a team of do-gooders who would turn up at flats and good-humouredly and sagely give lessons in how to mop a floor, or do laundry. A power-washer, a fumigator, an industrial disinfectant sprayer; they would have been more apt for where she'd been today. And perhaps, for good measure, an anti-contamination suit. The labours of Hercules, she thought; didn't he divert a river to clean the king's stables of horse shit? That would be handy; a raging torrent to summon up at will. An additional benefit would be drowning some of the neighbours.

She settled into the floor and closed her eyes. Her left calf was beginning to sing with cramp. Sleep was a temptation, at ten past seven on a Tuesday evening on her bathroom floor. When did her life become like this? Other single women her age might be dressing to go out to dinner. One of her lovers had accused her of paying him insufficient attention. She wondered if the same accusation still applied, but in relation to herself. It was wearily, compulsively, soul-destroyingly all consuming, this attempt to fix what would always mushroom beyond fixing. Her mother said once, a little tartly, *There'll be no room for marrying a man if you continue to be married to your job.*

She sat up and began to towel-dry her hair. She should call her mother and check she was okay. She should call Meg, and check Billy was okay; she hadn't had a minute and it had been on her list of things to do today. There was never the time to follow anything through, which was a separate endeavour from covering your back, for which many of her colleagues displayed genius talent.

She'd written to Elspeth and Malcolm, and said how sorry she was that it didn't seem to be a match. Malcolm's evident distress on the phone had almost undone her. *Well, that is a surprise,* he'd said, *we thought . . . but never mind what we thought. He's a lovely lad,* he'd added, *we enjoyed very much having him here.*

She was vexed as to what she might do with them now; maybe she could find a slightly younger girl? A little girl whom Elspeth might teach to knit and make flapjacks and scones, who might

love their quietness and their big, safe, solid house. She determined not to give up on the Bridges. After days like today, what
they had to offer was thrown into even sharper relief.

And as for Billy, she was mulling, mulling. She walked into
her bedroom, tossed down the towel and chose soft and comfortable clothes. Was it possible, she thought, to reach a lifestage
where wearing anything with a waistband in the evening seemed
intolerable? She went down to the kitchen and poured herself a
glass of Pinot Grigio from the fridge, and picked up a file she'd
brought home from work. No doubt if she had children of her
own to come back to and put to bed, the file would have stayed
on her office desk. She sighed and started reading.

Phil and Zoe Marshall. Sheila called them Brangelina. They'd
adopted three children from different countries already. It could
be argued they had form. Would an English boy fit into what
they called their *pick and mix* family? There'd be no single child
to antagonise, no oppressive adult-only house. Maybe it would
work?

Miriam opened the back door into her tiny garden and sat
down on a rickety chair. It wobbled as she adjusted its hinge. If
she had a partner, she wondered, would they go, at a weekend,
to a garden centre or to a funky artisanal store, and buy an
outdoor table, perhaps four chairs, choosing them carefully but
with a degree of merriment? Would they sit, on a summer evening
like this, having added a candle and some cut flowers arranged
in an old tomato can, and talk through their day, maybe one ear
cocked for the sound of infant wailing from the bedroom. It was
becoming harder to imagine; harder to convince herself as a
possibility. She'd have to get her skates on. She trailed her hand
through a clump of lavender, releasing a waft of scent into the
air, and tried to banish the thought of what would, no question,
be a heavenly cigarette. Even if she did marry someone, her
insight into other people's messes should have tutored her on the
more likely reality. They'd probably be quibbling about whose
turn it was to go up and try to settle the baby, or he would be
complaining that all she did was come home from work and

dump all her crap on him and expect him to function as her own personal focus group, miraculously coming up with the correct solution. Oliver, a couple of years ago, who wasn't so much the one who got away as the one who was married already, used to ruffle her hair, say *Rim, don't stress it*, and then have fabulous sex with her which was certainly distracting and absorbing if not professionally conclusive. Internet dating; her mother had actually suggested internet dating, and then gone one further and suggested a speed-dating evening that was happening in the town hall. *That would suit you Miriam*, she said, *what with you always being in such a hurry.*

Phil and Zoe Marshall. When she had assessed them, Zoe had asked her to call her Zu-zu. Miriam conspicuously hadn't done so. *No thank you*, she'd refrained from saying crisply. She'd bridled at Zoe's assumption that she was the one dictating terms. Zoe had been on a shaman retreat in the Welsh mountains three years ago, and the shaman had told her that four delphinium-blue lights were coming from around the globe to take seed in her womb. That, and something about a shell from the ocean and a whale bone, but Zoe's memory had gone fuzzy on the detail. At the time she hadn't eaten for three days and nights, so Miriam was impressed she had any recall at all. In the same position, Miriam was confident she'd have taken a bite out of the yurt. Phil's view on child rearing, now that three of the delphinium lights had come home to roost, was that all a child metaphorically needed was a smart phone and a wigwam, and this spectrum meant all bases covered. He owned a hugely successful company which designed subscription internet services targeted at the under sevens so maybe he had form there too.

She put down her file and realised she was hungry. She ought to make herself some supper. Perhaps she should call her friend Ruthie and see if she'd like to come round for some pasta. She went inside to the kitchen and picked up her BlackBerry. She tried to shake off her despondency. On current form, it was likely, should any decent man appear on the horizon, he'd realise quite quickly that beneath her bravado, she might require him to ride to the rescue. And that perception, she thought ruefully, would no doubt result in him abruptly turning tail.

Buck up, she said out loud to herself. *Buck up*. She'd always liked that old-fashioned expression; it conjured up reserves of doughty, emotional resilience and can-do. It was better than *Fuck up*, which she acknowledged she was more likely to do, or indeed *Fuck off*, which was where she had started her day.

She picked up the Marshalls' file and tried to concentrate on them again. Self-absorption, she'd long ago decided, was mostly a ticket to nowhere and best avoided. The Marshalls, the Marshalls. It was important – she dug deep for her professional demeanour – that whether she liked the prospective parents was of no significance. If they had passed the assessment, that was an affirmation of their worth and intent. The question was not whether she liked them but whether Billy did. It would pay her to keep that front of mind.

34

Billy was in Miriam's office after school. He looked a little dejected. Now was not the time, she thought, to ask him his view of the process. That he had been so visibly upset at the prospect of disappointing the Bridges had made her want to hug him. Looking at him, hunched and crestfallen in the chair opposite her, she reminded herself *Boundaries, boundaries*.

'Best foot forward? Spirits restored and ready for the off?' she said.

Billy nodded.

'No battle fatigue?'

He shook his head.

'Really?'

Billy nodded. 'Really.'

'Then onwards and upwards. We are going to crack this, believe me. We are going to find you a lovely home and a fab forever family. Say *Yes, Miriam, I believe you.*'

His eyes fleetingly met hers. 'Yes, Miriam I believe you.'

(Did he? She wasn't sure she believed herself.)

'Then we're putting our best foot forward, are we agreed?'

It would feel fitting, she thought, to march, in unison, perhaps once round the room. Maybe it would perk up her own flagging faith, if not his.

He'd nodded again. Miriam thought genuine enthusiasm might be too much to expect, but at least his spirits seemed to have rallied since he came into the room.

'Okay, so here we go. They're called Phil and Zoe Marshall. Shall I tell you why I think it might be a match?'

He gave the smallest flicker of assent.

'There's already three children, all adopted from different parts of the world. You'd be the only English one, and also the eldest, which could, in these circumstances, be a benefit. There's a little girl from India, called Shamina, and she's . . . let me check . . . eight; there's a boy called Dimitri from Russia and he's six; and there's another little girl, aged nearly three, from Croatia, who is called Nancy, although that might be an English version of a Croatian name, I don't know. There was meant to be a little Mexican baby at one time, but I don't know what happened there. Anyway, it means that everybody's adopted, so no cuckoo boy anxieties.'

Billy raised his eyebrow.

'Just a term we sometimes use,' she said, hastily.

'And,' she continued, 'because it's a house full of children it's definitely not quiet; not quiet at all. Zoe is a psychotherapist, which means someone who works with how people feel, and she works mostly from home. Phil has his own internet company – something children younger than you can subscribe to, you know, make their own house or look after a cyber pet. They decided they want what they call a rainbow family, and that's why they've adopted children from three countries.'

Miriam tried to suppress the memory of Phil, over a glass of Sancerre at their assessment, saying to her *The thing we all must recognise, Miriam, is that need works in a global market-place, it knows no national boundaries.* She'd nodded warmly. The Sancerre had gone to her head because she hadn't eaten lunch.

'A rainbow family?' Billy was saying.

'Yes, you know, all colours, all nationalities, all beliefs, one big merged rainbow.'

Billy's expression was unreadable. She made an arcing, sweeping gesture with her hand.

'Rainbow family,' he said again.

'That would be it. Worth a go, do you think?'

'If you say so, if you think so.'

Miriam achieved her most enthusiastic expression. 'Phil says if a child's got a wigwam and a smart phone, they've got everything covered. You can be the judge of that.' Billy blinked. Clubhouse? Wigwam? The Introduction process seemed to be revealing itself as a complex sequence of dens.

'A smart phone and a wigwam,' Joey said, sitting on the bench at break the next day. 'Bingo. Maybe this is where the gifts finally come in.'

'I don't think he means it like that. I don't think the other children actually have that. I asked Miriam. She says it means that children should have some traditional toys *and* technology so that they grow up and can use it in jobs.'

'So no gifts then.'

'No gifts.'

'But being able to use apps and still climb trees.'

'I think that's what it might mean.'

'Do you think there's a Find a Family app?'

'Miriam would be on to it if there were. My face would be all over it I'm guessing.'

'Perhaps you could suggest it to Phil – a new business idea. Not mind a pet, find a family. You could pass that on.'

Billy thumped his arm gently. At least Joey was still trying.

Billy laid the table for just him and Meg that night. The babies had both gone back to their mothers, who, Meg said, had straightened themselves out. Jayden had gone to a long-term foster carer, because it looked as if her mum wasn't going to straighten herself out in the foreseeable future. Matt, the teenage boy, had decided to give it a go with an aunt, and everything else was, as Meg put it, quiet on that front.

Billy tore off two squares of kitchen roll for them. Meg was flipping fish in a frying pan.

'Miriam says I'm going to the rainbow family house on Saturday.'

'Uh-huh.'

'The little girl, the one from Croatia, it's her third birthday, so they are having a party in the garden. I'm going to the party.'

'That sounds nice.'

'There won't be wigwams I don't think.'

'More likely a cake, I'm guessing.' Meg turned the fish on to the plates. 'Are you looking forward to it?' She asked as they sat down at the table.

'High wire, cricket match, Italian restaurant, lunch, allotment, Sunday lunch, sleepover, day on the boat, birthday party. Joey says Billy Morris's search for a new family goes on.'

Meg smiled, reached over and ruffled his hair. 'You will find someone,' she said. 'Someone is going to come along and scoop you right up. I know it.'

Billy cut into his fish. Perhaps it was trickier than anyone thought. Meg had been Introduced to him a lot, and she didn't look like she was thinking about offering to scoop him up and keep him. You might think, after all the years of children coming to and fro, it would be appealing to choose just one. She evidently wasn't tempted, which wasn't a good sign.

Later, in bed, he rummaged in his pillowcase and took out *Dear Zoo*. The giraffe got sent back because it was too tall. He pressed the audio button. It whinnied and whickered in a way that he'd never been sure was very giraffe-like. The Bridges hadn't sent him back. Perhaps he'd sent himself back because they made him too jumpy, just like the frog. Maybe the Marshalls would send him back because he was too dull for their rainbow. He was sure there were animals at the zoo that nobody really wanted to look at, animals they walked straight past, searching for something more spectacular.

Four more days of school and then he wouldn't see Joey anymore. In the holidays he went with his dad in his van, or to his nan's or to one of his grown-up sisters'. Miriam might go away on holiday, and probably Meg too. They might have to send him somewhere else, and give him a different key worker. It would be like a game of pass the parcel, but without it being any fun. He'd be like a gift in the middle that no one really wanted.

At school once, in Year One, they'd had to tell the teaching assistant about anything they found tricky, and she wrote it in a speech bubble next to a face with a downturned expression. Billy had said to her – he remembered her writing it carefully – *Joining in*. In the whirl of the playground, he had been unsure how to join in. Maybe not much had changed. His mum, who didn't properly know she had him, was gone, and now he was by himself and still not sure how to join in.

35

Zoe Marshall rolled up her yoga mat with a satisfying flick. She'd meditated, stretched, drunk her white tea, and felt ready for the day. She could hear Phil giving the children breakfast in the kitchen. Such a chattering, such busyness. It lifted her heart each time she thought of where they'd come from, how scarred they'd been, and how careful yet joyful their progression had been to what seemed to be miraculous normality. It was so life-affirming, she'd decided, to believe each day in the possible. Miriam Riley, who was always somewhat negatively terse, might benefit from adopting a similar philosophy. If Zoe could think of a way to suggest it, she was sure Miriam would be the long-term beneficiary.

She went upstairs to her bathroom and stood in front of the mirror. She gazed steadfastly at herself. Phil's birthday card to her said *Fab, fit and forty*. She tilted her chin. She applied her moisturiser with smooth, even, strokes, cleaned and flossed her teeth, and started to get dressed. Miriam Riley had called her about a child. An English child – that would strike a different note, even if she didn't really want to think about it in that way.

Zoe wasn't sure it was helpful to think of things in nationalistic terms; it was regrettably simplistic. She'd spent so much of her childhood living in different places because her father was an army officer, and then for part of her twenties she'd lived all over the States. She'd grown up, she'd liked to think, with a malleable sense of nationality. Nationality often emphasised differences between people rather than similarities, and if only the whole world could focus on what it shared, rather than how it differed, she was sure it would become a safer place. Cultural encounters, she would often say, do not have to result in conflict.

Another bugbear was faith. One Boxing Day, in a particularly robust conversation with her sister, Zoe argued it was best to see all faiths as basically the same but with different terms and conditions. Tess said that if you believed in everything you actually believed in nothing. Zoe had taken this to heart and subsequently evolved her own doctrine. It was a-religious, a-political, and based on something Tony Blair said about shining a light into dark places. That would be her mission. Search and rescue. As part of it, she resolved not to have any children of her own – Phil had been surprisingly compliant when she suggested it – and instead to adopt, adopt and heal. The world was full of children who would benefit from her skill set, the mind frame and sensitive emotional energy. The retreat in the Welsh hills with the shaman had confirmed it was all meant to be. She felt it with real zeal. So far it had worked with three; now maybe Miriam Riley would bring on the fourth.

She felt excited, slipping on her bracelets, lacing up her wedge trainers. Other women might become teary at the thought of children in need, but that wasn't her. She liked to think of it as a call to arms (if that wasn't too patriarchal, too military an image, and even if it were, she could excuse it on the grounds of being an officer's daughter). She would competently rally to another child who needed sorting and fixing. Without being smug, she could give herself – and Phil – a little credit. Three orphans successfully transitioned – that was how she saw it. Three damaged children robustly and happily – even now – scooting around outside with Phil, their laughter threading up through the wisteria beneath her window. Bring it on, she thought, applying lip gloss and giving her hair a confident tousle.

Billy woke up still tired. He gave himself a shake. Maybe the Marshalls were going to be it, maybe today would be properly good.

He got dressed. Meg was taking him to the Family Centre so that Miriam could take him to the Marshalls'.

A little later, he waited by the tree. Miriam was inside the

Centre getting a file, even though it was a Saturday and she wasn't meant to be working. Billy waited some more. Her phone was probably ringing, even though that wasn't meant to happen on a Saturday either.

A writer had come into school on Tuesday to read them a story. It was from a Greek myth and was about the Minotaur and his maze of a den. After killing the monster, Theseus the hero found his way out by following thread he'd unravelled on the way in and which led straight back to the entrance. Billy thought about it now. Thread wouldn't be useful in his own case. He wasn't so much finding his way out or on to somewhere else; he just kept coming back to the tree, to a scrubby piece of grass at the Family Centre, and waiting for Miriam. He touched the tree carefully, and took out his pen. The tree could be forgiven for wondering if there would ever be good news.

When Andrew arrived later to pick up some pliers he'd left in the tool store, Lorna asked, 'Can I see the tree? Which one is it?'

Andrew hesitated. Even with Lorna it felt like a betrayal. She was looking at him expectantly. He pointed.

'Do you think there will be a new note?'

'We can check, if you want to. He's off somewhere again today, Miriam mentioned it to me. He might have been here, I don't know.'

He bent down and reached into the hole. He flipped through the small bundle. There was a new one, folded in half. He opened it out.

'What does he say?'

'Just one thing. *It's like pass the parcel, only I'm not a good present.*'

Lorna put her hands to her mouth. 'But that's awful . . . That's so sad . . . You should tell Miriam that.'

'Why, so she can stop looking, stop sending him anywhere, and then he won't have the chance of another family at all.'

'But it's awful that he feels that way about himself. The process is making him feel worse.'

'And do you think me telling Miriam makes any real differ-ence? It hasn't changed anything so far.' Andrew was surprised by the heat in his tone.

'You don't need to be angry.' She cradled her bump. 'It just seems so unfair. Our baby is never going to feel that. He or she will know, all the time, that they're really loved and wanted. Whatever happens financially, wherever we live, whatever. Unconditional.' She spoke with determination, wiping her eyes with the back of her hand.

Andrew pulled her close. 'You're going to be a brilliant mum. Miriam would clone you if she could. That would be the perfect solution for all the children on her books.'

'Whatever my mother . . .' Lorna said, stifling a sob.

'Hush, I know, I know,' Andrew said. 'Don't. Come on.' He kissed her hair. 'Surely we can do better than this on a Saturday afternoon. Let's go somewhere – you choose where. I don't want you to be upset or I'll wish I hadn't shown you. I'm trying to work out a way to help him.'

Lorna smoothed back her hair and re-tied it.

'I cry in the supermarket, I cry at the news, I cry at work when a relative says goodbye at the end of a visit if their parent is unwell. Sobbing rather than blooming; you'd think my hormones could have made the distinction.'

'Sobbing *and* blooming I'd say, although maybe not looking your best right now.'

He took out a handkerchief and wiped her eyes.

'I love you,' he said, taking her into his arms. 'If you were a parcel, I'd be holding on for dear life.'

She felt cocooned by his body. She could feel his heart beating steadily, and pressed her ear to its pulse. There was about him a new awkwardness when he mentioned Billy. He seemed to shrink from even saying his name.

The baby would soon explode into their lives, changing every-thing. She pressed herself closer to his heart, soothed by the steadiness of its beat.

36

Billy had been inside the Marshalls' primrose-yellow hallway for less than five minutes before he was aware that Malcolm quoting a psalm as he left the house didn't even begin to cover it. Painted all along the wall of the hallway – as Zoe enthusiastically told him – were extracts from the Bible, the Koran, the Torah, the Vedas and the Tripitaka. *I think we've got it covered,* she said cheerfully with a wave of her hand at the words, *whatever your creed, we're good with it.* Suffer little children, Billy read, to come unto me.

Next to all the scripture extracts was a huge map of the world, and Zoe had painted on the geographical origin of each of the children, and then drawn arcing bright blue lines to the middle of England. This was told to me, she said a little mysteriously. *That's showing all my children, winging their way home.*

Billy thought it looked like an advertisement for an airline. If he came to live here, his trajectory would be shown as a straight line, a bit like the space shuttle. It wouldn't look, he thought, studying the map intently, quite so cool.

'This is Nancy,' Zoe said, pushing forward a chubby little girl. 'She had a horrible time for the first eighteen months of her life, but we've worked on it, and here she is, smiling and happy.'

Billy nodded.

'Ah,' Zoe said, 'you nodded. Just to reassure you, you don't have to agree with what I say. If you think something else, say it, just say it, that's the deal in this house. Every feeling is worth airing, every thought worth sharing. It's all healing.'

Billy checked the reflex to nod again. He looked at Miriam. It sounded exhausting. He also wasn't sure, from the expression on

Miriam's face, whether she was up for sharing whatever she was thinking at that moment. She looked as if she were chewing a thistle.

'Let me introduce you to the other kids; they're dying to meet you. They're out in the garden.'

Shamina and Dimitri were playing on a huge chequered rug. They had a dressing-up box, and were wearing velvet cloaks. Shamina was holding out a crown.

'Good sharing, Shamina,' said Zoe. 'Are you inviting Billy into your game? That's great. Here Billy, come and take the crown.'

Billy stepped forward. The crown had three words written on it: King, Rajah, Tsar.

'That's everybody's word for king,' Zoe explained, 'so that they stay connected to their cultural origins. I'm having a little trouble finding out the Croatian equivalent. Phil thinks it might be the Holy Roman Emperor but we'll figure it out and have it sorted by the time Nancy is old enough to understand.'

Enthusiastic, Billy thought. Zoe was definitely enthusiastic. She tipped her head on one side like a bird when she talked, and her eyes were a bright, clear blue. She stood in front of a leafy bush, and as she moved, her arm disturbed its branches. The dappled light within it shifted fleetingly and he was reminded of Elspeth. Zoe's beaming confidence blotted her out.

'All Nancy's little friends from nursery are coming in half an hour, and I've just got the cake to do and the little jelly boats. Maybe you'd like to give me a hand. Shamina, do you want to help Mummy ice your sister's cake?'

She turned to Miriam. 'This might be a good time for you to go if Billy is comfortable with that?'

Billy thought Miriam looked taken aback. People didn't give her tips very often. She looked at him.

'What do you think, Billy? Do you want me to stay or are you okay with helping with the cake and the jelly boats like Zoe suggests?'

Billy nodded.

Miriam looked at him intently. He nodded again.

Zoe said 'I think that will be for the best; it'll give us a chance just to be all together without any external pressure.'

Miriam looked as if she might disagree with being called external pressure. She took a deep breath.

'Have a lovely party, Nancy,' she said. Billy wondered when she walked out if it might be what was called turning on her heel. It was certainly brisk; Zoe didn't seem to notice.

'Here's what you need to do,' Zoe said brightly, taking out a plate from the fridge. 'See, I cut oranges in half, scooped out all the fruit, filled the halves with red jelly, and now it's set I've sliced them in quarters to make little boats. Aren't they cute? Then all you have to do is take one of these cocktail sticks, and thread on a rice-paper sail – I'd just cut these into triangles before you arrived – and then pop a couple of dolly mixtures on the top of the stick for the masthead, so there's no sharp point. Easy-peasy. Shamina, Dimitri, do you want to tip out all these Smarties and shall we see if you can arrange them into a big number three on the top of Nancy's cake? Nancy, you can put out all the sticky sausages on this plate; don't lick your fingers when you're doing it as that won't be nice. Okay team, are we set? Yay, ready steady go!'

Billy swallowed. One of the jelly boats quivered in his hand. He made a jaunty sail for it, and selected his dolly mixture for the masthead with care.

'Good work, Billy, good work,' Zoe said.

Caroline came to mind. Was it worse that Zoe was so encouraging when making jelly boats was properly easy? Maybe she was used to talking to a three year old, whilst Caroline was used to talking to Horatio who could do everything. Elspeth didn't seem used to talking to children at all. The only person who had been used to talking to him had been his mum, and she wasn't that chatty. Certainly not big on telling him everything he did was a great achievement.

He turned the finished jelly boat slowly in his hand, and made it bob over an invisible wave. It seemed an entirely separate universe, he reflected, where this was how a birthday party could be. Boats made from jelly set in orange peel. Might they ever have featured on his mum's list of things to do better, when she made a fresh start? If he'd known how to do this, he'd have tried to tell her. Broccoli soup seemed pretty lame in comparison.

'So Billy,' Zoe said, 'now we're all occupied but listening carefully, do you want to start with your story, tell us all about yourself? Shamina and Dimitri would love to know, wouldn't you, guys?'

Billy bit his lip. 'I think I'd just like to do the boats if that's okay.'

'Okay, that's okay for now. Shamina, maybe you could tell him about how birthdays used to be in the orphanage, about the nuns and the same pretend cake with the one cardboard candle and the paper flame that sometimes popped up when you pressed it?'

Shamina started to tell – Billy thought it sounded completely miserable – about 300 children in a room, mostly girls, nuns who got cross sometimes, and a dusty cake with faded Happy Birthday lettering. He wondered what the point was in making Shamina retell it; if it had been him he'd have preferred to stop thinking about it all together and focus on making the Smarties into a brilliant three. Nancy was licking the honey from her fingers. She also licked a sausage; Zoe didn't notice, she was so caught up in Shamina's telling.

'And now you're my darling girl and safe and loved here with us,' she said, as Shamina finished a little breathlessly. 'And you will always have a proper cake with candles to blow out and a new dress for your birthday.'

Shamina beamed. Billy thought she looked very grateful, although also possibly relieved. Maybe you would be, he thought, if you were constantly remembering what you'd left behind. It certainly looked like it made Zoe happy to hear it again.

'You see, Billy,' she said, 'we all have our stories. Sharing them binds us together. We listen to each other, and we understand each other better, and we become a family.'

She put her arms around all three children. 'Group squeeze!' she laughed, and gave them a collective hug.

Billy accidentally spiked his thumb with a cocktail stick.

He caught Dimitri's eye. He was fishing a Smartie out of his sleeve which had somehow upended there when the group squeeze happened. Did he have a stack of horrific birthday stories too? Perhaps he'd been in a terrible orphanage in Moscow without even a cardboard cake. He didn't look too bothered now; he was eating the purple Smarties which Shamina had decided didn't match the icing. Billy thought of Show and Tell in Year Two with Miss Clarke.

Every Friday afternoon she'd pick four people from the register and then on Monday they'd have to bring something in from home and talk about it. It was only marginally less bad than being chosen to take home Teddy Orph, who came with his own special diary in which to write everything he did. Such adventures Teddy Orph had. He'd been to Legoland, to the zoo, on picnics, to family birthday parties, to the seaside and the cinema. On the one occasion he brought him home, his mum had sat and read the entire book, laughing in a way that was cracked and harsh in her throat. *What shall we write?* she'd asked. *Teddy Orph got completely wasted and had the weekend of his life?* Billy had put him back in his rucksack. He'd written nothing in the book. He reflected, reasonably, that there was nothing to write. Miss Clarke had asked if he'd forgotten to do it. He'd shaken his head. She asked if he'd like Teddy Orph to visit the next weekend. He'd shaken his head more firmly. She left him off the rota then, and never brought it up again. Billy always thought Teddy Orph looked forlorn. Maybe he'd have preferred just to live in one place, to sleep in the same little bed each night and not always be out and about. Now that he thought about it again – and he hadn't for ages – it struck him that Orph was obviously short for Orphan. Teddy Orphan; that was properly descriptive, and perhaps not the kindest either. Billy Orphan – it would be better not to dwell on that.

Zoe was looking at him intently. 'Is there something you'd like to share with us, something you'd like to tell? We'd love to hear it.'

She said *love* with extra emphasis.

He shook his head. She looked disappointed.

Nightmare show and tell; that's what he'd tell Joey it was like. Completely the opposite from Miss Clarke's where it was meant to be happy stuff, although he'd been similarly taxed to fulfil that expectation. He shook his head again. Zoe couldn't quite disguise a little tut.

'Maybe you boys would like to play football in the garden. Dimitri never even had a football of his own, Billy and now he has a whole sack full, don't you darling? Phil will be here shortly; he's been running some errands. He's buying a piñata – you know the Mexican treats that you hang from a tree and whack with a stick until the casing breaks and you get showered with sweets? Have you ever done that, Billy? Have you ever been at a party with a piñata?'

'No, I've never seen one,' Billy said, not daring to shake his head.

'Oh great,' Zoe said, 'I really hope you love it. You're the biggest and strongest here so your whacks will be really key, and, by the way, great eye contact when you said that, good work.'

Billy blushed. Dimitri materialised by the kitchen door holding a ball. 'Do you want to play?' he said.

They went out into the garden, to a small set of goalposts.

'Do you want to be goalie or shooter?' Dimitri asked.

'The goalie I think,' Billy said. Dimitri lined up the ball. Billy tried to concentrate.

'Great save!' a man he presumed to be Phil said, striding across the lawn. 'It's great to meet you, Billy. We're so glad you can come to Nancy's party. Boys, do you want to help me hang the piñata? Dimitri, come and get the stepladder with Daddy. You're always such a star at remembering where everything is.'

Miriam hadn't been able to come and fetch him; she'd been called by a foster parent who was having what Miriam said was a flashpoint, so she'd arranged for a taxi to bring Billy back to Meg's. Meg was sitting in the garden when he arrived.

'How was it?' she said.

'Nancy looked like she loved it.'

'Did you enjoy yourself?'

'There was a piñata; you hang it from a tree branch and whack it with a stick until it cracks and sweets come showering down.'

'That sounds like fun.'

'It was, except the sweets come down quite hard. One of the little girls got one in the eye and cried for ages. Zoe said "Oh God they're coming down like hailstones".'

'And the two older children . . . what were they like?'

'Very nice. They play very nicely. They're very good and . . .'

'And what?'

'Well behaved and helpful.'

'Well, that's nice, and you are too so that's good.'

'After the party was finished, Phil downloaded and printed the photos he'd taken and they put them straightaway in Nancy's book.'

'Nancy's book?'

'Each of the children has a book. Zoe has written MY STORY in big letters on the front. It's like a scrapbook. It starts with where they began their lives; there's a picture of Nancy in a nappy in a cot, and then in a hospital looking all thin and scabby, and then Phil and Zoe holding her in a new blanket, and then at the airport, and then a welcome party, and then her in a new cot and a pink babygro, and then her second birthday and Christmas time and then on the beach in a turquoise wetsuit and then today. There's a photocopy of her adoption papers stuck in, and her birth certificate. Zoe says it will tell her everything she needs to know, if she ever wants to know.'

'I see.'

'They all sat down together and looked at it, and Zoe said *Thank goodness you are here now*, and *All that time, while you were in that horrid cot, we were waiting for you to come and be part of our family*. At the end of looking at it, we all had to give Nancy a big clap and a cheer for her being here now.'

'It sounds very caring. I think I've read that it's good to do things like that. Zoe obviously thinks about it a lot.'

'Mmmm.'

'Mmmm?'

'I'll just go upstairs and sort some of my things for a bit.'

'Okay. Come back down and talk some more if you want.'

Billy went upstairs. He lay on his bunk thinking about Nancy's book. It was like a scrapbook of awfulness. He hoped Zoe wouldn't suggest making one for him. Zoe said she liked rolling her sleeves up for a task and he thought she might jump right on to that. He could see it now: MY STORY in big letters on the front, and perhaps a cheesy picture of him holding the piñata stick or something. She'd stick a photo of his mum in. She'd probably choose one where she looked especially thin and bruised. He didn't actually have one – but Grandma would, and Zoe could be counted on to track it down. The stuff in his pillowcase; perhaps Phil would photograph all that. His shin pad would look pathetic by itself. *This is all my man had when he came to us*, Phil would say. Zoe would have completely ironed out the nodding by then, and he'd be answering all questions with good eye contact. She'd know about the singing ringing tree. Maybe she'd download an image of the dwarf, or the bear, and she'd probably stick a mini version of *Dear Zoo* in as well.

Elspeth's hesitant silence suddenly seemed more appealing and Caroline's chatter less demanding. He could hear Meg moving around in the kitchen downstairs. She said the books were a good thing and she was bound to know about stuff like that. He got up from the bunk.

When the phone rang later, it was Miriam. She didn't really ask him about the Marshalls; instead she said his mum's mum was in England and had asked to see him. She didn't call her his grandma – maybe that wasn't allowed anymore. She'd asked if he wanted to see her and he'd said yes. Maybe, if she did the scrapbook, Zoe would make a page that said he'd had a nice grandma but she'd been too threadbare to look after him. That was true. It might be helpful to be reminded there had been a good reason.

37

The plane touched down at Luton, and as the cabin door opened, Trudy Morris, who was sitting closest to it, felt the cool of a July early morning on her cheek. The shock of it caused an unexpected contraction in her chest; a sudden longing to be standing in the garden of her old house in Esher, the grass wet with a heavy, glittering dew, spiders' webs laced between the thorns of her roses, and a bunch of dahlias, freshly cut, in her hand. September had been her favourite month; the soothing chill of the mornings, the gentle warmth of the afternoon, the burned-sugar fragrance of the plums on the tree by her kitchen door.

The summer in Val de Lobo had been scorching. By eleven o'clock in the morning, to walk out on the pavement without a broad-brimmed hat felt like being felled by a heavy blow to the back of the neck. Ted had been on the golf course by six-thirty each day, his golf bag stuffed with chilled bottles of water. He was home by eleven-thirty, ready for light lunch, and by one he was asleep in their bedroom, the aircon turned up high, the sound of his snoring carrying downstairs where she sat in the shade on the terrace trying to concentrate on a book or her embroidery. She'd wallowed in the pool for hours; not swimming, hardly moving, just holding on to the rail with her outstretched arms, her neck pressed to the cool shiny steel, her legs wafting out like aimless tendrils of seaweed. The heat didn't lose its whiteness, its solidity, until about six, and then she and Ted would stroll the short distance to the beach and go for a drink at the club. Here, she drank things she'd never have drunk when she lived in England; mojitos, bellinis, and drinks that were coloured like bright jewels. She drank them through a straw, which she hadn't done since childhood. Afterwards, they would walk home for supper and she tossed salad, sliced avocados while Ted grilled some fish or some chicken. Alone, there were deep, steep, spools of silence between them. She showered before she slept, and applied huge handfuls of thick moisturiser to her legs, her arms. It seemed there was no quenching the deep thirst of her skin. When she fell asleep, it was to a rowdy chorus of cicadas and bullfrogs. One night she felt physically sick with longing, each muscle taut beneath the sticky gleam of her skin, her ear straining for the impossible sound of a pheasant crying out across a field of barley, or the sharp, clear bark of a fox down by the river.

She had not mentioned Billy. Some days she felt his name on the tip of her tongue, ready to spring into all that was unspoken between them, but she kept her peace; peace, she acknowledged bitterly, not being the right word. Ted gave no indication the child even crossed his mind.

He still seemed to love their life in Portugal, in contrast to all those years, grey-faced, commuting into the City. The annual scramble for promotions, for bonuses, for recognition. She hadn't doubted that it had been soul destroying. It had been his idea; the upping of sticks and going. Too many nights when she'd lain weeping about Lizzie; too many days when she'd dashed off in the car and gone to try and persuade her to stop.

I've had enough, he said implacably, one October morning two years after he retired, putting his spoon down neatly beside his porridge bowl. *I didn't spend all those years standing waiting for the six fifty-two, all those years paying bills for ponies and schools for this. I've had enough, and so have you if you had the guts to admit it. The exchange rate is the strongest it will ever be; I'm going to buy somewhere in the sunshine. It's not only her life.*

There had been compensations; Trudy knew there had been compensations. They'd made friends easily, she'd joined a bridge club, she'd grown to love the restless soughing of the sea. The things she thought she wouldn't miss she missed most of all: wood smoke from chimneys on charcoal-grey November afternoons; the fragrance of frosted darkness; the sound of sudden, sharp-smelling rain spilling from the gutter. And now, increasingly, Billy.

She had lied. She hadn't told Ted she'd decided to contact Miriam, that she'd phoned her some weeks ago, and was now coming to see him. She'd claimed she was coming to visit her sister, Marlene, who'd recently had an operation for a cataract removal. This made it partly true.

You do understand, though, don't you, Miriam had said in that pragmatic way of hers, *you understand there's no going back on the Placement Order you signed.*

Yes, yes I do, Trudy had whispered into the phone. *I understand fully, I would just like . . . it would just be . . . I would just like, so very much, to see him.*

Miriam's tone was crisp, abrupt. Trudy wondered if she despised her. Perhaps it was understandable; maybe contempt was understandable – even deserved – when family failed to step up to the plate.

I need to make the arrangement with his foster carer, just check the logistics work for her.

Would that be Mrs Oliver, is he still at Mrs Oliver's? Trudy faltered.

I'm afraid I am not permitted to disclose anything about Billy's situation.

I understand. I remember. Of course.

She was not permitted to know anything at all. She had forsaken that right. It had been her choice, she reminded herself. She thought back to the rawness, the bruisedness, she'd felt at the time of Lizzie's death. *You can't imagine; you can't imagine,* she wanted to say to Miriam Riley. She wanted to hear, for once, the crisp certainty, the brusqueness, waver in Miriam's voice.

She'd put down the phone and wept. What kind of grandmother was she? One who had evidently forsaken all rights to know even the barest details of her grandson. And yet, if she was going to dwell on it, what kind of mother had she been? That didn't bear examination either. One who somehow, unwittingly, unintentionally, but evidently stupidly, had not equipped her daughter to be stronger in the face of a man who had set in play her ruin; had not equipped her to be stronger in the face of substances which eventually were her ruin; and had not been able to keep her safe from harm, even when the harm was pitifully of her own making. It was this failing that lay most heavily on Trudy's heart. It curled round it like a cat, soft but tenacious, claws embedded, refusing to be shaken loose.

People were tactful. She acknowledged that, as she stood waiting for her suitcase to come round on the carousel. In the couple of years up to Lizzie's death, there were glimmers of a steadier footing and then the increasingly predictable slips and slides. Her friends had asked her, with concern, with grave voices, how Lizzie was faring. They'd squeezed her hand with solidarity when her eyes brimmed with tears, and raised glasses of chilled cava (*Long may it continue!*) after Lizzie had spent a week out there with them, completely clean.

Billy had spent that week with them being so quiet, so watchful. Ted hadn't the measure of him, of this she was convinced. *Make a little more effort*, she wanted to say. *Can't you try a little harder, find some kind of rapport?* Ted would be impervious to her chiding, after so many years of her steady stream of suggestions as to what might be best for Lizzie. To start talking about Billy in this way would have been redundant. Offspring, for Ted, had become a litany of woes. *You're the only man he's got*, she thought of telling him one night in bed. *How's he supposed to know how to relate? You walk so fast he practically has to hop, skip and jump to keep up*. She'd swallowed the words lest he interpret them as blame.

Now Marlene sat in a chair in her kitchen, a strap of bandage around her head and eye. She was in good spirits; she dealt cards, played patience. Her laugh had a raspiness, a merriment that Trudy realised she missed. She didn't mention Billy to her either; Marlene would have said something like *What's done is done*. For their whole sibling life, her default position seemed to assume that Trudy would intermittently mess up. *Here's to the harvest, nicely ripening*, Marlene toasted, knocking back a measure of ruby-coloured sloe gin. *Since when's crop ripening been any business of yours?* Trudy said, shaking her head. *It's ripening, though,* said Marlene, *it's ripening, even though it's not exactly my problem.*

The sloe gin tasted rich and heavy in Trudy's mouth. Later, as she lay motionless in Marlene's spare bed, she imagined it pooling in her oesophagus; a dark red puddle like a clot near her heart. Miriam Riley had left a message on her mobile, and texted it too for good measure.

You can see him at 4pm on Thursday. He breaks up for the school summer holidays the next day. It'll only be for a short while. Obviously I'm trusting you not to upset him in any way.

On Thursday Trudy caught a taxi from Marlene's which was probably inexcusably extravagant. She patched up some excuse about needing to sort something about a visa, a change to a visa condition that had to be signed in the presence of a bureaucrat. The good thing about Marlene was that she never enquired about anyone else's business. It was a form of selfishness, but it made things smoother.

When Billy walked into the room, Trudy thought she might falter. His eyes, just for a moment, seemed to leap out at her as Lizzie's. Lizzie's before all the lying, wheedling, protesting, and promising crept in. Lizzie's before the milky film of all the poison she was absorbing.

He hadn't grown much. Not noticeably, anyway. Was that normal, at his age, in two months, or should she be concerned? His hands were in his pockets. His shoes were a bit scruffy; one of his laces was almost undone. He wore a T-shirt with a VW beetle on. She couldn't remember him wearing that before. Was it new, had someone bought it for him, did someone get paid to shop for his clothes? Perhaps Miriam Riley or Mrs Oliver. Someone took care of such things, someone had stepped forward for that. Who made an appointment when his hair needed cutting? Maybe they trimmed it themselves with a pair of kitchen scissors? Perhaps she should have enquired about the detail more closely while she'd still been able. At the time, she thought, it had been about renouncing the emotional commitment. The practicalities of who bought him clothes hadn't occurred to her. Maybe his shoes were too small. It was a heartrending thought.

'Hello, Grandma,' he said. His voice was lighter than she remembered. It had a softness that suggested it could be blown away. She clasped her hands in her lap. Miriam hadn't said whether she was allowed to kiss or hug him. It probably counted as upsetting.

'How have you been?' he asked. 'How's Grandpa, how's Portugal? Have those trees grown at all, can you still see the water pipes running between them?'

'I'm well. Your grandpa's fine. His limpy leg's mostly better, and it doesn't keep him off the golf course anymore. The trees, yes a bit I expect, hard to tell when you see them all the time. I've never really noticed the pipes. I'll look when I get back. It's been hot. Very hot. Unimaginably hot.'

'The pool . . . I expect swimming in the pool is nice.' He paused. Understandable for him to have run out of steam. Impressive that he had taken the initiative. Had he thought up his questions, concentrating, on his way here?

'And you,' she said, 'how about you? How is everything for you?'

She would have liked to tell him that they talked about him often, but it wouldn't be true. She'd have liked to tell him that she thought of him often, increasingly often. That would have been true but she might start to cry. That would definitely be contrary to Miriam's instructions.

'How is finding you a, you know, a new family, a new, a fresh, a . . .'

She ran out of words. He was looking at her patiently, steadily.

'I'm visiting a family with three children; one's from India, one's from Russia and one's from Croatia. I went to their house for a birthday party and I think I'll be going to something else with them soon. I went with another family to a high wire climbing place, and with a couple for a day on their boat. There's a lot of day trips.'

What really undid her, what really killed her (and this she contemplated as she sat in the back of the cab, as the driver took the slip road for the motorway, and tried to pretend that the elderly woman in the back of his cab was not sobbing, unrelentingly, unabashedly) was the way Billy reached forward, and patted the back of her hand. Her hand was so mottled now, so spattered with age spots and wrinkles and snaking green veins, and his was so small, so fair and smooth. The nail of his index finger was bitten down to the quick. In the crescent of his thumb-nail there was a thin semi-circle of soil.

'It'll be okay, Grandma,' he'd said. 'You don't need to worry. They're on to it, they're sorting it. Miriam Riley's on the case. I'm not going to be spilt milk. Honestly, not spilt at all.'

Miriam Riley had come to the door to signal that their time was up. Billy stood and pushed his chair neatly under the table. And then, in a tiny gesture which had iron-branded its way scorchingly straight on to her heart, he'd stood taller, pulled back his shoulders and stiffened his spine, like a small soldier, standing to attention, ready to face and to take whatever came next.

He'd touched her arm again.

'Bye, Grandma, take care,' he said, and 'I'm remembering all my table manners.'

As Trudy stumbled out through the double doors, held open for her by a very tall man, she thought that if she ever again mustered the will to believe in God, He would have every right to damn her immediately to Hell. Damn every last scrap of her miserable skin, for abandoning Billy, her own flesh and blood, and leaving him to flounder in the uncertainty of finding a family who might one day love him but just as easily might not.

Two days later, she stood in the boarding queue for the return flight and anticipated going home to her garden which smelt of orange blossom and jasmine, but which would no longer disguise the smell of cowardice, and of abnegation. She knew that she'd lie in bed trying to sleep while the cicadas and bullfrogs jeered noisily at her, and she'd be consumed with self-loathing which would froth up from her bone marrow, and would slowly and surely cross the mattress to permeate Ted.

38

Andrew sat in his van tapping the steering wheel with his fingers.

It sucked. It damn well sucked.

The elderly woman he held the door open for – the woman who was patently dissolving into sobs, her hand pressed to her lips, her voice all choked so that her attempt to say thank you was barely discernible – was Billy's grandma. She'd got into a taxi and been driven away, and Billy had come out and told him who she was. Then, *How's your baby coming along?* he'd asked, as if it were a cake cooking, and then he'd told him about the piñata at the party. He'd gone and sat by the tree, and Meg Oliver had come to take him home – home, that would be a nice thought – and when Andrew fished for and found a new note, he could hardly bear to look.

1. *Caroline and Zoe think being a mum's always a smiley thing. It probably isn't – ask Grandma.*
2. *I think I make her sad, just like my mum made her sad, and that makes me sad.*
3. *Zoe would put it in a scrapbook like something that can be clapped about at birthday parties. Maybe she's found that works.*

Andrew looked up to see Miriam walking towards her car. She looked in a hurry; she was always in a hurry. He stepped out.

'I'm sorry, Andrew,' she said irritably, 'I haven't really got time for one of our roundabout conversations. I have to be somewhere. If you want to tell me something you have to get to the point quickly.'

'Just his grandma coming. I wondered what made you think

of that. He says he makes her sad and that makes him sad. How come she came?'

Miriam kept walking, her files bunched under her arm. Andrew kept pace.

'She asked to see him, and as the weeks went by I couldn't think of a solid reason to justify saying no. She hasn't done anything wrong, not legally wrong, just not taken him on. Other grandparents make the same decision. In an ideal world perhaps we'd have been able to offer her more help at the time of his mum's death, maybe that would have led to a different outcome. I don't actually know. His new placement – I don't know about that either. I don't know what he thinks, I don't know what they're thinking, and I don't know what I think yet, despite the fact I'm the one who's supposed to know, the one who's supposed to get it right, for Billy's sake. At this moment I've got a dozen others like him, and not enough resources, and definitely not enough time, and not enough certainties, all of which doesn't fix anything and means you make mistakes. Or, for the record, means *I* make mistakes.'

'I'm sorry. Sorry it's a bad day. Sorry about the fixing.'

Miriam opened her car door and turned to face him.

'Well, the thing you can console yourself with is it's not your job to fix it. You can focus on the fabric of the building whilst everything else comes tumbling around our ears. I have to go.'

She looked on the verge of tears. Her face flushed. She got into her car and drove away. Andrew stood in the car park feeling as if he'd overstepped a mark, and somehow made her feel worse. Did she have someone in her life who would give her a hug? She looked like she needed one. He walked back to Reception, where he overheard the receptionist on the phone.

'Yes, Miriam's on her way to the hospital. A child she didn't take into care, admitted with head wounds and burns – cigarette burns I think. Not life-threatening apparently but not good. She's frantic.'

Andrew winced. No wonder she had been short with him. Who could do that to a child?

He walked back to his van. He'd always been open, and expressed everything he thought or felt – sung like a canary since birth, his mother joked. For the first time in his life he didn't feel able to. Things that were unsayable log-jammed their way along the length of his ribcage; uncomfortable feelings which were hard to admit even to himself.

39

Zoe said it was a mystery treat. She reassured Billy that Miriam knew where they were going. 'But,' she said, 'it's one of our favourite things to bundle everyone up and go off with them guessing what the treat is going is to be.'

Billy felt Shamina and Dimitri were giving it their best effort. *Water slide park! Petting farm! Miniature village! Sculpture trail!* they chipped in from the middle row of seats in the car.

'Nope, nope and nope again!' Zoe said gleefully. 'Come on Billy, what do you think? Any guesses?'

Dimitri smiled shyly at him. 'Sometimes we go to the Animal Rescue Centre and look at the injured hedgehogs and the fox cubs which have been picked up from the road,' he whispered. 'You could say that.'

Evidently Zoe's interest in rescuing didn't just stretch to children. Billy wondered if it was much of a treat looking at an invalid hedgehog. He raised his eyebrow at Dimitri who leaned forward again.

'Last time we went, there was a hedgehog who'd put his head in a tin can and eaten what was left in it and then he got stuck and couldn't get out. When we saw him, it was right after they cut the tin off and you could still see the mark.'

Zoe turned round from the front passenger seat to face him. 'C'mon Billy, where do you think we might be going?'

Billy wondered why Zoe didn't see this was an awkward question to ask him. What if he said something really expensive and properly exciting, like Legoland or Thorpe Park, or the circus, and then it was actually going to see the equivalent of a now tinless hedgehog? He furrowed his brow; perhaps he should try to come up with something mediumish in terms of everything, and then no offence could be taken.

'The water mill,' Shamina said, 'the one with the big wheel where you can see the water rushing underneath?'

'The water fountains in the park that you run between and which stop and start? The model railway?' Dimitri shouted.

Their enthusiasm was impressive.

'No and no again!' laughed Zoe. 'Think of what time of year it is. July. July. Am I going to have to give you some clues?'

Nancy clapped. Billy wasn't sure what this chimed in with, as Zoe had explained to him that Nancy's speech was behind for a three year old as she had had so little verbal communication in the first eighteen months of her life. *I think she practically understands everything now, though*, Zoe had told him, *even though she's not yet verbalising her responses.*

Billy ducked his head to be on Nancy's level and mimed clapping back to her. Nancy chuckled.

'Come on, Billy,' Zoe said from the front. 'One guess before I start giving clues.'

Billy decided it probably said a lot that he didn't have a clue before the clues started. 'A farm?'

'No . . . although close-ish – that's close-ish.'

Dimitri smiled at him. Shamina said 'That means yours is the best guess so far.'

He looked out of the window; a bit of nature spotting would have been relaxing right now. He could copy Caroline and point out something to Nancy and teach her the word for it. Phil, however, was driving very fast and everything was going by in something of a blur.

'Okay . . . drum roll . . .' Zoe was saying (and here, Phil, who had said very little so far, added the sound). 'It's two words and they are both M. M and M are your clues.'

Shamina and Dimitri were coming up with lots of words that started with M. When they said milk machine it made him wonder if they were going to a dairy parlour – they'd had a school trip once to a farm and watched two cows being milked.

They pulled into a large, rutted driveway. 'Time up!' Zoe was laughing. 'It's the *Maize Maze*! It's grown high enough for them to open it up.'

'The A-maizing Maize Maze,' Phil added, pointing to a large painted sign.

'We're going to split into two groups,' Zoe said. 'Billy, you're coming with me and Nancy. Shamina and Dimitri, you'll go with Daddy. First one to the middle not only gets the ice lolly they give you but is also officially the family winner. Flags to the ready.'

They sat on hay bales waiting for the tractor ride to take them to the edge of the maze. Phil sorted them each a flag on a very long pole which could be waved above the maze walls if they got lost.

'Remember to look at the clues going round,' he said. 'They'll help you answer the question when you get to the middle. Get that right and you'll win a lolly!'

'But remember, you can't choose the flavour,' Zoe said to Dimitri, patting his leg.

Billy wondered what had happened about lollies the last time they came.

'Although, frankly,' Zoe said to Phil, over the children's heads, 'I still can't see how being able to shout up which flavour you want is too much to ask, particularly when children, these children, have had so little control over the rest of their lives.'

'I think you lost that battle last year,' Phil replied.

Billy thought if they allowed that, one flavour might never be picked and there would be a lot left over. No choice was always much simpler to manage. Maybe Zoe hadn't thought about that.

'Are you daydreaming Billy?' she said. 'I need all your powers of concentration and direction for the maze.'

Walking into it, Billy was struck by several things. First, by how tall the maize was. It was properly tall. He had a quick check to see that his flag did indeed hover above it. The second was how quickly it was disorientating. Three or four turns in and he had no sense of where the entrance was. It was like the Minotaur story; he'd be like all the other no-hopers who'd wandered in without trailing string and then died. The third thing, which intrigued him, was how the farmer had planted it. How could he stick to the shape when you couldn't see it properly from the ground? He squinted up at the slice of blue sky. Did he fly over it in an aeroplane and check the pattern was right? Phil said last year it was in the shape of a dinosaur. How could you see that standing on a bare field in January with some seed? He resolved to ask Andrew if he knew.

'Chop chop, Billy,' Zoe said. 'Let's sing from the same song sheet . . . Look, Nancy's pointing this way. Do you have any better suggestions?'

Billy shook his head. Following a three-year-old with limited speech was probably a better bet. They came upon a painted cardboard cut-out of a pirate with a huge cutlass. 'It's Captain Hook,' Zoe said. 'Read the question. Read the question.'

Reading aloud wasn't Billy's favourite thing. The words sometimes jumbled when he tried to read and speak at the same time. 'Auuh . . .' he said, looking at the words dance on the chalk boards in the shimmering heat.

'Who . . . wh . . . who was the girl in J M B- Barrie's *Peter Pan*?'

Zoe looked at him expectantly. She widened her eyes. 'Do you know the answer?' she asked brightly.

He shook his head. Should he?

'I'll have to read the book to you,' Zoe said firmly, 'fill in the gaps. That's my speciality. Every British child should be familiar with *Peter Pan*. It's Wendy, the girl was Wendy. The fairy was Tinkerbell, the dog was Nana. The boys were the lost boys.'

Billy looked at her steadily. A book about lost boys. Maybe that was a good thing. Perhaps it worked like her scrapbooks. Was there much difference between a lost boy and an orphan one? Maybe he'd turned into Boy Orph; taken out, just like Teddy Orph, for one day trip after another, but with Miriam, not a child, writing all about it afterwards. It was almost funny, and yet funny in a way that made him want to cry. Cuckoo boy, Boy

Orph; the Introduction process was turning into a collection of names he'd never have wanted to gather. He re-focused on the book Zoe was talking about. *Peter Pan.* Maybe it would contain something helpful to know.

'Come on, we're dawdling, let's be on our way,' Zoe said. 'Nancy, do you want to walk holding Mummy's hand? You're getting quite heavy on my hip.'

It was hot in the maze, hot and dusty. The ground was dry and cracked from so many footsteps. Small bits of chaff and leaf were working their way into his trainers. He wriggled his finger at the back of his heel to dislodge them. Zoe was fanning her face with her hand. 'I always forget that this is actually quite hard work,' she laughed. 'Where to next?'

Billy dared not shrug. He thought nodding or shaking his head would be similarly lame. He looked to Nancy.

'Nancy looks as if she's pointing that way,' he said.

This wasn't strictly true, but Zoe had taken off her flip-flops and was whacking them together so she hadn't really been looking at Nancy.

'Okay, but I asked *you* where you wanted to go, which direction *you* wanted to take.' The tone of her voice was less bright, more serious. 'Beyond this maze, that's an important question. Maybe that's a tricky thing for you? Do you feel anyone has asked you where you want to go, where you'd choose to go, before?'

A small boy thundered past him. A woman called *Rufus, Rufus, don't get ahead, you might get lost.*

'Rufus is evidently very bold,' Zoe said, nodding her head in the direction of Rufus's retreating limbs. Nancy blew a raspberry.

Billy blinked. He swallowed and looked up at his flag-pole. The blue triangle fluttered mournfully. A wasp buzzed near a discarded lolly stick.

'I think we should go back to the last turning and take a right,' he said.

'And you don't want to comment on or answer anything else,' Zoe said.

Billy shook his head.

'Okay, okay, in your own time, in our own time. I just want you to know that in admitting things, we own them, and we move on.'

Billy blinked again. 'Back to the last turning and take a right,' he said, beginning to walk.

There were three more clues to collect. One was guessing the name of an English cereal crop with six letters. 'Barley,' Billy said with conviction. Zoe punched the air when he got it right. 'Yay, clever you,' she said. It wasn't really clever, Billy thought, but it was nice of her to big it up.

He felt tired, and wondered what Meg was doing. She might be sitting in the garden in her stripy deckchair, or watching Wimbledon on the television. She loved the the tennis. She clapped at the television. He felt a sudden rush of warmth for her. She didn't treat him as if everything he said had to add up to an achievement or an explanation of himself. Maybe, he thought, squinting back up at the sky where a small plane was buzzing a loop the loop, maybe that was what love was like, when a grown-up loved you, and it was just easy and calm and not full of worries like it had been with his mum, and not full of all this trying like it had been with everybody since.

'Billy, Billy . . .' Zoe was saying. She sounded impatient. 'Phil's just texted me; they've reached the middle already. We must pull our socks up.'

When they got to the middle, finally, and Billy was eating his ice lolly, he reflected that Joey would have thought this was a hoot. He'd probably have dive-bombed his way through it and refused to carry a flag. It should have been fun. He was puzzled why it hadn't been. His heart felt heavier coming out than it had going in.

There was a roundabout by the exit, and Phil was helping the others on to it for a turn.

'Join in if you want to,' Zoe said, nudging his shoulder. 'Phil will stop it so that you can get on.'

Billy shook his head. He watched the roundabout spin.

'Is there anything you'd like to share with me, anything you'd like to say?' Zoe asked.

He shook his head again. His face felt as smooth as butter. He had a sudden flashback to his mum lying on a blanket by a river while he was fishing, and Grandma was asking her, asking her things, and her face looked just like his felt now. Was it starting, he wondered, was he turning into her, slowly and steadily, just like Grandpa had feared? What had he called her? He scrabbled in his memory for the word. *A wrecking ball*, that was it, a wrecking ball. His head felt metallic, smoothly round, on the soft stem of his neck.

Zoe pushed all her curls back from her face. She made a click-click noise at the side of her mouth, like when a horse is encouraged to giddy-up.

Giddy-up, Billy thought. Perhaps that was what he should be doing. Giddy-up and fit in somewhere and be wanted so that Miriam could concentrate on someone else and everything would be sorted. His bunk at Meg's could stop being Billy's bed. He rubbed his eyes. They felt dusty.

'In the car, gang,' Phil was saying, 'and how about a swim to cool down. Who wants to go? Don't all yell at once!'

'I don't think Billy's allowed to go swimming,' Zoe quickly said, with slightly pinched lips. 'I think you should have just run that by me quietly before you suggested it and got them all excited. I think we have to sign a form or something, like for school trips, if he's going to go in or near water. I can't contact Miriam to check on a Saturday afternoon, it wouldn't be fair.'

'Don't worry, I can watch, I'll be fine watching; the others all want to go,' Billy said.

And he did. He sat in a small balcony area behind a plastic rail and watched Dimitri and Shamina jump in pretending to be wide-footed penguins. There was a chute slide which coiled outside the building and came back in, and he waved to Nancy as she came down it on Phil's lap. He drank some orange squash from a paper cup, and watched as Zoe stood in the water and clapped to Dimitri and Shamina and encouraged them to jump in again. They made huge, confident splashes. He thought back to the little blonde girl who jumped into the river, to her daddy, when he was with Elspeth and Malcolm.

Maybe there were children – perhaps they were called lost boys? – who just never jumped in.

40

The visit the next day was to a French market. Billy was mindful of how Joey would have automatically thought it would be in France. He'd have whooped at that, and had the Channel tunnel – or a ferry – conjured up in no time, plus, he'd have included the Eiffel Tower somewhere in the background even if they'd been going to the town closest to the coast.

'It's a French market,' Billy explained to Meg when he got home from the Maize Maze and the pool, 'but it's not a French market in France, it's in the next town from here. The French stall-holders come and sell their things. They're the ones who go in the tunnel, or on the ferry,' he added, forgetting that that was a detail for Joey.

'That sounds nice,' Meg said. 'Maybe there will be crêpes and cheeses and bread. I'll give you some money to buy bread.'

He hoped there would be bread. He hoped he could come back with her favourite bread. It would be like bringing back the raspberries from Malcolm's allotment. He liked that memory. He thought back to the allotment, and wondered what Malcolm and Elspeth did on Saturdays when it was winter, the ground all bare and frosted and *The Girl Jane* taken out of the water. Maybe they just went outside anyway, but wearing all the jumpers Elspeth had knitted. Maybe when autumn came, she progressed to gloves and hats.

Meg sounded enthusiastic about the market. If she'd had any children of her own, would they have gone and spent Sundays together there? He thought of when she'd taken him to the boating lake after he'd been to the high wire centre with the Frasers. It had been very peaceful. He tried to imagine her with a husband

and two or three children. It felt a bit like trying to imagine Florence Nightingale or Mary Seacole with a regular family. Mrs Bailey said – in History – that Mary and Florence had given up their lives in the service of others. Maybe Meg had too. She was certainly going about it with fewer awkward questions than Zoe.

Now, she was in the kitchen making them a Spanish omelette for their supper, and he asked her if she'd watched the tennis in the afternoon and she laughed and said *Yes, can't you tell from the state of it in here.* Billy started laying the table and she said to him, 'So how did you find Zoe? Is she easy to be with?'

Easy wasn't the word he'd have used. 'She asks a lot of questions.'

'Maybe she just wants to find out things quickly so she knows you better.'

Billy put out the knives and forks neatly. It wasn't that; it was something he couldn't put his finger on. He thought of the hedgehog with the tin can on its head. Sometimes people got into positions which meant they needed help, but maybe it wasn't the best thing to keep asking them how it felt to have the can on their head in the first place.

'*Bonjour!*' Zoe said on Meg's doorstep the next morning.

Nancy waved from the car window. Billy waved back. Shamina and Dimitri were both wearing stripy T-shirts. 'They're looking very French today,' Zoe laughed. 'We've sung *Frère Jacques* all the way here. I hope you're in good voice this morning, Billy.'

Billy cleared his throat.

'You have fun now,' Meg said. 'I'll see you after lunch.'

'Say *au revoir*,' Zoe teased. '*Au revoir, au revoir*.'

The market was busy. Zoe got them all to hold hands as they walked along, and she clapped hers with pleasure at the sight of them, and got Phil to take a photo on his i-Phone. She bought them each a *pain au chocolat* and a round dimpled bottle of Orangina, and they ate them at a little table which was surrounded with bunting. Music was playing from a loud speaker, and all the stall-holders were calling out to each other, and Zoe bought a basket from a stall and said 'Isn't this lovely?'

'Are zey all yours?' a stall-holder asked, as Zoe bought four bars of lavender soap.

'Sort of. Almost!' she said cheerfully.

Billy looked at his toes. She'd caught Phil's eye and pulled a little face when she'd said it, and he decided she meant *Almost* because three out of four of them were hers, not because he was about to be.

'Come on, Billy, why not dance a little,' she said as she encouraged the others to dance to the music played by a man with an accordion sitting by the town hall. Shamina was making her skirt whirl in great swoops and Dimitri was jumping up and down holding on to Phil's hands. Zoe started waltzing with Nancy on her hip. They looked, Billy thought, like the happiest, most carefree, family in the world. He thought of Shamina's story and the cardboard birthday cake, and of Nancy looking scabby in a cot. Perhaps Zoe was right. Maybe if you kept talking about the past, thinking and thinking about it, you woke up one day and suddenly it had gone, like something evaporated – poof! – and you felt like dancing in a square to accordian music. Zoe was breathless from dancing and laughing so much. She gave Dimitri a big kiss and then ruffled Billy's hair.

'Are you having fun?'

He nodded. 'Yes, thank you.'

'You're so formal,' she said, giving him a little tweak on his ribs, and Billy remembered the time when he'd wondered whether bowing might be a good thing for Introductions. That wouldn't have gone down well with Zoe and Phil, not when you were meant to wing your way home to them, represented by a vivid blue line rather than a stiff little bow. Evidently you also had to be able to dance with enthusiasm.

Zoe bought some bread and cheese and white peaches and they sat down on the grass by the war memorial. Phil cut the cheese with a knife he produced from his rucksack, and tore off pieces of baguette for them all. Billy felt the warm, sweet stickiness of the peach juice on his fingers and his chin. The man with the accordion was playing a tune that went faster and faster. Nancy was clapping some more, and everybody was smiling and laughing, and Billy had the weirdest sensation of being separated from it all by the thinnest possible sheet of glass, so that everything sounded tinny and distant, and all their voices rang strangely in his ears, and everything he looked at was as if through the slightest of mists.

'Billy,' Zoe was saying, 'Billy, I just asked you something . . .' and he turned to face her, wondering what question he had failed to answer now, and he was struck with a sudden panic that maybe happiness was located with a switch, and, once it was switched off, it might never be turned back on. It was like a knack you lost. You couldn't find your way back to it, just like the entrance to the Minotaur's den.

Phil and Zoe lay in bed.

Zoe stretched beside him and laid her head on his chest.

'They all went out like lights,' she said, 'they're exhausted. Nancy was so sweet, insisting she didn't need her pull-ups, that she'd be dry in the morning.' She paused. 'You realise what a long way they've all come when you look at Billy. I just can't get the measure of him. I can't tell whether he's emotionally frozen, like the grief counsellor apparently said, or whether he's just not a giver, not a participant, not a joiner-in. His face is so difficult to read; it's hard to know whether there's anything going on at all. I ask him questions and he either avoids them or responds as if I've said something totally different. It rings a few alarm bells for adolescence I think.'

'So what are you saying?'

'I don't know really, I just feel a little bit uneasy. Maybe it's the process. With the others we committed from the off so I just rolled up my shirtsleeves and got on with it, and maybe because they were younger, properly shell-shocked, it made it easier. They knew a life-raft when they saw it coming. I just wonder whether this Introduction process doesn't cast something of an ambiguous shadow; we size him up, he sizes us up, that's what's going on beneath all the jolly activity, let's not kid ourselves. I'm sure Miriam has made it very clear to him that he has a choice. I think the other thing to bear in mind is that where he is, what he's comparing it to, isn't awful. Not by any stretch of the imagination. Meg Oliver seems really decent, she lives in a decent house on a decent street, he goes to a nice school. I have no sense of urgency coming from him. He doesn't feel like a child in jeopardy and maybe that's the stumbling block. We've said it loads of times: we're savers, we're rescuers. I'm just not sure Billy thinks he needs saving or rescuing at all. I'm feeling full of missionary zeal and he's avoiding meeting my eyes.'

'So,' (and here Phil began to cosy up to her in a way which signalled the direction the conversation was heading) 'what are you saying? This is your department.'

'Just because I'm a therapist doesn't make my instincts right. I'm just not sure – at this stage – whether he's the right child for our family. I haven't really noticed him making an effort with any of the others. Granted, Dimitri's three years younger but they're both boys. You'd think that was a starter for play.'

'But they weren't in the maze together, and Billy didn't swim. He's at an age that's a bit more self-conscious too.'

'So what do you think?'

'He seems sweet. But if he's not what you want, who you want, and if you think he doesn't fit and that a different child would work better, let's keep our options open. We always said four would be maximum, so you've got one last shot.'

'The shaman said it would feel right; that for all of them it would feel right instantly. It did with the others.'

'Problem is you're taking on board shamans, grief counsellors, social workers, as well as your own knowledge and instincts. It's a tough call.'

'The actual problem is I'm too sensitive. I take it all on. It's what makes me cut out for this, but also what makes it emotionally exhausting.' (Phil's hand began to make its way circuitously to her inner thigh.) 'I feel what they feel, and work twice as hard as anybody to process it all. Maybe I should relax. I guess there's no urgency. We can think about it, see Billy some more. I think I ought to share my concerns with Miriam though. She asked for total honesty, total transparency. Apparently, during the first Introduction the mother had a change of heart and it all came clattering down. Miriam didn't disclose any details.'

'Okay, talk to her. Maybe think of something else we can do with Billy. Maybe just have him over here and don't stage-manage it as much. Sometimes children find their own way while the adults around them try too hard.' (He began to tongue her ear.) 'A computer game's probably the best bridge between him and Dimitri, even though you'd prefer it to be an accordion.'

Zoe laughed.

'Except I know which side my bread is buttered, and that if it weren't for computer games none of this would be financially possible anyway.'

She arched her back, and rolled on to his chest.

41

Billy sat with his back against the picket fence at the Family Centre with Andrew. Andrew was eating his packed lunch, and seeing Billy waiting for Miriam had asked him to join him.

'Would you like some gingerbread?' he asked, proffering his Tupperware. 'Lorna made it; it's great.'

Billy helped himself to a slice.

'I've been saving up a question: have you ever been to the Maize Maze?'

'I've driven past it. Probably not intended for my age group, and I'm guessing the baby might not be up to it for a while.'

'Yes, but do you know how they make it? How do they know where to sow all the seed, and how can they see if they're doing it right?'

'That is the clever bit – and I *do* know. They just sow the whole field in April and when it's grown about half a metre but is still soft and easy to cut, then they go in and make the pathways, and then they leave it to grow until the middle of July and then open the maze. You can go through it like you did, in the daytime, but they open it at night as well so that older children can do it in the dark by torchlight. Clever business sense – you can make twice the entrance money. Then, in September, they cut it all down and the crop gets fed to the cattle. Win win.'

Billy whistled. 'That's smart.'

'Did you go there with the new family? Did you have a nice time?'

'She asks a lot of questions. She's made her other children a book each, a sort of scrapbook that's called *My Story*. She likes putting in photos of all the bad stuff from their lives before, and ones from how it is now so that you can see the difference.'

'Is she making a scrapbook for you?'

'Don't think so; not yet anyway. Maybe she's planning it. Even if she doesn't choose me, I think she thinks it would be a good idea.'

They both stared into the middle distance.

'Hard to know sometimes what's good for other people,' Andrew said. 'Sometimes they might not know themselves.'

Billy was grateful that Andrew hadn't asked another question. His words just floated between them for a bit, with no pressure to give an answer, and Billy took another bite of gingerbread and leaned back against the fence.

'We went to a French market too; there was music playing and everybody danced. I sort of did.'

'I'm not much of a dancer.'

'Aren't you?'

'Lorna says it's like watching a tree being felled – best clear the floor.'

'Were you a good dancer when you were my age?'

'More interested in other things I think, which is why I'm laying bets that if the baby is a boy it won't be ballet lessons he chooses. Especially not if he's my build. Picking up all those dainty ballerinas would look like tossing the caber.'

'Have you ever done that?'

'Tossed a caber? No! Don't you have to wear a kilt? I'd be game for a go though, should I ever get the chance. Look, here's Miriam she's after one of us. She's got that look.'

'Billy,' she called, beckoning him towards her.

'That would be you,' Andrew said, 'and it would be a braver man than me who didn't jump to it.'

Billy stood up and brushed the gingerbread crumbs from his lap.

'Take care, little man. See you soon,' he added. 'And you, by the way, are much better lunchtime conversation than Paul the electrician.'

Billy flushed.

'Hey Miriam,' he said, walking towards her.

He turned to wave goodbye to Andrew and felt a little spring in his step. If you were a hedgehog, with a rim mark on your neck which showed where something had been cut off, conversations like that could help you forget you'd ever had a tin can on your head in the first place.

42

Lorna, home from work and freshly out of the shower, lay on the bed and waggled her swollen feet and ankles. Today had been hot. Her skin felt itchy. She rubbed her hand over her bump; the baby kicked and her abdomen flexed. She kissed her fingers and planted them right where the baby had moved. *I forgive you for the ankles*, she said, and rotated them some more.

She heard Andrew come through the front door, closing it loudly behind him, and she heard him go into the downstairs shower which he used after work. Minutes later he came upstairs and into their room.

'Hey,' she said, 'how was your day?'

'Okay. How was yours? You look hot.'

'By that I'm guessing you don't mean hot in a good way, not with these ankles.'

'Hot and hot – you can have it both ways.'

'Thank you – I'll take any compliments going. George Roberts told me today that my chubby cheeks reminded him of a Coronation Toby jug he once had. I'm hoping my cheekbones make a reappearance after the baby's born.'

She smoothed her fingers across her face, and lay back on her pillow.

'Sorry?'

'I said George Roberts said that . . . Are you listening to me at all?'

'Sort of. Scrapbooks. The family he's being introduced to now, something about scrapbooks. Why would she want to make scrapbooks?'

'I don't know. Lots of adoptive families do that, especially when the child's from a different culture, a different country. It keeps a connection with their roots. Why are you so irritated by it?'

'Because that's not what he needs. He knows who he is and where he's from. He needs to be taken fishing, or to a football match, or to spend a morning at a work bench learning how to make a dovetail joint.'

'Okay, so why not tell that to Miriam? She might find it helpful.'

'She's got too much on her plate; she probably wouldn't listen anyway and yet it's obvious. I was nine once; some stuff doesn't change.'

'Maybe she hasn't got anyone queuing up to offer that.'

Lorna stretched. 'I'm going to lie here for ten minutes and then I'm going to get up and make us some pasta. Are you hungry, or just bad tempered?'

Andrew laughed. 'Both. I'm going to go outside and do a couple of jobs and then I'll cook dinner. You just relax.'

When Lorna rose from the bed, moments later, he was chopping wood. Chopping wood, she thought, what on earth for in July? She opened the window wide to let more air into the room and lifted her chin to let the breeze play across her body. The evening sun caught the edge of the axe and threw a flash of light. She watched as a small triangle of sweat appeared on the back of his T-shirt. The axe flew again and again at the logs. Demons, she thought . . . what demons was he battling? The baby kicked hard, and Lorna sat down again on the edge of the bed. Just by her ribs she could feel a small, persistent foot. She touched the solid little heel detectable beneath her thumb. *I love every scrap of you already*, she said, *every single atom*. She closed her eyes and felt a wave of emotion. Her skin flushed hot. Here came her faceless mother again, swooping and sweeping into every pore of her skin.

How had it been for her? Had she felt none of this? All of this? Or had she felt every increasing life-beat with a sense of horror and dread? The bedroom curtain flapped and the room felt full of long-ago decisions.

Her birth mother had not wanted her; that knowledge had

washed over Lorna time and time again during her pregnancy, as she watched her body change, her skin stretch and swell, breathing with a new consciousness that she was doing it for the baby as well. Her birth mother had handed her over, new-born, perhaps even unseen; handed her to her adoptive parents, to her adoptive mother who had been her mother in every sense of the word apart from this. It had taken being pregnant to realise the full impact of what *this* was: nine months of intractable connection, of belonging together in bone, tissue and blood. Knotted by cord. She rubbed her palm over the smoothness of her abdomen and traced the stretch marks which rivered across her skin. Tears welled in her eyes. Why, so many years after she'd come to terms with it all, was it making itself felt again, winding her with pain?

She'd watched so many television programmes where adopted children were reunited with their birth mothers after forty years. Grey-haired, teary old ladies with handkerchiefs saying to plump middle-aged women *Aren't you lovely, aren't you beautiful, I never stopped thinking about you. Every birthday, every single birthday.* Maybe her mother hadn't even started. That was a possibility.

Lorna had tried to trace her, and ten years ago she'd found her. The agency asked her birth mother if she would like to meet her and she'd said *No, it's best left as it was.* Lorna had sobbed; sobbed and sobbed in her mum's arms, too stung by rejection to think what a blow she might simultaneously be dealing, and all the while her mum stroked her hair and said *It's her loss, it's her loss, it always was,* until Lorna blew her nose, wiped her eyes and said *So that's that then,* and vowed not to think about her again. And so it had been, until pregnancy, and a disbelief that all this could happen to your body and leave no scar.

Her adoptive parents had saved her, on this she was clear. They had loved her, nurtured her, raised her, given her opportunities. She had been blessed. The baby kicked sharply. She looked out of the window. Andrew was sitting on the pile of freshly cut logs. What was he thinking? Whatever it was, he was not saying. She dared to think she might guess.

What was that film they had watched about playing a good deed forward? Perhaps there came symmetry. Her adoptive parents had saved her; perhaps it was her turn to initiate some saving. She opened the wardrobe door and looked at her nakedness in the mirror. It was lunacy. She hadn't even met him. Maybe her brain was adrift, like a small tugboat, awash on a sea of fluid chubbiness. She was awry with hormones. Who was the Hollywood actress who breastfed an orphan in a third world clinic? Perhaps motherhood did that to you: made you feel you could nurture and nourish the entire world by gathering it to your bosom. Billy had got under Andrew's skin. He flexed with it, itched with it; it was a new restlessness that he could not still. He had tried to disguise it, but she could intuit it. He would not bring it up. He seemed to be waiting, without intent or expectation, perhaps in the hope that she might reach it for herself. The baby kicked again. Perhaps she should construe that as consent.

She heard him come inside, and shower again. He came upstairs, this time wrapped only in a towel. His skin gleamed, and she felt a rush of love for his decency, his goodness, for his beautiful, muscled torso. Never, she thought, would she tire of touching him.

'Chased any demons away?' she asked. 'Now that we have enough logs to light fires everyday until Christmas?'

'I'm not sure. I might be clattering some pans while I make supper. Sorry.'

'Don't apologise.' She patted the edge of the bed. 'Here, come and sit with me. I have an idea I'd like to talk to you about.'

43

Miriam sat in Zoe's study. Zoe had beckoned her to sit in a way that had irritated her. She tried to shrug off the effect. *This is about Billy, not me*, she reminded herself. Through the window, she could see Nancy pushing a little horse on wheels. Dimitri was running around merrily with a water gun, and Shamina was sitting cross-legged on the grass making a daisy chain. It was harmonious and lively – an unusual equation. All credit to you, Miriam thought grudgingly, looking at Zoe who'd brought in two mugs of pepper-mint tea; you're definitely doing something right. Zoe turned on her rotating desk chair. She had the air, Miriam felt, of someone about to give her an appraisal. She swallowed a sense of indignation.

'I thought I'd ask you to come here, as, after the weekend I feel I've processed some observations about Billy and us, and some thoughts about where that might lead, and I just want to talk them through with you, just to confirm we're on the same page.'

'That sounds sensible.' Miriam scalded her tongue with the tea. She decided to view it as a displacement sensation.

'Good, because here's the tricky part and I'm not going to mince words. I'm not sure, on the limited exposure I've had thus far, that Billy is the ideal recipient of – something makes me want to say *participant in* – what Phil and I have to offer. Do you see?' She tilted her head to one side.

Was Miriam imagining it or was Zoe speaking a little slower, as if Miriam's own processing abilities might not be able to keep up with her own? She tried to cool the tip of her tongue by rolling it against her lip.

'I see. Tell me more.' (*I am all ears*, she refrained from adding.)

'The thing is,' Zoe continued, 'why I think we've been successful at family-building so far is because we understand our own strengths. You have no idea how powerful an enabler that is for everyone concerned. Phil and I are very clear: locate a child who's had the worst possible start in a complex culture, cultivate an awareness of their own narrative, encourage them to talk, to share, and then healing and growing and integration can begin. If to all that, you can also add a more global perspective, and a wider sense of what family means, you have a child who, put simply, gets it, and a child who will flourish as part of our family.'

Miriam was trying to tug her mind on from absorbing the fact that Zoe had just told her she had no idea.

'And Billy?' she mustered.

'Well, I might be being over-hasty here, too quick to jump to conclusions, but I'm not sure Billy is proving an ideal candidate. My hypothesis is Billy may have two issues which may make his progress with us either difficult or, frankly, unlikely, although I want to underline that my particular, personal jury is still out on this.'

'And the issues are?' Miriam could feel her tone becoming defensive. She breathed out carefully.

'I think he's not engaged enough with where he's been, and with what he's been through. He has an emotional reluctance to work with his back-story which may be very hard to progress from. The second element is, and this sounds horribly blunt, but he's almost not needy enough to benefit from what we have to offer. There's a kind of emotional gratitude which is a catalyst for change and I'm not sure Billy has that. I may be wrong, and it may manifest itself, but it's not apparent now, and Phil and I evidently, pragmatically, have only so many resources, and some-times it comes down to where those can be best deployed.'

How not to be provoked, Miriam wondered, by the self-justi-fication and self-regard at the heart of Zoe's philanthropy. She could supply Zoe's particular, personal jury with a few summa-tions of her own.

'So, to be equally blunt, as you said at the start, Billy's not fitting in, not benefitting from being with you and your family, because he's not needy or grateful enough? Have I got that right?'

Miriam tried to keep the sarcasm from her tone.

'Gosh, how awful you make it sound, but the truth is some-where in there. Miriam, this is where we're at. For Phil and me this isn't just personal. It's about how we can make sure what we have to offer goes the furthest, is best utilised. When it comes down to it, I'm just not sure it's Billy, thus far, obviously, although that may change. I've asked for this meeting in the spirit of keeping you posted.'

'It's quite a speedy conclusion.'

'As a therapist, Miriam, speedy emotional literacy is one of my particular skills. It's also prompted, I have to admit, by a call we had earlier this week from one of our in-country contacts, about two children who may be more ideally suited to what we have to offer. There's a South African child, aged one, an Aids orphan, and also a Chinese girl.'

'I see. Yes, I see.'

'Look Miriam, I'm not pulling the plug, I'm not asking for the whole Introduction process to stop instantly, but I just want to share with you my reservations. I just want to remind you about what Phil said when we first met, about need knowing no global boundaries, and I honestly feel that I have the most to offer where the need is greatest. There's some talk too of a Tamil Sri Lankan girl; you can't begin to understand the nightmare of what she may have experienced.'

Of course she couldn't even begin to understand, Miriam thought, not while Zoe owned the entire territory of human empathy and compassion.

'So I'm guessing Billy's experience doesn't even begin to rank on some kind of need-o-meter.'

'I think, Miriam, you know what I'm saying. I think you actu-ally may also have some reservations of your own. This experience with Billy is showing me, and this may sound terribly clinical, that the skill set I have may make me best placed to work in an international context. In the UK there just isn't the same kind of deprivation, the same kind of terrible need.'

Miriam thought about saying *Try telling that to the eleven year old kept in a coal bunker for three years, or the child locked in a bathroom for a year naked and covered in their own excrement and ultimately beaten to death.* She reined herself in.

'It's just a distinctly different agenda,' she said calmly, 'and it's good that you have such a clear understanding of your own role, what you have to give, and where you would best like to deploy that, and I appreciate you being candid with me. That always helps.'

The peppermint tea was beginning to taste rancid. In truth she felt wrong-footed. Whatever issue she had with Zoe's rationale, another child was going to benefit from it, another child would come zooming in a delphinium-blue arc from far away and would have a scrapbook and play in the garden and grow up loved and super self-aware. Just not Billy. She hoped, perhaps unprofessionally fervently, that Billy hadn't liked her anyway. He'd been typically tactful when she'd spoken to him two days before.

'I'll talk to Billy again. I'll sound out how he's feeling. He hasn't said much.'

'Therein lies the difficulty.'

Miriam wondered if Zoe's only index of emotional damage was something which would make the news. Maybe she didn't compute that children could be casually, off-handedly, unremarkably, frozen into emotional diffidence by a crappy – as opposed to a blatantly tragic – hand.

She got up to go. 'Thanks again for your honesty,' she said. 'It makes my job a lot easier.'

Sort of makes my job easier, thought Miriam driving away, wondering how she was going to broach this with Billy. Would he be upset? He'd look at his shoe laces and nod. Andrew would come in and tell her something heartrending three days later. *Shit,* she thought, whacking the steering wheel with the flat of her hand. What was worse, she had nothing else to offer; no other leads to follow. The school holidays had begun; everything was going quiet. Billy would feel that he had failed; failed to appeal, failed to be snapped up. Zoe Marshall was evidently angling to be let off this particular hook. Meg Oliver would surely need a break sometime soon; Miriam would have to find short-term foster care for him, disrupt him all over again. She sat at a traffic light and kneaded her forehead with her finger and thumb. She had nothing, that was the truth of it: no solution, no options, nothing to promise, as well as an irrational desire to take a swing at Zoe for having the presumption to conclude that Billy wasn't needy or grateful enough.

'You're looking crabby,' her mother said, as Miriam let herself into her house.

Stella was reclining on a navy blue velvet chaise longue which stretched the length of the bay window.

'I was driving back from a meeting. I thought I'd just pop in and see how you are.' Miriam on occasions wondered whether the obverse wasn't in fact true; that she popped into her mother's so that her mother could see how she, Miriam, was.

'I'm having tea,' Stella said. 'Would you like some? It's black-berry and nettle. Apparently it has fabulous purging effects. Your skin might glow a little more dewily even under all that unflat-tering yellow strip lighting in your office.'

Was her mother's unspoken inference that if the light had been a little more flattering, Miriam might have received the attentions of all manner of eligible men? It was not the occasion to restate that her case-load didn't include any of those, and anyway Stella would have considered it a conclusion born of Miriam's lack of resourcefulness. *Doctors, lawyers*, she'd say, *they are always a hair's breadth away from anything tragic.*

Stella got up to fetch another white china cup from the kitchen.

Amazing, Miriam thought, and absolutely to form. Five fifteen on a Thursday afternoon, and her mother had been reclining on a chaise longue wearing an emerald angora cardigan with marabou-trimmed cuffs, a full face of perfectly applied make-up, and a natty pair of wedges. Her nails were perfectly manicured. Miriam curled her fingers to tuck her own chipped ones from sight.

She tried to think of the number of occasions she'd seen her mother without lipstick. They were staggeringly few. Aged six? seven? she remembered her mother turning her face when Miriam went to kiss her mouth. *No, darling, you'll smudge me*, Stella said, *and anyway lips are for lovers, cheeks are for children*. It carried with it no hint of coldness or detachment, just a pragmatism which Miriam could see had steered Stella through life. Miriam, obediently, afterwards, always kissed her mother's smoothly powdered cheek.

Stella returned with the cup. She touched Miriam's hand lightly, and then briefly, the side of her cheek, tilting Miriam's face towards her.

'Perhaps not crabby,' she reconsidered, looking at Miriam carefully, 'more a little furious, tempered with a dash of glum.'

'What a face reader you are,' Miriam said brightly, thinking that her tongue had only just stopped throbbing from being burned by Zoe's peppermint tea. Perhaps this afternoon would be characterised by a series of scaldings, evoking the length and breadth of an English country hedgerow. The blackberry and nettle tea smelt sharp, consonant with her mother's presence.

Stella had raised her alone at a time when it was unusual; Miriam sometimes wondered if this didn't explain her fascination with Miriam achieving a life more ordinary. She had worked as a croupier in a club throughout Miriam's childhood, cutting and shuffling cards on the kitchen table to show Miriam how quickly it could be done. Maybe the casino was where she had learned to read faces: disseminate braggadocio, bluff, the panic of impending loss. Perhaps she's concluded that most men were chancers so best to try and snare one reliable.

'So,' Stella said, 'cut to the chase. How are you, and how are all the little lives you work so hard to fix?'

Miriam shrugged. Suddenly, she was no longer sure why she'd come. She didn't feel up to playing ball.

'No update on the mother with severe learning difficulties whose baby your department is trying to snatch away?' Stella persevered. She toyed with her large amber pendant. It glowed and gleamed at Miriam, who shifted her gaze. That particular piece of her mother's jewellery always felt like a third eye, seeing straight through to her heart.

'I'm not sure snatch is the word, Mother, there were some significant capability issues. And no, we failed. Sheila is furious. A freedom-fighter barrister tore strips off the case and argued that love is what matters. A little help with the domestic round and everything will be tickety–boo. I actually agree with her, but I'm alone in the department on that.'

'And the little girl you think you've found for the fuddy-duddy couple. Of course you'd never call them that but I can.'

'As a matter of fact, yes, the first couple of meetings have gone well. She's very keen on the woman. I don't dare hope for more just yet. The child would benefit from gentleness, from solidity. Who knows, I may well have cracked it.'

'A blessing indeed. And the boy child who has bounced between pillar and post? Again, my words not yours but again probably closer to the truth than the smokescreen you have to use.'

'No.' Here Miriam faltered. 'No, I have no good news about him.'

Stella paused.

'Who needs to watch soap operas,' she said, with a dip of her chin, looking at Miriam intently, 'when my daughter's choice of work means I can have all these vignettes? You remember Sadie Tyler's daughter, the one who works as a buyer for Selfridges? She's just been promoted to head of accessories, special respon-sibility for gloves. You have no idea of the beauty of the pair she's just given Sadie; she was able to buy them ahead of next Autumn's collection. The softest of leather, almost to the elbow and the most exquisite teal blue. As she showed me, I comforted myself that you, if not able to bring me objects of beauty, can turn up with scraps of moral worth and complexity. Perhaps I should say that to Sadie next time she's gloating over gloves; that when my daughter visits she brings with her a veritable moral maze. Postcards from the front line, that's how I'll put it.'

'They're not postcards or vignettes, Mother, you know that. They are people's actual lives. I'm going to stop telling you about my work if you persist in treating it as entertainment.'

'That would rather depend on how important you consider

entertainment to be. So what shall we discuss instead, then, Miriam dear, when you kindly call by? The man you don't know whether to marry or not? That your daughter wants a pony to ride? That you just cannot decide whether to build an extension on to the house or not?'

'Touché,' Miriam said. (If she concentrated hard on the marabou cuffs, Miriam decided they would metamorphose into paws, and her mother would become a precise, deft, cat, toying with her spirits with perfectly varnished claws.) 'And bless the day that any or all of them happen. In the interim I'll just stumble fallibly along. And this tea, by the way, tastes dreadful; even glowing skin would not be worth it.'

'And that attitude, my dear, is why you will not achieve it. I shall drain mine to the dregs by which time it will be time for a glass of fizz. Would you like to join me for that? Perhaps it may improve your mood?'

Driving to the hospital shortly afterwards, having received a call from Meg, Miriam reflected on the paradox that was at the heart of her relationship with her mother. If she thought about it carefully, analysing the content of what her mother said, she should leave her home feeling furious or crushed. Instead, perversely, it felt as if she had been the recipient of a bracing, windswept, seashore walk. Beneath the verbal fencing, the acidity, and the neat barbs which snagged in Miriam's skin, there was always the truth that her mother could read her like no other. Miriam had recently concluded, awake and alone in a violet dawn, that what appeared to be Stella's insistent, destructive combativeness was in fact a well-disguised recognition of Miriam's increasing despair, and a determined effort to whip up – in her only, much-loved child – an attitude of robust defiance and pluck in the face of an augmenting mutual desire to sit down and weep.

44

Miriam met Meg outside the children's wing of the A&E department, where she was waiting for a baby whose arm was being plastered, and who would go home with her that night. The child's parent was being questioned by the police. Miriam and Meg met on their usual bench. It was a depressingly familiar location. Before them was an enormous, polished stone statue depicting a woman holding an infant. She cradled it tenderly, although Meg had once remarked that the expression on the face of the statue was pained rather than fulfilled. *No wonder,* Miriam had replied, *she's just birthed something the size of a baby elephant.* They'd laughed, although Miriam reflected afterwards that many of the problems she dealt with were the upshot of what might be better understood as a mis-match of sizes: babies born into adult lives that didn't have the space or order to accommodate them.

The Marshalls had space and order, Miriam conceded. Zoe was so certain of her bountiful reserves of the latter that Miriam felt she would have looked smug and capable had she been called upon to put a small third world country to rights. She could probably sign up for Mama Africa, no less. Miriam checked herself. It was unprofessional to ratchet up dislike. It was an ongoing shortcoming; always, she felt, this reining in of her instinct in order to become the even-tempered, smooth-tongued, process-focused professional she should be. She toed the gravel at her feet, and concentrated on what Meg was asking her.

'So, did she say she doesn't want to go any further with the process?'

'She implied as much . . . She didn't exactly say game over, but it was a shot across the bows. She hasn't taken to him, that's the only handle I can get on it. The irony is I don't think she gets him, despite her elevated opinion of herself. She's got some notion of suffering and deprivation that's so black and white I want to slap her. Well, obviously not slap her.' She paused. Careless talk. Even with Meg that might count as careless talk. Meg reached over and squeezed her hand. Miriam bit her lip. Professional distance from colleagues, clients and charges. Every rookie social worker knew that; she should pay heed. And, one of her mother's assessments in her head again: *I would never have described you as careful, Miriam, not careless, but not exactly careful.* Careful might be something to shoot for. She could probably take a lesson from Billy in that.

Meg was talking again. 'So what are you going to do? Remember in all this that it's the doing that counts.'

As if she needed reminding.

'No idea. I'm out of alternatives. I could ask other regions to look at him but that will make logistics difficult, with more complex time-scales and the question of where he'd stay. I can't just stash him in a children's home or foster care and start parcelling him out at a distance. I don't want to transfer his case as that'll feel like abandoning him. I'm starting to wonder if I should just stop thinking about adoption and start pursuing long-term foster care. It feels wrong to give up on a forever family for him, but not as bad as this rolling on without achieving anything, and demoralising him and consigning him to a children's home which might be the actual outcome. I just thought, you know, with the speedy process, that something would come up.'

Meg hesitated. 'Your other problem,' she said, 'and I hate to say it to you now, is that he shouldn't stay with me for too much longer. It's starting to feel familiar, and he'll become attached to it, to me, even though it's not the right environment for a child to be in for any length of time. He can name-check half the Social Services' listed taxi drivers in the county, *and* the health visitors *and* the social workers. He shouldn't be able to do that. I'll go back with this busted-up little one tonight, and he'll ask

me about her and I'll give him as few details as I can get away
with, but he'll take it on, he'll infer what I haven't said, and it
will be logged away. His radar for what's normal is skewed anyway
with all he's been through, and all this can't help.'

'So what are you telling me? That I should start making alternative arrangements? This is turning into a firecracker of a day.
I'll be applying to foster him myself if this carries on.'

'No, nothing so drastic. All I'm saying is that I might be a safe
pair of hands, and he might be familiar with my ways and settled
and in a routine, but it doesn't make it good for him. We both
know that. I'm a short-term carer for a reason.'

One of the nurses approached. 'The baby's ready for you,' she
said to Meg.

Miriam sat on the bench a little longer. Might it all be beyond
her fixing? Might even the presumption that it could be fixed,
that all of these cases could be fixed, suddenly dramatically shatter
for her, like a vicar who wakes up one morning perplexed to
discover that God has wholly evaporated for him in the night?

A disaffected social worker who no longer believed in the power
of the state to intervene and ameliorate; Jesus, she thought, that
would be a point of no return. She tugged her jacket around her.
The image came to her of a lifeboat. Maybe if that was the image
she had of herself, and the role she provided for children like
Billy, it would be easier to retain a little faith. Lifeboats had a
robust, sturdy fortitude that was easier to believe in, to hold fast
to, than a code of conduct which wefted and weaved its way out
of her reach.

45

Miriam sat in her office opposite Lorna and Andrew. They'd asked to see her, and she couldn't fathom why. She looked at Lorna. All the blackberry and nettle tea in the world wouldn't achieve a dewy glow like she had, evident despite the yellow of the office strip lighting. If Lorna had been fruit, she'd have been a cherry: ripe, round and gleaming. Miriam resisted the urge to reach across and touch her bump; it had a magnetic draw. Might she be feeling envy or wonder? Lorna was reminiscent of a painting in a Catholic church; the Madonna, chock-full of goodness and holy life, reached up to by the hands of the uncertain and lost. More pragmatically, she didn't get to look at pregnant women like Lorna all that often; her clients were normally more battle-scarred, wary-eyed. They had about them a suggestion of a lifetime of inadequate nutrition. Lorna probably had a vitamin and haemoglobin count right off the scale. She looked grave though; grave was definitely the word, with perhaps a degree of hesitancy thrown in. Miriam began.

'Obviously it goes without saying that I'm very happy to see you both. I'd hazard a guess it's something to do with whatever you know about Billy. I'm grateful for any insights you can give me, so . . .'

'It's not that,' Lorna interrupted. 'No, it's not about what Andrew knows about Billy. It's what we've been thinking about Billy. We've been thinking and talking for two days nonstop so please don't think what I'm about to say is a moment of madness. What we want is for you to consider us as a potential family for Billy, to let us start the Introduction process with him, with the hope of it leading to us adopting him.'

Miriam was stunned. How could she have anticipated this? She paused then spoke gently. Sometimes people felt spurred into doing the wrong things for the right reasons.

'I realise how upsetting it must have been for you to hear about Billy from Andrew and to have insights into the difficulty and sadness of his situation. It must be like watching famine stories on the news and wanting to help and to do something. I'm really appreciative of your kindness and empathy in feeling that. I am trying as hard as I can to find a new family for Billy, and something will turn up. I have to be confident of that, just as I have to be mindful that you are – I don't know, seven months pregnant and you're telling me you'd like to be considered as an adoptive parent as well. You have to admit it's a pretty astonishing combination. Maybe Andrew has suggested it – I know he's found some of the details of Billy's case difficult . . .' She felt herself petering out.

'It hasn't come from me,' Andrew said. 'It's Lorna's idea, although she read my mind. It's what we both want, we both want to try – if Billy wants it too.'

'But Lorna, let's go to square one. I don't think you've even met him, have you?

'No, I haven't. But people collect children from orphanages in China or Russia and they haven't either. And I love Andrew, and I trust his instincts and his judgement and he has, and he's talked a lot about Billy and he sounds lovely, and anyway isn't that what the Introduction part is for?'

Even assimilating it quickly, Miriam saluted Lorna's logic. So that's what love is, she thought. Real, grown-up, proper love: being prepared to begin the process of taking on a child because you trust your partner's judgement. No wonder good marriages were scarce.

'Can you just . . . just talk me through your thinking because frankly I'm stunned, not in a bad way, just stunned because I would never have seen this coming.'

Lorna spoke again.

'I'm not underestimating how hard a baby can be; I know they can have colic and don't sleep and scream all the time, and I've seen enough husbands in the park with babies early on weekend mornings while their wives are obviously poleaxed with tiredness at home. I know that. But women have babies who have nine-year-old children too. I don't see how caring for a baby, with Billy alongside, would make it a double burden. If anything, it would be a good thing, for Billy too, in that he can start afresh with loving someone new who would always think of him as their elder brother. Billy's old enough to wash himself, feed himself, it wouldn't be like taking on a toddler who needed afternoon naps or nappy changing too. He wouldn't be jealous, he could do lots of things with Andrew. They have a connection, that's what prompted all this. This is not an impetuous madness. And I have other reasons too.' Lorna faltered.

'Then you need to tell me them, because – and I can't actually believe these words are coming out of my mouth – if I'm going to try and do some sort of fast-track parental assessment for you – you need to level with me, absolutely level with me on every single thing that's going through your head.'

Lorna sat tall.

'I'm playing a good deed forward. Blame it on a film we watched. I'm adopted too, and my adoptive parents saved me. I was given up by my birth mother, and she might as well have died for all the connection she chose to have with me – even when I traced her as an adult she didn't want to meet me. My adoptive parents love me and gave me a really lovely childhood. They saved me; I can't put it more simply than that. This is like bread bobbing back on the water, or what goes around comes around, I don't know. It's my chance, *our* chance, to make the same difference. I know how well adoption can work. I know it first-hand which sets me at an advantage to lots of people whose job it is to make decisions about it.' Miriam sensed the steel in her tone. 'I think it's my turn to do the saving now. My parents made a huge difference to my life; even more so because in the 1980s a white couple taking on a mixed-race child was more of a big deal. I'm paying it back. That's what I want to do, and I can't think of a child more deserving than Billy, even though I haven't had the pleasure, yet, of getting to know him.'

Bingo, thought Miriam, absolute complete bingo. There was no flaw to Lorna's logic.

'But what do you propose to do after the baby is born? Have you thought about the practicalities? Have you thought about childcare?'

'We're going to try and manage without me working. It won't feel right being paid to look after people's parents while paying someone to look after my child.'

Miriam paused. Her brain was racing ahead.

'Look, let's just say this idea goes through, let's say Billy's keen, let's say it all goes swimmingly, I may be able to offer you an alternative arrangement. I don't know how familiar you are with the different types of caring we offer as a service. Here's the key one: if you adopt a child they become legally exactly the same as your birth child, and you are financially responsible for all aspects of their care. If on the other hand we approve you as a long-term foster carer, you get paid to look after the child – it's close to two hundred pounds a week. He or she remains our legal responsibility, you get to parent, and, in your circumstances, you could be a full-time mother with two hundred pounds a week coming in which would go someway to meeting the financial shortfall of your wages.' Miriam smiled expectantly.

'No. Absolutely no,' Lorna said firmly, looking at Andrew who nodded in support. 'That would be horrible. That would be as if we were doing it for the money, being paid to take care of him rather than choosing to do so. No, no, no. If the Introduction goes well and Billy becomes part of our family it's on the same terms as the baby; our responsibility. We'll muddle through financially. I never want him to think we did it because of the money.'

Miriam paused. Today, so far, was one of the ones which made all the shit ones worth going through.

After they'd gone, Miriam sat at her desk. What a turn-up for the books. At so many levels it felt right. How perfect that Lorna should have been adopted. How perfect that, right from the get-go, Andrew seemed to be the only one Billy chose to chat to. Bradawl, was it a bradawl? She still had no clue what that was. She walked back to the window and pressed her forehead to the coolness of the pane.

What was truly uplifting, when so much of her time was spent dealing with the lowest expectation of behaviour, was how Lorna had rebutted her suggestion of the financial benefit of long-term fostering. Her dark eyes had blazed. She was doing it for the right reasons; Miriam felt she could write that in block capitals on the assessment form already. She determined to get Sheila on side and slice through any bureaucratic tape that might lie in the way. She wouldn't betray an inkling to Billy. Oh, what sweetness lay in thinking what might be in store for him.

46

Billy woke up early, feeling sick and sad.

Miriam had phoned last night and asked Meg to bring him in to see her. Their conversation on the phone had been short. Meg looked serious. He could hear her walking about now, downstairs, trying to stop the baby crying.

The baby was new; she'd arrived yesterday with a tiny broken arm in a pale pink plaster cast, and a sealed-up black eye that looked like a shiny tulip bud. This morning, for the first time, Billy thought that no matter how much he liked Meg, maybe it wasn't good to live here for a long time. All you got to see, to hear, was sad things; children whose parents drank too much, lashed out, didn't take proper care. Too many bruises, too many children who looked unhappy or cross. After a while, he thought, you probably stopped believing in the possibility of a mum and dad who loved their children, cared for them, fed them, kept them safe and didn't do anything cruel or violent or neglectful. Nothing shouty. It was starting to make him feel his future was doomed. That was what Miriam would likely tell him this morning.

Meg was like a huge sponge, absorbing all the sadness, all the wrongness, that came into her house; storing it away somewhere so that the children didn't have to feel it when they were there. Maybe that was why she was so solid. He waggled his limbs to confirm they were still soft. The baby cried on; it was an awful wailing.

He reached into his pillowcase and took out *Dear Zoo*. The Marshalls were going to send him back. He could feel it; that was what Miriam wanted to tell him. He flicked through the pages. Too big, too tall, too fierce, too grumpy, too scary, too naughty, too jumpy; it wasn't any of those things. It was something else, which he could see in Zoe's eyes when she looked at him. He wasn't – and here he scrambled for a word – he wasn't talky enough, wasn't sharing enough, wasn't colourful enough. He didn't count as a bright blue line. He was just too wrong; that's what he was. Same as he was wrong for the Frasers, and wrong for the Bridges. He started to cry.

The whole day yawned before him: a trip to the Family Centre to be told he didn't fit, that he was being sent back, and then returning to Meg's and trying not to get bored playing by himself in the garden. It was harder to fill up his time now he was not at school. He'd have loved to go and play with Joey, but Meg would be busy, so he didn't want to ask. Because of the baby there would be health visitors, doctors coming, perhaps even a solicitor.

Yesterday, he'd sat for an hour watching ants coming in and out of their nest, carrying tiny scraps which must have felt like boulders to them. He'd smoothed their runway, and used his fingernails to make a slight extra width in the crack of the paving. He felt like a God of small things, able to make things easier. He didn't want to think of the opposite, of how easy it would be to mess up all the ants' steadfast effort. One quick scuff of his heel. Overall, he wasn't sure how he was feeling about God. Malcolm thought there was one God; Zoe liked the idea of many. Miriam and Meg gave no clue; perhaps that was understandable with everything they saw. From his own point of view he thought it was probably best not to hold out for any gifts of love any time soon.

He heard Meg calling him from downstairs. 'Billy, wake up, I'm going to have to get you a taxi as I think this little one may need to go back to the hospital. She sounds as if something else might be hurting her.'

He quickly got dressed and pulled his duvet straight. He wiped his eyes, and went to the bathroom to splash his face. Meg mustn't know he'd been crying. She already had enough on her plate.

★

Miriam looked oddly smiley and twinkly; that was Billy's first thought. She got him to sit down, and opened his file which was properly fat now.

'So, any update on what you're thinking about the Marshalls and being part of the rainbow family? I'm guessing it's a no-go for you, much as you don't want to sound ungrateful or to criticise, and that we can move swiftly on.'

Billy was startled. 'But that's quick.'

'I think that's neither here nor there. Let's cross them off anyway. I'll phone her later to say. Between you and me I found her a bit of a phoney. Phoney, is that the right word? Do you know what that means?'

'But . . . but . . .'

She put a big line through the page. She almost seemed pleased. Billy was mystified. Had Miriam lost her mind from too much work?

There was a knock on the door.

'Come in, come in,' she said almost merrily.

Billy turned to see Andrew walk in. He wasn't wearing his work clothes; he looked sort of scrubbed up, and a bit uncomfortable in a collar and tie. Beside him was a pregnant woman who he presumed was Lorna. She smiled at him too.

'Hey,' Billy said to Andrew. 'Is there something to fix?' Odd that Lorna had come too. He looked round the room expectantly. There was no tool box, or paint can, to give him a clue.

Miriam laughed and clapped her hands.

'No, not really, Billy, there's nothing to fix; they've come to talk to *you*.'

Billy blinked. They were all smiling, and he was bewildered, clueless.

'Here's the thing, Billy,' Andrew said, kneeling down by his chair. 'We've been to the hospital for a scan and the baby's a girl. Bets off on the fishing rod, and probably thumbs-up for ballet classes. I think it's time for me to act now before I'm outnumbered. I need an ally. What do you think about being Introduced to me and Lorna?'

47

Trudy sat in her white cotton dressing-gown in the garden on an August morning. She sipped from a mug of hot water infused with a slice of fresh lemon. It tasted pure and clear, as if it might clean her, purge her, from the inside out. That was perhaps too much to hope for. The morning light was already fierce, the heat in the air already thick enough to cut. She squinted across to the pool. A turquoise lizard darted across the terracotta tiles. Ted was at the golf course; he had left without waking her. Last night they had argued, and this morning their bitter words were strewn around the bedroom like leaves. She'd picked her way through the memory of them, feeling as if her feet might scorch.

She'd sat on the edge of their bed and abruptly, out of the blue, her words came volcanically. Some things, evidently, refused to be contained.

'Do you think we failed him?' (Her tone was even, despite the force behind them. Why was she even asking, she thought. Of course they'd failed him. What did she want Ted to say? Make it better, make it different?)

'Failed who?' Ted asked.

'Billy of course. Don't pretend you don't know who I mean.'

She sensed his spine stiffen. His tone was icy.

'I thought you'd gone quiet on that. I'd hoped you'd reached some kind of acceptance. I see you're still tormenting yourself. There's no point, Trudy. You spent enough of your life tormenting yourself about Lizzie. What's done is done. Your hand-wringing anguish didn't work then and it won't achieve anything now. It's over, and I don't want to talk about it.'

'But don't you think of him at all? Surely you must think of him?' (And all the time, his back remained turned, as if to look at her would be to reach a point of no return.)

'Not if I can avoid it, and I've become skilled at that. And where would it lead anyway? Nowhere, that's where. Like all the blind alleys Lizzie danced her way up, paved with good intentions and all your useless fretting.'

'But don't you wonder about what's happening to him? He's our own flesh and blood, our *only* flesh and blood for God's sake, and yet we live here and go about our antiseptic, plastic days and and just pretend he doesn't exist, waiting for someone else to rescue him and make it right, whilst we look the other way. How can you, how can we, how could we? Don't you look at yourself in the mirror and see how badly we failed?'

Ted remained motionless on his side of the bed.

'Don't you see, we made all of it, all of it about Lizzie,' she continued. 'Your precious girl. It wasn't actually ever about him. He's a child, and he was and is innocent of it all. We were so washed up with his mother that we deserted him; that's the word we should face up to using. And now, now that I can see everything more clearly for what it is, that makes me sick. *We* make me sick. And you look the other way, just like you're doing now.'

He turned to face her.

'You want to know how I can look the other way? How can I? I'll tell you how. I listen to all the other chaps at golf talking about their children, their grandchildren, their new jobs and new houses, and planned holiday visits here, and piano exams and sports teams and A stars at GCSE, and gap years and university places, and all I can see, all I can conjure up in its stead, is her sitting on that mattress, eyes like glass, bloody computer on and him sitting there wordless like a small pale, shadow next to her and that's how I don't think of it, because thinking of it's too bloody awful and you can dwell on it if you want but I won't. I damn well won't. You were ineffectual then, and you'll be so now.'

He'd stalked out of bed, slammed on the landing light and gone and slept in the spare room. Trudy had lain on top of the bed, even a sheet too stifling, and wept copious tears. She'd failed everyone she ever loved, she saw that truth clearly, as if someone had thrown it like a ball, into the room. She saw herself as a young woman qualified for little else than to be a wife, housekeeper and mother. She saw herself holding Lizzie on her christening day, wearing a pill-box hat and pale lemon leather gloves – she could remember their softness, their suppleness – and Lizzie in her arms, so tiny, so perfect, so miraculous. She remembered standing with a bridle in her hands, threading a bit into the pony's mouth, and Lizzie, aged nine, pulling on her boots, her hacking jacket, with fierce determination. She remembered carrying boxes of Lizzie's stuff into grotty university flats, and standing at drinks receptions as a loyal, socially capable wife, or preparing complex dinner parties to entertain Ted's colleagues, and through it all, she had lacked spine; lacked bravery, lacked courage to assert what was right. She should have been more insistent with Lizzie about Milo; she should have confronted her when the drugs first started; she should have taken Billy away to their home in Esher when he hadn't even registered on Social Services' agenda. She had not fought, she had not fought at all. She saw that clearly, now. It had taken her sixty-eight years to see the truth of herself. She'd thought that attempts at persuasion, her soft, insistent nibblings of love, could stop it all happening, stop disaster in its tracks. It had not.

And now, in the morning, her head light as gossamer from lack of sleep and new knowledge, there was this. A letter from England, franked not stamped. She guessed it was from the Social Services: it could only be Miriam. Maybe an arrangement had been reached, something signed, something irreversible. Job done.

She thought of Billy as he'd sat before her on the morning in July, dressed in his VW beetle T-shirt, his eyes clear, his voice soft. The way he'd stood before her, stoical, taking it all on the chin. How could she ever have thought he'd be flighty like Lizzie? He was braver than them all. She opened the letter.

Dear Trudy

I have good news about Billy. After three faltering attempts at matching him with new families, a couple came forward who are a perfect match. The man is a carpenter who works sometimes at the Centre, and Billy had contact with him in all his comings and goings and they formed a bond and it all went from there. The irony is, I tell him, he put me out of a job and found his new family for himself. Like a homing pigeon; that's how I'm thinking of it.

His new mum Lorna (and I hope it doesn't upset you reading that because I have to tell you in the circumstances it shouldn't; it's a reason for real joy) is expecting their first baby in October, so Billy will have a sister. Lorna was adopted herself and so knows more about the reality of it than any of us. This will stand him in good stead. They are a lovely couple and Billy is blossoming.

What's even more extraordinary is what I'm about to write. Lorna says that Billy technically has five sets of grandparents; yourself and your husband, his absent birth father's parents, her birth parents, her adoptive parents and Andrew's parents. Of the five, Lorna says, they don't have a clue about two, so all the more important to hold on to the ones he does have. She thinks it's healthy and right for Billy to maintain contact with you. Apparently Andrew saw you when you came to the Centre in July – perhaps you recall that? So, they are happy for you to have contact; to write, to phone, to visit if you choose. It is an extraordinarily generous offer and I hope you will take it up. I've put all their details on the attached sheet. I told them I would write to you, and so that's my part done.

I'm sure Billy will tell you more if and when you see him.
With very best wishes –
Miriam Riley.

Trudy wept some more, and then she dressed, prepared lunch, and sat, very still, on the terrace with the letter in her hand, waiting for Ted to come home. When he came through the door, she was struck by how wary and uncertain he looked. What words had she thrown at him last night? *Your precious daughter.* The words had a startling, fresh power.

Oh, how she had been his very precious daughter. She was his darling girl child, for whom he would have done anything. When he could not save her, when she stole from him, lied to him, refused to be helped, she saw now his only refuge had been in turning completely away.

He had not come to the mortuary because he could not bear to look at her dead body. What she thought was rejection, she saw clearly now as frailty. With Billy, he had decided not to risk his love again, so stalked ahead of him on a beach and refused to engage, in the knowledge that love could crack open the heart and leave it rawly weeping pain.

Ted stood before her, now, and she realised her own wounds had been so compelling they had blinded her to his. Long ago, when Lizzie was a child, in the blue cold of winter mornings he had broken the ice on the pony's water before he left for the station. *That's how I know Daddy loves me*, Lizzie had merrily told her. How prescient that love carried the wounding potency of long, broken shards of ice. Perfect for piercing the heart.

'Look,' Trudy said, 'look . . . read this before you do anything. I can't believe it came today, after last night, after . . .'

Ted came towards her and she gave him Miriam's letter, and he sat down and started reading, his hand over his mouth, and when he got to the end he placed his face in his hands and wept; huge great racking sobs that shook through his body. He looked older, frailer. She understood his stroke for what it had been: a rocket of pain that had ricocheted right through him, marking Lizzie's loss with the limp he still carried. She held his trembling hand and sat silently as he wept, and she knew that he was weeping for his darling girl in her cherry-red pullover, chin tilted up, eyes bright, hair swinging in plaits, unaware of the darkness that would overtake her, of how she would fall. Ted wept, saying nothing, but the silence between them was complicit, and Trudy sat, straight-backed, beside him, knowing that there were no words for that moment, but that it was a bridge between them, and she knew that he wept not only for Lizzie but also for the hope of Billy, of a fresh start, of a new path. She resolved to be brave, to be proactive, to embrace the couple who had saved him, and she squeezed Ted's hand, and said with conviction 'It's going to be all right; everything's going to be all right.'

48

It was a bright April morning.

Andrew's van pulled into the Family Centre car park. He turned to Billy.

'I'll just pick up a couple of tools to make the crayfish trap, and then we'll go and get Joey and go fishing. Do you want anything else to eat? Are you happy to wait in the van?'

'I haven't been here for ages,' Billy said. 'There's just something I want to do over there if that's okay.'

'Sure. I'll be ten minutes or so.'

They both got out of the van. Andrew made his way towards the store, and Billy walked towards the tree carrying his rucksack. He looked around. The car park was empty. Miriam must be having a proper Saturday off; she deserved it. She'd been at his forever family ceremony a week ago, when the adoption papers were formally signed. She'd arrived holding a huge great bunch of turquoise balloons and told him, breathlessly, that she had actually blown up every one herself. 'I'm so light-headed that on reflection it might have been an error; I could float up and off.' Meg Oliver had come too, and given him a huge hug, and sat in the front row looking solid and safe and in no danger of floating anywhere, and she clapped really loudly when Judge Joan signed the papers. After she'd signed them, the Judge said *Hooray*! and asked Billy if he wanted to sit in her chair. She'd fetched her wig and asked if he wanted to try it on. He'd done so, and had his picture taken with Sophie on his lap gurgling and pulling at the horsehair plait.

During the ceremony, Miriam stopped looking breathless and instead seemed as if she might cry. Lorna – who said he could now officially call her Mum – sat with Sophie who babbled her way through the whole thing, blowing bubbles at Billy and clapping her hands together. She was as cute as it was possible to be. Andrew had stood with his hand on Billy's shoulder – not as if to pump him up into anything bigger but as a reminder that he was solidly there – and when they handed him the papers he lifted him right off the floor and said *That's my boy*. Joey sat in the front row with his nan, who cheered, and Joey saluted the judge, which he said afterwards he thought might be incorrect but that he hoped he'd never be up before one and actually find out what was. His nan said better not to count on that.

Afterwards, they'd stood out on the pavement on St Aldates, and asked the court usher to take a photo, which was on his bedside table now: Miriam and Meg with their arms up like football champions, and Lorna kissing the top of his head with Sophie dangling down, and Andrew crouched down beside him, with the most massive smile ever. Joey was laughing, and his nan was clapping, and smiling so widely you could see where her teeth stopped.

The photo next to it was one taken when Grandma and Grandpa visited from Portugal at Christmas. Grandma had hugged Lorna, and kissed Sophie, and cried and cried but she said this time it was for happiness and it looked properly true. Grandpa had held his face in his hands. They'd invited them all to Portugal, and they were going for two weeks in the summer.

Billy patted the tree. The bark still felt cool in the mild Spring sunshine. It didn't need to sing or ring. He knew what love was; he felt full to the gills with it, and he felt so happy it was as if he might sing or ring himself.

He reached down into the hidey-hole and found a damp, mildewed clump of paper. He squashed it back in, and pulled up a small clump of grass. He pushed it in on top, tucking them away for ever.

He reached into his rucksack and took out a small trowel. He knelt by the roots and started digging carefully, his brow furrowed in concentration, using both hands in his effort. He dug until he'd made a shallow thirty centimetre by thirty centimetre hole, and reached into his rucksack again and took out *Dear Zoo*. He held it close to his chest. It was saying goodbye to so many things. He'd thought about keeping it for Sophie, but decided that when she was bigger he'd save up his pocket money and buy her a new one, so that the animals would be able to call out fresh and loud. He read the text one last time, kissed the cover, and laid it into the hole.

Nobody would send him back now; he'd found a home that was perfect. His birth mum's jazz-hands turned into a fuzzy, faraway wave.

He carefully buried all trace of the book. He thought of Caroline, Toby and Horatio, and a cricket ball whacked far. He hoped Horatio was happy and that Caroline was still enthusiastic about everything. Toby, he expected, would always be jolly. He thought of Elspeth and Malcolm; Miriam had said she'd successfully placed a little girl with them, and that it was all going beautifully. He was happy for them both. He pictured Malcolm trying to teach the girl to play draughts – he hoped she was better at it than him – and the girl sitting beside Elspeth on *The Girl Jane*, eating freshly made flapjacks and wearing an identical broad-brimmed straw hat. The girl would like doing the jigsaw puzzles, of that he was sure; the soft click of the pieces, and Elspeth's careful hands. He thought of the Marshalls and the map with the arcing-blue lines. Another child would no doubt be zooming towards the rainbow family soon. Zoe would be on to the next scrapbook, and would do her best to make them a new life story.

He finished covering *Dear Zoo*, and strewed some beech leaves around to disguise the disturbed soil. Just as he finished, he heard someone approaching.

'Are you all set, Billy?' Andrew asked. 'I've got the crayfish stuff. Your mum's just rung and she's going to bring Sophie down to the river later in the pushchair. Are you ready to go and fetch Joey?'

'Yes, completely ready,' Billy replied.

He turned to face his dad.

His smile was dazzling.

Acknowledgements

Many thanks are due.

I have been gifted with two editors in the writing of this book.

At the time of writing, Sue Fletcher is shortly to leave Hodder and Stoughton to begin a drama degree. I am proud and grateful to have been one of the last recipients of her formidable editorial ability and experience. She is a trail-blazing role model and will be much missed. Suzie Dooré has been brilliant; I value greatly her insight and sharp eye.

It is a mark of both Sue's and Suzie's abilities that the tandem editorial process has worked so seamlessly and I am happily the beneficiary.

Swati Gamble, Assistant Editor, has guided *Choose Me* to press with her customary efficiency and grace.

My agent, Helenka Fuglewicz, has steadfastly been with me at each step of the way. I am grateful to the many conversations with her which shape me as a writer. Thanks also to Ros Edwards and Julia Forrest at Edwards Fuglewicz.

To Barbara Bradshaw, Linda Longshaw and Claire Batten; always key.

Georgia Stevenson, again, read the manuscript first. Her instincts belie her years, and I am hugely appreciative of her interest. And to Sebastian Maskrey, who was an insightful early reader, and to whom Joey owes a debt.

And finally to Hamish . . . Where to begin?

In the best books, the ending often comes as a shock.
Not just because of that one last twist in the tale,
but because you have been so absorbed in their world,
that coming back to the harsh light of reality is a jolt.

If that describes you now, then perhaps you should track down
some new leads, and find new suspense in other worlds.

Join us at www.hodder.co.uk, or follow us on
Twitter @hodderbooks, and you can tap in to a
community of fellow thrill-seekers.

Whether you want to find out more about this book,
or a particular author, watch trailers and interviews, have
the chance to win early limited editions, or simply browse
our expert readers' selection of the very best books,
we think you'll find what you're looking for.

And if you don't, that's the place to tell us what's missing.

We love what we do, and we'd love you to be part of it.

www.hodder.co.uk

@hodderbooks

HodderBooks

HodderBooks